The Survivors
A Glen Haven tale

By Michael Breakfield

Table of Contents

Prologue

Chapter 1: The Survivors Club

Chapter 2: Autumn's Story

Chapter 3: The Lawmen

Chapter 4: Spirit

Chapter 5: Cat's Story

Chapter 6: Mr. Nobody

Chapter 7: Tesla's Story

Chapter 8: Anne's Story

Chapter 9: The Final Chapter

Epilogue

Prologue

The full moon reflected off the glasslike surface of the lake's still waters. The clear night sky was dotted with countless white specs, light from stars far, far away. Out here, the stargazing was the best. You can see forever. A slight breeze kissed her soft skin giving her goosebumps. The young very attractive woman strode gracefully along the quiet shoreline. Her tight white t-shirt hugged her body and exposed her flat, pierced midriff. Around her slender waste was wrapped a rainbow beach towel. Her firm, slender frame was carried along by long toned legs. With each step, her bare feet plunged into the soft sand of the lake shore. She gleefully squeezed the warm sand between her toes, as she made her way down the beach.

Here and there along the shoreline, the young woman would venture a bit closer to the water's edge, each time dipping a toe or two into the warm, calm waters. This ritual repeated itself several times before the woman; hands on her hips and with a mischievous smile had decided she found the right spot. With long, nimble fingers she opened the towel and tossed it nonchalantly to the sand. She adjusted her baby blue G-string as she once again dipped a toe into the waters of the lake. She looked over her right shoulder, then her left, and then she pulled her tight half-shirt off and tossed it to the sand next to the towel. Her bare, ample breast bounced and swayed as if relieved to be free

2

from their constricted confinement. A small wooden figurine hung snug between her breast from a leather string that was tied around her long neck. Slowly, she pulled her G-string down and stepped out of it and dropped it next to her other garments.

The killer's breath and heartbeat quickened. Not with any kind of carnal desire, but from the anticipation of a predator stalking its prey. From his unseen vantage point in the shadows of the trees that lined the lake's shore he watched her. The pupils of his dark, almost black eyes dilated. There was something familiar about this one, but then again, there was something familiar about all the sheep. The killer watched as the attractive naked woman waded into the shallows of the water and then dove beneath its rippling surface.

For several minutes, the woman swam back and forth in graceful circles. She moved through the calm waters with the ease of a creature that belonged there. She would dive deep into the black waters and curl around to pop out of the surface with a glee and freedom few ever experienced. She began to float on her back, a trick her father had taught her when she was a child. If she could find the right center of balance, she found she was able to float like this for dozens of minutes. Much longer than anyone else she knew.

For a long while she floated there a few dozen yards off the shore and stared up at the stars in the night sky, her round breast buoyed in the water. The moon was as full as she had ever seen. The forest surrounding the lake was still. Only the typical sounds of chirping crickets and night fauna echoed here and there throughout the darkness. Then there was another sound, an unnatural sound.

She started and sank beneath the surface of the water for a moment as she gathered herself. Treading water, the woman gazed along the shoreline and the dark shadows of the tree line beyond. Tilting her head to the right and left trying to pinpoint the sound. Her mouth went suddenly dry, and a chill ran up her spine when she realized that all the other sounds of the forest had ceased. The night was deathly silent, unnaturally calm. It was unnerving.

Then the sound came again.

It was faint, and to pinpoint from where it came was impossible. It would seemingly be coming from the right, then the left, then echoing from a great distance, then suddenly right off the shore itself. Her eyes darted from right to left, desperately trying to catch a glimpse of who or what could possibly be making that god-awful sound. She had heard that sound once before. If she had to describe it, it sounded like a lamb, or goat mixed with the crying of an infant. It was unsettling.

Even more unsettling was when the sound stopped. The night was quiet, still. The only motion at all was her treading water. Then a breeze picked up. For a moment, she could have sworn she saw movement in the shadows of the trees along the shore or was it just her imagination fueled by her heightened state of perception and the suddenly eerie setting of her surroundings. She began to swim to the shore.

The rapid dart took longer than she had anticipated. She must have floated out further than she realized. When she finally reached the shore, she crossed her hands over her breasts as the breeze was far colder than it had been before. She was relieved to feel that her little wooden totem was still there. She looked for her towel, but it was not there. She assumed she must have come ashore further down the beach than where she entered the water. Holding her breasts protectively, she trotted up the shoreline, looking for her garments. She arrived at the spot where she was sure she had left them, but they were not there. She looked down the beach in both directions, the clear night sky and bright full moon illuminated the beach, and she could tell her belongings were nowhere to be seen. Could they have been carried into the water by the current? That thought quickly left her as she stared at the calm, still waters of the lake. A sudden feeling of dread washed over her.

Once again, a cool breeze enveloped her. As the wind rippled through the trees, she thought, again, she heard movement through the brush. Spinning to investigate the tree line, she was startled to see her baby blue G-String, swaying in the breeze as it hung suspended from a low-hanging branch. This was very unnerving, and she could almost feel eyes upon her.

"Whoever you are, this isn't funny!" She called out to the darkness.

With all the modesty, she could muster while standing totally exposed and naked, she strode over and retrieved her bottoms. As she pulled them on, her blood ran cold as suddenly the awful sound once again began resounding from the dark. Again, the sound was impossible to pinpoint for it would echo in the distance to the right, then suddenly closer to the left, and even almost seemingly right next to her. It was a terrible noise that would haunt her dreams.

As she looked here and there something caught her eye. In the distance, surrounded by shadows and darkness, she could make out the faint almost glow of her white T-shirt hanging off another low branch. Swallowing hard, she ventured into the dark woods to retrieve it. With each step, she winced as her bare feet navigated the rough, poking and cutting floor of the forest. The closer she got to her shirt, the darker her surroundings became. The leaves and branches high above blocked out the light of the moon and stars. When she was mere feet from her prize, her mouth went dry and her heart began to pound as that awful sound resonated once again, but this time it was lower, almost guttural, and it was literally right on top of her. Without seeing it, she could feel the presence of another standing directly behind her. She could hear his heavy breathing and feel his hot breath on her bare back. For a moment, she could not even breathe.

On pure instinct, she fell to the side narrowly ducking out of the way of the large hunting knife as it slashed down, splitting her white T-shirt in half. Rolling onto her back, the rough ground cutting and scratching her tender bare skin in several spots, she looked up to see her attacker. He was an extremely large man, a giant man, bare-chested, and wearing worn, dirty grey pants held up by fraying suspenders. He stood over her like a mountain, his broad chest heaving. He looked down at her through the hallow sockets of an animal skull, a skull adorned with a shaggy mane of matted hair that he wore as a mask over his face.

She screamed in terror. He reached for her. In a crazed frenzy, she fought back with all her terror-fueled might. Somehow, she avoided his attempts to grab her and just barely rolled out of the way of his knife which plunged hilt-deep into the exposed root of a tree. She scrambled to her feet and ran screaming into the forest. As she ran through the forest, jutting branches and rough brush tearing at her delicate skin, she could hear her attacker pursuing. She dared not look back for fear of dying of fright, but she could hear his heavy plodding and boots snapping the brush under his feet. She could feel the near misses as his giant frying pan-sized hands reached out for her. She could feel his heavy, hot breath on her neck. She ran as fast as she could.

She came sprinting and screaming into a small clearing deep in the woods. Her bare feet bleeding, her naked body bruised and bleeding from dozens of cuts and scratches gained from her mad dash through the woods. Inexplicably, she trips on her own accord and stumbles to the ground, the sheer force of her terror seemingly making it impossible for her to go on. The killer entered the clearing behind her.

"No...No!" She pleaded as she rolled over onto her back and back crawled desperately away from her attacker. "No, God, please!"

The killer slowly, methodically stalked toward her. As he did, he unsheathed a second large hunting knife from one of three sheaths strapped to his leg. His prey pleading, her back now braced against the trunk of the tree, had nowhere left to run. Saliva dripped from his cracked lips. Only another two steps and she was his. He raised the large knife high above his head, ready for the kill.

Suddenly, a light, brighter than the sun, engulfed the clearing. Several industrial-sized spotlights blazed to life and washed the killer in a light so blinding that he became disorientated. His balance was compromised. He brought his giant hand up to cover the sockets of his mask to shield his eyes from the light, but his vision was already full of spots, and he was dizzy. Blindly, he lashed out with the knife, swinging it in wide arcs trying to slash and kill an assailant he had yet to lay eyes on. For the very first time in his life, the killer was vulnerable. That's when the first round of Tasers hit him.

Two small darts pierced his chest sending 50,000 volts of electricity surging through his body. Staggered by the attack, the killer instinctively tore the electrodes from his chest only to be hit by four more darts. The electrifying surge caused his muscles to involuntarily seize, causing him to drop his weapon. The vulnerable moment passed. He once again blindly tore the electrodes from his chest. And, once again, he was hit with another round of Tasers. This time it was six darts sending excruciating amounts of current through his body. The killer slumped to one knee. It took him a moment to recover as he, one-by-one, plucked the electrodes from his skin. He spits a tooth out that he had cracked off during his last seizure, along with some blood.

The brilliance of the spotlights still blanketed the clearing. Standing on unsure legs, his vision was still blurry. The killer could barely make out shadowy figures surrounding him on the perimeter of the clearing. He reached for his third knife, but as he unsheathed it, a large tranquilizer dart thudded hard into his chest. The impact set him back a step. With an animal grunt, the killer swatted the dart away breaking the needle off in his chest. Then the thud of another tranquilizer dart hit him in the chest, then another…and another...and, another one after that.

With a thunderous sound, the killer collapsed hard onto the unforgiving ground.

On the verge of consciousness, the killer looked up through the hallow sockets of his animal skull-mask. He could not make out the details of the blurred figures standing over him. He recognized the first voice he heard as the voice of his elusive prey from earlier.

"Do we kill him now?" She asked.

"No," another female voice, a voice also vaguely familiar to the killer, answered. "No, we finally got him and he's going to get what's coming to him. You hear that?" she asked, following her question up with a swift kick to the killer's ribs. "Your day of reckoning is at hand, you son of a bitch."

The killer's world began to spin out of control. He could barely make out the motion of his assailant raising something above her head. She brought the blunt instrument down on his head with all her might, and the killer's world went black.

Chapter 1: The Survivors Club

The void is calm. The nothingness is soothing. Then there is a voice, a vaguely familiar voice, then another voice, also vaguely familiar. The black void begins to swirl as the light of consciousness begins to crack through. A sense of awareness spreads like a virus. The sensation is rushing, faster and faster…until.

The killer opens his eyes.

To his right, two women are engaged in a heated discussion.

"You're positive this will hold him?" Asked a tall slender woman, her long curly blonde hair vibrating as her entire body shook with adrenaline. She pointed toward the killer emphatically. Her voice cracked and her manner almost pleading. "You're positive? If he gets loose, God help us all."

"Trust me," answered a shorter woman with equally long and curly, but dark hair. This woman spoke with a calmness and confidence that seemed to put her counterpart at ease. "I have been planning this for years. He's not going anywhere. He's ours now."

The killer's eyes scanned the room. There were three other women there as well. Standing next to the first two women, thoroughly engaged in their conversation, was a very attractive woman with an athletic toned body. Her cutoff shorts accentuated her long firm legs. She wore a tight-fitting half shirt that revealed a pierced naval. This was the skinny dipper who had led the killer into the trap. To the left, sitting on a work bench, was another woman. Her legs crossed; they swayed as they dangled above the floor. She absently flicked on and off a small green plastic lighter, staring intently at the fleeting tiny bursts of flame. If she was paying any attention to anything else going on in the room, nobody could tell. Finally, there was another woman, a young woman, so young in fact that her adult status was only recently obtained. She stood as far away from the killer as physically possible in the close quarters, her back to the wall, her arms crossed in front of her. Her huge brown eyes went even wider at the sight of the nightmare before her. She had turned her body as if to shield herself. Her body vibrated violently as waves of fear washed over her.

She whimpered, followed by a bladder spasm.

The young woman caught the attention of the others in the room, all except the woman with the lighter who continued to flick the small instrument on and off. The tall blonde and the equally tall woman in the half shirt were immediately at the young woman's side comforting her and reassuring her.

"Autumn, honey, it's okay," the tall blonde coaxed as she put her slender arm over the young woman's shoulders. "Please, sweetheart, it's okay. Tesla is here. I won't let anything happen to you." She spoke with a motherly tone and attempted to calm the younger woman the way a parent would.

"Autumn, sweetheart," the attractive woman in the half shirt tousled the younger woman's hair. "What's the matter, darling?"

The younger woman inhaled violently, trying to catch her breath. She welcomed the calming embrace of two older women trying to calm her down. She felt a little safer with them, but not completely. Still shaking with fear, she extended her hand meekly and pointed in the direction of the killer. All the eyes of the women present looked over at their captive and all the air seemingly left the room as they suddenly realized he was no longer unconscious.

Nobody said a word as the killer's head slowly turned right from left. He looked at them from behind his mask, a fashioned animal skull with a long shaggy mane of animal hair which had been stenciled into the base of the mask. On the right side of the forehead on the mask was a small, chipped hole with small spider web cracks spreading out away from it. He stared at them, peering through the hollow sockets of his skull mask. His eyes were black, soulless eyes, like a shark. Like a predator. He slowly, methodically looked at each woman in the room. Each time his gaze fell on one of them, he would cock his large head to the side, as if trying to remember a lost memory. This ritual went on until he had studied each woman present.

He then turned his attention to himself. He looked down to see he was sitting in a large metal chair. It was bolted to the cement floor. His legs were shackled at the ankles with very thick iron chains, also bolted to the floor. Across his chest were thick leather straps which secured him firmly against the backrest of the iron chair. His enormous forearms were also securely shackled by chains to the armrests of the chair. For a moment, he tested his bonds but quickly realized even his inhuman strength would not be able to break them.

"Don't even try it," the short dark-haired woman to the right ordered. "Those chains are strong enough to hold a silverback. Psycho-strength or not, you aren't going anywhere."

The killer went back to taking in his surroundings. There was a large workbench with tools, anyone of which he could use to maim and kill his captures if only he could get his hands on one. Over against the far wall was a rolled up old mattress, a bucket and dirty mop, and rolled up rope. Beyond the women he saw an open door leading to a stairwell which led up. Above was a single bulb, the only source of light in the entire room. Its light shinned down; casting shadows that gave the man in the skull mask an almost otherworldly look.

"Shhhh, it's okay, honey," Tesla comforted Autumn as the younger girl buried her face in the older woman's bosom.

Emotions were running so high that the tension in the dark room was palpable. However, the woman to the left went back to flicking her lighter and staring at the flame. Her thin lips were painted black and shoulder length hair was died jet black except for a thin purple stripe dyed into it. The flickering flame of the lighter reflected in her green eyes. If she were shaken at all by the situation, none could tell.

"Diana, do you think he remembers us?" The attractive athletic woman in the half shirt asked the shorter dark-haired woman. "Do you think he knows who we are?"

"Well, if he doesn't, Anne" Diana replied as she adjusted the gun belt on her waist that holstered her .44 magnum, "he soon will."

Anne chuckled. "You hear that, you son of a bitch?" She bravely took a few steps toward the killer. "We've got big plans for you."

Seemingly unfazed by her threats, the killer slowly tilted his head from side to side.

"By all the rules of the horror movie I should be dead," she scoffed at their captive. "Yeah, I was having sex when you tried to ghost me." Her voice was becoming more agitated with each word. "Does murdering people get you off, huh?" she asked, stepping even closer. "Does it?!" She screamed in his face. She stepped back and pulled her half shirt up, her ample naked breasts exposed. "The big bad Goatman of Azlewood. Well, you missed, fucker!" She reached up and pushed her breasts together right in front of him mockingly.

The killer stared back her from those hollow sockets of his macabre mask, his soulless eyes piercing her soul and causing a shiver to run up her spine. She fell back a step as her captive's ominous presence threatened to overwhelm her. A sudden feeling of humility washed over her. Absently she pulled her shirt back down and covered her exposed breasts. She could feel an uncontrollable fear begin to engulf her being and at that moment, all she wanted to do was make a break for the door. Right before her fear overwhelmed her, Anne felt a comforting, firm hand on her arm.

"Relax, girl," Diana assured her. Diana had a way of reassuring all of them. There was something about her, an unexplainable quality that made them all trust her. "Relax," she said again. "Remember why we are here, and who we are here for." Diana's words strengthened Anne's resolve. She felt her confidence rise and her swagger return.

"Diana, Autumn needs to get out of here," Tesla said from behind them. "I'm taking her upstairs."

"Yes," Diana retorted. "Let's all go upstairs." She looked over at the killer and said, "He's not going anywhere."

Tesla, still holding the sobbing younger woman close to her, led her out the door and slowly up the stairs. Diana gave Anne another reassuring squeeze on the arm, and then Anne followed the others out of the room, her head hung low, momentarily ashamed by her actions. Diana started for the door when she realized the last member of their party had not joined them.

"Cat," she called. The woman with the purple stripe in her hair did not respond. She simply continued to flick her lighter and stare blankly. "Cat!" Diana raised her voice, this time getting the other woman's attention. She looked over at Diana, her face as expressionless as can be. "Come along, honey," Diana urged, reaching her hand out. "Let's go upstairs."

Without a word, Cat hopped off the workbench, made her way to the door, and ascended the stairs. Diana walked after her, but she paused at the doorway. She turned back to see the killer staring at her with those cold, dark eyes.

"I wouldn't get any bright ideas," she warned. "That chair you are sitting in is rigged with enough electrodes to fry an elephant." He could see the wires running from the chair, across the floor and attached to a large throw-switch mounted on the wall next to the doorway. "If you even attempt to escape, I'll fry your ass." Diana nodded toward the throw-switch. "You better try and get some rest because believe me, your last few hours on this earth are going to be miserable."

Without another word, she turned the light off, exited the room, and shut the heavy door behind her. The sound of several heavy bolts being locked into place could be heard. The killer sat unmoving, alone in the darkness. The only sound in the black was his breathing.

Autumn allowed Tesla to lead her up the stairs and into her designated room. She felt tired, physically, and mentally. She felt weak, and she had a nauseating knot in her stomach. As she fought back the urge to vomit, she allowed Tesla to lay her down in bed.

"Here you go, sweetie," Tesla said as she pulled the sheet and covers up to the younger girl's chin.

"I'm sorry," Autumn said weakly. "I just…just seeing him there, right there like that, I just…I just…"

Tesla gently ran her fingers through Autumn's long blonde hair, an act that seemed to have a calming effect on the girl. "It's okay, darling," she said in a low, soothing voice. "It's a tough pill for us all, but don't you worry, honey. You're safe. I invested a lot of money in this plan to make sure of that. Okay?" Autumn nodded; her eye lids were becoming heavy. "Get some sleep, Autumn," Tesla leaned over and kissed her on the forehead. "If you need anything, anything at all, you just call out, okay?"

Autumn was already out by the time Tesla reached the door. The girl's steady breathing brought a smile to the older woman's face. She turned off the light in the room, but she left the door slightly ajar. As she stepped into the upstairs hallway, Tesla found Diana waiting for her.

"How is she doing?" Diana asked genuinely concerned but, in that rigid, stern manner that they all have come to associate with Diana.

"She's shaken up," Tesla replied. "She should not have been down there."

"She's a tough kid," Diana said as she padded Tesla on the shoulder. "She has to be to have faced down that monster and lived to tell the tale."

Tesla had a pensive look on her face as they walked side by side down the hallway and descended the stairs together. When they reached the first floor, they found Cat and Anne waiting for them. Cat was in the kitchen preparing sandwiches. Anne was in the living room leaning against the fireplace, her fingers gently tapping against a revolver that was lying on the mantle. Her bare foot was tapping impatiently on the hardwood floor.

"So, how's the little one doing?" Anne asked. The anxiousness in her voice was palpable.

"She's resting," Tesla responded in a manner that suggested Anne should not push the matter.

"Well, good," Anne retorted, the small wooden totem she wore around her neck resting on her crossed arms. "So, what are we waiting for?"

"What do you mean?" Tesla asked."

"Let's end this fucker, right here, right now," Anne responded without hesitation.

Tesla's expression turned hard. "You're ready to make the decision right here and now, are you? You're ready to take a human life?"

"You're goddamn right I am," Anne leaned forward. "That son of a bitch down there, that thing, isn't a man, and he murdered my sister."

"We all know what you lost, Anne," Diana interjected. "We have all been hurt by this creature."

Tesla flinched at the sound of that word – *creature*. She shot Diana a look of concern that did not go unnoticed.

"Then what's the debate?" Anne asked. "We take this gun," she snatched the revolver from the mantle, "we point the barrel right between his soulless eyes and pull the fucking trigger!"

"And you're willing to do that?" Tesla protested. "You're willing to murder another human being just like that, in cold blood? What the hell is the matter with you?"

"I'll tell you what's wrong with me," Anne stepped toward Tesla aggressively. "I can't believe we are even discussing this. We have that motherfucker, and we can end him right here, right now!"

Anne's anger subsided in an instant when she suddenly noticed the look of terror on Tesla's face. She followed the woman's gaze down to the revolver in Anne's hand, the revolver that was now pointed directly at her friend.

"Anne, give me the gun," Diana's stern voice commanded. Her hand was resting on the hilt of the gun she kept holstered at her side. "Now," Diana said even more forcibly than before.

"Oh my God," Anne exhaled. She quickly lowered the revolver to her side and did not resist even a little as Diana disarmed her. "Tesla, I'm sorry," Anne pleaded. "I would never…" Her voice failed her as she sank back onto the couch sobbing.

In the kitchen, if Cat even noticed the drama unfolding in the living room, nobody could tell. She was slicing a nice big tomato for the sandwiches she was preparing. As the extremely sharp blade of the kitchen knife slid through the juicy vegetable, it came out the other side a bit faster than Cat had anticipated and cut into her thumb right at the base where the digit meets the palm.

Cat winced at first at the sting of the cut. She brought her hand up to her mouth and gently sucked it. The taste of copper hit her tongue as drops of blood ran through her lips. She pulled her hand away and studied the wound. For a long moment, she just stared at the little slit the knife had cut into her pale skin. When she used her fingers to squeeze her hand just on both sides of the small cut there was a slight sting that ran up her arm. The sensation brought a smile to her lips.

Before she even realized she was doing it, Cat had taken the kitchen knife and made two more small cuts on her hand right next to the first one. The stinging sensation reverberated through her body and mind. An unexplainable sensation of feeling washed over her. Absently she rolled up her sleeve. There on her arm were dozens of small pink scars, each one a memento of the times before when she sought that feeling, that sensation that allowed her to feel anything at all. As she rested the cold steel of the kitchen knife on her arm, she was suddenly aware that someone was calling her name. The voice seemed very far away at first, but then it was not very far away at all.

"Cat, honey, please," Tesla's voice was right beside her. She felt her gently remove the kitchen knife from her hand.

"Oh, hi, Tes," Cat said absently. "I was just fixing everybody a sandwich."

"I know, honey," Tesla said as she gently led Cat out of the kitchen and into the living room to join the others. As they walked, Tesla pulled a handkerchief from her pocket and gently wrapped Cat's bleeding hand. "Here, honey, sit right here." Tesla sat Cat down on the sofa and then she sat down beside her and gently rubbed her shoulders. "It's okay, honey, you are among friends. We are here for you."

"Oh, I know," Cat smiled. "I was just going to make everybody a sandwich." When she gestured to the kitchen with her thumb a stinging little pain shot through her arm, and she noticed the handkerchief Tesla had wrapped around her hand. Blood was seeping from the sides of the cloth. "Oh, yeah…," Cat said sheepishly. She looked around the room and saw genuine looks of concern on the faces of her friends and in that moment, she felt a bit ashamed. "Sorry," she whispered as she hid her hand under her arm.

Tesla pulled a knitted blanket off the backside of the couch and wrapped it around Cat's shoulders.

"I think we have had enough excitement for tonight," Tesla said. "I believe you all already know where I land on this subject. I suggest we all take a day to think about it. Think hard on what it is we should do. We live in a world of law and order for a reason. I for one cannot even begin to fathom the ramifications of taking a life, no matter how putrid that life may be."

"Tes is right," Diana added, reaching over to gently squeeze Anne's shoulder. "We are all wound up a little tight right now. We should get some sleep. Tomorrow we'll put it to a vote. Let's get some rest and come at it again with clearer heads. Agreed?"

For a split instant Anne lingered on the revolver Diana had taken from her. Then she nodded in agreement. Tesla took Cat by the shoulders and gently led her up the stairs.

"Come on, honey," she said as they ascended, "let's get you cleaned up and ready for bed."

Anne followed, but she paused at the bottom of the stairs for a moment. She turned back toward Diana and said, "We have a chance here to end this evil once and for all. You know that." She rubbed her fingers across the little wooden totem hanging from her neck. "We have a chance to avenge our loved ones, Diana."

Without another word, Anne turned and walked up the stairs.

Diana walked over to the table that held the monitor which was linked to the camera in the basement. Cat had set it up. On the screen, she could see the killer chained to the metal chair. Though the room was dark with no light, the camera had night vision tech and showed the basement in clear high def. For a long moment, she just stared at the killer, his massive shoulders and chest heaving with every breath he took. He was just staring straight ahead.

"What would you do?" Diana asked out loud as she stared at the monitor.

As if in answer, the killer slowly turned his gaze straight into the camera. She knew there was no way he could possibly have heard her. Those dark black eyes staring at her from behind that macabre bone mask unnerved her. Diana could feel her legs going numb and her hands shaking. For one moment, she felt like she was back in that dark hallway, frozen with fear and watching in terror unable to move or even scream. Watching, as this monster murdered her sister. Diana exhaled and squeezed her hands into fists so tight that her fingernails drew blood.

"One way or another, you son of a bitch," Diana said defiantly to the image on the monitor, "this ends tomorrow."

Chapter 2: Autumn's Story

1 year before the trap…

As the tree line passing quickly by outside the window thickened, Autumn could tell they were getting closer to their destination. It was not a destination she was looking forward to seeing. She had come to terms with that notion, sort of, a few hundred miles back. There was nothing she could do about it, so why dwell. Instead, she decided to try and focus on the beauty flying by as they drove down the highway.

The leaves had already changed colors from green to that beautiful burnt orange and red signaling the onset of her namesake. From her position in the backseat of her mom's minivan, Autumn had cracked her window. The air blowing in was cool and crisp. The cabin of the van had become almost unbearably hot, a biproduct of Jeffery being constantly cold and constantly whining about it enough to get his way. Jeffery was Autumn's annoying little brother. Sometimes she did not mind him, especially when he left her alone. Unfortunately, as little siblings tend to do, Jeffery was always around and always up in her business.

"We're almost there," her mom said cheerfully from the driver's seat.

"Yay!" Jeffery exclaimed, sounding about as annoying as he could possibly be.

Outside her window, Autumn saw the city limit sign which read *Welcome to Glen Haven, Home of the Screaming Bats Pop. 11,334.*

"You have got to be kidding me," Autumn scoffed.

"What's that, honey?" Her mom asked.

"My new school's mascot is a bat?" Autumn's face wrinkled as she spoke the words.

"Oh, well that's kind of cool, right?" Her mom offered.

"Hell, yeah that's cool," Jeffery added. "Batman!"

"Not Batman, you little turd," Autumn snapped. "A bat, as in a flying rodent, a rat, like you."

"I'm not a rat," Jeffery retorted. "Hell, if anybody is a rat around here it's you, Rat Queen. That's what you are, the Rat Queen. That's what I think of you." He trailed off in a fit of laughter.

"Jeffery, knock it off," Autumn's mom scolded, "and stop saying hell."

"Sorry, mom," he apologized and straightened up in his seat. Meanwhile, he was sticking his right hand around the side of his seat and giving Autumn the bird.

"You little turd!" Autumn exclaimed as she reached out and seized his little digit and twisted it.

"Mom, mom! Help! The Rat Queen has me!" He shouted.

"Autumn!" Her mom snapped. She released her brother's finger which he immediately started shaking. "That's enough out of both of you. I mean it. Straighten up now; we're almost at your father's house."

"Yes, ma'am," Jeffery replied as he complied.

Autumn just fell silent.

She could feel her mom's eyes on her in the rearview mirror.

"Autumn?" She nodded.

"Why are you making me do this?" Autumn asked as her eyes began to well. "It's not fair. I don't want to be here. You don't want to be around dad, so why should I want to. You're just selfish. This is all bullshit!" She knew her protest was worthless, but she could not help herself. She fell silent, crossed her arms, and went back to stare out the window.

The rest of the drive was spent in silence.

Autumn's mood sank even lower as her mom's minivan made that left turn off Route 666 onto

Ferndale Drive which led to her father's home. She pulled out her phone, but she already knew what it would say even before she clicked it on – *No Service*. As she had found out in previous visits to her father's country home, Azlewood, the woodlands which surrounded the town of Glen Haven, was notorious for being a dead zone. At least the woods were pretty she thought as they continued down the country road another ten miles.

She could see her father's house coming into view over the horizon. It was a two-story home of brick and wood. Her father, a retired contractor, built the house himself. As they rolled to a stop in the driveway, which was covered in fallen orange and brown leaves, Autumn could see her father waiting for them in the front yard, a big smile etched across his chiseled face. The minivan had barely rolled to a stop when Jeffery quickly unfastened his seatbelt, but before he could leap from the vehicle his mother gently tugged on his arm.

"You weren't planning and going on without telling your mama bye, now, were you?" she asked with a warm smile.

Jeffery leaned over, hugged her, and kissed her on the cheek. "Buy mama, I love you," the boy said then he quickly leapt from the minivan. "Daddy!" He cried with joy as he ran into his father's embrace.

"How you doing, kiddo?" Autumn's father said scooping Jeffery up off the ground with the greatest of ease and engulfing the happy boy in a monstrous dad hug.

"Guess what." Jeffery said.

"What's that?" His father asked.

"I know who Glen Haven's mascot is," the boy declared.

"Oh?" His dad retorted gently placing the boy back down on the ground.

"Batman!" Jeffery exclaimed.

His father laughed and tousled his son's hair. "Close, Little Champion," he said referring to Jeffery by the nickname he had given him years ago. "What you meant was bats. Bats are Glen Haven High's mascot. Don't worry, we'll get to that. Hey, why don't you run up to your room and check out what's waiting for on your bed?"

"Alright!" Jeffery exclaimed as he took off toward the house in a dead sprint.

Autumn's father smiled after the boy. When he turned back toward the minivan, his smile did not dissipate, but it did weaken.

"Honey, go say hello to your father," Autumn's mom encouraged her.

Autumn hesitated and scowled. She looked at her mom one last time, pleading with her eyes. Her mom just slowly shook her head.

"Whatever," Autumn said as she stepped out of the minivan.

Her father walked over to greet her with a hug she did not return. At six-foot-four with long limbs, Autumn's father was a physically imposing man. He was older than her mom, probably by four or five years. Even at his advanced age, her father was in a fantastic shape with a physique any man half his age would kill for.

"How you doing, sweetie?" he asked, not yet ready to release her.

"Your beard is scratching," she complained.

"Sorry," he apologized releasing her from his bearlike embrace. She would not make eye contact with him. He took his index finger, placed it under her chin, and gently brought her gaze up to meet his. "Honey, I know this is tough on you, but let's try and make the best of it, okay?"

She shook free of him and started toward the house. "Whatever," she muttered as she walked away.

For just a moment, he hung his head. Then he walked over and leaned on the driver's side door of the minivan. The window lowered to reveal Autumn's mother running her fingers quickly through her hair and smiling back at him.

"Good morning, Beverly," he smiled. "How are you?"

"I'm doing well, Ryan," she replied, pulling her long hair back behind her ears. It was something she always did when she was nervous. Ryan had seen her do it a thousand times and it always made him smile. "You are looking good," she said, eyeing his tall lean frame up and down.

"Oh, I keep busy, working on the house, the yard, hunting…," he trailed off as he made a wide arc with his hand. "There's plenty fishing and hiking around here to keep a man fit. How was the drive down?"

"It was fine," she lied. Ryan could always tell when she was lying. She would get a little crinkle right above her nose. "Jeffery couldn't wait to get here."

"And Autumn…?" Ryan asked, "How is she taking the…the move?"

Beverly exhaled. "She's a teenager, Ryan," she tried to explain. "Of course, she's not taking change well."

"Well, what did you expect, honey?" Ryan retorted. "First, the separation, and now this, Beverly, she's a seventeen-year-old girl. How else is she supposed to be taking all of this? It must be hard on her, moving to a new town, a new school, leaving all her old friends behind. Everything she knows is back in Frisco. As far as she's concerned, her entire world just came to an end."

"Don't you think I know that?" Beverly snapped back a little harsher than she had intended. She took a deep breath and continued. "Look, someday when the kids are old enough, they'll come to realize that sometimes relationships just don't work out."

"Relationship?" Ryan scoffed. "Hell, I thought we were married."

She shot him a look he had become all too familiar with in the last few years. That *don't push it too far* look.

"Why don't you stay for a while?" Ryan asked with all sincerity.

"No, I really can't," Beverly declined. "I really must get back out on the road. My job is flying me to Hong Kong in two days and I need to get back home and get a few things in order first."

"Seriously, stay," Ryan politely insisted. "I'm sure the kids would love having you around a little longer before you fly off," He paused for a moment and then added, "I would love to have you around for a little while. It would be great for all of us to spend a little time together again as a family."

Beverly leaned back and smiled as if she were considering the invitation.

"Sorry, honey, I can't," she politely declined. "I really should be going. Will you be able to get the bags with your back like it is? How are you sleeping?"

"The back is fine actually," he said stretching to emphasize his point. "I sleep pretty well. I had a good dream last night. I dreamt about you and the kids and me and we were all actually happy."

"Don't do this," Beverly scolded.

"Open, honest and no bullshit," Ryan replied unhindered, "I'm really confused right now. I miss you. I miss the feeling of being loved by you. I am a little lost right now. I feel alone…sad. Do you not love me anymore? Or have you decided that you just don't want me in that way? If you don't, what changed? I thought we were meant for each other. If you do still love me then what is it, we are doing here? Haven't we missed out on enough time? Why would we spend any more time apart? You say this is how it must be, that you don't have any left for me? That doesn't sound like love. Tell me you love me. Tell me you want me. Tell me, I'm your man. I'm dying here without you. I'm starting to withdraw. I don't feel the closeness we once had. I feel you slipping from my grasp. Tell me we are going to be okay."

"I'm really glad you didn't have a bad dream," Beverly's poor attempt at humor fell flat. She exhaled and replied, "All I can tell you is that I do love you, and I do hope for a future with you. That's what I want, but I just can't do it right now. I just can't. I am sorry that I made you feel this way. It's the last thing that I want to do. I am just trying to be as open and honest and no bullshit as I can be. I know how…," she paused for just a moment. "I feel the distance as well. I see you withdrawing, and I feel my walls going up. Believe me when I say, I am as lost as you. I don't understand why things are the way they are. I just know they are. I am sad and confused too and of course I miss you, too. I just know that I need this right now. So, I guess the question really is can you handle the way things are right now? Are you going to be okay with it? If not, then you need to tell me so we can figure it out."

"I guess I just don't understand," Ryan shook his head. "If we want to be with each other, why can't we? It makes me feel like you have one foot in this marriage and one out the door. Like you thought this is what you wanted then when it was in your face, you realized it isn't what you wanted. Or worse, you may be holding out for something better. Either of these break my heart."

"That's not what's going on," she tried to reassure him. "I just know that I can't keep going down this path right now. I want us to at least have a chance to make this work at some point and right now can't be that time. I know me and I don't want it to come to a point where there is no future because we pushed for something I can't give right now. I am seriously going to have a breakdown and at times I feel it happening from the inside. I'm sorry that you don't get it but I'm trying to tell you and you keep thinking it's something more or different than what it really is. I wish you will take it as what I'm saying and know that I do love you and I do miss you and it's hard, very hard for me too, but I really think it must be this way. I just need you to figure out for you if you can be okay with it?"

"What does *right now* mean?" He asked. "Today? Next week? Next Month? Next Year? When will you be ready? Never? You don't know?" He started to wring his large hands. "I get it. But, if you truly love me and want to be with me and want to be with me romantically and beyond, doesn't this seem like something we should talk about and work on actively, not shelve it for potential future revisiting? That doesn't seem fair or healthy for either of us."

"I have no answers," she shook her head. "I just don't know. Does that seem fair or healthy? Probably not, but I just don't know. I wish I knew. I wish I understood so that I could help you understand, but I don't. I'm sorry that things are not the way we thought they would be right now. You are asking questions I wish I had answers to, but they are impossible for me to answer, and I just can't answer them when I don't know myself. Do I love you? Yes. That, I can answer." He just stared back at her blankly. She continued, "I love you. It kills me knowing that you are hurting, and it makes it even worse that it's my fault."

"Killing you, huh?" He scoffed. "…obviously not enough to stay and try to fix our broken family. From the bills, I also noticed you changed your last name back."

"Please, Ryan, don't do this," she shook her head.

"Pop the hatchback," he said sternly.

"What?" She asked, confused.

"The hatchback," he answered, pointing to the rear of the minivan. "Pop the back so I can get the kids' bags."

"Oh, yes, of course," Beverly reached down and pulled the small lever.

Ryan unloaded the luggage and sat it on the front lawn. He then walked back over to the driver's side of the minivan. He leaned in the window and kissed his estranged wife on the cheek. His scent engulfed her and for a moment her defenses failed. There was just something about his scent that always overpowered her will. Absently, she reached up and grabbed him by the back of his head, her long slender finger forking through his short-cropped graying hair. She gently turned his head and kissed him full on the lips. For a moment, just a moment, they both remembered why they loved each other. But the moment was fleeting.

"Sorry," she apologized, regaining her senses, and quickly releasing him.

"It's okay," Ryan smiled. "Have a good trip, honey. We'll all be here, awaiting the return of her majesty." His last statement was equal parts flirtation and sarcasm.

She smiled and started the engine. He watched with sadness as she aptly turned the minivan around in the large driveway. Just before she pulled away, Beverly blew Ryan a kiss. He stuck his hand up and closed his fist miming catching the invisible gesture. As the minivan disappeared down the drive, Ryan tossed the invisible kiss over his shoulder.

As she ascended the stairs to the second floor, Autumn could hear Jeffery screaming with joy from his room.

"O-M-G! O-M-G! O-M-G!" He kept screaming repeatedly.

As she walked past his open door, he came running into the hall so fast that his enthusiasm nearly took them both over the second story railing.

"Oh my god, Autumn!" he exclaimed at the top of his lungs. "Oh my god! Oh my god! Oh my god!"

"Calm down you little spas," Autumn shook free of his clutching grasp.

"Autumn, dear sister, you don't understand!" He tried to explain.

"Understand what?" Her patience was reaching an end.

"Look!" He pointed into his room. "Just look!"

"Ew, no, you little freak," she refused.

"Just come on!" he insisted, grabbing her by the arm and leading her into his bedroom.

As they entered the room, there were posters of movies and assorted comic book characters thumbtacked to the wall. *Spider-Man, Batman, Thor, Wolverine*, and many others in various ridiculous poses covering nearly every inch of wall space. A few of the posters, movie posters - *The Goonies, The Monster Squad*, and *Stand by Me* - were neatly framed and centered. There were several bookshelves with assorted books, graphic novels, and stacks of comic books on the shelves. On top of the four-drawer dresser stood more than a dozen models and statues of various robots and mechanized heroes – *Transformers* and *Robotech* mostly, with a large statue of *Voltron* in the back, towering over all the rest. In the far corner was a plastic chest, no doubt full of *Star Wars*, *Teenage Mutant Ninja Turtles*, and any other action figure one can possibly imagine. On the nightstand next to Jeffery's bed was a *Hot Wheels* car, a small green plastic flashlight in the shape of a lightsaber, and a *Batman* alarm clock that projects the Bat-Signal on the wall when it goes off.

Autumn just shook her head. "It's like a ten-year-old boy's wet dream just exploded in here," she teased. "Dad sure has wasted a lot of money on you, you little dirt bag."

"Stop it!" Jeffery snapped. "Stop being you for just a second and bask in the gloriousness." He gestured toward the bed.

Autumn followed his gesture to where he was pointing and sitting there on the bed was a long box, no, not a box, a slipcase that was a little over a foot long and about eight or nine inches tall. Within the slipcase were at least two dozen books. The outside of the slipcase was adorned with artwork featuring various characters in dynamic poses.

"So," Autumn rolled her eyes. "So, it's just more comic book crap. As if you don't have enough of that garbage already." She made a wide arching gesture with her hand, referring to the décor of the bedroom.

"Don't you get it?" Jeffery asked as he walked over to admire the slipcase. "This is the second Premium *Naruto* Box Set! It includes volumes twenty-eight through forty-eight! I finally get to see what happened after *Naruto* left to train with *Jirayia*!"

"Na-what?" Autumn asked completely confused.

"*Naruto!*" Jeffery exclaimed.
"*Naruto! Naruto! Naruto!*"

"What the hell is a Nay-root-oh?" Autumn asked in a way where Jeffery could not tell whether she was teasing or not.

"*Naruto Uzumaki!*" Jeffery exclaimed. "He's the earthly host of *Kurama* the nine-tailed fox. He's the protector of the people of Konoha. Any of this ringing a bell?"

"You know something?" Autumn scoffed. "Mom and dad should really have you checked out for mental issues."

"I assume you liked your gift?" Their father asked as he entered the room carrying the children's luggage, a suitcase in each hand, a duffle bag tucked under each arm, and three large bags with long straps hanging off each shoulder and around his neck.

Jeffery sprinted across the room and nearly knocked his father off balance with his over enthusiastic embrace.

"Daddy, thank you, thank you, thank you!" Jeffery screamed with joy.

Ryan chuckled as he caught his balance. "I'm glad you like it, little buddy. Now, give the old man here a hand, will you?"

"Sure thing, pop!" Jeffery exclaimed as he grabbed the large suitcase out of his father's right hand. But the over enthusiastic ten-year-old misjudged the weight of the case and buckled under it. He tumbled backwards to the ground with the large suitcase crashing down on top of him.

"Whoops!" Jeffery smiled. "Heavier than I thought."

Ryan and Jeffery were laughing as Autumn made her exit out of the room. She walked down the upstairs hallway to the right. Her room was the next door on the right. Across from her room was the upstairs bathroom. Further down, at the end of the hallway was another room, a much larger room. This was what her father referred to as the game room. Back down the other way, at the other end of the hall was the master bedroom where her father slept.

Autumn turned the knob and entered her designated bedroom. She noticed that it was exactly how she had left it when they were down for their visit last summer vacation. Everything was tidy and neat and in its proper place. The vanity was polished and all its drawers and little compartments which contained all her make-up, jewelry, and knick-knacks were closed and unmolested. She picked up the ivory-handled brush and studied it for a moment. All the loose hair had been plucked from the bristles. She noticed the mirror had been wiped clean and did not have a smudge on it.

She opened the closet. There were dozens of thick white plastic hangers for her clothes. Several blankets and linens were neatly folded and stacked on the shelf above. There was a stackable case for her shoes. To the left of her bed was a small desk. She would sit at this desk and write her stories and poems. Next to the desk was a large window. From the window, Autumn had a fantastic view of the forest which surrounded her father's home. The top of the trees was like a blanket of brown and orange this time of year. Way off in the distance, she could see the blue waters of Eagle Mountain Lake.

She turned back toward the bed. On the stand, next to her bed was a pad and a pencil next to the bejeweled alarm clock. She always kept the pad and pencil there just in case an idea struck her. On the bed was a large brown box. There was no marking on the outside of the box that would give any indication of what was within. The box was quite large though. Autumn just assumed it was an over-sized stuffed bear, probably pink with a giant red heart on its chest, a gesture of love meant for a much younger girl.

"I'm not a little girl, dad," she said to herself. "I think I'm a little too old for stuffed animals."

However, her attitude quickly changed tune once she opened the top of the box to reveal what was inside.

"Oh my god," she breathed. She stepped back with her hands over her mouth. That's when she heard her father's voice from behind.

"Do you like it?" he asked.

She turned to see him standing large in her doorway. He was only carrying half the luggage he had before, having dropped Jeffery's off in his room.

"I figured if my little girl was going to be a writer then she needed the right tools," her father said as he neatly stacked her bags against the wall.

He walked over and carefully pulled out the contents of the box revealing a brand-new laptop computer. He carefully placed it on her old desk and flipped it open to reveal a fifteen-inch monitor. The whole time, Autumn just watched, speechless.

"There, it all fits perfectly," he stood with his hands on his hips admiring the set up. "Now you won't have access to the internet out here, but you should have enough memory in there to write another *War and Peace*."

He barely had time to finish his sentence as she was already embracing him in a tight hug. He smiled and hugged his daughter. He was happy that she was happy. She released him and that sad look crept back over her round face. Her thoughts were many miles away.

"Honey, I know this is a big deal," he assured her. "Uprooting your life and moving to a strange new place is hard on anybody, especially a teenage girl about to enter her senior year."

"Yeah, that really sucks," she said walking over to the window, "but that's not why I'm upset."

"Oh?" Ryan crossed his arms and leaned his tall frame against the wall. "Then what's the matter, honey?"

"It's…mom!" Tears were beginning to well up in her big brown eyes. "She's so damn selfish. First, she made you leave without any warning or reason that I've ever been given, and now, she's basically leaving Jeffrey and me as if she never cared at all. What kind of person abandons her children?" Anger prevented her from breaking down into a full-blown cry, but nonetheless, tears began to stream down her face.

"Oh, honey," Ryan said walking over to her and once again taking her into his long, strong arms. His heart was breaking with each word. "Listen, Autumn. Your mother is not abandoning you. She loves the both of you very much. It's just that she has a really big opportunity with her company that in the long run could mean a much better life for you and your brother."

"I don't care about that," she said as the tears continued to fall. "I just want us all back to the way things were before. I want us to be a family again."

"I know, honey, I know," he lovingly stroked her hair. "Sometimes two people, no matter how much they may love each other, just aren't meant to be together. Your mother and I have a long and complicated history. Somethings you may know, somethings you certainly will never know. Someday, when you are old enough and have had a few more years of life experience under your belt, you'll begin to understand a little better. I'm not saying you'll have all the answers. God knows I don't, but someday you'll be able to look back on this time and you will have a better perspective, okay?" She nodded. He kissed her on the forehead and brushed her tears away. He said, "Okay, honey, unpack your things and meet me downstairs. Since we don't have cell phone reception in these woods and no landline that comes out here, I'm going to go over with you and your brother on how to use the CB radio."

"Okay," she replied as she wiped her face with the sleeve of her shirt.

Ryan walked toward the door, but before he exited the room he turned and said, "Autumn, I love baby girl."

"I love you too, daddy," she replied with a smile.

*****

"Come on, Little Champion, we're almost there," Jeffery's father called back from up the trail some ways. "Your sister is already there. Come on, son, you're too damn young to be this out of shape." His father laughed and continued up the trail, his rifle slung over one shoulder and a large pack over the other.

Jeffery was finding it hard to keep up with his father and sister because the only exercise he was used to would be the required fifteen minutes of calisthenics at gym class, which consisted of a half dozen jumping Jacks, touching his toes a couple of times, and mowing down zombies with the latest shooter on his PS4. He paused for a moment to catch his breath. With his hands on his knees, he breathed deeply. The air here was much cleaner than back home. Well, back in Frisco anyway. He had not quite gotten used to referring to Glen Haven as his home yet. The air also had a sweet aroma to it. They had trees back from where he came from, but nothing like what surrounded him now. From his vantage on the sloped trail, he could see for miles in all directions, trees, giant majestic trees, small trees, and everything in-between.

"Get a move on, boy," he heard his father call from quite a distance up ahead.

Jeffery took one more deep breath, and with a second wind, trotted the rest of the way up the trail. The trail opened to a wide flat plateau overlooking the Lake and forest below. His father and sister were already sitting and relaxing on a blanket they had laid out for the picnic. Autumn was pulling out sandwiches and various plastic containers filled with fruit and potato chips. Jeffery came stumbling into the picnic and made an over exaggerated pratfall onto the soft blanket.

"There he is!" His father exclaimed playfully patting him on the back. "There's our Little Champion."

"Wow!" Jeffery breathed. "That was quite a walk."

"It was a mere a hop, skip, and a jump from the house, my boy," his father teased. "You, my boy, need to spend a little less time in front of the computer screen and a little more time outside."

Ryan reached over and tousled the boy's hair playfully.

"Here you go, dad," Autumn handed him a sandwich.

"Thank you, honey," he replied, as he began to un-wrap the sandwich. He took a deep whiff and declared, "Egg salad…yummy!"

For a few minutes, Autumn and her father sat there enjoying the picnic and enjoying the view. Meanwhile, Jeffery lay flat on his back, his chest heaving, and staring up at the clouds in the sky. Far below them, the waters of the lake rippled as gusts of strong wind blew in from the north. That same breeze rustled through the trees of the forest and caused leaves of many colors to fall like rain all throughout the land. Below their vantage, was the roof of the forest with many dotted spots of fall orange and brown mixed in with even more sections of evergreen, it appeared almost like a flat solid surface running the width from horizon to horizon. Birds were chirping all around, squirrels, armadillos, and other various critters were scurrying here and there, going about their daily activities, showing no interest in the three people resting on that large comfortable picnic blanket.

"Dad?" Autumn broke the silence.

"Yes, honey," he nodded.

"Why did you move here?" She made a gesture toward the picturesque scene surrounding them. "I get it. Really, I do. It's super pretty here and the air is fresh and sweet..."

"What is that smell," Jeffery chimed in. "It's strong."

"What you smell is the loblolly pine," Ryan answered. "See all those trees out there that are still green even as others are turning colors and losing leaves for the winter to come." The kids nodded. "Those are what are known as loblolly pines. They are evergreen trees."

"Wow, dad, you are wicked smart," Jeffery said without an ounce of insincerity.

"Oh, I don't know about how smart I am," Ryan chuckled. "I grew up here, kids. I was born in Glen Haven. That's why I built this home here. Y'all have only been here a couple times for a few weeks in the summer, but I had always planned for this to our home…all of us, together."

"Isn't this where you met mom?" Autumn asked.

"It is," Ryan answered. "We were in school together."

"Why did y'all leave?" She asked.

"Your mother…," Ryan paused for a moment, then said. "Let's just say that Glen Haven, or more specifically Azlewood, isn't your mother's favorite place."

"Are there bears here?" Jeffery's imagination was beginning to run. "Are we in danger? Is that why you brought your rifle?"

"Bears?" Ryan scratched his chin and shook his head. "Nah, not in these parts. Maybe once every blue moon but not really. For bears that would be much further east... Louisiana, maybe, but not here. I brought the rifle because there have been the occasional cougar sightings, not to mention the occasional white-tailed deer."

"Deer?" Autumn gasped. "Dad, you're not going to shoot a deer, are you?"

Ryan laughed. "No, no," he said. "Just teasing. No, I brought my rifle along because while there may not be any bears that I know of you never know what you might run into out in the wild. It's always good to be prepared."

"What about Bigfoot?" Jeffery asked, crossing his fingers.

"Why, you believe in Bigfoot?" Ryan teased.

"Yes!" Jeffery exclaimed.

Ryan chuckled. "Well, I've never seen him, but that's not to say there aren't other critters scurrying around in these here woods."

"Well, I did some surfing on the web and rumor has it these woods are haunted," Jeffery again spoke without a tinge of irony.

Ryan smiled but did not reply, not right away. He thought carefully for a moment about how to respond. Then, he said, "Haunted is not a word I use to describe these woods."

"What word would you use?" Autumn asked.

"Magical," Ryan answered.

"Magical?" Jeffery and Autumn asked in unison.

"Oh, absolutely," Ryan smiled.

"What like fairies and unicorns and Leprechauns?" Jeffery asked, his eyes getting wide.

"Don't be silly, Little Champion," Ryan smiled, "Leprechauns don't exist."

"What do you mean magical?" Jeffery was practically begging. "Come on…tell me!"

"Calm down, Little Champion," Ryan patted his boy on the back. "Let's just say that this forest here has been here for a very long time, a very long time. Way longer than any town, or settlers, even longer than the Indian tribes that used to live in this area. And, during that time many, many stories about these woods have been told. Many legends."

"Scary stories?" Jeffery asked.

"Yes," Ryan replied, but noticing the look of fear on his young son's face, he quickly reached over and reassured him, "but many good stories as well."

"Before mom forced us to move here, I also did some studying up on this area," Autumn said. "According to the internet, the town of Glen Haven, and more precisely Azlewood, is a notorious hotspot for supernatural activity."

"You read this on the computer?" Ryan asked.

"Yes," Autumn replied. "There are entire websites devoted to the topic of Glen Haven.

"Did you know that back in the 1800s, a bunch of miners went missing, and then people in town started to go missing?" Autumn continued. "The town was practically a ghost town and then suddenly, the disappearances stopped. Nobody knows why exactly, but there are theories."

"What kind of theories?" Jeffery asked.

"Lots of theories," Autumn said. "Did you know that in the 1950s there was this rancher whose wife went missing, but the townsfolk charged him with her murder? They tried him and sent him to the electric chair. They say that on some nights, if you stand on the shores of the lake, you hear her sobs in the winds. Some legends say she cries because she was violently murdered by her husband and her soul cannot rest. I've also read that she cries because her husband was an innocent man, and the guilt of his wrongful execution weighs so heavily on her soul that she can never rest until the mystery surrounding her disappearance is solved."

"Really?" Jeffery asked nervously staring down at the lake below. "She's really out there?"

"Did you also know that there have been a rash of murders in these woods that have happened just in the last few years?" Autumn continued.

"What?" Jeffery asked with a shaky voice. He was becoming nervous and slid closer to his father who put a reassuring strong arm around his shoulder.

"Yeah," Autumn smiled. She could see her stories were getting to her little brother and she could not help but antagonize him. "First, a summer camp was attacked, and then a group of college kids on vacation. All of them, cut into pieces by a serial killer they call the Goatman."

Unbeknownst to the children, at that moment, Ryan's right hand involuntarily shifted toward his rifle.

"Goatman?" Jeffery asked. He was beginning to shiver despite the comfortable seventy-eight-degree temperature of the afternoon. "Why do they call him the Goatman?"

"There are lots of theories on that as well," Autumn replied. "You said you wanted to see Bigfoot?"

"I never said that," Jeffery retorted, shaking his head. "I just wanted to know if he was ever seen in this area."

"Well, they say he's called the Goatman because he's half-man/half-goat, you see," she explained. "He has the body of a man, but the legs and head of a goat, and he's seven feet tall." She could see her little brother becoming more and more squeamish with each word. She was enjoying making him uncomfortable. "They also say that he just doesn't murder people, but that he also eats them as well."

"What?" Jeffery had heard enough. He squirmed so far into his father's side that he nearly knocked the large man over.

"Alright, honey, he's had enough," Ryan told Autumn.

"Well, it's all true," Autumn declared.

"Don't believe everything you read on the internet, okay?" Ryan said as he coaxed his frightened son back into his space.

"What about the witch?" Autumn asked.

"Witch?" Jeffery jumped.

"What was that, honey?" Ryan asked, not because he did not hear what she had asked, but because he was stalling for time.

"Well, as I was doing my research on the web about all the legends surrounding this town and these woods, there was one name that kept coming up time and time again," Autumn explained. "Agatha Warden. They say she was a witch and that hundreds of years ago she plagued the people of this land, and her ghost still haunts these woods to this day."

Ryan did not answer, not right away anyway. He leaned back on his large hands, crossed his long legs, and stared out over the horizon. He let the cool fall breeze wash over him. His thick graying hair wafting in the wind. With his eyes closed, he smiled, as if remembering something, something good. He seemed completely relaxed, and this influenced Jeffery. Watching his father become completely at ease helped the boy to also relax.

"That internet sure is a something," Ryan chuckled. "Well, I can't tell you anything about that. I've had no firsthand experiences, but I'll tell you what. I can tell you a legend about these parts my granddaddy told me when I was about your age." Ryan nodded at his son. "Would you like to hear that?"

"Yes, please," Jeffery answered with a smile, sitting with his legs crossed, his elbows on his knees, his chin in his hands.

Autumn crossed her arms and looked at her father suspiciously.

"Okay," she said.

"Y'all have heard of Christopher Columbus, right?" Ryan asked.

"Of course," Autumn replied.

"Yes!" Jeffery exclaimed. "He discovered America."

"Well, that's not entirely true," Ryan corrected. "What he did do though was inform the Europeans of this whole New World that lay across the sea, a vibrant, virtual paradise just waiting to be explored and, unfortunately, exploited. Besides, the Americas were already inhabited by many, many tribes of Native Americans. So, Columbus was by far not the first person to discover this great land of ours." Ryan paused to let his words sink in. "Do y'all know who Leif Erickson is?"

Jeffery's eyes squinted, and then eventually he just shook his head.

"No, well, I think I remember his name…who is he?" Autumn asked.

"Really?" Ryan's question was met with blank stares as both his children shook their heads. "I weep for the modern school system." Ryan chuckled. "Columbus made his historical journey to America in 1492, and for centuries he was thought of as the guy who quote 'discovered America.' Christopher Columbus wasn't even the first European to make it over to the shores of America. Leif Erickson was an explorer from Iceland who had sailed to the North American shores over five hundred years before Columbus came to America."

"Whoa!" Jeffery gasped.

"I thought that might capture your imagination, Little Champion," Ryan padded his son on the head. "Now, though history tells us Leif Erickson was the first European to set foot on American soil, there are legends of others, even before him, before Leif Erickson, of others who braved almost certain death and unknown dangers and crossed the harsh Atlantic Ocean to come to discover this virtual paradise. These were strong, rough, hard men, men from a harsher way of life, men who lived and died by the sword, by the axe, and arrow. They were raiders, reavers, men who took what they wanted and pillaged and vanquished all who stood in their way. Empowered by old religions and old gods, these were hardened warriors, forged in combat."

"Wow, who were they, dad?" Jeffery asked.

"They were Vikings, son," Ryan replied.

"Vikings?" Jeffery gasped. "Whoa! Like Thor!"

"Well, not exactly like the Thor you know, but Thor was probably one of the many deities these men worshiped."

"Hey, wasn't Leif Erickson a Viking?" Autumn asked.

"Yes, but he was from a much later time than the men in this story," Ryan replied. "These men were said to have actually walked the shores of America one-hundred years before Leif Erickson set eyes on Greenland. They sailed across the Atlantic in their longships, great wooden vessels with a dozen long ores on both sides and a massive dragon's head carved into the bow and a serpent's tail in the stern. Their journey was long and quite arduous."

"What does *arduous* mean?" Jeffery asked.

"It means their journey was difficult," Autumn answered.

"Oh," Jeffery replied, rubbing his nose.

"Yes, their journey across the Atlantic Ocean was quite difficult," Ryan continued his tale. "You have to remember that this was over one-thousand years ago. Back then, many people thought the world was flat, and if you sailed too far out to sea, your boat would simply fall off the edge and plummet forever into a great void. So, for these men to attempt a journey like this one took great courage. Vikings by nature were a stalwart lot, nearly fearless in their endeavors."

"Whoa," Jeffery exhaled.

"Now, don't go idolizing these guys just yet, Little Champion," Ryan warned his son. "What do you know about Vikings?"

"Well, they live in a magical place called Asgard," Jeffery answered in an earnest tone. "Their leader is Odin; he's an old guy with an eye-patch. Their greatest warrior is Thor, who has a hammer that can defeat anybody." Jeffery brought his little fist down into his other hand making a slapping sound to mimic the hammer he was referring to.

"Those are stories from your comic books," Ryan corrected. "Real Vikings lived a very hard and violent existence; especially during the time my grandfather's tale takes place. Vikings were known throughout Europe at that time as raiders and pillagers. Their warriors would load up in their longboats and sail along the coastline of northern and western Europe and raid and plunder any settlement they came across. These raids were not what you'd call a pleasant affair. They would slaughter the men of these poor villages and enslave the women and children." Ryan saw his son's expression change from happy to sad in an instant. "Don't fret, Little Champion," Ryan said, taking his forefinger and tapping his son under the chin. "Keep your chin up. I'm not telling you this story to bum you out. I'm passing down a tale my grandfather told me, a tale his father had told him. This tale ties into the history of our town here and it addresses some of those questions y'all seem to have found on the internet. Would you rather wait until another time to hear the tale?"

"No, I want to hear it now," Autumn answered immediately.

Jeffery was silent, but just for a moment. "I want to hear it, too," he said. "Please, dad, so what happened?"

"Okay," Ryan said and then continued his tale. "Among these raiders was a particular group of extremely ruthless Vikings known as the *Sons of Fenris*. They hailed from Iceland and their capacity for violence and mayhem was legendary even amongst their own kind. They not only raided and plundered, but they would slaughter every male, of all ages, every woman over the age of twenty and under the age of twelve, and then burn the village to the ground, leaving nothing behind but death and ash.

These *Sons of Fenris* were led by a ruthless warrior named Bjorn, a mighty warrior whose face and body bore the scars of countless battles, but his sword never knew the sting of defeat. All who challenged him fell before his monstrous blade, which to most men would require two hands to wield in combat. Bjorn only needed one. Legends say he could cut down two to three men at a time with a single swipe of his giant sword. Some say the secret to Bjorn's invincibility was due to the black magic of the Norn-witch he kept among his crew, a female whom he captured on one his raids. The Norn's name was Eden. Some stories say Eden and Bjorn were lovers from the start. Others suggest that Bjorn allowed the witch to live so long as her magic proved useful and that they fell in love over time.

Bjorn and his crew were making quite a reputation for themselves. It was said that they were feared, even by their own people. However, after their last raid on the shores of what is now Ireland, Bjorn and his crew set sail for home, but they were never seen in Iceland again. Though the exact reasons why they set out on their harrowing trek across the ocean are not known, some legends say they were tricked by stories of treasures beyond imagination in a land that was paradise on earth. Another version says that the acts of violence and the massacres committed by the *Sons of Fenris* in the name of the gods offended the *Aesir*, and Odin, the king of the gods, most of all." Noticing the confused look on Jeffery's face, Ryan explained, "The *Aesir* were the Norse Gods. Odin, Thor, Sif…they are who those superheroes you read about in the comic books are loosely based on." Jeffery nodded. Ryan continued his tale.

"Odin had become so enraged by the slaughter committed in his name that he cursed the *Sons of Fenris* causing them to never be able to find their way home," Ryan said. "When they had set out for home, their detail was comprised of four longboats, sixty battle-ready Viking warriors, twenty-one enslaved Irish girls, and one Norn-witch. For over a year, some versions of the tale say up to even ten years, the *Sons of Fenris* sailed the torrential waters of the Atlantic lost and aimless. Miraculously, they eventually found themselves in the Gulf of Mexico.

How they survived so long at sea is anybody's guess. Some theories suggest that once the food ran out the Vikings turned to cannibalism to keep from starving to death. The first victims were the enslaved Irish, but as time wore on, and morale began to fail, crew members began turning on each other. At first the stronger members of the crew would kill the weaker members, but as time wore on some more it is suggested that a full out mutiny broke out and warriors who once fought side-by-side as brothers-in-arms now tried to slaughter each other to stave off starvation. Other rumors suggest that this could not have been enough to save them, and that the resident Norn used blood magic to overrule the curse placed upon them by the gods. Whatever the case may be, by time they had reached the New World all that remained of Bjorn's once mighty force was a single battered ship, barely seaworthy, twelve men including Bjorn, and one Norn-witch."

"What is cannibalism?" Jeffery asked.

"It means they ate each other," Autumn answered before Ryan could.

"Ate each other?" Jeffery asked, trying to work out the details in his head. When the light went on, his expression changed to one of revulsion. "That's gross!"

"Haven't you ever heard of the *Donner Party*?" Autumn asked. "They had to resort to cannibalism when they got stuck in the mountains for the winter on their way to California."

"That's okay that you are offended by that, Jeffery," Ryan said. "Cannibalism is a terrible thing. Let's hope we never have to be put into a position where we'd have to make that life-or-death decision."

After a moment of contemplation, Jeffery asked his father, "So, what happened next?"

"Yeah," Autumn chimed in, "how does this tie into the witch Agatha Warden the internet was talking about?"

"Bjorn and his crew, weakened by starvation and the ordeal of their journey, found what we know today as the Mississippi River. However, wherever they made land fall, they were seemingly always greeted and dogged by the hostile natives that inhabited the area along the Mississippi at that time. Their journey up the Mississippi brought them to a branching waterway we today call the Red River. Who knows how long they would have continued but the decision was made for them as their longboat simply gave out and collapsed under their feet. Two more men, not having the strength to make it to shore, drowned in that moment.

Bjorn, the surviving crewmen, and his witch made their way to shore. Though they were still dogged by hostile natives and only able to eat whatever the land could provide, somehow, they survived and eventually made their way south, to here."

"Here?" Jeffery patted the ground.

"Yes," Ryan answered. "They made it here to what we today now call Azlewood. That probably would have been the end of their story too if a local tribe of Native Americans known as the Caddo had not intervened. The Caddo embraced this strange group of foreigners. They fed them and nursed them back to health. They allowed Bjorn and his surviving crewmen to live alongside their tribe in these woods, woods the Caddo held high respect for. However, the decision to help Bjorn and his men would be a decision that would come back to haunt the Caddo."

"What happened?" Jeffery asked.

"The Caddo were a peaceful people," Ryan explained. "They lived in harmony with nature, never taking more than they needed to survive. Bjorn and his men were after all Vikings, and a soft peaceful existence did not sit well at all with these warriors born. It started when Bjorn and his men, now fully recovered from their harrowing ordeal at sea, began raiding neighboring tribes. The whole sale slaughter of their neighbors did not sit well with the Caddo. When a party of Caddo, led by the chief's son, confronted Bjorn and his men about the transgressions, they were ambushed and subsequently slaughtered by the Vikings. With their strongest tribesmen dead, the Caddo were powerless to stop Bjorn and his men as they turned on the tribe that had only a year before saved their lives.

The elders of the tribe called upon the spirits of the forest for protection. Their prayers were answered as Bjorn and his men were mysteriously struck down by some sort of debilitating sickness, a rapidly acting decay suddenly coursed through their bodies. At first, they became weakened, unable to even hold up their weapons. Then they were stricken and deprived of the strength to even stand. They lay there on the ground, their muscles shrinking away, their skin rapidly shriveling, their bones softening, and their breath slowing.

Do you know what a *straw death* is, son?" Ryan asked Jeffery. The boy shook his head. Ryan explained, "Vikings were a warrior class. They lived and died by the sword. Their goal was to die in glorious battle so that they could sit side-by-side with all the great warriors from history in *Valhalla*, the great Hall of Odin. However, to die of old age or weak and sick in your bed was considered the absolute worse way for a Viking to meet his end. They called it the *straw death*.

Well, as Bjorn and his men lay there, rapidly aging, and quickly withering away to dust, Bjorn called out to the Norn. She was not a part of the Viking raid and therefore not inflicted by the woodland spirits herself. Suddenly, she appeared at his side and knelt. The sight of her mighty warrior lover so stricken horrified the Norn and sent her into a fit of rage and anguish. In the last moments before Bjorn and his men were snuffed out of existence all together, Eden called upon the darkest of magic, blood magic.

66

She unsheathed a dagger and sliced it across her palm. As she spoke the words of a long-forgotten language, she walked to each of Bjorn's inflicted warriors and splattered blood from her hand upon them. She finally came to Bjorn himself, who could no longer speak because his tongue had long since recoiled into his throat. She knelt and kissed her lover on the forehead where the bone of his skull now shown through his thinning skin. She wiped blood from her hand across his forehead. She then stood and screamed the final incantations of her unholy spell. With wind, dirt, fire, and rain swirling all around her, she turned to face the elders of the Caddo tribe. The old men were chanting, praying, calling on the spirits of the forest for protection. Eden plunged her own dagger into her heart and with her dying breath her curse was implemented."

"Curse?" Jeffery asked. "What happened next?"

"Who knows?" Ryan answered. "I've heard it described many ways, but the one that has always captured my imagination was the maelstrom."

"The what?" Jeffery asked.

"The maelstrom," Ryan said holding his hands out wide and then crisscrossing them back and forth rapidly to illustrate his point. "In that moment of the witch's death there was a great release of power. Some say that the woods lit up as bright as day in that moment. They say that in that moment the holy spirits of the woods and the dark forces the Norn had called upon waged a battle in the spirit world for the fate of this land."

"Who won?" Jeffery asked emphatically.

"Nobody, you spaz," Autumn teased. "It's just a stupid ole fairy tale."

Ignoring his daughter's taunts, Ryan finished his tale, "That's just it, Little Champion; neither side could get it over on the other. It's a war between light and dark that some say is still going on to this day. I asked my grandfather the same thing you just asked me, and I'll try to explain the same way he explained it to me. There are things in this world that no man can explain. Good, evil, mankind is susceptible to both, and both are vying for control. These woods here, Azlewood, are a vocal point for something that is beyond my ability to explain." Ryan turned to his daughter and continued. "Now, over the years, have there been terrible things that have occurred in and around these woods? Yes, but no small town is without its secrets. Some say that this land was a virtual paradise before the Norn cast her curse over it. I've heard some people refer to these woods as cursed, like you've no doubt read on the internet, but I have also heard many people refer to these woods as blessed. Cursed...blessed...? That's not a question I can answer, but I can say I was born here, I grew up in these woods. I've been all over the great state Texas, been to California, hell, I've even been to New York City a time or two, and there's one thing I can tell you for sure, there's nowhere on God's green earth I'd rather be then right here, right now with you two."

"Wow, dad, that was some story," Jeffery said. "Your grandfather told you that story?"

"He sure did," Ryan replied. "Your mother's father tells it as well, but he has a little different spin to it."

"Really?" Jeffery asked. "What does he say?"

"Maybe you should ask him some time," Ryan said patting his son on the shoulder. "I bet he'd just love to tell his version."

"So, what did that tale of *Dungeons and Dragons* have to do with Agatha Warden?" Autumn asked.

Ryan's brow furrowed as he tried to think of the best way to address his daughter's question. "Honey, there are no such things as witches," he said.

"But I read on those websites…," she replied.

Ryan cut her off by holding up his large hand and said, "Honey, you can't believe everything you read on the internet."

"But what about that story you just told us with the witch and the Vikings and spirits?" Jeffrey asked, as he squinted his eyes against the light of the sun which had begun its descent in the western sky.

Ryan cleared his throat and said, "Kids, that's just a story. Those rumors on the web are just stories. They are stories old timers tell each other and pass them down to try and explain things they don't understand. Now, come on. Let's head back to the house. It will be dark soon."

They gathered their belongings in silence. As they started back down the trail, Autumn paused for a moment and looked out across the endless bed of trees below. A cool breeze swept over her, giving her a chill. She exhaled and then started off after her father and brother.

*****

The next morning, Autumn sat at her desk, ready to begin writing her thoughts down, her memories, her dreams, and her desires. She sat there and stared at the blank screen. Long quiet moments passed by. She stared so long she felt like she was in some sort of trance. In fact, she shook herself to clear her vision.

"Well, just like every great writer has said before," she said out loud as she reaches over and closed the laptop, "I'll start tomorrow."

Autumn decided to stretch her legs. She walked out into the hallway. There was no other sound coming from anywhere in the house. In fact, the only sound she could hear at all was the natural ambient sounds one would hear in the woods coming from outside. That and something else caught her ear. A mild thumping sound. There would be a few moments pause and then a *thump*. There it was again. Autumn looked left and then right and decided that from the right was the direction this *thump* was coming from.

She slowly walked down the hallway. She poked her head into the bathroom. There was the *thump* again, but not coming from the bathroom. She opened the door to her father's game room. This was the largest room in the whole house. As she entered, on her left, was a long case made of wood and glass, no doubt crafted by her father. It ran the length of the left wall. The bottom of the long case was made of sturdy wood, and it had a wood frame around the glass. Inside the long case were several levels, each one filled with all sorts of trophies, awards, and ribbons. Every single award her father, brother, and herself had won over the years was prominently displayed in this case.

To the right on the far side of the room were two stand-up arcade machines – *Asteroids* and *Ms. Pac-Man*. Relics from a time when her father was her brother's age, a time when kids used to gather at the malls across America in arcades and spend endless hours and countless quarters trying to get what her father called the *High Score*. Autumn smiled and shook her head.

Along the wall behind her was a wall-stand holding pool sticks, brushes, and several pool balls racks of various shapes. In front of her were two very large windows looking out onto the side lawn. Off in the distance, Autumn could see her father's guest house. Between the two large windows was an old-fashioned dart board carved out of wood. No doubt yet another one of her father's creations. The board had six darts embedded in its checkered field.

In the center of her father's game room was his prized possession, his pool table. It was a nine-foot regulation beauty with pine green felt and leather pockets. Her father, of course, designed and constructed the pool table himself. He carved, cut, and sanded the wood to perfection, glued and bolted each piece into place by hand, and even tanned the leather for the pockets himself. He loved this pool table.

Thump.

There was that sound again. From here, Autumn could tell the sound was coming from outside. She walked over to the large window and stared down into the yard. Below, she could see her father and brother. Jeffery was sitting, leaning up against a tree, his nose buried in one of his comic books. Her father had his flannel shirt tied around his waist and was chopping wood with his giant axe. The thumping sound that drew Autumn's attention was the sound made every time her father's powerful swing would come down, split a log in twine, and embed itself into the large tree stump he used to cut wood.

For a long moment Autumn just watched them and wondered *what they could possibly be talking about*?

Down below…

"I've read in some comics that Wonder Woman is supposed to be second in strength only to Superman," Jeffery said still holding the comic book in front of his face. "If that is true, then who would win in a no holds barred throw down - Wonder Woman vs. SHAZAM?"

"SHAZAM?" Ryan asked. "The wizard?"

"What?" Jeffery lowered the comic. His forehead crinkled in contemplation. "What wizard?"

"You know SHAZAM, the wizard," Ryan halted his next chop. He leaned the ax against the chopping stump and grabbed a water bottle which was resting on the ground next to him. After a big swig, he clarified, "You know the old man that gave Billy Batson his superpowers. You know, he shouts the wizard's name – *SHAZAM!* – and a bolt of lightning comes down and transforms him into Captain Marvel."

"Captain Marvel?" Jeffery asked completely confused. "The blonde super lady in the Avengers?"

"The Avengers?" Now it was Ryan who was confused. "The Avengers are in Marvel Comics. I thought we were talking about DC characters?"

"We were," Jeffery said. "I mean we are. You are the one that brought up Captain Marvel."

"Captain Marvel is who Billy Batson turns into when he says the word *SHAZAM!*" Ryan explained.

"No," Jeffery laughed. "Captain Marvel is the pretty blonde lady who fights alongside Captain America and Iron Man in the Avengers. Billy Batson turns into the DC superhero known as SHAZAM whenever he shouts the word *SHAZAM!*"

"Huh," Ryan said taking another swig of water and then tossing the nearly empty bottle back to the ground. Grabbing the ax and preparing for another swing he declared, "Comics sure have changed since I used to read them."

"I say Wonder Woman would win," Jeffery said, answering his own question from before. "Billy doesn't have the combat skills to take down Wonder Woman. He's strong and fast, he has courage and mental fortitude, but no real combat skills. Then, you add in the Thunderbolt, and other weapons she has gathered from Olympus, and SHAZAM is toast."

"Thunderbolt?" Ryan asked, bringing the axe down and splitting another log with one chop.

"Yeah, she is the daughter of Zeus, Wonder Woman can now use his Thunderbolts," Jeffery explained.

"Daughter of Zeus?" Ryan asked. "I thought Wonder Woman was made from clay?"

"No, no," Jeffery shook his head. "They retconned all that. She's a true daughter of the gods now. The Queen of the Amazons, Hippolyta, and Zeus are her parents."

"Oh, okay," Ryan said as he stood another log up on the chopping stump.

"Anyways," Jeffery continued, "I think Wonder Woman would win in a fight with SHAZAM."

"Seems to me like you're selling the Big Red Cheese a little short," Ryan replied.

"Big Red Cheese?" Jeffery asked, as his nose crinkled in thought.

Ryan smiled and explained, "Captain Marvel." After seeing Jeffery's crinkle rise to his eyebrows, Ryan corrected himself. "SHAZAM," he said.

"How so?" Jeffery asked.

"I think you are forgetting that SHAZAM has the Wisdom of Solomon," Ryan said, "and that means he might be able to figure out a way to beat Wonder Woman." Then he shook his head. "No, I agree with you. Wonder Woman wins."

"Hell, Wonder Woman fights Superman to a standstill," Jeffery said. "Add in the Thunderbolt of

Zeus to her arsenal and she drops SHAZAM like a sack of potatoes. He hasn't really tapped into his full potential of powers. Eventually I think he'll get better."

"I think Superman is always holding back, even against a powerhouse like Wonder Woman," Ryan said as he split another log. "I can think of a couple of occasions when he unleashed on her, and she couldn't even slow him down let alone beat him. That storyline called *Absolute Power* written by Jeph Loeb comes to mind. And Jeffery, don't say *hell*."

"Sorry. Oh yeah, no question," Jeffery agreed. "It's been said several times the only ones he doesn't hold back on are Doomsday and Darkseid, and even then, he still holds back a little because the shockwaves of his punches could hurt the people around."

"Agreed," Ryan smiled. "The only time I can ever recall seeing Superman truly use his entire potential is when he KO'd the Anti-Monitor at the end of *Crisis of Infinite Earths*."

"Even in *Injustice*, where he's a big jerk, he's still holding back," Jeffery added. "If he really wants, there is nobody that can stop him."

"Agreed," Ryan said. "That's why the whole notion of Batman vs. Superman always bothered me. It's just implausible."

"What are y'all talking about?" Autumn asked as she came walking up the stone walkway to stand by her brother.

"SHAZAM!" Jeffery exclaimed with glee.

"You see, apparently SHAZAM no longer refers to the wizard who gave Billy Batson his superpowers and ability to transform into Captain Marvel," Ryan explained. "In fact, Captain Marvel is SHAZAM."

"Yeah, but we still think Wonder Woman can take him," Jeffery mused.

Autumn just shook her head. "I'm sorry I asked."

Across the way, over at her father's guest house, a blue jeep pulled up, coming to a skidding halt. Loud rock music blaring from the jeep's speakers subsided when the vehicle was turned off. Three teenaged boys leapt out. Two of them began unloading boxes from the jeep and carrying them into the house while the third, a particularly attractive shirtless teen, trotted toward where Autumn and her family were.

"Hey, *Bossman*," he called out as he came striding up to her father.

"How's it going, kid?" Ryan replied as he brought his axe down to cleave another log. "You and the guys come to set up the house for your big night?"

"Yes, sir," the teenager answered with a big smile.

He was tall, not quite as tall as Ryan, but tall for a teenager, and quite handsome. He had wavy sandy brown hair that framed an angelic face. His body was lean and toned. He had an athletic build. However, what really captured Autumn's attention were the teen's eyes, large perfectly placed green eyes. Autumn was by no means a wallflower, but even she felt a warm flash wash over her as she studied this attractive young man.

Ryan, noticing his daughter's reaction to the young man worked through several sensations in only a few seconds. He felt the natural protectiveness a father feels for his daughter, but he also liked this kid and could think of way worse for her to be drawn to. Deciding to shelve these feelings for the moment, Ryan introduced the young man to his children.

"These are my children," he nodded toward them, "my son, Jeffery and my daughter, Autumn."

"Whoa," the teen gasped when his eyes met Autumn's and a large devilish smile spread across his angelic face.

Ryan reached over and placed his very large, callused hand on the boy's shoulder and repeated, "My daughter," with great emphases on the word *my*. The boy nodded emphatically. Ryan continued. "Kids, this charming young man here is Jonathan. He works for me from time to time, even helped me build the guest house over there."

"How y'all doing?" Jonathan waved, but despite his respect for Ryan, he could not help but wink and smile toward the pretty girl to whom he was being introduced.

Autumn smiled. Jeffrey nodded and then went back to reading his comic book, indifferent to the teen's presence.

"Nice to meet you," she replied unconsciously pulling her hair back behind her ears.

Ryan patted the boy on the back, an act that caused the kid to stumble a step. Not that Ryan meant the boy any harm; it was just that Ryan sometimes did not know his own strength. He patted the boy on the back once more, this time taking great care to do so gently.

"Ole Jonathan here is a local hero," Ryan boasted. "Not only did he take the high school baseball team to the State Finals, our boy here pitched a no-hitter!"

"Oh, so you are an athlete?" Autumn asked. She wanted to engage in conversation with him for as long as possible.

"Yes, ma'am," Jonathan smiled.

"You also work in construction with my father?" She asked.

"Yes, well, part time," Jonathan replied. "Your dad lets me apprentice with him from time to time. He's teaching me the ins and outs of carpentry. I figure it's a good skill to have just in case this whole star athlete thing doesn't work out."

"Ah, don't let him fool you, hon," Ryan interjected as he set another log on the chopping block, "Jonathan here is a damn fine athlete and a damn fine carpenter in the making. He'll do fine in which ever endeavor he winds up in."

"So, Autumn, are you living here with the *Boss* now, or just visiting?" Jonathan asked.

Autumn hesitated for a moment and then replied, "I live here now." This was the first time that notion brought a smile to her face.

"Wow, that's great," Jonathan said. "So, you'll be going to the high school then?"

"Yes," she replied with a nod. "I start next week."

"Awesome," Jonathan smiled.

There was a long awkward pause as the two teens just stared at each other, neither of them realizing for how long. Ryan clearing his throat brought them back to the present.

"Oh, well, I have to get going," Jonathan gestured back over toward her father's guest house. "But hey, some friends of mine and I are having a Halloween party next door tonight. Would you like to come? Since I helped your dad build the house, he's letting us use it this weekend."

Autumn almost shouted *YES*, but she paused to look over at her father who had just centered another log. For a long moment, he let the question dangle, then a warm smile edged onto his grizzled face, and he nodded. Autumn shook her head and answered, "Yes, I'd love to go. Oh, but wait. I don't have a costume."

"Oh, that's okay," Jonathan reassured her. "It's not a costume party. Actually, it's my birthday."

Jeffrey looked up from his comic and asked, "Your birthday is on Halloween?" Jonathan nodded to which Jeffrey replied, "That's so cool." And, then he returned to his comic.

"Yeah, but you should come," Jonathan said. "We'll have a blast. Oh, and hey, you can meet my friends. They'll be the people you'll be going to school with so that should be cool."

"Sounds great," Autumn smiled.

"Hey, Leap frog, let's get to it!" A curly haired teenager cried out from across the way. He was gesturing for Jonathan to come back over to the guest house.

Jeffrey looked up from his comic and asked, "Why did he call you Leap Frog?"

"Nothing," Jonathan snapped comically. "I mean no reason. It's just a dumb nickname. Anyway, I should go and help set everything up, but I'll be back in a few hours to escort you over. Sound good?" Autumn nodded. "Okay, great," Jonathan said waving bye, but as he turned to leave, Ryan spoke up.

"Jonathan," he said getting the teen's attention.

"Yes, Boss?"

"Just remember, she's *my* daughter," Ryan reiterated and then brought his axe down with a mighty swing that split another log cleanly in half.

"Yes, sir!" Jonathan said. He waved to Autumn and then hurried back over to the guest house.

Off in the distance, a low rumble of thunder could be heard. A bed of gray clouds rimmed the sky and proceeded to roll in.

"Looks like rain," Ryan said.

Three hours later, a rumble of thunder in the distance was followed by a knock at the door. Ryan pulled the large wooden door open to reveal Jonathan. He was wearing jeans, a purple T-shirt, and a pointy paper party hat that said *Birthday Boy*. In his mouth was a multi-color blowout. He blew and the party favor's long tail unfurled and produced an obnoxious sound.

"Jonathan," Ryan nodded.

To which the teen replied in an almost cartoonish voice, "We've come for your daughter, Chuck." Jonathan smiled quite proud of himself.

Ryan did not react. He just stood there staring down at the teen. Jonathan was tall for a seventeen-year-old, but Autumn's father was still easily a head taller than him. Ryan replied, "Nineteen eighty-seven called and Michael Keaton wants his joke back."

Jonathan's smile faded. "Oh, sorry, Ryan, I was just playing around." The teen straightened up and sheepishly removed his party hat.

Ryan let him squirm for a moment longer, then let him off the hook with a smile. "I'm just giving you a hard time, Jonathan."

Jonathan relaxed and smiled. Autumn walked over to join them, and the teen's eyes lit up once more.

"Wow," Jonathan breathed. "You look amazing."

Autumn smiled back at him, and the moment suddenly became too uncomfortable for her father. Ryan cleared his throat to remind them he was still standing there. "Have fun, sweetheart," Ryan said leaning over to kiss his daughter on the cheek.

Jonathan extended his arm out for Autumn to take, which she did and as they turned to leave, he said with a smile, "Don't worry, pop, we'll take really good care of her."

Jonathan suddenly felt Ryan's large, strong hand on his shoulder. With great ease, Autumn's father leaned the boy back to just inside the doorway and nodded over to where two rifles sat mounted on the wall, a deer rifle with a scope and double-barreled shot gun.

Ryan leaned in real close and whispered to the teen, "You just remember that's my daughter, and I'm a really, really good shot." Feeling he made his point quite clear; Ryan released the teen.

Jonathan straightened up and cleared his throat. "You got it, chief," he said. "Shall we, my dear?" He asked Autumn once again extending his arm, which she took with a smile.

"Y'all have a great time," Ryan called out to them and waved as they walked onto the path that led to the guest house.

"Don't let him get to you," Autumn reassured him. "That's just my dad's kind of sick humor."

"Get to me?" Jonathan patted his chest. "No, no, your dad and I are super cool. I've been doing odd jobs and apprentice work for him for like a year now. He's letting us use his guest house for free to throw this party. Your dad is super cool."

Though it was kind of odd for someone her age to refer to her father as *super cool*, Autumn still could not help but appreciate it. "Yeah, he's all right I guess," she smiled looking back over her shoulder to see Ryan standing on his porch and watching them. "I have to tell you, I'm not sure about this. I mean, your friends...are they cool?" Autumn asked.

"They're cool," Jonathan answered without hesitation, and then he chuckled. "I mean, I hope you think they're cool. Look, you're about to start up school next week, right?" Autumn nodded. "Okay, then it will be good for you to get to know some of the people you'll be going to school with, right? Think about it, you're getting an opportunity to do something most new kids in school don't get to."

"What's that?"

"You'll get to make friends before your first day at a new school," Jonathan smiled, "plus, even if you don't like my friends, I'll still be your friend." He winked.

"Boy, you are quite the charmer, huh?" Autumn smiled.

"I have my moments," Jonathan smiled back. Rain started to fall, so they picked up the pace. Jonathan said, "Come on, let's go meet the gang."

They entered her father's guest house. Electronica dance music was blaring from the stereo. To the left, over in the dining room, three guys sat at the table, two of them were engaged in a heated discussion and the other, a curly haired kid with big dark eyes, was watching them. There was a very handsome couple sitting on the couch making out and oblivious to anything else going on in the room. To the right stood three girls engaged in their own conversation. Whether it was a glass of wine or a red plastic cup of beer, everyone at the party was drinking. The entire interior of the house was completely decked out and decorated for a birthday celebration. Hanging from the vaulted ceiling was a very large banner that read *Happy 17th Birthday – Leap Frog*!

"Who's *Leap Frog*?" Autumn asked leaning in real close so that Jonathan could hear her over the music.

Jonathan just shook his head and smiled in defeat. "Never mind that, it's just a stupid nickname," he confessed.

Autumn smiled, "That's you? You're *Leap Frog*? Oh, I must hear all about this."

"Not if I can help it," Jonathan replied. "Come on, let's go meet the gang."

As Jonathan led her over to the couple on the couch, Autumn noticed that one of the girls, a very tall, very beautiful blonde, from the group to the right was watching them intently. It took Jonathan a moment to pry the couple on the couch away from each other's lips. The guy, a very attractive well-put together boy with light brown hair and a wicked grin smiled up at Jonathan and leapt up to hug him.

"Hey, *Leap Frog*!" he exclaimed wrapping Jonathan in a bear-like embrace. "Happy birthday, buddy...I love you man!" He planted a big kiss on Jonathan's cheek.

Their arms still over each other's shoulders, they turned toward Autumn.

"Autumn, this is Blane. Blane, this is Autumn, Ryan's daughter from next door," Jonathan introduced them.

Jonathan's very handsome friend smiled as he looked right into Autumn's eyes and said, "Oh my, now aren't you a pretty little thing." Autumn felt her face flush. "Darling, have a look what Jonathan brought to the party." Blane said as he reached down to help the girl who had been sitting next to him up off the couch. "This lovely young girl is my angel, Cindy," Blane introduced her.

As attractive as Blane was this very young tan lady was even more so.

"Nice to meet you," Cindy shook Autumn's hand. "So, you live next door?"

"Yes, well, I mean no…it's our summer home, I mean…," Autumn realized she was stammering and flustered. "It's my father's home and my brother and I are now living with him. Our folks are separated. I'm new to town," Autumn had to consciously try to stop talking.

To their credit, neither Blane nor Cindy burned her on it.

"That's cool," Blane smiled warmly wrapping his free hand around Cindy's very thin waist.

"Say, is your father that extremely tall, extremely hunky lumberjack looking man?" Cindy asked tapping her long fingernail on her rosy bottom lip.

"I guess?" Autumn shrugged.

"Honey, he is gorgeous," Cindy replied.

"You think my dad is gorgeous?" Autumn asked her jaw agape.

"Oh, God, yes," Cindy nodded her head emphatically with a giggle.

"All right, all right, honey," Blane lovingly snuggled her. "Hey, *LP*, we're headed to the kitchen for some more drinks, you want…?

"In a minute," Jonathan replied. "I want to introduce Autumn to the rest of the gang first."

"Okay, buddy," Blane hi-fived Jonathan and then reached over to shake Autumn's hand. "It was nice to meet you, darling, this guy right here," he poked Jonathan in the chest, "he's a good guy. You kids have fun."

"Nice to meet you, honey," Cindy smiled then started giggling as Blane hoisted her up onto his shoulder and carried her into the kitchen hi-fiving the curly haired guy at the dining room table as he walked on by.

"They seem cool," Autumn said.

"Blane and Cindy…? Yeah, they're the best," Jonathan replied. "I've known Blane since we were in second grade. He's always had my back. It's good to have someone who is always on your side. Come on, let's go meet the others."

As Jonathan led her over to the dining room Autumn could hear the tail end of the heated discussion that had been going on this entire time.

"There's more to music, bro, then just the Mount Rushmore of Grunge," said a baby-faced guy with a

89

mop of brown hair flowing into his eyes. He was constantly brushing it away from his eyes to no avail as it constantly fell back into place.

The guy he was talking to had long, bushy dark hair that hung down to the middle of his back. He wore glasses that had a thick frame and a tight black T-shirt with the sleeves cut off. He was rolling a joint and retorted without hesitation, "*Pearl Jam, Nirvana, Alice N' Chains*, and *Soundgarden*." He sounded off with such confidence, as if his response could not even possibly be challenged.

The kid with the mop of hair bushed his hair back and indignantly replied, "Of course, but that's not the point. The point is that there is more music out there than just the *Seattle Sound*. There are some truly great songwriters out there like *Adele, Beck*, and *Bruno Mars*."

"You lost me at *Adele*," the guy in the glasses said flippantly as he continued to meticulously roll his joint. "And please, my dad told me I was conceived while the *Yield* album was playing. What can I say, my parents taught me all about good music and your parents failed you in every way?" He chuckled while his mop-haired friend just scowled in silence.

The curly hair guy chuckled and added his two cents, "You both are Neanderthals when it comes to music. You need some *Marvin Gaye*, some *Otis Redding*, some mother-fucking *Earth Wind and Fire* in your lives."

"Jesus, Grandpa, time to update the MP3 player," the guy in the glasses scoffed.

"There's a reason why you two never get laid," the guy with the curly hair replied smugly. "Show a little kindness, a little tenderness, and maybe, just maybe, you two might go home with something more than your right hand." As he spoke a tall attractive young woman with a giant hive of jet-black hair came out of the kitchen, handed him a cup, and sat on his lap. "Isn't that right, Baby?" He asked her.

"That's right, Baby," she said with a smile and planted a big kiss right on his lips.

"Nah," the guy in the glasses waved off his friend's remark, "I use my left. It makes me feel like I'm with a stranger." Then, he noticed Jonathan and Autumn walking up to the table. "Well, well, well, look who decided to join the party. Happy birthday, *Leap Frog*!"

The guy with the curly hair and the girl sitting in his lap stood to greet them.

"Hey, my man!" The guy with the curly hair smiled and clasped Jonathan's hand with one hand and threw his other hand over Jonathan's shoulder in a *bro-hug*. He said, "Happy birthday, partner."

91

The girl hugged Jonathan and kissed him on the cheek, "Happy birthday Baby."

"Thanks," Jonathan replied with a smile. "Hey, everyone, this is Autumn, she lives next door and will be starting up school at Glen Haven next week." Jonathan pointed to the curly hair guy and the girl and said, "This is Jack and Iona, they are a couple."

"How you doing, darling?" Jack smiled and bowed his head.

"Hello, cutie," Iona shook Autumn's hand then turned to Jonathan and said, "We're a smoking hot couple, and don't forget it."

Jonathan held his hands up in mock apology and smiled. Then he nodded toward the baby-faced kid with the mop of hair in his face, "This is Elisha, we call him Eli for short." Eli nodded allowing his mop of hair to fall in front of his eyes. He did not brush it aside and kept his gaze firmly on the table. "Oh, he's not being rude," Jonathan assured Autumn, "he's just shy." Then he gestured toward the guy with the glasses who was just putting the finishing touches on his hand-rolled masterpiece. "This lovely fellow here is Steff."

"How you doing, doll," Steff replied as he licked the paper to seal his joint. He held it up proudly and asked, "You like?"

Autumn replied, "I've never tried."

"Oh, well in that case, step into my parlor," Steff gestured to the empty chair next to him.

Autumn just stood there not really knowing how to respond.

Jonathan stepped in and said, "Don't let him bother you, he doesn't mean any harm. If you're not into it, don't feel pressured, okay?"

Autumn nodded.

"Well, just let me know if you change your mind, honey," Steff said with a wink as he lit his joint, took a drag, and began passing it around the table.

Jonathan turned to Autumn and asked, "Are you thirsty? We have beer and wine, and if that's not your thing, I'm sure I can find..." He never finished his sentence as a snarky female voice from behind them interrupted.

She said, "Well, if it isn't the birthday boy himself, *Leap Frog*, and uh, who is your little friend here?"

Autumn and Jonathan turned and came face-to-face with the three girls who had been engaged in their own conversation on the other side of the room ever since they entered the house. Autumn instantly recognized the owner of that question as the very tall blonde who had been intently eyeing them when they first came in.

Autumn could tell she came from money just by looking at the clothes and jewelry she wore. She wore a form-fitting black skirt which stopped high up on her perfectly shaped thighs. Her three-inch heels accentuated her toned legs and made what was already a statuesque beauty even taller, towering compared to Autumn's five-foot three-inch frame. With one hand on her hip, the blonde beauty held a glass of white wine in the other. She studied Autumn intently. Flanking her on the right was a girl of medium height with shoulder length red hair and enormous breasts barely being held in check by a pink halter top. She was also sipping a glass of white wine. Flanking her on the left was a girl of about Autumn's height who was built slightly heavier than the other two girls. She wore a little too much make-up.

Jonathan took a deep breath and exhaled as if preparing himself. He then forced a smile and said, "Hello, girls. I'm so glad y'all could make it out."

"You don't have to lie, *Leap Frog*," the tall blonde retorted, really emphasizing the nickname.

"Yeah, *Leap Frog*," the other two girls repeated almost in unison and then started giggling.

"Girls, this is Autumn," Jonathan introduced her, ignoring their teasing. "Autumn this is Ronda," he said gesturing to the well-endowed red head who nodded. "This is Andie," he gestured toward the short, stocky girl whose face lit up with an enormous smile which fled as soon as she saw the look on the tall blonde whom Jonathan introduced as, "and this is Kate."

"Nice to meet you," Autumn smiled and nodded.

The two girls flanking Kate stood stoic and silent, waiting for her reaction before giving theirs. They did not have to wait long.

"So, Autumn, how long have the two of you known each other," She asked in a way that could have been meant for either of them.

"Oh, we just met," Autumn answered. "My father lives next door. This is his guest house."

"Right, right," Kate repeated then looked directly at Jonathan. "It must be nice to find the love of your life for like what…the third time in two years?"

Jonathan chuckled nervously. "Take it down a notch, huh, Kate," he pleaded. "Autumn just moved here and will be starting school with us next week. I thought it would be good for her to meet the gang and maybe make some friends. You know, have a few familiar faces to greet her in a new school."

"Uh-huh," Kate snarled. "Well, that's okay…what did you say your name was? It really doesn't matter. Our staff, as you can see, is all full. Come back in the springtime and maybe there will be an opening, but I wouldn't count on it."

Kate stood there with her arms crossed, tapping her wine glass, and scowling as if she had just made a real point. Behind her Ronda and Andie looked at each other a little puzzled. They shrugged and assumed similar stances. However, their scowls were obviously quite forced.

"You know why they call him *Leap Frog*, honey?" Kate continued. "It's because when he's fucking, he always pulls out before his partner finishes. Just like a little frog leaping away to another pad. He just doesn't have what it takes to get the job done, if you know what I mean."

Jonathan exhaled and was about to respond but Autumn beat him to the punch.

"Oh, you're one of those," Autumn said nodding knowingly.

"One of what?" Kate snapped back.

"A catty bitch," Autumn explained. "Thank you, that's good to know. I could have wasted time trying to get to know you but now I don't have to worry about it. You know, my dad always told me if someone hates you for no reason then maybe you should give them one." In one deft movement, Autumn took Kate's glass of wine from her hand and poured the contents over her blonde head. "Maybe that will cool you off."

Kate screamed bloody murder and stormed away to the bathroom.

"Holy shit!" Jonathan exclaimed. For a moment, Autumn thought she may have taken her retaliation a bit too far, but then he exclaimed, "That was awesome!"

Ronda and Andie were both giggling.

Ronda leaned forward, "I just want to say that I'm sorry for Kate's behavior."

Andie jumped in wiping some wine spittle from her cheek, "Me too."

Ronda continued, "Jonnie, I'm sorry. You know how she gets when she's around you. Autumn, we're sorry. I promise you, once you get to know her, she really isn't this *catty*." Ronda paused and looked at Andie. They could not even begin to keep a straight face as they broke out into hysterical laughter. "Who am I kidding," Ronda said, "She's a bitch, but she's our bitch. I'll let Jonnie explain the history, but please don't take this all personally."

Just then, Stef, Elisha, Jack, and Iona joined the group.

"Is everybody in, is everybody in...?" Stef asked in an obvious impersonation, "The ceremony is about to begin..."

"Yo, Jim Morrison called, and he wants his swag back," Jack scolded.

"Hey, man, where Morrison is he won't need it," Stef shot back as he produced two newly rolled joints to the group. "Now, who's with me?"

"I'm in." Ronda replied with a big smile slithering up next to the long-haired teen.

Stef draped his arm over Ronda's slender shoulders and pulled her tight to his body. "Ada girl," he smiled. "Let's light these babies."

Stef and Ronda plopped down on the vacated couch with Jack and Iona right beside them. Stef lit the first joint but before putting it to his lips he offered it to Ronda and said, "To my voluptuous queen I offer the first drag."

"Why thank you, kind sir," Ronda took a deep drag off the joint as Stef held it in place for her.

"Y'all in?" Steff offered the next drag to Autumn.

Autumn replied, "No thank you."

Stef offered to Jonathan who hesitated and then replied, "That's cool, Stef. Y'all go on." He turned toward Autumn realizing how uncomfortable she was becoming. "Hey, the rain is letting up...take a walk with me?"

Autumn smiled. "Yes."

He snagged an umbrella from the closet and led her out the front door.

Back on the sofa, Stef, Ronda, Jack, and Iona continued to pass the joint around. This left Elisha and Andie standing next to each other off to the side. Not that anyone else in the room would notice but these two wallflowers were painfully shy, and obviously attracted to each other, neither of them knowing how or having the courage to strike up a conversation. For long moments, they played an awkward game of not meeting the other's gaze. Every time one of them looked over to see the other staring they would both immediately avert or turn their gaze.

Elisha was medium height with wavy hair that hung in his face. This was accentuated by the fact that he always kept his shoulders slumped and his head hung low. His tan slacks and sweater vest suggested that he was not what someone would call a fashion savant. He did like Andie, but he had absolutely no idea how to express that to her.

Andie was short and plucky. She had spent her entire life struggling with her weight. Though she had known Ronda and Kate since they were all children, the fact that her friends seemingly were gifted with bodies that men would die for always left Andie feeling a little sad, a little overlooked. However, Ronda was busy in the circle and Kate was nowhere to be found, so Andie mustered the courage and took a chance.

"Are you enjoying the party so far?" She could barely utter the words. In her mind, she sounded like audio that had been slowed way down, but to Elisha, she sounded like an angel.

"Yes, yes, I am," he said straightening up a bit. He ran his slender fingers through his hair, moving it out from in front of his eyes. He swallowed deeply and mustered a reply. "I saw something happen with Kate and the new girl. Is everything alright? Are you okay?"

His concern brought a smile to Andie's face. "Yes," she replied. "I'm okay. It was nothing. Just more of that Kate/Jonnie drama we all love so much."

"Yeah, the *WB* should hire a writer to follow them around and they'd have enough material to fill an entire season in just one week," Elisha's joke drew a laugh from Andie.

"Eli, you always were funny," Andie said reaching over to pat him on the shoulder. Her touch caused him to stiffen, a reaction she misread. "Oh, sorry, I didn't mean to…I mean I wasn't…," she trailed off.

"Oh, no, it's okay," he explained. In fact, he caught himself off guard with an over explanation. "It's just that you're so pretty and…and, oh shit…I've said too much. Sorry…I mean…"

He began to squirm in his skin. He did not even want to look over. When he finally did, Andie was staring right at him, her big brown eyes even larger than normal, her hand placed firmly in front of her gaping mouth. He misread her look as one of horror, but in fact, it was one of stunned surprise. For a moment, he wished he were anywhere else but right there, right now, but then she spoke.

"You think I'm pretty?" She asked.

"Yes," he answered, slumping his shoulders, and hanging his head, allowing his shaggy hair to fall into his face. Though he had no idea where the courage came from, he was uttering the next sentence before he was fully conscious he was even speaking. "Andie, I think you are the prettiest girl in school, and I have always had a crush on you. Ever since the second grade."

With tears welling in her eyes, Andie reached over and brushed the hair away from his round face. She placed her plump hands on his cheeks and gently pulled him in close and kissed him full on the lips. For a long moment they held each other, locked in a kiss they had both needed for so long. And then, with a little help from the *Peanut Gallery*, the moment was over.

"Come on you two, get a room!" Stef yelled out over the music.

"We were always rooting for you kids," Ronda added.

"Damn, Elisha, hit that!" Jack dog-piled with a hardy laugh.

Elisha and Andie gathered themselves. They were both bright red with embarrassment.

"Hey, would you like to take a walk with me?" Elisha asked taking Andie's hand into his.

"Yes," she replied with a big smile. "Just let me go freshen up first."

"Okay," Elisha said. "I'll grab us a couple of drinks from the kitchen and meet you out back by the tool shed. There's a trail back there I've been dying to explore."

"Great, I'll grab an umbrella in case it starts to rain again."

She squeezed his hand, they smiled and then darted their separate ways, if only for a moment. Since Kate still occupied the downstairs restroom, Andie had to use the one on the second floor which was fine since her bag with all her make-up and perfumes was up there in the room she was staying in that night. As she darted up the stairs, Elisha made his way into the kitchen where he heard a sound coming from the pantry. It was a muffled, guttural noise, almost animalistic.

Elisha cocked his head and tried to make it out. He could not tell what it was he heard. It sounded kind of like someone was in the pantry, but why would the door be closed. Something in the back of his mind told Elisha not to open that door, but his curiosity was firmly in control. He slowly made his way across the kitchen. That guttural sound was growing louder with each step closer to the door. He reached forth, slowly turned the knob, and pulled the door open to reveal Blane and Cindy locked in the throes of passionate love making.

Cindy was bent forward bracing herself against the shelves of the pantry which were rattling with each forceful thrust from Blane who stood directly behind her. Blane paused for a moment, sweat glistening down his muscled back. He looked over his shoulder and caught Elisha's gaze.

"Dude, either join in or shut the fucking door," he snapped.

"Oh, shit!" Elisha exclaimed completely embarrassed. "Sorry, shit, sorry!"

As he slowly closed the pantry door, Elisha could hear Cindy giggling and then the rattling of the shelving as the two started going at it again. That noise continued to reverberate from the pantry even as he gathered up four beers from the ice tub and made his way out the back door.

As Autumn and Jonathan walked down the dark woodland path, a slight drizzle of rain began to fall. Jonathan quickly unfurled the umbrella he had brought and held it over both their heads. He absently put his arm around Autumn's shoulders and gently pulled her close to him so that she was well covered under the umbrella. She did not mind the gesture, in fact, it brought a comforting smile to her face.

They walked another fifteen, twenty feet before Jonathan realized what he had done, and he realized she seemed okay with it, and this brought a comforting smile to his face. And, just like that, the rain stopped. The two came upon an alcove nestled on the side of the trail. There was a wooden bench. It was mostly dry thanks to a large outcropping tree.

Jonathan gestured toward the bench, "Like to sit and talk for a while?"

Autumn nodded and joined him on the bench.

"I remember when my father made this bench," she said. "It must have been seven years ago. He even cut out this alcove. He was so proud of it. When he showed it to my mother, she was less than interested."

"Sorry to hear that," Jonathan responded in earnest. "He stills brags about this bench though."

"Really?"

"Yeah, he loves to point out how he carved it out of a single piece of wood," Jonathan explained. "I believe he said he used the trunk from a tree that had fallen in the woods. He actually pays me a little scratch to come out and trim back the branches and brush and weed-eat the grass here."

"My dad mentioned something about you being a ball player?"

"Yeah, baseball, that's what I do," Jonathan nodded. "I'm the starting pitcher for our team. Coach really seems to think I have talent. He even said I may get drafted into a Major League farm system next spring, but my folks really want me to go to A&M and get a degree. I don't know."

"What do you want to do?" She asked him.

Jonathan cocked his head and blinked his big beautiful green eyes. "You know? Nobody has ever really asked me that before. Mostly people just tell me what can do, or what I'm going to do, or what I need to do. Nobody has ever really asked me what it is I want to do. Well, nobody except for your father."

"How long have you worked for my father?" Autumn asked.

"Me? About a year," Jonathan replied. "Your dad comes in my father's hardware store all the time. Apparently, they have known each other since they were kids. My dad asked yours if he'd take me under his wing and teach me a thing or two about construction. See, my dad thinks I need to have something to fall back on in case my baseball career doesn't take off."

"And I thought my dad was retired," Autumn said.

"Oh, he is," Jonathan responded. "I just think he loves working with his hands. The people in town love him. He helped erect the new score board for our stadium, and he oversaw the construction of a whole new add-on at the high school. You know, we had help for the big stuff, but it was just your old man and me mostly that worked on that guest house. He tells me I have a knack and that I'm good with my hands. Whatever that means...," he trailed off.

Autumn took the teenager's hands in hers. His hands were much larger than hers. She gently squeezed them and asked, "These hands right here?"

"Yes, ma'am," he flashed her that sexy smile of his.

Autumn was not even going to wait for him to make a move. She leaned over and kissed him full on the lips. For a long moment, they sat there on the bench embracing each other. When Autumn leaned back a sheepish smile spread across her face.

"Wow," Jonathan exhaled.

"Sorry about that," Autumn apologized. "I just couldn't help myself."

"Oh, no," Jonathan playfully held up his hands. "No need to apologize to me, but there is something I should tell you."

"What's that?"

"I never go all the way on the first date," he said with a devilish smile.

They both laughed. Then, the rain began to fall again, not hard, just a sprinkle. They were kept quite dry by the large overhanging tree above. For a long moment, they sat in silence. Then Autumn's curiosity got the better of her.

"So, what's up with you and Kate and how long did y'all go out?" She asked.

"Yeah, I was wondering when we were going to get to that topic," he chuckled nervously. He straightened up and cleared his throat. "Well, as you have already guessed, Kate and I dated," he said.

"How long?"

"For about a year," he said. "We were pretty serious, but as time went on, she began to show a really shitty side."

"Yes, I think I was a victim of that tonight," Autumn nodded.

"Yeah, I'm sorry about that," Jonathan apologized. "I should have given you heads up, but truthfully, I wasn't even sure she would be here tonight."

"When did y'all break up?"

"Almost a year ago," he answered.

"She seems to still be carrying a torch for you," Autumn said. "When you say y'all were serious, how serious is serious?"

"Well, I think some of her anger may be my fault," he tried to explain. "I may have misled her, not on purpose mind you, but she may have misunderstood something I did."

"What?"

"Well, I had never been in a serious, committed relationship before Kate," Jonathan explained. "Sure, I had gone on dates and to dances, and I had little puppy-love romances in elementary and junior high, but nothing that I'd call a real relationship. I guess I just didn't know the rules."

"What did you do that was so bad?" Autumn pushed.

Jonathan took a deep breath and said, "Well, it was last Christmas. I was trying to think of something to buy for her, something nice. I thought hey, girls love jewelry, right? So, I know, I'll buy her a ring. I didn't think anything of it."

"Oh, no," Autumn shook her head in anticipation of where his story was going.

"Oh, yes," he said. "So, me being the big dummy I am, I think I'm getting my girlfriend a really sweet gift but when I give it to her, she takes it all wrong."

"She thought it was a *promise ring*, didn't she?" Autumn asked.

"She did," he shook his head. "I thought I was just buying a nice Christmas gift for my girlfriend, and she thought I was making a promise to someday ask her to marry me. I got spooked. I mean, I liked her, and we got along great, but married? It was the furthest thing from my mind."

"So, what did you do?"

"This is where I'm probably at fault here," he said sliding in his seat. "You see, instead of actually talking to her and explaining things, I just broke up with her."

"Ouch."

"Yeah, at school."

"No."

"In the hallway between classes."

"No!"

"With everybody we know in the world standing all around us," he winced.

"So, what happened?" She asked.

"She stormed off crying," he said hanging his head low. "I felt horrible. She got about ten feet away then turned and whipped the ring at me like it was a ninja star. It cut me right below the eye." He ran his finger over a spot just below his left eye. Autumn could still make out the tiniest of scars. "Later that day, after school, she showed up at my house," he continued.

"What happened?" Autumn asked.

"We were in my room and…," he paused for a moment. "I am really not proud of this next moment."

"What happened?" Autumn asked again.

"We were in my room and she's just standing there bawling her eyes out. She had this look on her face, this desire to understand. She was beside herself. I wasn't very forthcoming with an explanation. When she asked *why*? All I could say was that it's over and that's just the way it is. I wasn't man enough to just explain it to her, I think I didn't really understand it myself. Just the fact that she thought I wanted to get married and that she was happy about that, I don't know, it really scared me."

"At least now I see why she's so catty," Autumn replied. "Jonathan, you have to know that was pretty harsh, right?"

"I agree, totally," he said. "I feel so bad. I guess that's probably why I let her give me so much shit. I guess she deserves to get her licks in, especially after what I did. I will tell you this, though. Ever since that misunderstanding, I have made a conscious effort on my part to always be up front with everybody. I don't ever want to have another misunderstanding like that again. Open and honest and no bullshit, that's what you get from me, every time."

"Is that why you are being so open with me right now?" Autumn asked.

"Yes, well, no, I mean…," he hesitated. "What I mean is that I really like you. You're pretty, you're smart, and you don't take shit off anybody. I like that. And you are really easy to talk to for some reason."

"So," Autumn smiled and hung onto the word longer than normal, "you think I'm pretty, do you?"

Just now realizing he did just say that Jonathan smiled and replied, "Yes, yes I do. I think you are absolutely beautiful, Autumn."

Autumn leaned in real close and smiled. "I think you are beautiful, too," she said and then kissed him.

"I'll tell you something else about that story," Jonathan declared. "After I told her it was over and that's all there was to it. I turned my head to turn up the volume on my stereo. Well, Kate reared back and punched me square in the jaw. Rocked my world! I tell you; I've played football and I've been in my share of rough-n-tumbles, but I haven't ever been hit as hard as she hit me that day."

They both started laughing, and the rain started falling just a little harder than before.

*****

In the back yard, Andie slowly made her way to the tool shed. She was giddy with excitement, all at once nervous and happy. She had what they call butterflies in her stomach. Her smile grew wider with each step. She was quite unaware of the eyes that followed her from the dark shadows of the tree line that framed the backyard, dark cold eyes.

As Andie reached the door to the shed, she paused. She tried to listen, but she could not hear any sound coming from within. She cupped her hand in front of her mouth and exhaled. Satisfied with the aroma of her breath, she straightened up, took one last deep breath, and opened the door. The inside of the shed was dark.

"Eli?" She called out in a quiet voice. "Eli, it's me…Andie. I'm here to take you up on that moonlight stroll. Eli?"

As the door to the shed swung fully open, the light from the full moon peeking out from behind black clouds above illuminated the inside of the small hut. The wet ground reflected the light, highlighting the macabre scene within. Elisha's frame hung limp, as he had been impaled through the throat by an old rusty pitchfork. The tool had been forced through his neck with such force that the sharp metal prongs tore through flesh and bone and embedded into the thick wood of the support beam behind him. The murder was only minutes old as gouts of crimson blood were still leaking from the vicious wound, streaming down Elisha's frame, and puddling up on the floor below.

In that moment of pure terror, Andie's world froze. Her body tensed as she was about to scream, but just as her voice began to register; she was violently seized from behind. A large, dirty hand, the same hand responsible for the murdered youth impaled in front of her, engulfed her face, covering her mouth and stifling her scream. She barely had time to register her dire situation as the blade of a large hunting knife suddenly stabbed through her skull, her brain, and out the front of her forehead. The killer released her, and Andie's limp body fell to the floor of the shed in a lifeless heap.

It was unclear to everybody in the house – Jack, Iona, Steff, Blane, Cindy, Kate, and Ronda - when and why the killing started, but when it did, the celebration of a friend's birthday was turned into a massacre in a matter of a few dozen minutes. Slowly, methodically, the killer made his way through the house, one-by-one coming upon one teenager after another and taking their lives in the most horrible ways possible. Their dying screams of terror resonated throughout the house and outside.

"What is that?" Autumn asked startled and looking back over her shoulder.

"It's coming from the direction of the houses," Jonathan deducted.

"Oh my God…!" Autumn exclaimed. "Dad…Jeffery!"

Autumn immediately stood up and ran back up the pathway toward her father's home with Jonathan close behind her. As they sprinted up the trail, the rain began to fall harder.

In the moments before the screams started, Ryan was sitting in his chair and reading the paper. Jeffery was lying on the floor on his stomach reading his manga comics. When the first cry for help echoed over from the guest house, Ryan leapt from his chair and rushed to the large double window. The rain outside was picking up steam. Even over the torrent of rainfall Ryan could hear the cries for help from across the way. He turned to see Jeffery standing in the middle of the living room, his eyes wide with terror, his body quivering with fear. Ryan walked over and placed calming hands on the boy's shoulders.

"Listen to me very carefully, son," Ryan said in as calm a voice as he could, "I need you to be brave right now. I have to go over there and find out what is going on."

"NO!" Jeffery cried out, tears beginning to stream down his face. "Daddy, don't go out there!"

"Son…Jeffery, please listen to me," Ryan looked the boy right in the eyes, "I need you to be brave and I need you do something for me. Can you do that? Can you be brave for me?"

Ryan's inner strength gave the boy fortitude. "Yes, father," Jeffery answered. "I can be brave."

"Good, that's my Little Champion," Ryan gently tousled his son's hair. "I have to go over there and find out what is going on. Your sister is still over there. I need you to get onto the radio and notify the police, the way I showed you, okay? Can you do that for me?"

"Yes, father," Jeffery said wiping his nose with his sleeve.

"Okay, son, get to it," Ryan hugged his son and then directed him in the direction of the CB radio.

As Jeffery set to his task, Ryan turned and pulled his *thirty-aught-six* down off the wall. He grabbed a fist full of rounds from a box and was loading his rifle as he darted out the front door. He leapt off the front porch in a dead sprint nearly barreling over Autumn and Jonathan as they were running up toward the house. Ryan scooped up Autumn in his giant's embrace.

"Oh, honey, are you okay?" He asked setting her back down on the wet ground.

"Yes, daddy, we're fine," she reassured him. "What the hell is going on?"

"I don't know," Ryan answered. "Get into the house and lock the doors. Your brother is calling the authorities. Stay with him while I go check it out."

"But, dad…!" Autumn protested, but Ryan cut her off.

"Don't argue with me, Autumn, not now," Ryan was forceful but the love and concern in his voice was palpable. "Please, go to the house and your brother." Ryan turned to face the young man at her side. "Jonathan."

"Yes, sir," The teen answered.

"Stay with Autumn, please, keep her safe."

"Yes, sir."

Ryan patted the teen on his shoulder, gave his daughter one last look, and then started off toward the guest house running. As he did, another scream came from the guest house.

"Oh my God, that's Kate," Jonathan said and started to follow Ryan, but he was stopped by a surprisingly strong pull on his arm.

"Jonathan, no!" Autumn yanked him back toward her father's house.

In a bit of shock, Jonathan allowed her to lead him on. They scramble up onto the front porch and out of the rain. They entered the house, Autumn slamming the front door behind them and locking the dead bolt.

She called out for her little brother, "Jeffery! Jeffery, where are you!" The shaken ten-year-old came walking into the living room from the den. Autumn rushed over to him and hugged him. "Jeffery! Are you okay?"

"Yes," Jeffery replied weakly. The boy just stood there, not returning her embrace.

"I think he's in shock," Jonathan said.

"Jeffery, did you contact the police?" Autumn asked as she reached for a throw blanket which was on the back of the couch and wrapped it around her little brother's shoulders.

"Yes," Jeffery answered his voice low and horse. "They are on their way. Where's father?"

The question sent a shiver down Autumn's spine. "He'll be back soon. He went to check on the kids next door."

"Does this work?" Jonathan asked reaching for the double-barreled shotgun hanging on the wall.

"Yes," Autumn answered. She walked over to the table below where the shotgun was mounted and pulled the drawer open. She pulled out a small box and handed it to Jonathan. "Here are the shells."

Jonathan took the box of shells from her. He held the box under his arm as he tried in vain to figure out how to load the gun. Autumn could not help but be semi-amused by the spectacle of him standing there trying to bend the gun in half, struggling with no results.

"Here, let me see it," Autumn reached for the weapon which Jonathan gladly handed over to her. With her thumb, she pressed the latch that released the break-action of the two barrels and revealed the dual chambers ready for shells. She loaded two shells and snapped the barrels back into place. "There, now it's loaded. You've never shot a gun before, have you?" She asked.

"I've never even held a gun before," Jonathan answered honestly.

118

"I better hold onto this then," Autumn said securing the weapon under her arm. She opened the coat closet, pulled out a wooden baseball bat and tossed it to him. "Here, Slugger," she smiled. "You should have no problem with this."

Jonathan smiled and asked, "Did I mention that I play baseball and hit twenty-five homeruns and knocked in seventy-five RBIs last season?"

"Yeah, you might have mentioned it," Autumn winked at him.

Their moment of levity was startlingly cut short as another scream echoed through the rain. Autumn checked the lock on the door and then rushed to the back door to lock it as well. She and Jonathan then went to the large double window of the living room.

"I can't see anything, can you?" Autumn asked frantically wiping the fogging glass with her hand.

"No," Jonathan replied, "it's raining too hard."

"Where's father?" Jeffery asked again.

Autumn came over, leaned the shotgun against the wall, and put her arm around her little brother. "I know you are scared, little brother," she said, "I'm scared too. So is Jonathan." Jonathan came over to stand beside them. "But right now, we have to be brave. The police are on their way and dad is the biggest, strongest man I know, okay? Everything will be alright."

"Are you sure?" Jeffery asked.

But, before Autumn could answer, the three of them jumped at a knock at the door. They all turned and stared. Then there was another knock that made them all jump again.

"Should we open it?" Jonathan asked.

"Hell no!" Autumn replied. "Not until we know who is on the other side."

"What if it's the police?" Jonathan reasoned.

"What if it's dad?" Jeffery asked.

With his bat firmly in hand, Jonathan slowly made his way toward the door. Then, another knock followed by a weak plea caused them to jump again.

"Please, let me in," they heard coming from the other side of the door.

"Oh my God!" Jonathan gasped. He darted for the door and quickly released the deadbolt, too fast for either Autumn or Jeffery to protest.

He swung the heavy door open to reveal Kate standing in the portal. She was soaked from the rain, her hands and feet caked in mud, and her clothes were torn and ripped and covered in blood. She had a deep cut over her right eye where blood flowed from freely. She was weeping as Jonathan leaned his bat against the wall, took her by the shoulders and led her into the house. Autumn quickly rushed over to the entrance and looked outside. There was nothing but darkness and the rain. Then, for just the briefest of moments, Autumn could have sworn she heard the call of some kind of animal. It was far away and barely audible over the torrent down pour, but it sounded like the baying of a lamb. She closed the door and bolted the lock back into place.

Autumn grabbed a blanket from the closet and handed it to Jonathan who wrapped it around Kate's shivering frame. She was obviously shaken. Her speech was barely audible and decipherable as she spoke through quivering lips and chattering teeth.

"He's coming…coming…," she stammered.

"Who?" Jonathan asked trying in vain to comfort her. Autumn handed him a small towel she retrieved from the kitchen that he used to dab and wipe the blood from her eyes. "Who is coming?" he asked. "Kate, what happened? Who did this to you?"

Kate suddenly stopped shivering and grabbed a hold of Jonathan by the arms so tight that he winced. Her eyes went wide, and she began to scream, "He killed them! He killed them all! Murdered them! Murder…murder…murder…!" She just repeated herself until her voice faded away into another bout of whimpering.

"Autumn," Jeffery called to his sister. The boy was quickly reaching his threshold of being able to deal. His sister rushed to his side.

"It's okay, sweaty," she tried to reassure him.

"Autumn, where's father?" Jeffery asked again.

They jumped and screamed as a large object suddenly came crashing through the giant double window of the living room. Shattered glass and splintered wood exploded and rained down all over the room and its occupants. A small shard of glass gashed Jonathan right under his left eye only an inch away from taking the eye. The object that had come flying through the window landed on and demolished the wooden coffee table. As pieces of the table and magazines flew in all directions, the object landed with a sickening thud and limply rolled to stop mere feet from where Autumn and Jeffery stood.

Autumn, her eyes welled up with tears, reached over with a shaking hand. It took all her strength, all her inner fortitude to reach out and roll the body over. Autumn screamed out in anguish and terror as she realized what, or better yet, who the object was. It was a dead man. A very tall, lean man with the blade of a large hunting knife buried to the hilt in his temple. It was her…

"Daddy?" Jeffery asked in disbelief, his voice low and shaky.

"Oh my God," Jonathan breathed as he looked back over his shoulder to scope the distance from the shattered window to where the body finally came to a stop. "What could have possibly had the strength to throw him that far?"

"No!" Kate suddenly screamed. "He's here! He's here!"

"Kate, Kate, shhhh…," Jonathan tried to calm her down, but she forcefully shoved him aside and ran to the front door.

"We're all going to die!" She screamed. "I can't…I have to get out of here!"

Kate frantically unlocked the front door and swung it open. The air simply went out of the room as everyone gasped. Kate stopped in her tracks as she was suddenly face-to-face with the killer.

This man, this monstrous thing filled the entire frame of the door. His shoulders and the top of his head extended pass the boundaries of the doorframe. He wore dirty grey pants and frayed suspenders with a large tool belt strapped around his waist which was adorned with many knives in sheaths. He was shirtless with a barrel chest covered in curly, dirty, matted hair. A foul stench permeated off him, amplified by the rain.

His face was hidden behind a macabre mask fashioned from the bone of some indeterminate animal. A dingy brown shock of stringy, dirty hair framed the mask and his thick neck. Autumn's father was the tallest, strongest man she ever knew, but this thing standing at the front door was a monster compared to her father. The behemoth held her father's axe in one hand.

Before Kate even had a chance to protest, the killer buried the axe blade into her face. Using the axe handle as leverage, the killer, as easily as a child would a doll, hoisted Kate's limp body up off the floor and with the axe still in place flung her lifeless body across the room. Her body slammed into Jonathan with such force that it carried him back over the couch and out of sight. The killer then turned his attention toward Autumn and her brother. He took one menacing step forward as he slowly unsheathed a hunting knife from one of the many sheaths which adorned his tool belt.

Autumn stumbled backward in fear and slammed up against the wall. A rattling sound drew her attention down to where she had leaned the double-barreled shotgun up against that wall earlier. As she reached out for the weapon, the killer's hunting knife embedded into the wall next to her head, narrowly missing her by just a hair. The killer had flung it across the room with such force that the knife buried itself hilt-deep into the wood panel. Autumn screamed and jumped backwards away from the gun.

"Autumn!" Jeffrey cried out from his vantage halfway up the stairs.

The Killer sprang forth.

"Jeffery, run!" Autumn cried out. "Run! Run!"

The scared boy ran up the stairs as fast as he could. Autumn rushed up the stairs after him. Just as her foot reached the fourth step, a large hand with a grip like a vice snatched her by the left ankle. Autumn fell face first onto the stairs, cutting her lip on the corner of a step. As the killer pulled on her leg, Autumn tried to hold on with all her might. Her nails were digging into the wood of the stairs, gouging deep groves as she fought as hard as she could. But she knew she would never be able to break free from this monster's grip.

"No!" She protested as the killer slowly drug her back down the steps.

"Get away from her!" Jonathan demanded as he brought the wooden baseball bat down on the killer's back with all his might.

As two wooden shards bounced across the hardwood floor, Jonathan looked down in astonishment to see he only held what was left of the bat's handle in his hands, hands that throbbed with pain from the blow. Hitting the killer in the back was like smashing the baseball bat into an oak tree. The act did get the desired result, though.

The killer released Autumn's ankle. She sighed in relief but the pain from that vice-like grip still registered. The killer turned to face his assailant. Jonathan was blinking his eyes feverishly trying to clear his vision as blood from a wicked gash on his forehead flowed freely, a gash he had received when Kate's skull had smashed into his. Jonathan saw that the bat fragment he still held had broken off into a very sharp end, a very sharp weapon. He reared back and brought the sharp handle-shard down toward the killer's chest, but the killer proved to be much faster. The monster caught Jonathan's wrist, the wrist of his pitching hand, in his mammoth-sized hand and squeezed. The killer squeezed so hard that Jonathan winced and dropped the shard to the floor. Everyone alive in the room could hear the tendons and bones of Jonathan's wrist snap and crack as that monstrous grip tightened even more. As Jonathan tried in vain to free himself from that vice-like grip, the Killer casually knelt and retrieved the sharpened bat handle. The killer studied the makeshift weapon for a moment and then raised it above his head.

"No!" Jonathan pleaded. "No…no…no…!"

"No, please," Autumn also pleaded.

He reached up with his free hand to try and hold back the monster's thrust, but to no avail. The killer brought the sharpened wood of the broken bat handle down repeatedly, stabbing over and over. Gouts of crimson blood spraying as the makeshift weapon punctured arteries. Autumn screamed in anguish at the horrible sight of Jonathan's murder.

"Oh God! Oh God! He's killing me! He's killing me!" Jonathan screamed over and over until he could not scream anymore.

Even after the teen had long since stopped screaming, the killer brought the handle down a few more time. Jonathan's lifeless body just dangled a few inches off the bloodied floor held aloft in the killer's monstrous grip. The killer released Jonathan's shattered wrist and the massacred teen's bloodied remains fell to the floor with a sickening splash of blood. Once more the killer took a moment to examine the makeshift weapon, turning it side to side. Then it was obvious he had reached some sort of conclusion and simply, and nonchalantly, tossed the broken wooden handle to the floor.

He turned his attention back toward Autumn. She was shaking, her eyes glazed over with tears. Her mind was swirling in chaos. All she wanted to do was close her eyes, curl up into a ball, and hope this was all just a bad dream. Then a voice, a familiar voice, brought her back to reality.

"Autumn!" Jeffery called from the second floor.

Autumn was instantly in motion. Even though the pain in her left ankle was excruciating, her adrenaline kicked in and she sprang up the stairs like a puma. This time she could avoid the killer's lunging grasp. She did not even look back when she heard him crash hard into the wall at the bottom of the steps. Jeffery was crying and quivering with fear.

"Stay strong for me, Little Champion," Autumn told him. "Stay strong!"

She grabbed Jeffery by the hand and drug him swiftly to his room. She coaxed him into the room, but the boy resisted.

"No…no…no!" He protested, reaching for her in tears.

"Listen to me," she pleaded with him. "Listen to me Jeffery. I'm going to lead him away. When I do you get the hell out of here. Understand?" He shook his head violently, tears streaming down his face. "Jeffery, listen to me," she took him by the shoulders and looked into his eyes. "I need you to be strong. I need you to be Batman. Can you do that for me, Little Champion? Can you?" He nodded. "Good, now get inside and lock the door. When I say go, you get the hell out of the house and just keep on running. Got it?" He nodded.

She feverishly guided him into the room. She heard the lock mechanism click. She looked over her shoulder to see the killer now standing at the top of the stairs less than ten feet or so away. His monstrous shadow cast darkness over the whole hallway. He cocked his head to the side as if studying her. He looked the same way a dog looks when it is trying to decipher a human's words. This act was made even more chilling by the presence of that macabre animal skull mask the killer wore.

Autumn limped back down the hall toward the game room. Every step was agony. She knew her ankle was probably broken. The killer slowly walked after her. Autumn looked back over her shoulder and noticed that the killer was not following her anymore. He had stopped at Jeffery's door. The killer looked at the door as if contemplating what to do.

"No!" Autumn called out. "Come on you son of a bitch! Come after me!"

The killer looked over to Autumn who stood at the door to the game room. Then he turned his attention back to Jeffery's bedroom door.

"Son of a bitch!" Autumn cursed, looking around frantically.

Autumn pulled a framed picture of her, Jeffery, and their parents down off the wall. It was a quaint Christmas themed picture of them all smiling. Her mom used it as their Christmas cards that year. She pulled the framed picture down and flung it at the hulking killer. The corner of the frame caught the killer in the temple and the glass from it shatter all over him. He barely flinched, but it did get his attention. He started marching toward her at a rapid pace.

Autumn stumbled back into the game room, slammed the door shut, and quickly locked it. She barely had time to dive out of the way as the monstrous killer came crashing through, blasting the door off its hinges. Autumn grabbed a pool stick off the wall rack and swung it with all her might. The thin stick broke across the killer's face. The impact barely caused a reaction from the brute, but the force of the blow knocked Autumn backwards. She tried to regain her footing, but her wounded ankle collapsed under her weight. She crashed to the floor with a hard thud.

The killer once again lunged for her, but she somehow managed to roll out of his grasp and under the pool table. She quickly belly-crawled to the other side. When she regained her feet, she was on the opposite side of the pool table as the killer, who just stood there looking at her with his head cocked to the side.

"Jeffery!" She cried out. "Run! Run, baby, run!"

Autumn took a step right toward the door, but the killer stepped to his left ready to head her off. She then stepped to the left, but again the killer stepped to his right showing that he could reach her no matter which way she went. Desperate, Autumn retrieved a couple of pool balls from the side pocket in front of her and flung them at the killer with all her might. The first ball missed to the killer's right and shattered the framed poster of Troy Aikman which hung on the wall. The second ball smacked against the killer's bare chest with a sickening thud and then fell to the floor and rolled up under the pool table. If the attack hurt the monster across from her, Autumn could not tell.

Keeping her eyes on him, she frantically reached back and retrieved a couple of darts from the board which hung on the wall between the two large windows of the room. In rapid succession, she whipped the darts at the killer, both darts stabbing into his barrel chest. The killer winced but then slapped the meager darts away. Having had enough of this game, the killer walked to the end of the pool table closest to the door, immediately sending Autumn down to the other end. The killer reached down and clasped the pool table and in one violent motion turned the massive table over onto its side. The pool table, which probably weighed nearly one-thousand pounds, slammed hard on its side into the wall. Now there was nothing between Autumn and the killer.

She screamed as he rapidly made his way across the room. His giant hands were only inches from her neck when the room was suddenly engulfed with the deafening sound of a shotgun blast. The impact of the blow slammed the killer up against the wall just below the window. He sat there slumped over, blood pouring from the vicious wound in his right shoulder.

Her ears still ringing, Autumn looked over to the door to the room to see Jeffery stand there with the double-barreled shot gun held fast in his small hands, one barrel still smoking.

"Oh my God, Jeffery!" Autumn limped over and embraced her little brother.

He weakly handed her the shotgun and planted his face in her chest, no longer able to hold the tears back. When he raised his head, he fell back a step, a look of stark terror edged across his face. Autumn, noticing her brother's startled reaction whirled around with the shotgun poised. The killer just stood there, towering over them like some kind of monstrous troll out of a children's storybook. He looked down at Jeffery who cowered behind his sister. Then he looked at Autumn. His eyes were black, like those of a shark. He cocked his head to one side and then the other. As he did this, he slowly unsheathed another knife from one of the many sheaths which adorned his tool belt.

Autumn simply said, "No," and she pulled the trigger, unloading the second barrel of the shotgun at point blank range.

With an explosion of sound and flash, the killer was sent flying backwards through the window, shattering glass and wood, to fall end-over-end down to the ground below where he landed with a sickening thud. Autumn limped over to he shattered window and looked down to see the killer lying on the muddy ground, sprawled out in a bloody and broken heap. Jeffery came over to her side. Brother and sister both collapsed into each other's arms, the events of the evening finally overwhelming them emotionally. For a long moment they just cried, taking solace in the fact that they survived. Rain and wind were pelting them from the shattered window, but they did not notice.

"Are you okay?" She asked.

"Yes," Jeffery answered, his voice shaky. "What about daddy?"

Autumn's eyes began to well up once more, as the thought of the truth threatened to overwhelm her. Not having an answer for him right now, she just hugged him as hard as she could.

"The police should be here any minute, okay?" She assured him. "You were so brave, Little Champion. You were so-so brave."

Autumn, emotionally and physically exhausted, slumped back against the wall. She let the shotgun, its barrel still smoking, fall to the floor. The pain from her ankle was shooting throughout her body. The reality of the night's events kept coming to her wave after wave. She placed her face in her hands and began to weep some more. Then, she heard her brother's voice.

"Autumn," fear resonated from the sound of his voice.

Autumn opened her eyes to see Jeffery looking out the window. Painstakingly, she made her way to her feet. She followed her little brother's terrified gaze down to the ground. Down below, on the wet and bloody indention where her attacker had fallen, stood the

133

killer. He just stood there, his chest and shoulder bleeding and the flesh torn from two shotgun blasts. He just stood there as the rain poured down in sheets. He just stood there and stared back up at her and Jeffery. He stared at them with those cold, black eyes, piercing their souls from behind that macabre animal skull mask.

Autumn could not even breathe. Jeffery grabbed onto her with all his might and buried his face in her stomach. Autumn was quaking with fear. This could not possibly be real.

"What are you?" She whispered through quivering lips.

Over the torrent of the rain, there was no conceivable way he could have heard her, but he reacted as if he did. The killer cocked his head to the side. He placed his bloodied forefinger in the spot of his mask where his mouth would be as if to say *shhhh*. Off in the distance, Autumn could hear the echo of police sirens getting closer and closer. She scanned the black horizon of the woods and could see the flashing lights coming closer through the trees. When Autumn looked back down below, the killer was gone. She scanned the yard and all the surrounding area, but he was nowhere to be seen. As the first police car came skidding to a halt in front of the house, Autumn could almost swear that somewhere in the distance, somewhere out there in that black forest, she could hear the *baying* of a lamb.

*****

Six months later, the Gaia Institute…

Doctor Pleasence McDowell had been practicing her craft now for twenty years. Over the years she has witnessed many different, disturbing, and quite strange cases. From her behavior and relationship studies at Oxford to her time abroad exploring the jungles of South America in search of lost tribes to even a stint at sea, studying the mindset of deep-sea fishermen and modern-day pirates, these exploits and more she has written about in the dozen books she has seen published, even winning a *Pulitzer* for investigating and writing an eye-opening expose about *ISIS*. She has been described as quite adventurous by her colleagues. It is this very *adventurous* nature, this search for understanding that brought Dr. McDowell to Glen Haven in the first place.

In the academic circles she inhabits, the historical and oft times unexplainable nature of certain events surrounding the history of this small east Texas community is the source of great discussion and contemplation. So, two years ago, when the administrator of the Gaia Institute retired, Dr. McDowell immediately pulled on some strings and cashed in a few favors to shoot to the head of the line for the open position. Glen Haven is a well-known geographical hot spot for supernatural phenomenon and unexplainable events. She could think of no better way to get informed about these events and compile enough data for a new book than as the administrator of the local psychiatric institution.

Her very large office set in the center of the third floor of the five-story hospital was quite impressive. The walls were adorned with dozens of degrees and awards, all framed and meticulously hung with care. Her many bookshelves were packed with volumes upon volumes of textbooks and medical research. The books she authored were displayed prominently on a free-standing shelf in full view of the comfortable couch in the lounge area of her large office space. She sat behind an eight-foot mahogany desk. Behind that, the entire back wall of her office was a giant window looking down into the grounds of the institute with a beautiful view of Azlewood, the tree line stretching off into the horizon.

Dr. McDowell sat, the fingers of both hands pressed in front of her, looking out that very window. For a long moment, she rocked in her apparently very comfortable leather chair, her nose slightly crinkled in contemplation. She swiveled her chair around to face her visitors, two women. One was an athletically built Hispanic woman with shoulder length curly black hair. She had an edge in her eyes, a fire one might say. She was clearly one who wore her emotions on her sleeve like a badge of honor, but she was obviously quite practiced at controlling these emotions. Dr. McDowell mused about how she would love to dive into that psyche for a session or two.

The second woman Dr. McDowell recognized. She was the widow of the late renowned fiction writer Ross Lawry. This woman was a few years older than the first woman. She was a little taller than the other woman, and a little heavier, but not at all overweight. She was quite healthy looking for her age, and attractive. She had a warm quality to her, a nurturing quality. The horrendous details of her husband's murder and her own harrowing experience were a public record.

Either of these women would make a fascinating case study, but they were not here for Dr. McDowell's expertise. No, rather they were here to ask to visit with one of her patients. Given the older women's experience, Dr. McDowell could clearly see the coalition between her and the patient in question. And, with that revelation, it would not be very hard for someone to make the connection and decipher just who the younger Hispanic woman was as well. Glen Haven was after all a small town and the details of murder cases, especially cases with connections, were amplified even more in such proximity.

"I see no problem with your request," Dr. McDowell smiled. "In fact, I think it could be quite encouraging."

"Excellent," the older woman responded. "May we see her?"

"Of course," Dr. McDowell answered. "Come…I'll take you to her."

The two women stood and followed the doctor out of her office and to the elevator where they descended to the second floor.

"Is she confined to her room?" The younger curly haired woman asked.

"Oh, no," the doctor assured them. "This wing is an *open unit's* wing. The patients are free to come and go as they please. They are here voluntarily. Our crisis stabilization and long-term care facilities are located on the fourth and fifth levels. Our girl has made quite a bit of progress since she arrived."

"So, she can leave whenever she wants to?" The curly hair woman asked.

"Well, yes and no," the doctor replied. "Her living family, a mother and brother, live overseas. So, her next step is probably a halfway house before full release. She still needs to be monitored and there is the matter of her medication."

The doctor led them down a long corridor, past a nursing station and several inhabited rooms. The nursing station was a moving living thing, as five nurses moved like a well-oiled machine answering phones, pulling files, checking charts, and separating meds. In one room, a resident had family who had brought balloons and a cake and hats. It was obviously her birthday. The women smiled as they passed by, and the patient blew out the candles. In another room, an elderly man sat in a wheelchair staring out the window as an orderly changed the linens on his bed. As they passed another room, a very tall older man stood in the doorway wearing an open bathrobe and striped pajamas. His mouth was agape, and a long string of drool clung to his bottom lip. Without missing a beat, Dr. McDowell pulled a napkin from her pocket and wiped the man's lip. Using her index finger, she gently pressed on the man's chin, closing his mouth.

"I know, Mr. Goldberg," she smiled and straightened up his robe tying it in front for him. "I know, these women are very beautiful, so how about we look our best, okay?"

If the older man understood a word she was saying, they could not tell. They proceeded down the hallway, and he remained motionless in the doorway to his room. At the end of the hallway, there was a double-swinging door. The doctor easily pushed one door open and guided the two women into a large cafeteria. There were only a few patients here and there, eating and conversing. Dr. McDowell looked around for a moment and then smiled.

"There she is," Dr. McDowell nodded toward a blonde teenager sitting all alone at the furthest table. She was staring out the window into the courtyard not touching the food on the tray in front of her. "Now, before we go over, I just want to remind you that she may not be very responsive."

"Is she catatonic?" The curly hair woman asked.

Dr. McDowell studied her inquisitive guest for a moment. "You are quite extroverted, a real go-getter," she observed. Then she explained, "No, she is not catatonic, but it does take a little coaxing to get her to talk. Given the shared histories you three have, I'm sure you ladies may have quite a bit to talk about."

The two women looked at each other a bit startled, and then back to Dr. McDowell.

"Oh, don't be so shocked," Dr. McDowell smiled. "Observing and deducing is what I do for a living. Come on, I'll take you over."

The two women followed her over to where the teenager was sitting.

"Autumn?" Dr. McDowell said as they approached. "You have a couple of visitors."

At the sound of the doctor's voice, Autumn looked over. There was the ever so fleeting glint of hope in her brown eyes, but it was instantly gone the moment she did not recognize the two women. Autumn's empty stare went back to the window. Doctor McDowell leaned over and placed an arm around Autumn's shoulders.

"Autumn, honey," she spoke in very dulcet tones, "I think you'll find that if you listen to what these women have to say, you'll find that you three have a lot in common."

Autumn slowly nodded.

"That's a good girl," Dr. McDowell smiled and gently squeezed Autumn's shoulders. Then she stood, placed her hands in the pockets of her lab coat, and nodded her head toward the two women. "I'll let you two do the introductions. If anybody needs me just ask one of the nurses to give me a ring. Autumn, I'll speak with you later, honey." And she walked away leaving the three of them alone.

"Hello, Autumn, how are you doing?" The older woman asked.

Autumn did not respond. She sat there, one foot up on her chair, her arms wrapped around her knee, her other foot dangling just off the tile floor. She sat there staring out the large window of the cafeteria, staring at nothing. Outside the sun was shining bright, the sky was a perfect baby blue Texas sky, and the grass and trees were a vibrate green. It was a perfect spring day. Yet, Autumn did not smile. She just stared.

The older woman began to speak again. "My name is Tesla...Tesla Lawry," she introduced herself and then her companion, "and this is Diana Roa. We thought we'd come and talk to you...about your incident." Tesla could see Autumn's entire body tense up at the sound of the word, *incident*. "Oh, it's okay, honey,"

141

Tesla reassured the teenager and even reached across the table and placed a comforting hand on Autumn's shoulder. "I know it's a terrible thing to discuss."

"Trust me when I say that if there is anyone else who can relate to what it is you are feeling right now it's us," Diana added.

"Yes," Tesla agreed. "We are part of an exclusive group, a group of women like yourself, women who have," she paused for a moment searching for the right word, "endured an extreme incident. We just want you to know that you are not alone, honey."

The sound of Tesla's voice was soothing and maternal. It really put Autumn at ease. The teen stopped staring out of the window and looked over and stared right into Tesla's earnest big brown eyes. A warm smile spread across Tesla's perfectly round and quite beautiful face. Though Autumn did not quite return her smile, the teen's posture did relax a bit. She turned toward the two older women and for the first time in days, spoke.

"Tell me more about this *group*."

Chapter 3: The Lawmen

Ranger Maverick leaned back in his leather chair and smirked, the top of his thick handlebar mustache tickled his nose. He stared down at the letter on his desk, a letter he had just finished reading, and a letter that provoked the grin on his grizzled face. The letter had the official seal of the governor on it, so it was official. Glen Haven will soon be receiving a guest, a special guest from the Federal Bureau of Investigation.

Now, this would not be the first time the government had sent out a representative to his shady little corner of the world. There have been federal agents in the past to come through town putting their stamp on this crime and that one, and this would not be the last time the ranger's quaint small town would play host to an agent of the F.B.I. In his nearly four decades as a Texas Ranger, Emmitt Maverick has dealt with many Special Agents of the F.B.I. Some he has liked others not so much. For the most part, they are only sent out because one of Glen Haven's more notorious *happenings* has made the national news. The unexplainable makes folks nervous, and when folks get nervous, government officials get nervous. When government officials get nervous, enter the F.B.I.

What was up in the air is what kind of visit this one would be?

Ranger Maverick's thoughts were interrupted by an elderly woman's voice on the intercom, "Emmitt…Emmitt, honey can you hear me?"

Despite countless such exchanges, that voice had a way of nearly making the veteran ranger jump out of his skin every time.

"Katheryn, honey, you have a voice that could peel paint, you know that?" He replied.

"Enough of the pleasantries, you have a visitor," the elderly woman replied. "There's a Special Agent Christoph Edison here to see you."

"Special A…," Ranger Maverick's voice trailed off for a second as he tried to make it add up. He snatched the letter from the governor off his desk and looked at the date – *October 14th*. "Two weeks ago," he said out loud. "This letter is dated from two weeks ago. Why am I just now reading it?"

"Oh, Emmitt, that's a question only you can answer," she responded in a scolding fashion. "I've been after you to clear out that In-Box now for months."

Ranger Maverick looked over at said In-Box only to find a stack of envelopes and memos stacked so high they were leaning and threatening to fall over. "Yeah, yeah, I'll get on that right away," he said absently. "Okay, send him in."

A few moments later, there came a knock at the ranger's door.

"Come in," Ranger Maverick called out.

In walked a young Asian man, the ranger pegged him to be in his mid to late twenties. He had chiseled features and the ranger could tell he was quite fit. He wore a white collared shirt with a black tie, black sports coat, black pants, and black shoes shined so clean, the ranger would swear he could see his reflection in them. Over his ensemble, the young agent wore a long gray trench coat. The bulge in the young man's coat told the ranger he was armed.

Ranger Maverick stood to greet the young man. "Well, you definitely look the part of an F.B.I. Agent," he smiled and extended his hand. "I'm Ranger Emmitt Maverick. Welcome to Glen Haven."

The young agent took the ranger's hand in his, pointed to himself, and replied, "Special Agent Christoph Edison. Good to meet you, Ranger Maverick."

"Nice grip," the older man said with a smile. "You may look like a fed, but you shake hands like a real lawman." Agent Edison received the backhanded compliment with a smile and nod. Ranger Maverick gestured to a chair in front of his desk and said, "Please, have a seat. Before we get started, I'd like to get something out of the way first."

"Of course," Agent Edison replied and obliged.

Ranger Maverick sat back behind his desk and leaned forward with his fingers crossed in front of him. He studied the young man sitting in front of him for a moment and then began to speak.

"When it comes to Special Agents visiting my small town here, they usually break down into two categories – the *Hoss* or the *Boss*. The *Hoss* is usually an easy fellow to get along with. He is not here to step on any toes or upset the apple cart. He works alongside the local law enforcement in a joint effort to solve the matter at hand. The *Boss*, however, is the kind of government spook that can rattle a small town like Glen Haven. As far as they are concerned, the local authorities are his personal foot soldiers to be used and be at his beckon call anytime, day or night. The *Boss* is unconcerned with sharing information or evidence, he is unconcerned with rattling the locals with over-the-top, and often unnecessary, procedures like curfews, roadblocks, and mandatory forums." Ranger Maverick paused and leaned back in his chair. Then he asked, "So, Special Agent Christoph Edison, what type of F.B.I. are you?"

Ranger Maverick watched the younger man very carefully as he took a moment to contemplate the ranger's words. There was something about the way he carried himself, he had confidence without ego, intelligence without arrogance. Before the young man even spoke, Ranger Maverick had already decided right then and there that he was going to like this Special Agent Edison.

"Well, I am certainly not here to step on anybody's toes," the young man assured. "I'm here to help, Ranger Maverick, in any capacity I can. You shall have my full cooperation, as, I assume, I shall have yours."

"*Hoss* it is then," the older man smiled. "So, Edison…," Ranger Maverick paused and scratched his grizzled chin. "Uh, if you don't mind me asking, you don't look to be from around these parts. How did you come about with the last name Edison? Marriage? Adopted?"

"My father was a Captain in the United States Air Force," Agent Edison answered. "He met my mother when he was stationed at Osan Air Base. I was born state side, Oklahoma City."

"Ah, a *Sooner* fan, huh?" Ranger Maverick smiled and teased, "Well, we don't take kindly to *Sooner* fans 'round these parts."

"Well, you have nothing to worry about then," Agent Edison replied. "I have absolutely no stakes in the *Red River Rivalry*. I'm not exactly a football fan."

"Not a football fan?" Ranger Maverick scoffed. "Boy, you do realize you're in the great state of Texas. We live and die football 'round here."

147

"Yes, I understand it is quite an obsession around here," Agent Edison replied without the slightest bit of irony.

"You under…," Ranger Maverick huffed. "Boy, just what is you are a fan of?"

"Chess."

"Chess?"

"Yes, Chess."

"Sweet mother of…." Ranger Maverick leaned back in his comfortable leather chair and exhaled. "Well, I sure as hell ain't inviting you over Sunday night for a round of Chess." The veteran ranger broke out into a hardy laugh, a deep belly laugh. His boisterous outburst was met by Agent Edison's own laugh, a lighter, throaty rapid-fire laugh. "Alright, son," Ranger Maverick gathered himself and continued, "what do you know about our fair community here?"

Ranger Maverick noticed the Special Agent straighten up even more so than he already was. He could almost see the wheels turning in the young man's head as he prepared to speak.

"Glen Haven was established in 1690," Agent Edison said. "Originally it was a Spanish mission, one of many established in what would one day become east Texas because of Spain laying claim to the territory before the French could. Very soon after, due to the hostilities by the natives, a fort was erected, Fort Charles, named after Charles II, last of the House of Hasberg, known as *The Bewitched* for his many ailments both physical and mental.

In 1723, a settlement began to grow around the mission and fort. Glen Haven became a destination for settlers moving west and up from Mexico. In 1860, just before the outbreak of the American Civil War, the settlement struck it rich with silver. The silver rush made Glen Haven an important asset to the United States and the government stepped in to make sure not only that the town prospered but that it remained part of the Union. For nearly ten years the town flourished and grew. They even brought the railroad through, but then the silver ran dry. By the time the 1900s rolled around, Glen Haven was little more than a ghost town.

Then in 1912, Swedish immigrant Peter Skarsgaard struck oil and his fields brought work and settlers in, and once again, Glen Haven flourished. Glen Haven was one of very few places unaffected by the Great Depression. However, just like everyone else, Glen Haven lost many sons to World War I, even more to World War II. The town is widely recognized as the home to Purple Heart honoree and recognized national hero for his bravery and sacrifice at the Battle of Attu, Stellan Larsen. A statue of him was erected in Shady Grove Park.

In 1951, the U.S. government established Grimlock Air Force Base on the former site of Fort Charles. Much of what happens on this site is shrouded in mystery. The Paparazzi has taken to calling the site *Area 52* as an obvious reference to Groom Lake. What is known is that Grimlock is used for developing and testing experimental aircraft."

Ranger Maverick held up his hand and the younger man stopped speaking.

"So, you going to recap the entire textbook for me or just give the *Cliff Notes*?" the older man asked. "Son, I bet you must have been some kind of wizard in school. Straight 'A' student, were you?"

"I had a 4.0 G.P.A. at the University of Oklahoma," Agent Edison replied. "I finished top of my class at the Academy, excelling in behavior and forensic sciences, I…"

Ranger Maverick once again held up his hand and the younger man stopped speaking.

"I'm going to ask you a question and I want you to really think about your response before you answer," Ranger Maverick said. Agent Edison nodded, and the older man asked, "What do you really know about Glen Haven?"

The young man sat stoically for a moment then replied, "The F.B.I. does not make a habit of trying to investigate or look into the…," he pauses a moment, "…the paranormal. However, files do exist, files containing many unusual cases. Many of these files are classified and above my pay scale, but if you are asking if your small town is on the government's radar the answer is yes."

"Do you believe in the supernatural, Special Agent Edison?"

"I believe in phenomenon and that anything that can be experienced can be explained," the younger man answered sincerely.

"Do you believe in spirits, Special Agent Edison?" Ranger Maverick asked.

"What do you mean?" Agent Edison's brow furrowed. "Spirits? Like ghosts? The afterlife? Ranger Maverick, are you asking me if I believe in heaven and hell? Are you asking me if I believe in God?"

"Maybe."

"I'm agnostic," Agent Edison replied. "Is there a God above looking down on us? I don't know. It'd be kind of cool if there was, no? Do I believe we all have little angels and devils sitting on our shoulders pulling us this way and that controlling our actions and motivations? Absolutely not. I believe every man and woman is responsible for their own actions and thus the consequences for those actions. I believe in being a good person, fundamentally. Ranger Maverick, I don't lie, I don't cheat, and I don't steal. I will not pull my firearm except in self-defense or in the defense of others. If there is a heavenly reward after this mortal coil is through and that is not good enough to get me through the gates, I can live with that knowing that I conducted myself the best way possible. And I know I don't need to give ten percent of my income to the local house of worship to appease an omnipotent invisible man who has no need for cash."

The older man rubbed his grizzled chin for a moment then smiled and said, "Damn, son, I'm not trying to recruit you for some cult here."

Both men laughed.

"My main reason for coming here is to assist in any way I can with the *Goatman Murders*," Agent Edison said.

"Jesus H., those newspapers sure do love to give these cases a colorful name, don't they?" Ranger Maverick stood and walked over to a filing cabinet and pulled out a vanilla envelope, its string fastens holding on for dear life against the weight of papers it held. He pressed the button on the intercom on his desk and asked, "Katheryn, can you make a copy of the file we have on the Azlewood murders for Special Agent Edison here?"

"It's what I live for," the elderly voice came back through the speaker.

"Where you staying?" Ranger Maverick asked the younger man.

"The bureau has me at the Sunset Lodge right off route 666 across from a roadhouse whose name escapes me," Agent Edison answered. His eyebrow arched as he tried to recall the name of the roadhouse.

"The Vikings Hub," Ranger Maverick said. "That's ole Marge Thompson's joint. It's a shame you don't like football because that's the best joint in town to catch a game." He paused a moment to shake his head. "Don't like football? Jesus H..." he pressed the button on the intercom and again and said, "Katheryn, honey, send those copies over to...," he looked over at Agent Edison and asked, "What room are you in?"

"237."

"Send those copies over to room 237," Ranger Maverick said, but when there was no reply, he asked, "Katheryn, honey, did you get that?"

"Shall I pull down his covers, pull out his slippers, and place a mint on his pillow while I'm at it?" The elderly woman's voice was matter of fact and without a trace of malice.

Ranger Maverick smiled and replied, "Just the copies of the case files will be fine, thank you." He stood and retrieved his cowboy hat from the rack and placed it on his head. It was a dark felt hat with a red bandana wrapped around the crown and a string of beads wrapped around the bandana. A single black feather was held in place by the bandana. "Long drive in, Edison?"

The younger man stood and stretched out the ache of the road. "It was quite a jaunt," he replied.

"You must be hungry?"

"Starving."

"Great," the ranger smiled. "Let's grab a bite. I know just the place. Plus, I can drive you around a little so you can get to know our town."

"Sounds terrific," Agent Edison smiled.

*****

Steven coughed as the smoke hit his lungs. His friends, Eric and Brian fell into a fit laughter. In-between whoops that seared his throat, Steven found he was involuntarily giggling. He was not particularly happy about anything, in that moment, he just found it easier to give in over to the silliness of it all. He passed the joint to Eric and leaned back against the concrete wall and slowly exhaled, his feet resting easily on his skateboard. He closed his eyes and let the warm sunshine down on his face. His thoughts began to wander, and he dreamed about the day when he could leave this old town, his insane mom, her asshole boyfriend, and his three bratty sisters behind.

Through the fog of thought he heard Eric coughing. This time it was Steven's turn to join Brian in pointing and laughing.

"Goddamn," Eric muttered between deep, throaty coughs, "that's some good shit."

He passed the joint to Brian who took a small puff. A puff he almost immediately exhaled. With a big grin, Brian tried to pass the joint along back to Steven, but Steven was having none of it.

He waved his hand and said, "Don't be such a puss. Take a real drag."

"Yeah," Eric added. "Just think about it like it's the dicks you suck in the bathroom at school."

Eric was tall, extremely tall for a fourteen-year-old. At Six-foot four inches, he towered over the other two boys. Quite aware of this size differential, Eric often used it to his advantage. Though he had been called a bully by others, Eric never saw it this way. He just saw

155

it as getting others to see the right way, his way. He padded Brian on the back with a heavy hand, causing the smaller teen's entire body to shift.

Eric snatched the joint from Brian's hand and held it up to the smaller teen's lips and said, "Suck it. Suck it like you're in love, you little bitch."

Brian complied and inhaled deeply. As he began to cough, Eric and Steven fell back in a fit of laughter. Brian swallowed hard; his eyes glossed over. He gave the thumbs up then continued to cough violently. This act only made his friends laugh even harder. Despite his burning lungs and tearing eyes, Brian could not help but join them in laughter.

Wiping tears from his eyes, Steven asked, "Is it just me or was that *Riverdale* TV show better the first time around when it was called *Twin Peaks*."

"I have not seen or watched anything regarding that travesty," Eric replied. "It is abundantly clear that it's just another *CW* teen-fluff show with an *Archie* skin with no actual regard or respect to the source material. It's somehow even lower in my esteem than *Gotham*."

"I've never seen *Twin Peaks*," Brian added as he wiped a bit of spittle from his lips. "It was a bit before my time. Isn't that a TV show our grandparents used to watch or something?"

"You have *Netflix*?" Steven asked.

"Not at the moment," Brian replied. "I was using my dad's account, but he turned it off when he moved again. I should probably ask my mom and stepdad if we can get one of our own."

"Both *Netflix* and *Hulu* keep it in pretty heavy rotation," Steven said as he took the joint from Eric. "When you have one or the other, do yourself a favor and binge *Twin Peaks*. You won't regret it."

"This may seem like a sin, but *Twin Peaks* has never looked interesting to me," Eric said as he wrung his hands nervously. "I know very little about it, but it just hasn't caught my eye enough to look into it."

Passing the joint back to Eric, Steven, ignoring the larger teen's critique, looked at Brian and said, "I have the *Blue Ray* that includes the TV series and the follow up film if you'd like to barrow it."

After a look, over to Eric who was slowly shaking his head as he puffed on the joint, Brian answered, "I'll pass. I appreciate the offer, but I know it would just sit and I'd never get around to watching it."

Steven leaned back against the concrete wall and once again let the warm rays of the sun wash over him. Eric and Brian were his friends, perhaps his only friends, and that made him feel sad. On his mental checklist of things to do once he blew out of this town, Steven added *find new friends*.

"I recently went back and read *Secret Wars* from 2015," Brian said waving off his turn at the pot.

"Suit yourself," Eric said taking another puff.

"So, in this story, in Doom's new world, he and Sue Richards are a couple, right?" Brian mused. "Does that mean ole Doom was plugging Reed's wife? If so, is there anything more villainous than that?" The smaller teen began to chuckle.

"Yes," Eric replied in all seriousness. "How about having a witch seduce your brother, then drugging him up with mind control potion, then forcing him to watch while you sleep with the witch that your brother is now in love with." Eric started laughing almost manically. "Then, you turn your brother into a frog!"

"Man, Walt Simonson's Thor is the best ever," Steven interjected.

"Yeah, but Loki at heart is a trickster," Brian explained. "What he does, he does for a good laugh. Doom covets Reed's wife. That's a sin." Brian made that goofy face he makes when he thinks he has made a point.

"What is sin to Doctor Doom?" Steven asked seriously. "The man has stolen from Satan himself?"

"Exactly," Eric said, his hands steady, his eyes squinting against the light of day. "He's so villainous that sin is an afterthought. He's the ultimate bad guy."

"It's not that Doom is villainous or sinful," Steven corrected. "Those are concepts for lesser men. They are beneath him. The crux of Doom's character is that he is better than anyone on the planet. Hell, he is better than anyone in the cosmos. Everyone else is beneath him. Damn Reed for a fool for not being sensible enough to realize that and not standing aside to let Doom remake the world into a better place."

"And, to give Reed's wife a better boning," Eric giggled as he thrust his hips several times to emphasize his point.

"Well of course. Doom doesn't need stretchy tricks to light up her eyes," Steven added with a smile.

"Worry not, Reed old boy," Eric said in a faux voice. "Now that I've stolen your wife, your mother is no longer the only person to call me *Daddy*!"

"No!" Brian exclaimed in a cartoonish voice of his own.

They were all laughing so hard that they did not even notice the white Bronco pull up, a Bronco with the distinct logo of the Texas Rangers on the side of it.

"How you boys doing?" Ranger Maverick asked with a smile that made his handle-barred mustache curl wide around his lips like two hairy cobras.

"Oh, Shit!" Eric exclaimed.

He grabbed Brian by the collar and darted off down the alley in the opposite direction, practically carrying the small teen along as he ran. Steven, lost in his foggy thoughts, was a bit slower to react. When the old ranger's smiling face came into view, Steven bolted to his feet, skateboard in hand, and ready to follow his friends in flight.

However, just as he turned to go, he heard the ranger's stern command, "Don't even think about it, Steven Tyler Jenkins! You stay put right there." The sound of his name coming out of that man's mouth halted the teen right in his tracks. He looked over to see the old ranger beckoning him with his long, gnarled finger. "Step on over here, young man."

His head a little foggy, Steven still knew what this meant when his mother found out. He would be grounded, that goes without saying, but not only would she probably hit him; her asshole boyfriend would probably want to get in a few shots of his own. Steven shuffled on over to stand next to the driver's side window. His eyes staring at the asphalt.

"Look at me, son" Ranger Maverick said.

Steven gradually brought his eyes up to meet the old lawman's stare. What he saw in those stark blue orbs was something that rocked young Steven Jenkins to his very core. It wasn't anger. It wasn't frustration. And it was not annoyance. All of which he had grown used to in the eyes of his mother, his teachers, and all the other adults in his life. No, what he saw in those stark blue eyes of the law was disappointment.

"Hand it over," Ranger Maverick commanded.

Steven slowly handed the old lawman the last remnants of the smoking joint, a crooked smile edging across his young face as he did. In a quick move, the veteran ranger took the joint and flicked it past the teen's left ear. Steven could hear the sizzle as it flew by.

"Don't be a wiseass," Ranger Maverick said sternly. "Hand it over."

For a moment Ranger Maverick remained vigil as the teen rummaged through the pocket on the front of his hoodie. Then, Steven pulled out a small zip-lock sandwich bag which contained about a half an ounce of weed. The teen reluctantly handed the crumbled-up baggy over to the ranger. Ranger Maverick sat the baggy down on the seat next to him.

Steven noticed the ranger's companion and asked, "Who's this…Tonto?"

"You just never you mind about who this is," Ranger Maverick scolded. "Now, Steven," just the sound of his name coming out of the old ranger's mouth caused the teen to straighten up, but he still found it hard to meet the gaze of those stern stark blue eyes. "You are not a stupid kid. You know if I see you smoking weed, I'm going to bust your ass. Surely you and the dynamic duo you call friends can find a more discrete place to hang out than in a back alley behind a condemned K-Mart, right? Where'd you get the weed from?"

"It belonged to my mother's boyfriend," Steven answered, still not meeting the lawman's gaze. "I stole it from his dresser drawer."

"Well, I suspect retribution in your future," the ranger said shaking his head. "Everything going alright back at the homestead?"

"Yeah, it's cool," Steven lied.

"Cool, huh?" The old ranger nodded skeptically. "Listen, Steven, you're a good kid, maybe not the sharpest tool in the shed, but hell, you still have plenty of years left to go before you have to try and figure things out. You have any problems at home; you give me a call, okay?"

"Yes, sir," Steven replied.

"Now, go on, get," Ranger Maverick gestured with his thumb.

"Seriously?" Steven exhaled.

"Yeah, but don't let me catch you smoking out so blatantly in public again," the ranger smiled and gave the teen a wink. As Steven took off in the direction his friends had departed, he heard the old ranger calling after him. "And Steven, tell your buddy, the one that looks like the Jolly Green Giant, and his little sidekick that when I see them, I'm giving them both a stern kick in the ass for running off."

"Yes, sir!" Steven called back as he leapt onto his skateboard and zipped off down the alleyway.

Ranger Maverick smiled as he saw Steven disappear around the corner flying on his skateboard. He reached over and retrieved the small bag of weed and held up to his hawk-like nose for a moment. Then he deposited the baggy into his shirt pocket. To his right, Special Agent Edison was leaning on the window seal, his dark sunglasses reflecting the image of a smiling old Texas Ranger.

"Interesting law enforcement procedures practiced out here in the sticks," Agent Edison said with a straight face.

"Ah, hell," Ranger Maverick said as he pulled the Bronco back out onto the main road, "What good is busting the kid and giving him a record before he even has a chance to discover who he is going to be? Steven may have some hurdles to jump ahead of him, but he's a good kid. Most of them are. Who knows what minor little indiscretion could be the catalyst that sets one of these buggers down the wrong path? Besides, the prisons are overpopulated enough, mostly due to some trumped up charges and/or antiquated laws against weed. Look to the future, Special Agent Edison. Weed is already legal in many states, and it won't be long before it is in the rest of them. Though I imagine our great state here will be the last holdout. No point in starting a kid off on the wrong foot over something that isn't going to mean a hill of beans a few years from now."

Agent Edison chuckled. "I was just referring to the interesting choice of evidence storage."

"Oh this?" The old ranger patted his breast pocket. "Shit, I'm smoking this shit tonight." He laughed. "For my arthritis, you see."

Of course," Agent Edison smiled.

As the Veteran Texas Ranger turned the Bronco right onto the next street he began to point and explain, "This is Main Street. It's one of the older parts of town so there isn't that much traffic, at least during the day anyway. Over there is *Dave's I like Tacos*. You open the tortillas, and their tacos look like a used baby's diaper, but it's good eats if you're in a hurry. There to your right, now that's some good eats. That there, my friend, is *Limits*, best damn chicken fried steak this side of the Red River. Ah, see this?" Agent Edison followed the ranger's gesture to see an array of black and white streamers swirling in the wind and empty plastic cups rattling around in and alongside the curb. "The football team just had their Homecoming parade yesterday. Remind me later to get on the horn and have Katheryn get Carl the Street Sweeper over here."

The brick on the buildings that lined both sides of the narrow street were chipped and weatherworn. More than half of the buildings were empty and closed, some of them even boarded up. There was a feeling of desolation, almost despair-like. Agent Edison had been through small towns all over middle-America. It was the same story one right after the next. This factory shuts down or that farm is bought out by a big corporation and before long jobs begin to dry up and locals move on. Agent Edison did not even realize he was frowning.

Noticing this, Ranger Maverick chuckled and said, "Don't you fret none, Special Agent Edison, sure the recession back in oh-eight hit us pretty hard, but we're doing alright. Most of the local mom and pop fronts have moved on over to Stewart Street to be closer to the traffic coming in and out of that new Cineplex over there. This is an all but abandoned side of town. The local teens use this strip of road to hang out on the weekends. They'll usually start over at ole *Dave's I like Tacos* and then cruise down this strip and all meet back up over in the parking lot of the *Winn Dixie*."

"You ever have any trouble with drag racing?" Agent Edison asked.

"Oh, we've had our fair share of incidents," Ranger Maverick mused. "I'd say about fifteen years ago; a couple of Hot Rods were swinging their dicks around and decided to go head-to-head. You know, a couple stubborn grease monkeys too dumb to back down and wanting to prove whose car had the most muscle. Well, they come tearing down the strip when one of them loses control of his car and ends up plowing right into a group of kids that were lined up on the side of the street cheering them on. Happened right over there. Tragic, really. Well, the kid behind the wheel of the car that ran those kids down was haunted by the guilt of it all. He couldn't live with it and took his own life. Yes, sir, put the dick end of a .44 magnum in his mouth and *boom*." The Ranger turned the Bronco right onto another street and continued. "So, the local authorities don't really have to do too much policing. That story alone is a nice deterrent for the kids. Sure, every now and then the Sheriff will send a unit over to do a drive by. It's good for them. Let's the kids know that there's still someone watching just in case they decide to get a little too rambunctious."

"Every small town has their stories," Agent Edison said. "Every small town has their tragedies."

"Yes, sir," Ranger Maverick agreed, but added. "Some more than others."

166

*****

A charming little bell rang out above their heads and announced their arrival into the quaint diner. Six booths upholstered in burgundy lined the walls, three along each wall, framing the main counter which was lined with round spinning stools. Locals occupied all the booths, all enjoying meals and casual conversation. A few of the residents looked up from their coffee or toast and greeted the Ranger with a nod and smile. The aroma of coffee was strong in the air but even that paled in comparison to the aroma of blue berry.

Ranger Maverick gestured to the counter and Agent Edison followed and sat down beside him. Waiting for them on the other side of the counter was a diminutive elderly Asian woman with a warm smile and hot pot of coffee. Her round face showed the cracks of age. She had a few long grey whiskers hanging from her chin. Her spine was slightly curved.

"Good morning, my fine-looking Ranger," the elderly woman behind the counter greeted, pouring Ranger Maverick a steaming cup of coffee. "My, and who pray tell is your handsome young friend?" She asked.

"Good morning, Coco," Maverick replied with a smile, "and this here chap is Special-Agent-Christoph-Edison who's come to us all the way from the F-B-I." The Ranger's emphasis on his name and profession was not lost on Agent Edison.

Noticing Coco to be of Korean descent, Edison stood and spoke to her in a very polite manner using a formal greeting in the Korean language. Coco's small nose crinkled, and she smiled warmly and replied in a thick southern accent, "I'm sorry, Honey, but I don't speak Spanish." This drew a boisterous laugh from the Texas Ranger to Edison's left.

"Sorry," Agent Edison apologized with a nod and sat back down. "Nice to meet you, Coco."

"Ah, don't get your balls in a bunch, Special Agent Edison," Maverick said with a firm pat on the Agent's back. "Coco here makes not only the finest cup of Joe west of the Mississippi, but she owns this here diner and this diner is world famous for its mouth-watering, delicious, freshly baked blue berry empanadas." He pauses to inhale deeply. With a smile spreading across his chiseled face, the Ranger said, "Just take a whiff, Special Agent. Do you know what that is?" Edison could smell the enticing aroma wafting into the eating area from the kitchen in the back. "That there, my boy, is a little slice of Heaven just waiting to make your day better."

Just then the door to the kitchen banged open and a young man, Edison estimated him at around nineteen or twenty years old, came stumbling into the dining room, lugging a large bag of garbage. He had a very lean frame. His apron was stained and his mop of curly hair unkempt. The weight of the bag of refuse was obviously right at the young man's threshold as he stood on unsure feet, his body trembling with the effort of hoisting it up.

"Dagnabbit, Jared!" Coco's expression switched from warm to stern in an instant, "How many times have I told you, the garbage goes out the back? You can't bring garbage through the dining area, you numbskull!"

The young man flinched as if smacked across the chin. His unsure footing caused him to stumble, and he fumbled mightily with the large bag of trash. As his feet shuffled crazily below, with one hand he would be catching small bits of trash that would spill out the top of the bag and with the other grasping desperately to get control of his burden. It was a cartoonish sight to behold, for sure.

"I'm sorry, Ms. Buck…I mean Coco…I mean Ms. Coco…," he stammered as he finally wrangled in his awkward load.

"Well, you never mind all that," the elderly woman's voice switched back to that warm tone. "Now, take that trash on out back like I said, and hurry on. We got us a couple of brave lawmen right here that would like themselves a helping of our world-famous blue berry empanadas."

"Yes, ma'am…I mean Ms. Coco…I…," the young man trailed off as he stumbled back through the swinging door from which he came, lugging his giant bag of garbage with him.

The elderly woman behind the counter turned back to her distinguished guests but paused a moment as a loud crash came echoing from the kitchen. A few of the patrons burst into laughter as the young man reemerged from the kitchen, his entire front side completely doused in white glazed and powdered sugar.

"It may be just a few moments on those blue berry empanadas," he said sheepishly as he licked frosting off his lips and wiped powdered sugar out of his doe-like eyes. And then once more, he disappeared back into the kitchen.

"Jeezus-H-Christ," Ranger Maverick said, "Coco, the boy's a walking train wreck."

"Well, young Jared may not be what you'd call a great thinker," Coco smiled warmly, "but he sure does come in handy."

"Darling, you have the patience of *Job*," the Texas Ranger smiled, "and you have quite a burden on your hands dealing with that there potato-head."

"Oh, don't worry, my handsome Texas Ranger," Coco said as she turned away, "I'll straighten him out real quick, okay? Just give me a moment and I'll be back with your order."

She walked back to the kitchen where the boy waited. He had that kind of *puppy just got caught peeing on the rug* look about him. Coco closed the door to the kitchen behind her. At that point, the lawmen could only imagine what was being said back there.

Agent Edison stood and removed his trench coat. He folded it in half and laid it over his stool.

"Restroom?" He asked. "I'd like to wash my hands."

"Over yonder," the ranger pointed around the curving counter to a door at the back of the diner.

Agent Edison made his way along the counter to the door. As he walked through the swinging door he came into a narrow hallway. On his left was the door to the Ladies Room. Directly in front of him was the door to the Men's Room. Before he entered though, something to his right caught his eye. The narrow hall went along about fifteen feet to an open doorway that led into the kitchen. From his vantage, Agent Edison could see Coco dressing down the boy. She had her small finger right in his downturned face and she was really laying into him. For a moment, the Special Agent began to feel sorry for the young man.

He entered the restroom which was surprisingly clean and well kept. He imagined for a moment the tongue-lashing the boy would get from Coco if it were ever otherwise. He washed his hands and dried them. Then, he pulled out a small black comb from his pocket and ran it through his hair. Even though he had washed his hands, he could never be sure who before him had not. So, he used a paper towel to grasp the handle of the door and open it. Holding the door open with his foot, he turned and tossed the paper towel into the trash.

Exiting the restroom back into the hall, Agent Edison looked to his left to see if the situation in the kitchen had resolved itself. To his surprise, it had, but in a most peculiar manner. Just beyond the open door that led to the kitchen, Agent Edison could see Coco and young Jared locked in a loving embrace and kissing each other passionately. The boy could not have been more than a few years younger than the Special Agent, and Coco was old enough to be their grandmother. The scene was both startling to the senses and romantic at the same time.

"Welcome to Glen Haven indeed," Agent Edison said to himself as he pushed the swinging door open and reentered the dining area.

After a round of chicken fried steak, mashed potatoes, green beans, and a pair of dinner rolls to die for, the lawmen got their blue berry empanadas to go. Agent Edison decided not to mention what he had witnessed in the hall. He felt it was nobody's business save Coco's and the boy's. Agent Edison offered to pay for the meal and Ranger Maverick let him. As they left the diner, Coco called out from behind the counter.

"You handsome men be sure to come back and visit old Coco, you hear?"

Chapter 4: Spirit

Agent Edison awoke a full hour before dawn. Silencing the chirping of his watch, the young man leapt out of bed, fully refreshed and ready to take on the day. After a quick visit to the restroom, he set about doing his morning workout. One hundred push-ups immediately followed by one-hundred sit-ups. His father always used to preach - *If it's good enough for Herschel Walker then it is good enough for you.* Now that his heart was pumping and his blood flowing, he started stretching. Touch the toes, right foot over left foot, then left foot over right, wide stance, lean to the left for the groin, now wide stance lean to the right for the other groin, and finish with a backbend into a handstand. Though his frame did not show it, Agent Edison's lean body housed quite a lot of strength for man his size. Many pugilists sparring partners at the Academy learned that lesson the hard way.

Now, ready for his morning run, Agent Edison put on a pair of gray sweats, his Oklahoma University sweats, and set out. Stepping out into the brisk morning air, unusually brisk even for a Texas fall morning, he thought he would give the trail on the other side of the road behind the *Vikings Hub* a try. The old gentleman that rented the Agent his room mentioned it and said it ran back into the woods about three miles or so with several branching pathways. Agent Edison thought a quick paced six-mile jaunt would be just what he needed to get this day started right.

The town was deathly quiet. A blanket of fog had rolled in with the cool morning breeze. Somewhere in the distance a rooster crowed, and somewhere beyond that, another rooster answered. Before crossing the four-lane road that separated him from his destination, the Agent looked both ways. Not a sound, not even a hint of traffic. Even though the fog was thick, he determined that the passage across was safe enough. He trotted across Route 666 over into the empty parking lot of the tavern. Circling around to the backside he came upon a quaint little abode, a nonintrusive single-story house. Smoke rose from the chimney and a warm glow illuminated the windows on the front of the house. Agent Edison assumed the house to be the living quarters for the proprietor of the Norse themed tavern. Beyond the house, he spotted the entrance to the trail the motel manager had mentioned and made a B-line for it. There was a short but steep incline entering the trail.

Running along the forest trail, Agent Edison started making mental notes of the numerous branching trails. He would have to make a concerted effort to explore each of them before his time in Glen Haven was done. Even though the sun was now peaking over the eastern horizon, the trail was still quite dark, shaded by a blanket of trees above. Even with the shade and the quickly dissipating fog, Agent Edison was having no difficulty navigating the path and seeing in front of

175

him. However, there was something somewhat off putting by his surroundings. Though he could not put his finger on it, there was something different, something odd.

Reaching the end of the trail he came to a small clearing. Someone had erected a small wooden sign that said – *3 miles, now just 3 more to go*. It was obviously placed here by a local as a motivational tool. Perhaps the owner of the bar. Agent Edison paused for only a moment, taking a deep breath. The aroma of pine was almost intoxicating. He cocked his head as the ambient sounds of the woodlands came alive all around him. Small critters darting through bushes no doubt looking for the day's meal. Birds, high in the branches, chirping back and forth, having a conversation amongst themselves no human being could possibly understand. Somewhere not far off, he could hear the running water of a stream or *creek* as the locals might call it.

About halfway back down the trail, something caught his attention. It was an object moving swiftly through the woods, off in the distance to his left. However, when Agent Edison looked over the object was gone. As he continued down the path the object reappeared in his peripheral, but when he turned his head, it was gone. Again, he continued down the path and again the object returned, but this time Agent Edison did not turn his head. He tried to make out the object from this askew vantage.

Whatever the object was, from this view, it appeared to be a man, or a woman, it was hard for him to make out using peripheral only, especially when coupled to the bouncing of his jogging. He discerned that the blurry object was roughly thirty or forty meters out and pacing him. He stopped jogging and looked over, but the object was gone.

"Hello!" Agent Edison called out; his voice echoed throughout the forest. "Hello!" He called out again, his voice reverberating through the trees.

There was no response. Agent Edison suddenly felt very alone. He was painfully suddenly aware of his surroundings. The forest seemingly ran on and on forever. Shadows and strange sounds all around him. He was also quite aware that he left his sidearm back in the motel room. The fog seemingly thickened. The ambient sounds of nature seemingly grew louder. The trees seemed taller and the shadows they cast darker. Agent Edison began to jog again and once again the object appeared in his peripheral.

He quickened his tempo, and the object kept pace. He slowed to almost a walk, and the object slowed with him. It was not so much fear that gripped the Special Agent as it was frustration, uneasiness. He continued along the path back the way he had originally come. Surely, he should have seen the entrance to the trail by now. He ran nearly every single day of his life. At this point, Agent Edison could nearly tell how far he had run just by feeling alone. His pace quickened, as did the object mirroring him.

Faster and faster, he ran until he was in a dead sprint. Every time he looked over his shoulder, the object following him would not be there, but every time he turned away, it would return. The fog was thickening, and it was becoming even harder to see the ground beneath his feet. According to his inner odometer, he must have gone at least another three miles beyond the initial three marked by the sign. His heart began to pound and sweat began to pour down his face. He looked over his shoulder once more and his foot caught on a jutting tree root that stretched across the path. He tumbled forward. However, years of training allowed him to catch his balance and the fall turned into a forward roll, allowing him to avert injury as he rolled head over feet down the incline on the entrance to the trail.

He came to a rough stop at the bottom of the incline, scraping his forehead on a small rock. He stood up and checked himself for injuries. Everything seemed fine. Over by the small house, an older woman was clapping. She wore a Minnesota Vikings jersey that countered as a night gown and a pair of brown, fuzzy puppy dog slippers.

"You alright, son?" She asked.

Agent Edison felt around and decided he was not injured. "I'm okay." He gave her the thumbs up.

"I'll give that dismount a ten," she chuckled as she turned and walked back into the house.

The young man was more than a little embarrassed. Not so much because of the fall he took, but more due to how he allowed his imagination to take control of him like that. Curiosity took him back up to the top of the incline which led to the trail. Agent Edison felt a sinking feeling in his stomach as the trail was all but engulfed by thick fog. Fog so thick that to even attempt to walk the trail would be dangerous. As he walked away, scratching his head, he could almost swear he heard childlike laughter coming from somewhere deep in that fog.

Agent Edison brushed himself off and made his way back to the highway. A truck was motoring up. So, he decided to let the vehicle pass before crossing the road back to the motel where he was staying. As the truck drew closer, it became painfully obvious that the truck was slowing down. It rolled to a stop right in front of Agent Edison. There was a very large, portly man sitting in the passenger's seat. He eyed Agent Edison up and down. The scowl on his round bearded face was a bit off putting. The driver, a thin, older man with glasses stared as well. As the window on the passenger side of the truck slowly rolled down, the large man pulled something from the glove compartment. Agent Edison again suddenly became painfully aware his sidearm was back in his motel room.

"Here, boy," the passenger said thrusting something toward him.

Agent Edison was relieved to see the man holding a *Band-Aid*. "Thank you," he said taking the small bandage from him.

Then, the passenger pointed a large, meaty finger at the young man. Both he and the driver shook their head. He held up that same meaty hand, his middle and ring finger were bent and held in place by his thumb while his index finger and pinky were pointing straight up.

"Hook 'em Horns!" He bellowed.

The driver held out the same gesture on his side. They laughed and then drove away.

At first Agent Edison was a bit perplexed but then he looked down at the crimson *O* and *U* on his sweatshirt and pants and it all came together.

"Hook 'em Horns indeed," he said to himself as he crossed the road back over to his waiting motel room.

After a long hot shower, Agent Edison felt something more akin to himself. The chill of the unusually cold morning and his woodland experience firmly behind him, the young man dried off and combed his jet-black hair. A smile cracked his lips for he knew all too well that once his hair dried, it would poof out into that mop of hair he has become all too known for. He could probably use moose or gel to hold his locks in place, but it had never been a major concern for him. He dressed in standard attire – black shoes, black pants, white button up shirt, black sports coat, and black tie. He retrieved a complimentary cup of hot coffee from the motel lobby and was quite surprised at just how good that coffee tasted. Filling up a second cup and snagging a pastry, also complimentary, Agent Edison headed back to his room.

He had another hour to kill before the ranger would arrive, so he decided to once again go over the case files provided by the ranger's staff. Sitting at the small table in the motel room, by the light of a lamp, he started to go through the papers again.

Early sightings and reports of what the news has dubbed the *Goatman Killer of Azlewood* were cryptozoic in their description. Some reports described him as an animal that walks like a man, a bipedal creature with the legs and hooves that resemble the hind legs of an animal, the torso of a man, and the head of a demon. There was a couple of hikers that swore they saw Bigfoot. A clear picture of the assailant does not exist. These woods are well known as an odd dead zone when it comes to cell phones and technology in general. The sightings go back as far as five years. Some locals have reported sounds at night coming from the woods, an animal call of some sort, almost like the bleating of a baby lamb. It is from this sound which the media drew their inspiration for the killer's colorful moniker.

There were even a few incidents where local teens were caught trying to cash in on the media hype and local paranoia by pulling pranks on locals using various Halloween costumes. There have been half a dozen missing cases and three other murders that have been linked to this case through the media, but at this point, which is just conjecture and there is no evidence to support that they are linked to the *Goatman Murders*.

However, Agent Edison was not interested in any of the fluff and window dressing of the case. His only concerns were facts.

The murders began almost three years ago. The first victim of this *Goatman* on record was Christmas Roa. She was attacked in her house. This case was different since the victim was strangled to death. The murder weapon, which has never been found, used in most of the cases was a large knife, perhaps a hunting knife. The murder was witnessed by the victim's twin sister, Diana, who herself was the sole survivor of another yet unrelated series of murders. Agent Edison made a mental note to request those case files.

The second attack occurred three months later at the residence of renowned author Ross Lawry. He and his then pregnant wife, Tesla, were home alone when the killer invaded their home, murdered Ross, and severally injured his wife. She survived the attack, though their unborn child did not.

Another six months passed before the third attack which happened at the lake. A group of college kids on their way to summer vacation decided to stop in Glen Haven and visit the infamous location they had been hearing about on the news. Unfortunately, for these kids they got way more than they bargained for. They were joined by two local girls, sisters Angela and Anne Lee. In total, nine murders with Anne as the lone survivor.

The fourth, and probably the most compelling of the attacks, occurred when a group of film students came down from UNT to film a documentary about the infamous murders of Azlewood. What makes this incident stand out amongst the others is that there is actual film footage of the days and the hours leading up to the attack and of the attack itself. Caitlin Bachman was the sole survivor in this instance. Her camera man, Adam Hyde, and boyfriend, Joshua Foreman, were not as fortunate. Agent Edison committed another mental note to ask the ranger about the found footage.

Finally, the last known murders that have been officially linked to the *Goatman* occurred last October at the home of Ryan Carpenter. The victims included Ryan himself along with ten local teenagers who were renting Ryan's guest house that weekend for a Halloween/Birthday celebration. Miraculously, Ryan's teenage daughter, Autumn, and ten-year-old son, Jeffrey, both survived the experience.

The description of the attacker correlates from each case. Each survivor describes the killer in the same manner. He's a monster of a man. In size if not origin, Agent Edison mentally added. He is described as wearing worn, dirty pants held up by suspenders. He has never been seen wearing a shirt. His massive shoulders, chest, and arms are covered in matted, curly hair almost as thick as fur. His hands are reported to be enormous with long sharp, dirty fingernails. He is reported to have an almost overpowering, pungent odor. A couple of the witnesses have described his odor as putrid and even rancid. However, it is the killer's most distinct feature that has peaked the Special Agent's curiosity. It is reported, and confirmed this with every eyewitness account, that the killer wears some kind of as yet unidentified animal skull over his face. Other than the fact that he has a long thick beard with matted hair just as unkempt as the rest of his ensemble, none of the survivors have seen their attacker's face. It remained hidden behind that macabre mask and a giant mane of matted animal hair which the agent assumed was stitched into the skull. A couple of police sketches accompanied the files.

Police Case File #6946-1

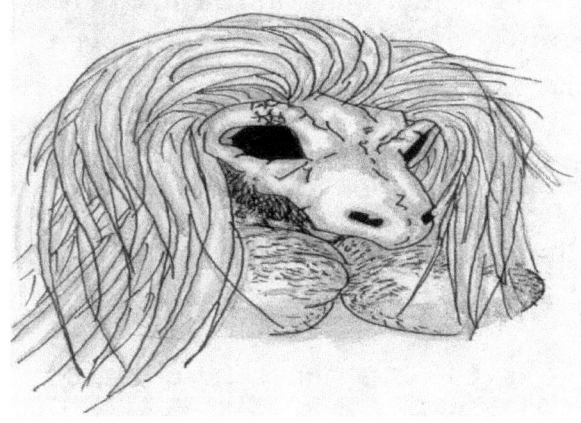

"Monstrous," the Special Agent said out loud.

A knock at the room's door startled him from thought. He walked over, checked the peephole, and opened the door. Leaning against the frame in that laid-back way he always seems to exude was Ranger Emmitt Maverick, arms folded casually.

He tipped his cowboy hat and asked, "Sleep well?"

"Four solid, uninterrupted hours," Agent Edison replied in earnest.

"Four hours?" The older lawman chuckled. "Jesus H, son, you must be exhausted."

"On the contrary, Ranger Maverick, I find that four hours a night is all anyone needs to maintain a healthy, productive life," the young man said as he gestured for the ranger to come in.

"That can't be true." The older man said as he entered the room. "Everybody knows you need at least seven to eight hours of sleep every day."

"That would be true in most cases," the Special Agent said as he shut the room's door behind his guest. "That would be true for the average person who still has to experience all four stages of sleep."

"And, uh, you don't have to experience these stages?" Ranger Maverick asked skeptically.

"Years ago, I mastered a technique of meditation which allows me to slow my breathing, heartrate, and my body's core temperature, allowing me to enter a deep stage of sleep sooner," the Special Agent explained. "By doing this I have found that I do not require any more than four hours of sleep a night."

"Witchcraft," the veteran Texas Ranger scoffed.

"Excuse me?"

"Never mind," the older man chuckled then he pointed to the small bandage on the Agent's forehead. "Cut yourself shaving?"

Agent Edison absently ran his fingers through his bangs covering up the small wound, "No, no, jogging accident."

Ranger Maverick nodded as he scanned the motel room. "I see you have filled your time by going over the case files?"

"Yes," he answered as he donned his trench coat. "As a matter of fact, there are further case files I'd like to look at concerning one of the surviving eyewitnesses. A Diana Roa I believe her name is? Then, there's also that found footage the film students shot. I'd like to set up a viewing. Plus, if possible, I'd like to visit a few of the attack sites." He paused and held his hand up. "Not that I think local law enforcement missed anything in their investigations. I'd just like to add a visual of the situations to the text for my own frame of reference."

"I'm sure all that can be arranged," the ranger nodded, "but first, how would you like to go and meet the *Survivors Club*?"

"*Survivors Club*?"

"Yes," the ranger replied. "Get your things. I'll explain on the way."

The older lawman exited the room and headed to his Bronco. Agent Edison took a moment to take stock. He was suddenly reminded of his morning jog and the peculiar incident he had in the nearby woods. He made a mental note to inform the ranger about it as he secured his sidearm in its holster under his left arm.

*****

The morning sun had barely crested over the eastern horizon and Diana was coming back up the trail that led to the house. She tried to get in at least five miles every morning. Though her GPS watch was not operating in these woods, according to her manual step-counter, this morning she knocked out nine miles. She just assumed the extra energy was from the adrenaline boost from the previous night's events. It could also just be a byproduct of her being in the best shape of her life. Yet another byproduct of her previous harrowing encounter with the Azlewood Killer.

In the years since that fateful, horrible night that took her sister away from her, Diana has spent almost every waking moment honing her mind and body to physical perfection. Now, she was not going to win any gold medals in the Olympics anytime soon, but she was as physically fit as a twenty-nine-year-old could be. As she jogged up toward the house, past the mailbox with the address *308 Saranell Court* on it, Diana was quite aware of the eyes that were upon her from the front porch. Ever since her encounter, she has been in a constant state of alertness. She did not immediately jog over to the house because she still had one final exercise to complete for her morning routine.

She trotted up to a large tree at the foot of the driveway. This tree towered over the others in the yard. It had dozens of jutting branches that snaked out in all directions. About six, six-and-a-half feet off the ground were two particularly large branches the extended forward and parallel to each other. Nestled between these two branches was a metal pole. Diana stepped forward and leapt up to grab hold of the pole with an underhand grip. She steadied herself, took a deep breath, and began to pull herself up until her chin was above the pole. She slowly lowered herself back down into a hanging position and repeated.

1...2...3...

From the front porch of the house, Tesla sat in a wooden rocking chair with a quilted shawl pulled tight around her shoulders, and a steaming cup of coffee in her hand. She watched as Diana continued her morning exercises. Anne and Cat stepped out of the front door to join Tesla on the front porch, the screen door closing shut behind them. Both had cups of coffee of their own, both still in their pajamas. Anne had a blanket thrown over her shoulders. Underneath she was

189

wearing a see-through nighty which barely reached her thighs and a pair of red underwear that left little to the imagination. Cat had thick gray cotton pajama top and bottoms and large fuzzy gray slippers on her feet.

4...5...6...

"Super woman is at it again, huh?" Anne asked as she sat down on the wooden bench to Tesla's left.

Tesla did not reply. She simply nodded and lightly blew across the rim of her coffee mug.

7...8...9...

Whether Cat was interested in Diana's morning routine no one could tell. She walked slowly to the other end of the porch, sat on the porch's wooden railing, and drank her coffee in silence.

10...11...12...

"Jesus, how many is that now?" Anne asked sipping at her mug.

"I would imagine she is just as worked up as the rest of us," Tesla replied enjoying how the mug warmed her slender hands. "We all have our own ways of dealing with...with our situation."

Cat absently pulled the sleeve of her wool pajama top up to reveal several small cuts on the inside of her forearm from her wrist to her elbow. Most of them, the older ones had faded to small white scars. The fresher cuts were now scabbed over. As she looked at her work, Cat could not help but wonder where she had left her pocketknife.

13...14...15...

They continued to watch in silence.

16...17...18...

Diana released her grip on the pole and dropped down to the ground where she landed with the gracefulness of a cat. As she walked over to join the other women on the porch, Diana was stretching her toned arms and shoulders and wiping herself down with a pink hand towel.

"Good morning, ladies," Diana said as she ascended the three wooden steps of the porch.

"Good morning, hon," Tesla replied warmly. "There's coffee in the kitchen."

"Thank you," Diana said, "but I think I'll just grab some water."

"Damn girl," Anne teased, "you make Sarah Conner look like a bitch."

"Sarah Conner?" Diana cocked her head. "Is that the one from that movie with the creatures that burst out your chest?"

"No, that's Ripley from *Aliens*," Anne said. "I'm talking about the jacked up, machine gun-toting, ass-kicking, she-bitch from *Terminator*."

"*Terminator 2*," Cat corrected.

"Right," Anne agreed. "*Terminator 2*."

"Oh yeah," Diana smiled, "she's cool."

The ladies all laughed. It was a rare moment of levity which came to an abrupt halt by the sound of a vehicle coming up the driveway. It was a white Bronco with the distinct emblem of the Texas Rangers on the side.

"Oh shit!" Anne exclaimed. "What the fuck is he doing here?"

Tesla and Diana's leadership instincts kicked in.

"You two go inside and make sure the package is secure," Diana ordered. "We'll find out what this is all about."

Anne and Cat reacted without a word.

"Also, check on Autumn," Tesla said as she reached over and gently grabbed Anne by the arm. "Plus, Anne, can you put on some proper attire?"

This drew a devilish grin from the younger woman.

As Anne and Cat entered the house to set about their tasks, the Bronco came to a stop a few yards from the front porch. Out of the driver's side stepped the familiar tall, lean Texas Ranger Emmitt Maverick. The women had come to know Ranger Maverick quite well over the last few years during his investigations into the *Goatman Murders*. Ranger Maverick was an older man in his early-fifties, but that long gray hair and the long gray handle-bar mustache did not detract from the fact that he was a strikingly handsome man. He wore a cowboy hat adorned with a tribal sash and single crow's feather sticking out the side of the sash. Even from this distance, the ladies could see the Ranger's silver badge proudly pinned to his leather vest and glinting in the light of the morning sun. The ladies were quite familiar with Ranger Maverick, but they were not at all familiar with his new partner.

Stepping out of the passenger side of the Bronco was a much younger Asian man. He was probably younger than Diana. He had similar lean frame to Ranger Maverick but was a few inches shorter than the grizzled old lawman. He was boyishly handsome with a mop of jet-black hair that waved in the breeze revealing a small *Band-Aid* on his forehead. He wore a white button-up shirt and black tie with a long grey trench coat that billowed in the wind around his legs.

The two men strode up to the bottom steps of the front porch.

Ranger Maverick tipped his hat and greeted, "Ladies."

Diana and Tesla both nodded and smiled and replied almost in unison, "Ranger Maverick."

"Why, Diana," the older man smiled, "dear you are glistening and positively stunning this morning. How are your workouts coming along? Ready to don a cape and cowl and fight crime yet?"

Wiping sweat from her arms with a towel, Diana responded in the same teasing manner, "That's your job, old man. To what do we owe the early morning visit from the Lone Ranger and Tonto here?"

"Oh, I just thought I'd pay a visit," he said. "It's been over a month since I've been out this way and I thought I'd drop in and check on you lovely ladies."

"Who's your handsome friend," Tesla asked as she sipped her coffee and continued rocking in her chair.

"This here is Special Agent Christoph Edison," the ranger gestured toward his partner. "He was sent down by the governor to see if he could help us country folk with our case. But no need to fret, ladies, ole Special Agent Edison here is one of the good ones. At least so far. Edison, this lovely woman here is Tesla, the matriarch of this household." They both nodded. "And this little spitball of muscle and beauty over here is Diana."

"And I would prefer Special Agent Edison or Edison or even Christoph or Chris to Tonto if you don't mind," the young man nodded toward Diana who smiled back.

Both women decided right then and there that they were going to like Special Agent Edison.

"As I understand it there are five of you living here?" Agent Edison asked as he pulled a small pocket notepad out and confirmed with his notes. "308 Saranell Court, correct?"

"Yes," Tesla answered. "This is my home. I'm so glad the F.B.I. sent you all the way here to confirm those facts."

Agent Edison smiled, put his notepad away, and asked, "I was hoping that I could possibly interview each of you about your encounters with the so called Goatman Killer?"

As the young man spoke, he unconsciously ascended the first step. Tesla immediately stopped rocking and stiffened in her chair. Diana instinctively took one step to her right placing herself between the young agent and the front door. These subtle actions did not go unnoticed by the lawmen.

Tesla cleared her throat and replied, "That sounds like fun, however, right now would not be the best of times."

"Oh, and may I ask why?" Agent Edison inquired politely.

"Oh, you know how it is, right?" Diana interjected. "You get a bunch of women all living together in the same place and pretty soon not only are they using the same shampoo they're all on the same cycle."

For a long uncomfortable moment, Agent Edison and Diana stood staring into each other's eyes before the young man responded, "I see."

"I tell you what I see," Ranger Maverick said smacking his young counterpart on the back as he came to stand next to him on the bottom step. "I see a beautiful future for you two, two-car garage, white picket fence, the whole nine. But, as entertaining as the sexual tension is between you two, I was wondering, how is the little one fairing?"

Tesla stood up and came over to stand next to Diana. Now, instinctively, both women were directly between the two lawmen and the front door.

"She's…she's resting right now, Ranger Maverick," Tesla answered.

"Is everything okay?" The ranger took another step up. Even from two steps below them, he towered over the two women. "May I check in on her?"

Both ladies tensed up.

"I don't think that would be a good idea right now," Tesla replied.

"Why not?" The ranger asked in all earnestness.

"Emmitt," Tesla said just as earnest as she reached out and touched the tall lawman on the shoulder, "she had another episode last night. The child's nerves are raw right now. I think it's best if we just let her rest today. We can do Special Agent Edison's interviews another day."

Before either man could protest someone cleared their throat from behind the women. Diana, Tesla, and the lawmen looked over to the front door. Standing there in the frame, her barefoot propping the screen door open and holding two cups of steaming fresh coffee, was Anne. Now, it was not the unexpected gesture that drew the perplexed looks from the men and women. No, it was the young lady's attire.

Anne had lost the blanket from earlier. So, now she stood there wearing nothing but her totem necklace, that see-through nighty and a very skimpy red thong. A cool morning breeze amplified her already ample breast, as her nipples pressed against the transparent material of her nighty. Her audience could see the goosebumps on her flesh from across the porch. She had a cup of coffee in each hand and a smile as big as Texas on her pretty face.

"I just thought you handsome boys would like a hot cup of coffee," Anne said as she sauntered across the porch in her bare feet. As she came to stand directly in front of Special Agent Edison, she said with a charming smile, "Oh my, aren't you a cutie."

Making extra effort to maintain eye contact, Agent Edison smiled and replied, "Ma'am."

"Wow, and polite too," Anne chuckled.

Ranger Maverick cleared his throat and said gruffly, "I can see we caught you ladies at an inconvenient time. We'll come back another time. Tomorrow perhaps." He tipped his hat and started back toward the Bronco.

"It was nice meeting you," Agent Edison said as he backed down the steps to follow the ranger. "Please, call if you need anything." He paused to pull a card with his number on it and handed it to Diana.

Before stepping into the Bronco, Ranger Maverick paused and said, "Anne, honey, put some clothes on before you catch your death." He winked and then hopped into the Bronco.

As the Bronco drove away, Diana turned toward Anne, whose nighty was even more see through than before in the rising morning sun and scolded her.

"Are you out of your fucking mind?"

"What?" Anne replied with a mischievous smile.

"You could have ruined everything with that asinine stunt," Diana was visibly upset.

"Y'all looked like you needed some help," Anne retorted.

"We had it under control," Diana snapped.

"Not from where I was standing," Anne snapped back.

"It doesn't matter," Tesla interjected. "They are gone, for now, but they will be back. It's time for us to decide what it is we are going to do. No more putting it off."

Tesla turned and went into the house.

Anne poured the coffee out onto the lawn. "Damn it's cold," she said through chattering teeth as she quickly followed Tesla into the house.

Diana took one last look over her shoulder as the Texas Ranger's Bronco disappeared around the bend. Then a determined look came over her and she said out loud, "Yes, it's time to finish this."

*****

A few miles back down the road, Special Agent Edison stated, "They seemed a bit stand offish."

199

"Those women have been through quite a lot, Special Agent Edison," Ranger Maverick retorted as he pulled his Bronco out onto the main road heading back into town. "In fact, I'd go as far as to say that those women back there, son, are about as tough as they come. Most people, men or women, who have been through what they have would be sitting in a diaper in some asylum somewhere with some ole nurse wiping drool from their lips."

"You referred to them as a *Survivors Club*?" The younger man asked.

The older lawman had a stern look about him. His eagle-like stare scanning the horizon as they drove along. The trees of the forest lining both sides of the country road were almost a blur as they sped on down the road.

"I assume you've read the files?" The ranger asked as he lit a cigarette.

"Twice."

"Then you have a pretty good idea what it is those women have been through," Ranger Maverick said. "At least as good as one can have without experiencing it for yourself." Agent Edison nodded. The old ranger took a long drag off his cigarette and continued. "I for one think it's a damn miracle they all found each other. Probably gives them strength to be around others like themselves, those that have experienced exactly what it is they have."

"Kind of like the VFW," Agent Edison said absently.

Ranger Maverick looked over at his young counterpart out of the corner of his eye. He exhaled and a huge billow of smoke engulfed the cabin of the Bronco.

"That's pretty astute for someone who has never served," the ranger said as he cracked his window, "at least not in hostile territory anyway."

This time it was the young agent's turn to look at his older counterpart with a crooked eye.

"How could you possibly know that?" He asked. "Background check? Friends at the Bureau?"

"Nah, nah...," Ranger Maverick chuckled. "No, nothing like that. You just still have innocence in your eyes. The way you walk, the way you carry yourself...you still have that look about you."

"And what look is that?"

"Hope."

"And you are without hope?" The younger man asked.

The ranger contemplated the question for a moment, the ash on his cigarette growing long. A line of smoke encircled the ranger's head. For a moment, the Special

Agent could almost swear the smoke took the shape of a halo right above the older man's head. The moment was fleeting as a gust of wind stole the smoky apparition away through the cracked window.

"I wouldn't exactly say that it's hope I lack, young Edison," Ranger Maverick said. "Let's just say I've seen things in this world that definitely makes a man reevaluate the notion of his place in it."

As cryptic as the old ranger's words were, their conversation brought the morning's odd events back to his mind. For a long moment, Agent Edison contemplated whether to even bring up the subject, or. Surely it had nothing to do with the case at hand, and the young Special Agent was quite sure that most of the incident could be easily explained away as a figment of his imagination. A dark, strange new setting coupled with the disturbing information gleaned from the case files from the night before simply left his mind vulnerable to suggestion. Of course, the whole issue was just a matter of imagination run wild.

"Either you have something you'd like to get off your chest, or you need to drop some wolf-bait," the ranger declared.

"Why do you say that?" Agent Edison asked.

"Your face," Ranger Maverick responded. "You're contorted it in a way that suggests deep concentration. So, either you have something to say, or you're holding back the flood, and let me tell you son, that second option never turns out good for anybody."

The Special Agent decided to tell the old lawman what happened. After a brief explanation about his jog into the woods, the feeling of being shadowed by some unseen entity, and the strange feeling of confusion and disorientation as he tried to return to the entrance into the woods, Special Agent Edison sat back and waited for the ranger's taunts. Instead, what he received was a knowing nod.

"It sounds to me, my friend, like you just met your first *Will-o-the-wisp*," the ranger said with a knowing smile.

"*Will-o-the-wisp*?" The Special Agent repeated. "I'm sorry, I'm not familiar with the term."

"Oh, there are many legends and folklore that speak of them," the ranger explained. "Some tales suggest that they are flashes of light to draw lost travelers to their doom. I've heard other tales of them being described as lost souls that have returned from beyond the grave to bedevil the living. Sailors have long since sworn to their existence and believe they are benevolent spirits that warn ships away from dangerous shallows and rocky shorelines."

"And, you believe this," Agent Edison asked.

"Oh, it doesn't matter what I believe now does it, Special Agent Edison?" The old ranger answered his question with a question of his own. "My experiences are my experiences. Only you can know what it is you don't believe and what it is you are willing to accept as truth." He tossed his spent cigarette out the window and continued. "I told you when we first met that Glen Haven is not like most other towns. These woods here," he pointed to the left and right side of the road to the rapidly passing tree lines, "these woods have a way about them. It's in the details, the way the wind moves through the trees, the way the wildlife moves through the brush…," his words trailed off for a moment, but then he continued. "I asked you once before if you believed in spirits. If you are asking me the same thing my answer is yes. Yes, I do."

"Why do I feel like I've just arrived in *Roswell*?" The younger man asked, shaking his head.

"We prefer *Smallville*, sir," Ranger Maverick chuckled.

The young F.B.I. Agent's eyes lit up.

"Familiar with the Last Son of Krypton, are you?" He asked.

"I can't say I'm a fan of where the character is today," the old ranger mused, "but I've read my fair share of comics back in the day. My son-in-law was a big fan, and my grandson, *whoa*. That kid can't get enough of the stuff. You?"

"When I was younger, I loved them," the young man paused for a moment and stared out the window in contemplation. Then he said, "But, these days there really hasn't been anything that blows my hair back. Good? Yes. Great? No. I guess I'm just too old for that medium."

"The problem is they forgot that guy has *MAN* in his name," the ranger retorted. Noticing a perplexed look on the Special Agent's face, he continued. "Look here, he's supposed to be a super-MAN, right? Not some pretty boy that caters to the popular beliefs of the times. He's supposed to be a two-fisted hombre that takes on the corrupt and the immoral and makes the world a better place for the common man. Now, he's a poster boy for modern day angst."

"You like George Reeves, huh?" Special Agent Edison teased.

"Yes, sir," Ranger Maverick snapped back without hesitation. "Truth, justice, and the American Way…yes, sir, that's my kind of hero."

"Funny thing about that old show," Agent Edison mused, "the criminals would empty their guns at him, and George Reeves would just stand there laughing, but then, after they were out of bullets, they'd throw their gun at him, and he would duck. I mean, what's that about?"

Ranger Maverick chuckled. "George Reeves was the best."

"Christopher Reeve was the best," Agent Edison countered. "One of the greatest things ever in the history of cinema is that montage in the first Chris Reeve movie when he's like," he drops his voice an octave to approximate the actor's tone and says, *"Something wrong with the elevator?* And *Bad vibrations?* Greatness!"

"Yeah, that was a pretty good one too," Ranger Maverick smiled and then he also affected his voice to imitate another line from the film, *"That's a bad outfit! Woo!"*

The two men burst out into laughter.

"It's a shame those guys are no longer with us," Agent Edison said.

"Yes, it is," Ranger Maverick agreed. "I tell you what, Special Agent Edison, how about I drive us over to Coco's Diner and I'll let you buy me a cup of coffee."

"Sounds like a plan," Agent Edison chuckled. "Welcome to Glen Have indeed."

Chapter 5: Cat's Story

Sheriff Marcus Wyatt's hands were shaking as he lit the cigarette. It was his first one in six months. He had quit at the doctor's behest. He had promised his wife. He had kept the last cigarette from the last pack he smoked in his desk drawer as a reminder, kind of like a trophy. It was hard to explain, even to himself, but keeping that last crumbled pack with that last cigarette in his drawer gave him the strength of will to not smoke. At his advanced age and his retirement firmly in sight, Sheriff Wyatt had promised.

However, after what he'd just seen, he had no willpower left. He had not watched the footage in over eighteen months. But, upon the request from the Texas Ranger, the sheriff thought he had better reacquaint himself with the case. Now, he wished he had not.

He sat at his desk, staring blankly at the wall as he smoked that last cigarette. By the time his guests had arrived, he was smashing the butt on the corner of the desk. Two men entered his office. The first, an older gentleman, he knew quite well. There was no mistaken the tall, lean build, the hawk-like nose perched atop one of the most impressive handlebar mustaches, and confidence that just oozed out of every pore. He was a fellow law officer, a Texas Rangers, an extremely active lawman in these parts. The second fellow, Wyatt did not recognize. He was a much younger man of

Asian descent and by the way he carried himself, Sheriff Wyatt could tell he was trained. He wore a dark suit and tie, with wavy black hair. The bulge in his jacket suggested he was armed. Sheriff Wyatt figured the young man must be government.

"Texas Ranger Emmitt Maverick," the Sheriff greeted the older man as he stood and shook his hand, "glad you could make it."

"How are you, Marcus?" Ranger Maverick asked. "How's the heart? I thought you had quit," the Texas Ranger took a couple of sniffs, "but from what I can detect, you've jumped back in the ring."

"Yeah, yeah," Sheriff Wyatt nodded absently. "I haven't had a cigarette going on a year now." He lied. "I just…well, never mind all that. We pulled the footage you asked for and…, well, let's just say I won't be joining y'all for another screening."

"I understand, Marcus," Ranger Maverick nodded.

"Yes," Sheriff Wyatt said absently as he nodded toward the Ranger's companion. "And who do we have here?"

"Oh, this is Special Agent Christoph Edison," Ranger Maverick introduced. "He's F-B-I, sent all the way from Big D."

"Oh?" Sheriff Wyatt nodded.

"Yes, sir," Ranger Maverick continued. "It seems ole Big Brother doesn't seem to think old law dogs like you, and I can handle our jurisdictions, so they sent us our very own Wonder Boy to help us out."

"I'm not here to step on any toes, sheriff," Special Agent Edison said, extending his hand to the sheriff. "I'm just here to help in any way I can."

The sheriff accepted the man's hand and became painfully aware that the young man's lean frame belied the strength of his grip. Shaking his hand, the sheriff urged the two men to take a seat.

"The files provided by Ranger Maverick stated you have visual evidence of the attack on Caitlin Bachman?" Special Agent Edison interjected.

"After the girl showed up on the roadside covered in blood, not all of it hers, for three days, my men and a dozen volunteers from town combed the woods, looking for the other two missing students," the sheriff said. "Finally, we came across an abandoned makeshift hut or deer stand deep in the woods and inside we retrieved the camera they were using to film their documentary. There were no fingerprints on the camera other than those of the film students."

"Documentary?" Special Agent Edison asked.

Sheriff Wyatt and Ranger Maverick both nodded knowingly.

"Yes," the sheriff answered. "It seems they were film students come down from Denton in order to film some sort of documentary about one of our local, how should I put this, urban legends."

"Urban legends?" Special Agent Edison asked, as his brow furrowing. "You are, of course, referring to the Goatman Killings, right?"

The old Sheriff shot the ranger a look.

Ranger Maverick nodded and said, "It is okay, Marcus. Agent Edison is here to help."

"Let's just say, young man," the sheriff swallowed and then addressed the agent's question, "that Glen Haven is a town with a very," he paused, "eccentric history. The woods surrounding this town have an essence, a life of their own and for those who aren't prepared, it can even tend to swallow them whole."

"What are you saying, the woods are haunted?" The younger man asked, as the events of his morning run came bubbling back to the surface.

Again, the two older men shot each other a knowing glance.

"When you are ready," Ranger Maverick said padding the younger man on the arm, "you'll know." He turned back toward the sheriff and asked, "So, we're here to review the footage."

Sheriff Wyatt looked down at the crushed butt of his last cigarette and for a fleeting moment, he wished he had another.

"Marcus," Ranger Maverick interrupted his thoughts, "the footage?"

"Over my twenty years as sheriff of this town," Sheriff Wyatt said still staring at the extinguished butt, "I've seen many things, many strange, unexplainable, and yes, disturbing things. What we found on that camera ranks right up there with the worst." He pointed to the television on a rolling stand with the film camera they retrieved from the woods plugged into it. "I have no wish to watch it again. It's set at the beginning. Just push play."

The sheriff stood and walked out of the office.

"Alright," Ranger Maverick nodded to his younger counterpart. "You ready?" Special Agent Edison nodded compliance. "Okay, here we go."

Ranger Maverick leaned over and pressed play.

*****

The screen came to life with a single shot of a young woman smiling and staring directly into the lens. Behind her is a large sign that reads *Welcome to Glen Haven*. She is an attractive young woman in her early twenties. She is petite and clothed in all black and white. Her lipstick is a darker shade of red than most wear and the black liner and shade around her eyes is a little heavier. Her shoulder-length black hair has a single purple stripe dyed into it that frames the left side of her alabaster face.

"And four…three…two…one…you're a go," a male voice from off camera said.

The young woman hesitated for a moment and then began to speak.

"Hello," she smiled. "I am Cat Bachman. My fellow film students, Adam, Josh, and I" she nodded toward someone off camera, "are from UNT and we are here in Glen Haven, a small town located about a four-and-a-half-hour drive southeast of Denton. Across America, every small town has its secrets, its urban legends. Well, we have come to Glen Haven to shed a little light on just such an urban legend, the infamous Goatman murders of Azlewood." She paused and nodded toward the thick woodlands off in the distance.

"For nearly two years now," she continued, "it seems this small hamlet has been under the shadow of a serial killer that still remains at large. Some say it all started at Pelican Bay Summer Camp when a group of camp counselors were viciously attacked and one-by-one murdered. There was only one survivor from that horrible incident. Her name – Diana Roa.

Now, these first attacks were conducted by a woman named Salvia Vasa. Very little is known about this woman and even though I have done extensive research on these killings, and those involved, all I have been able to come up with is that Salvia Vasa is of Scandinavian and Native American descent. She was well known in these parts as a soothsayer. She was also known for her rants and warnings against anyone committing crimes against nature in the woodlands surrounding this area. She protested vigorously when it was announced the summer camp was being built and was even arrested several times when she attempted to sabotage the construction of the camp. Her protests started out with putting sugar in the gas tanks of the bulldozers and earthmovers. When that did not stop the construction, her attempts escalated to starting fires and vandalism. She was known to paint strange symbols on the walls of the cabins and hang strange pagan objects and animal skins from the trees all around the campsite.

Weeks before the summer camp was set to open, Salvia took her protest to a whole other level when she systematically stalked and murdered the half-a-dozen counselors who were preparing the campground for the summer season."

The camera cuts to Cat approaching an elderly couple exiting a grocery.

"Hello," Cat greeted them, "May I ask you a few questions about the Goatman murders?"

The elderly couple just shook their heads and pushed their cart of groceries past Cat. Undeterred Cat turned toward another man exiting the grocery. He is a robust fellow in a worn red flannel shirt with a case of beer securely tucked under his trunk-like arm. His thick beard spread wide to reveal a warm smile as Cat and her camera crew drew closer.

"Hello," Cat said, "may I ask you a few questions about the Goatman murders?" She extended her mic.

The robust man chuckled and replied, "What is this? Some sort of TV reality show?"

"No, sir," Cat responded. "We are film students down from UNT and we are filming a documentary and trying to get to the bottom of the Goatman mystery surrounding your town."

"Oh, the Goatman huh," he said, as he ran his plump fingers through his thick beard. "Why would you kids want to go and get involved with a mess like that?"

"Like I said," Cat replied. "We are filming a documentary. Please, any information you could provide would be helpful."

His brow furrowed. "Well, there's not much I can say about the Goatman that you can't read in a paper, but the first thing you need to know about Glen Haven, darling, is that this town has a long history of strange and, how should I put this, bizarre occurrences," he said. "My granddaddy used to tell me a tale when I was kid that used to just chill me to the bone."

"Really," Cat goaded, "and what was that?"

"Ye see," he pointed to the north, "a few years after the war between the north and the south the railroad was being built and Glen Haven was having a silver rush. However, strange murders plagued this here bourgeoning mining town, and some believed the town cursed."

"Cursed?" Cat asked. "What do you mean by cursed?"

"Ye see, darling," the man continued, "some believe these woods here," he made a wide circling arc with his beefy hand, "have vitality, a life, if you will, of their own. The Natives that were here before us called them *Canotila*."

"Chawn-oh-tee-lah?" Cat asked.

"Yes," he replied. "*Canotila* are what you would call a spirit or a ghost. The Caddo and Sioux who inhabited this land long before we came along believed these spirits protected these woods and them as well, as long as they lived in harmony with nature."

"This sounds like a bad episode of Scooby-Doo," Cat winked at the camera. "So, are you saying these ghosts cursed Glen Haven?"

He rubbed his fuzzy chin. "Let me put it this way," he said. "At least this is how my granddaddy put it to me. There must always be a balance between man and nature. One cannot take from the other without giving back. So, going back to the silver rush and the railroad coming through, when they cut a swathe through the forest to make way for the railroad and pulled that precious metal from the earth, perhaps the *Canotila* took offense, no?"

Cat starred for a moment blankly. "So," she hung on the vowel for a long time, "you're telling me that these woods surrounding Glen Haven are haunted?"

The large man ran his beefy fingers through his thick beard, smiled, and then replied, "The word I would use is *alive*."

"Alright," Cat said turning back toward the camera. "Let's see if anyone else has anything to say about this."

The robust man, his case of beer still firmly tucked under one arm, holds his other hand high in the air with his index finger and pinky pointing straight up and his middle and ring fingers bent down, he shouted, "*AC/DC* rules!"

Cat placed her hand on her hip and shook her head. "We're getting nothing here," she said in disappointment.

216

The camera began to focus on an elderly black man on the sidewalk behind Cat. He was very tall, very skinny and dressed in black trousers, a white button-up, and a thin black vest. On his head, he wore a worn fedora. Two braided pigtails hung down from the hat and framed both sides of his weathered old face. In his gnarled very large hands, he held a broom which he pushed up and down the sidewalk. What the camera picked up was that every now and then, this elderly man would stop and look over at Cat with a very inquisitive look. Then he just lowered his head and began to sweep again. Then he would stop and look toward Cat once again.

The camera tilted and bobbed a few times in the direction of the elderly man. Cat's brow furrowed. "What?" She asked with her palms up. "What, Josh?"

"Talk to that guy," Josh's voice came from off camera. "He seems very interested in what we are doing. "

Cat looked over her shoulder just in time to see the elderly man look away and go back to sweeping the sidewalk. Cat walked over to where the elderly man swept, and the camera followed her.

"Excuse me." He ignored her at first and quickened his pace down the sidewalk. The much, much younger Cat overtook him easily. "Excuse me, Sir, can I ask you a few questions?" she asked as she stepped in front of him.

The elderly man stopped short of her feet and stood straight up. He towered over Cat. A look of concern spread across her face. *Maybe this was not such an excellent idea* was the vibe she expressed. Then, she was completely put at ease as the elderly man smiled down at her warmly.

"Yes, ma'am, what can I do for you?" His voice was deep but not overpowering, in fact, it was quite soothing, almost hypnotic.

"Hi, my name is Cat. We are students from the University of North Texas, and we've come down to your town to hopefully shed some light on the Azlewood murders. We'd really just like to get the point of view of locals and hopefully try and make some sense of what is quickly becoming a modern-day urban legend."

"Oh, I don't know about all that," he said with a smile. His body language took a comfortable stance as he casually leaned upon his broom. "You folks are from out of town you say?" Cat nodded. "And y'all are here to what?" He pointed one of his long, gnarled fingers toward the camera. "What is this here for? Are y'all filming a movie?"

"A documentary, yes," Cat nodded. "May I ask, what is your name, sir?"

The elderly man leaned back and smiled. A warm smile spread across his wrinkled old face nearly ear-to-ear. "Who me…? Oh, I'm nobody." There was a hint of laughter in his reply. For an old man in tattered clothes, he was quite charming.

"Nobody…?" Cat asked. "Surely you have a name. "

"Oh, most folks 'round here don't say much to me at all," he replied. If this revelation affected the elderly man either way, it did not show on his face.

"People don't just come up to you and say 'hey, you,' do they?" Cat persisted.

The elderly man rubbed his grizzled chin for a moment. "What is in a name?" He asked. "What is your name?" Just as Cat was about to speak, he continued. "What is his name?" He pointed once again toward the camera. "Do our names define us? If I had no name, would I no longer exist? If y'all had no names, would your lives no longer have any meaning?"

Undeterred and defiant as ever, Cat asked, "What the fuck does that even mean?"

The elderly man just smiled, he leaned in real close, and replied, "I'd be careful to whom you reveal all, little girl. Too much insight to your world can leave you wide open to suggestion."

When he spoke, there was absolutely no malice in his tone, it was a warning issued in the friendliest way possible. Cat stood there for a moment, blinking.

She turned toward the camera and said, "OK, nothing here. Let's move on."

She started to walk away, and the camera followed her. Then a voice came from off camera. It was the smooth, friendly voice of the elderly man. The camera swung back around, and his tall, lean frame came back into view.

"If y'all plan on venturing into these woods," he said, "be sure not to cross the threshold. The place beyond is cursed and there are very old, very angry spirits that dwell within. If you kids enter their domain, you will awaken these angry spirits."

"Spirits...?" Cat shot back. "What...like ghosts?"

"Don't cross the threshold," he repeated. Then he leaned forward and swept his way down the sidewalk without another word.

Cat watched him for a moment then turned toward the camera and asked, "What the fuck just happened?"

The camera cuts to Cat smoking a cigarette.

She was sitting on a bed next to a young man. He was a skinny lad dressed in a tight-fitting black t-shirt with the words *The Smiths* in red on the front. His hair was dyed black and combed straight back. He wore a spiked wristband on his right wrist. The décor of the room suggested they were in a motel room. They were flipping through a stack of papers and maps.

"So, tomorrow we'll head out to the campsite," the young man said. "What do you make out of what Grizzly Adams had to say?"

"About what?" Cat asked absently as she studied a map.

"About the woods being haunted," he replied.

"Come on, Josh," Cat replied, her eyes still scanning the map in front of her. "Don't tell me you believe in that shit."

Josh's brow furrowed. "Well, don't we all kind of believe in that shit?" He asked. "Isn't that why we are here?"

Cat looked up from her map. "What the fuck are you talking about?" she asked with a little venom in her voice. "We're here to do this documentary and win that grant. You remember, that grant that will fund the movie we want to make?"

"Of course," Josh replied sheepishly. Cat went back to flipping through the papers and old newsprints. Then Josh said in a faint voice, "I believe in ghosts."

"What?" Cat asked absently still ruffling through pages.

"I said, I believe in ghosts," Josh repeated. This time raising his voice to an octave that could be heard clearly.

Cat looked up. For a moment, she just stared at Josh. Then she said, "Do I actually let you fuck me?"

"Don't be like that, Cat," Josh replied. "I'm serious. I believe in ghosts."

"Okay," Cat said stacking the pages neatly in front her and crossing her legs. "You obviously want to tell me about it. So, what do you have?"

"Cat, I'm being serious," he said. "I used to be just as skeptical as the next guy, but after what happened, I can't help but believe."

"So, now you're religious?" Cat asked, crossing her arms. "Now, you believe in God and Jesus and all that shit?"

"That's not what I'm saying," Josh said reaching over to place a comforting hand on Cat's arm. "That's not what I'm saying at all."

"Then what are you saying?" She asked.

"Look," Josh said crossing his legs and turning to face her, "I'm not saying that I automatically believe in heaven and hell, an afterlife, and all that voodoo mumbo jumbo. What I am saying is I believe in something." He swallowed hard. "I can't speak for anyone else in this world about what they do and do not believe in. I can only tell you what I know based on my own experience." He paused for a moment. "And it scared the living shit out of me."

"Alright, honey," Cat said, as she pulled her hair back and tied it into a tail. "Let's hear your story, but I'm warning you now, if I smell bullshit, I'm making fun of you."

"It happened last semester," Josh said. "Now, before I get to my experience, I have to tell you about the footsteps."

"Footsteps?" She asked.

"Yes, footsteps," Josh answered. "As you know, our apartment is two-stories." Cat nodded as Josh continued. "Several times, in the middle of the night I have been awakened by footsteps coming up the stairs."

"So," Cat scoffed, as she blew smoke in his direction. "It was probably just Adam getting in late from one of his binges."

"That's what I thought, too," Josh shook his head. "At first. But then I would be awakened by those footsteps on a night when I knew Adam was home and in bed. Our rooms were right next to each other. So, one night I heard those footsteps and stepped out into the hall to see who it was. I looked down the stairs and there was nobody there. I just assumed it was some late-night booty call Adam had given a key to and I went back to bed. But the next day when I asked him about it, he said he didn't have anyone over and that he was in his room all night by himself. I asked if he had heard those footsteps and he said no.

Well, the next night, I was awakened by the footsteps again only this time it sounded like someone was running up the stairs. I jumped up out of bed and stepped into the hallway. This time Adam heard the footsteps too because he stepped into the hallway at the same time as me. He asked what the hell I was up to, but after I explained the noise wasn't coming from me, we both went to the stairs but there was nobody there. We turned all the lights on in the apartment and checked the downstairs and upstairs. The front door and sliding door that led to the back patio were both still locked. There was nobody else in the apartment but us."

"So, Adam heard these footsteps too?" Cat asked.

"Yes," Josh answered. "But that was the last time either of us heard them, at least for a while, so we didn't think anything else of it. We just chalked it up to probably some rodent in the walls or something. Then a week later, it happened."

"What happened?" Cat asked.

"Adam had gone back home for the weekend to see his folks and I was at the apartment by myself," Josh said. Cat noticed his hands were shaking as he continued. "I don't know exactly how to explain what happened and I cannot even begin to tell you what it means, but here it is as best as I can." He paused for a moment to wring his hands. As he spoke, Josh began to sway slightly back and forth as the nervous energy coursed through his body. "I have no idea what time of the night it was, but I know I was asleep and then suddenly I wasn't. I don't know how to explain it, but I was wide awake, and I could not open my eyes. A kind of fear I've never felt washed over me. I just lay there in the dark. Then I heard them."

"Heard what?" Cat asked.

"Those footsteps," Josh answered. "But this time they were slow, methodical. I could hear each foot fall as they slowly ascended the stairs. I could hear those footsteps walking right up to the doorway of my bedroom. The weird thing is that I always close my door before I go to bed yet that night, my door was open. Again, I was wide awake but for some reason I could not open my eyes. My mouth went dry as I could suddenly sense that I was not the only one in the room. I could not see this other," he paused, searching for the right words, "this other presence, but I knew I was not alone in that room.

I heard those footsteps now inside my room and could feel someone standing over me. I was terrified as I felt someone sit on the foot of my bed. I have never been so terrified in my life. I could not open my eyes, and for some reason, no matter how hard I tried, I could not sit up. Something kept me from physically sitting up. I just lay there in the dark, unable to speak or move, and whimpered. I could physically feel someone sitting on the foot of my bed, and there was nothing I could do."

"What happened?" Cat asked, as she reached over to comfort him.

"I don't know," he answered.

"You don't know?" She repeated. "How can you not know what happened next?"

"I just woke up the next morning," he said. "My sheets were soaked through with sweat. Like I said, it's hard for me to explain."

Cat's face twisted in an inquisitive fashion. Then she said, "What a load of shit."

Josh looked up in disbelief. "No, I'm serious," he said. "That really happened."

"Oh, Okay," she said mockingly. "So, that was your big ghost story." Cat shook her head in disbelief. "I cannot believe I actually sleep with this man. Do you believe this shit?" Cat asked looking over her shoulder toward the camera. Then, her nose wrinkled, and a scowl formed on her alabaster face. "Adam!" Her tone was not pleasant. "Are you filming this bullshit?"

"Of course," Adam answered from off camera. "For posterity, of course." He chuckled.

Cat shot her camera man a harsh look. She pointed her index finger toward Josh, "You," She scolded, "grow some balls, and you," her attention was now firmly on the man behind the camera, "stop wasting memory space and battery on bullshit. Come on guys, this is serious. This documentary is important."

"Adam," Josh pleaded, "you heard those footsteps, right?"

"Yeah, buddy," Adam answered from off screen, "I did."

"Enough!" Cat exclaimed. She stood up, stormed over, and reached for the camera. "Turn the goddamn camera off!

The Camera cuts to hiking boots coming into and out of frame with each step. It is daytime and from the ambient sounds of nature and the twigs and brush crunching under foot, the location must be in the woods outside of town. For a few minutes, the camera films the march with the labored sounds of breathing taking center stage. Then, the camera rose to focus in on the supple buttocks of a young woman walking a few yards ahead. The hiking shorts hugged the woman's rear like a lover and with each stride, the tone muscles of her smooth legs and rear-end rippled. Then she stopped, and so did the camera. The camera rose again to see Cat turning back toward it.

"Did you hear what I said?" She asked.

"Huh? No, what…?" Adam asked from behind the camera.

"I said stop staring at my ass and film our surroundings," she scolded, as she pulled a joint from her pack. Her hand disappeared once again into the pack, and she searched for something in vain. The struggle was real as her face twisted into a mask of confusion and disappointment. Even with her features twisted like this, Cat was a still an attractive woman. After searching the pockets of her hiking shorts, Cat asked absently, "Where is that Goddamn lighter?"

Coming into frame from the bottom of the screen Adam's left hand held out a small green plastic lighter. "You didn't mind me filming your ass last Thursday," Adam said from behind the camera, an unmistakable glint of mirth in his voice. "And," he continued," you didn't seem to mind the way I appreciated your ass in the van last night after Josh fell asleep."

Cat exhaled in frustration and snatched the lighter away from her cameraman. "Stop it," she scolded as she lit the joint. "Don't say things like that on camera."

"Don't worry, darling," Adam reassured her. "I'll edit this part out."

Cat's exhale was followed by a small cough. "Goddamnit, you better," she said wiping her mouth on her sleeve, "and don't call me darling."

"Why not?" He asked.

"Because it's just creepy," she answered. "Josh and I are together." Then she quickly gestured to herself and the camera and said, "What we have…what we do…what we did," Cat inhaled and contemplated her next words, "it's just wrong, and let's just leave it at that. I love Josh. You and I are just…," she paused before exhaling, "we're just co-workers. It's not going to happen again."

"We'll see," Adam responded flatly.

"I'm serious," Cat snapped. "I swear to God, you better edit this shit out. Now, stop fucking around and start filming for real."

"Filming what?" He asked.

After a few more puffs, she handed the joint to Adam. His exhale of smoke engulfed the screen, and the camera shook as he coughed. He handed the joint back to Cat who swept her hand in a wide arc and nodded toward their surroundings.

The camera tuned slowly, taking in the landscape. They were on an obviously highly trafficked trail. To the east was a gorge thick with brush, to the west a fast-running creek. The camera caught a doe drinking from the fresh water. The deer's head shot up and looked in the direction of the camera. For a long moment, it just stared at the film students, cocking its head to the right and left, and then darting off, disappearing into the thick brush.

"Cat! Adam!" Josh called from up ahead of the trail. The camera whipped around to see him about thirty or forty yards ahead waving them over. He was standing next to another man who was holding a fishing pole and tackle box. "Get over here and meet this guy," Josh called again.

Cat dropped the smoking bud and stomped on it. Then, she and Adam hurried over to Josh and his new *friend*. The stranger was a tall, lean older man with a handlebar mustache, a hawk-like nose, and a cowboy hat with a single feather tucked in the band. He greeted the young people with a warm smile.

"This is Emmitt," Josh introduced the man. "He's a local and maybe able to point us in the right direction."

"Howdy," Emmitt extended his free hand.

"Hello," Cat shook his hand.

"Josh here tells me y'all are here to film some sort of movie?" Emmitt asked.

"Yes, well not exactly," Cat replied, her fingers absently twirling the purple dyed streak in her hair. "We're here to film a documentary."

"Documentary?" Emmitt asked. "Like for PBS or something?"

"No, no, for our film class," Josh interjected.

"Film class?" Emmitt rubbed his rough chin.

"Yes," Cat answered. "We're students up at the University of North Texas."

"University of...," Emmitt's words trailed off. "That's all the way up north of Dallas, isn't it?"

"Yes, sir," Josh answered. "Denton."

"Well, I'll be," Emmitt smiled. "What are you kids doing all the way down here? What's this documentary all about?"

"We're here to shed some light on the Goatman Killer of Azlewood," Cat said with confidence. "We're here looking for answers."

Emmitt's inquisitive ice-blue eyes narrowed for a moment, but the moment was fleeting. His expression quickly softened. "Y'all would do better to pick another topic for your documentary."

"Why?" Cat snapped. "Does this town have something to hide?"

Emmitt smiled warmly. "Not at all darling," he said. "I'd just be careful what it is you are looking for; you just might find it."

"Can you tell us how to get to the Pelican Bay Campsite from here?" Josh asked.

"You kids really want to go and stir up some old ghosts, don't ya?" Emmitt asked leaning back to study each of them. "You kids ever hear the expression – *Don't poke the bear?*"

"Look, man," Adam said from behind the camera. "We're just trying to film a cool documentary for our class. We're not here to start any trouble."

Emmitt stood straight up. He towered over the film students. He was a very intimidating presence to them. He rubbed his bristling chin. He looked at them not with anger or agitation, but rather with the concerned look a parent gives their child when they are about to do something foolish.

"My advice to you would be to not take this project of yours any further than that abandoned campsite," Emmitt said with all earnestness. "These woods here," his ice-blue eyes made an arching half-circle before coming back to rest on the film students, "they just have a way of swallowing up folks looking for too many answers."

"Is that a threat?" Josh swallowed.

Emmitt chuckled. "You kids have nothing to fear from me," he said with a smile. "I'm one of the good guys."

Right then, as if to emphasize his point....

"Ranger Maverick...Ranger Maverick, come in...over." A muffled disembodied voice came from a pocket on Emmitt's fishing vest.

"Excuse me," Emmitt held up a finger and retrieved his phone from his vest pocket. He activated the walkie-talkie app with a push of a button and responded, "Maverick here...over."

"Uh, Ranger, we got us a situation here," said the disembodied voice from the other end of the phone. "We have a 10-80 in progress. Three bad hombres knocked off a bank in Dallas and made one hell of a mess out of some state troopers that were in pursuit. They were last seen hauling down Route 666, we believe heading right toward your jurisdiction. Over."

"On my way, "Emmitt answered, as he flipped the other pocket on his fishing vest to reveal a shining silver badge.

It was an engraved star that read – TEXAS
RANGERS.

"It was nice meeting y'all," Emmitt tipped his hat.
"Now, if you'll excuse me, I have to go to work." But,
before he left, Ranger Maverick leaned in real close to
Cat and said, "If you are going to smoke a doobie in
my woods, honey, you better be damn sure those buds
are put out when you're done."

With his fishing pole and tackle box in tow, Ranger
Maverick made off down the trail, the same way the
film students had come in.

"But you never told us how to get to the old campsite,"
Josh called after him.

Ranger Maverick stopped. For just a moment, his head
sank. He slowly turned and said, "Head up the trail
about another click, when you reach the lake, head due
east. Stay close to the shore and you'll eventually
stumble on it." He looked to the ground for a moment
then said, "Y'all seem like good kids…y'all carrying
protection?" he asked ominously.

Cat pulled a small handgun from her pack. "Don't
worry, Grandpa, I'm registered," she said.

Ranger Maverick smiled. "You've got spunk, little
lady," he said. Then his face turned stern once more.
"Heed my warning; don't take this documentary of
yours any further than the campsite."

He tipped his hat, and without another word, Ranger Maverick turned and walked up the trail, stopping only for a moment to pour the contents of his canteen out dousing the still smoldering bud Cat had dropped.

The camera cuts to a shot of a derelict campground.

The grounds were overgrown with foliage, vines and moss had claimed the cabins, and the wooden shudders on the windows, the ones that had not already been blown away by the elements, were hanging on for dear life on rusted hinges. Those shudders made an eerie sound as they swayed in the wind and thudded against the sides of the cabins. The overall feeling of the scene was isolation. There was Crime Scene tape here and there on a few of the cabins. At the foot of the trail leading into the campsite was a wooden sign that read – *Condemned. Keep Out.*

Cat came to stand in the camera shot with the rundown campsite behind her.

"It's been about an hour maybe two since we ran into that handsome Texas Ranger," she said placing her hand on her forehead to shade her eyes against the sun. "As you may be able to tell by the sun it is late in the afternoon, but I must be honest, it is getting hard to tell. The passing of time seems somewhat off in these woods. I'm feeling a bit disoriented." She looked over her shoulder at the campsite. "These desolate surroundings add to the uneasiness I'm feeling."

The camera slowly panned around to show the scope of the campgrounds. There were five large cabins. The boys' and girls' barracks were in the foreground, clearly marked by signs, and set roughly twenty meters from each other. The land sloped up from there with two more wooden buildings beyond those, and even further up the hill was a slightly larger building. When the camera view came back to rest on Cat, she was pointing to something off screen. The camera swept around to land on a tall wooden pole with half a dozen arrow-shaped signs nailed to it. Two arrows pointed to the closest buildings confirming they were the campers' dormitories. Another two signs referred to the next two buildings as the *Councilors' Quarters* and the *Chow House (Cafeteria)*. And the largest building up on the hill was referred to as *Town Center*. Two more signs pointing in opposite directions read *Restrooms/Showers* and *The Docks*, and they pointed down two long since overgrown trails.

Then, the camera followed Cat's gesture over to the far side of the campsite where a wooden barrier had been erected with a sign that read – *Road Closed*. Josh was standing beside the barrier and peering into the forest.

"Yeah, there is no way we could have possible gotten the van up here this way!" He shouted. "There are trees collapsed on the road and holes dug into the ground!"

The camera cuts to a single shot of Cat standing directly in front of the directional arrows.

"We rolling?" she asked in a hushed tone. The camera gave a slight nod. "Okay, while Josh takes a look around, let's run a segment." Cat took a deep breath, rolled her neck around, stretched her jaw, and then began to speak. "I am standing here on the sight once upon a time known as Pelican Bay Summer Camp. This now abandoned campsite was the scene for one of the grizzliest mass murders of the modern era. On the night of June 1st, just a week before the camp was to open for dozens and dozens of campers, Salvia Vasa systematically stalked and murdered five councilors. Two young men and three young women who had come aboard to help the camp owner Sonny Peterson get the campsite ready for the summer season."

Cat motioned for the camera to follow her. She headed up the overgrown path which led to the cafeteria. As she walked, with the camera trailing her, she began to speak again.

"As the reports have indicated, one day before the killing started, Sonny Peterson had headed into town for supplies. Along the way, he was ambushed by Vasa and murdered. His jeep and remains were found hidden in these woods three days after the murders."

She came to a stop in front of the cafeteria. She turned to face the camera and continued.

"Salvia Vasa entered the camp masquerading as Virginia Miller. Mrs. Miller was to be the camp chef for that summer. Days later, the authorities found Mrs.

Miller, along with her husband Bernie, both murdered in their home, still lying in their bed. Their throats had been cut. Since none of the councilors had ever met Mrs. Miller and had no idea what she looked like, they didn't think twice when Vasa introduced herself as the campsite's cook. This should be a lesson for all young people. If the councilors had kept up on current events and news, they may have been able to recognize Salvia Vasa before her reign of terror could begin.

Over the course of the next twelve hours, Vasa would cunningly isolate the councilors from each other using lies and subterfuge and murder each of them until only one remained. Diana Roa, the sole survivor of this harrow massacre was asleep when the power to the campsite was suddenly disconnected. She and two other councilors, Ruby Goodman and Ben Coleman, were together in the Councilors' Quarters when the lights went out."

As Cat spoke, she walked across the way to come and stand in front of the abandoned Councilors' Quarters.

"Having no reason to believe anything was amiss, Ben set out to check the generator while Ruby left to take a shower, leaving Diana, who was awake now, all alone," Cat paused. Her head sank for a moment, and she exhaled. "Time passed, much too much time passed and this whole time Diana was sitting there alone in the dark. Can you imagine sitting alone in the dark surrounded by nothing but these woods and the sounds of nature? My heart is pounding just thinking about it."

Cat started down a side pathway that eventually led to a small shack. The door to the shack had long ago fallen off its hinges and was nowhere to be seen. Inside the small shack was a worn, rusty gas-powered generator.

"After more time passed, Diana decided to investigate and see what was taking her bunkmates so long to return." Cat gestured toward the shack and said, "Here she found Ben murdered. His Achilles tendons had been slashed and his throat cut. Obviously, he had been ambushed from behind. In a state of terror and pure panic, Diana raced to the shower facilities to find Ruby. There she found her friend, brutally murdered, lying naked on the cold floor of a shower stall with an axe buried between her breasts. The water from the shower was still running and indifferently washing Ruby's blood down the drain."

"Indifferently?" Adam's voice asked from behind the camera.

"Yes, indifferently," Cat scolded. "Don't interrupt. I'm trying to paint a picture here. Now, stop fucking around, and you better be able to edit that out."

The camera cuts to Cat who was back at the Chow House.

As she made her way up the steps and into the main dining hall of the Chow House she explained, "In stark panic, Diana desperately goes from building to building looking for her friends. In the Boys Barracks she finds the remains of David Mason and Sarah Lockhart. The young couple was ambushed and murdered in the act of loving making. They were hacked to pieces by what was later confirmed to be a machete. Diana then ran to the vehicles, but all the tires had been slashed.

Suddenly, power was returned to the camp, but the only building at the campsite that had any lights on was the Chow House. Diana then made her way to the cafeteria. There was no one in the main dining hall. Reduced to a quivering wreck, Diana called out for help. She called for the only two others she had not found, yet. *Amy! Amy!* She cried. *Mrs. Miller!* She cried. In pure desperation, she even cried out for Mr. Peterson. But there was no reply." Again, Cat paused. She shook her head. Then, rubbing her eyes, she continued, "These woods are known for not being cell phone friendly. Pelican Bay Summer Camp's motto was - *No phones. No computers. Unplug and have fun in the sun*. I cannot even begin to imagine the fear and isolation Diana must have felt.

She made her way into the kitchen where a peculiar and pungent smell was wafting. When Diana first entered, the kitchen was as empty as the dining hall. There was a very large pot on the stove, the flame underneath it was on, and the water inside was boiling over. Diana slowly walked over and removed the lid. She wanted to scream but her voice was gone. In that boiling pot was the severed head of Amy Johnson, the last unaccounted-for councilor.

Diana turned to flee but standing between her and the door was a crazed-looking Salvia Vasa. The elderly woman was holding a giant butcher's knife and her cook's apron was splattered in blood, obviously not her own. There was a brief exchange between the two women and Diana quickly figured out that this woman in front of her was not Virginia Miller. As the crazed elderly woman methodically stalked Diana around the large silver cutting table that adorned the center of the kitchen, she meticulously explained how she murdered each of the councilors. When Diana asked her why, Vasa gave a brief explanation about how long ago an atrocity was committed on the grounds this campsite was erected, an atrocity that quote 'bent' the land, whatever that means."

Cat started making motions and gestures with her hands as she spoke.

"In a brief scuffle," Cat said as she swung her left hand in a wide arc, "Diana was able to defend herself against the older woman's vicious attack by using an iron skillet. Parrying the knife, Diana smashed the skillet across her attacker's face. The blow threw the elderly woman to the floor and Diana fled out the door. Vasa, incredibly, recovered quickly and pursued Diana out the door."

The camera cut to Cat walking past the directional post with the arrow-shaped signs and down the path that led to the docks.

"Diana fled this whole way with Vasa right on her heels, slashing at her, barely missing with each attack. The old woman was screaming curses and using language Diana had never heard before. The chase brought them right down this path, the whole time Vasa taunting and threatening the frightened young councilor like a crazed banshee."

"Crazed banshee?" Adam asked, scoffing from behind the camera.

Cat paused and turned to face the camera. She kicked with her right foot. The blow caused the camera to shake violently. For an instant, the camera showed Adam rubbing his shin vigorously where she had kicked him. Then, the camera came back to rest on Cat.

"I told you not to interrupt," she scolded. "Now, keep up."

For the next few seconds there was a hitch in the shot as the cameraman was obviously limping. By the time they reached the docks, the shot was steadied as the pain had probably subsided. Cat positioned herself so the docks and the water were to her back.

"Right here is where the final confrontation went down," she gestured back toward the docks. "Vasa had relentlessly pursued the young, battered councilor down to the docks here. Cornered, Diana ran out to the end of the pier. The elderly woman taunted her as she slowly walked the length of the dock and slowly made cutting gestures through the air."

"Okay, now you are just embellishing for embellishment's sake," Adam said from behind the camera.

Cat shot her cameraman a dangerous look. She took a moment to collect herself, and then continued.

"Diana knew that if she jumped into the water, she would be a sitting duck. She looked around desperately for something to help protect her. Down in one of the row boats she spotted a wooden ore. She reached down and brought the paddle up just in time to deflect the stabbing butcher's knife. Diana used all the strength she could muster to push her attacker away. Vasa stumbled backwards off balance. Diana swung the ore with all her might and landed a fierce blow right across the older woman's face." Cat was acting out the encounter as she spoke. "Stunned by the blow, Vasa shook her head clear and lunged once more at her would be victim. Once again, Diana swung the ore as hard as she could, this time smashing it against the older woman's right temple.

Completely dazed, Vasa weakly stabbed into the air with her knife. A vicious wound opened on the side of her skull. Blood was pouring from the gash freely into her eyes and soaking her clothes. The butcher's knife fell from her hand and clanged to the dock, as Vasa stumbled back and forth. Instinctively, Diana reached for the knife, seized it, and buried it in her attacker's stomach. Salvia Vasa released a sound akin to air leaving the body and then fell over backwards off the dock and plunging into the waters of Eagle Mountain Lake. Never to be seen or heard from again."

Cat took a moment to catch her breath. Then she pointed back up another pathway leading away from the lake.

She explained, "Alone, exhausted, and in shock, Diana made her way over to the playground. The next day, when the rest of the camp's staff arrived, they found the massacre and they found Diana curled up and shivering, hiding in the treehouse. Later, Diana told the authorities that all through the night she could hear noises, sounds coming from the woods. Sometimes the sound was right below the treehouse and sometimes it was far away. She heard sounds coming from the woods and coming from all throughout the campsite. When asked what the sound was, she described it as the sound of a crying animal."

Cat paused. Then she looked directly into the camera and said, "To this day, the body of Salvia Vasa has never been found."

Cat paused for a moment as her stance took on a more relaxed look. It appeared as if she was switching from an on-air persona to her more relaxed off camera self. She began to casually walk back up the overgrown pathway back toward the rundown campsite. The camera followed along behind her. The shadow of the camera and its operator stretched into view as the sun was getting low in the western sky. As they walked, Adam's voice came from off camera.

He asked, "What does the *Pelican Bay Camp Massacre* have to do with the Azlewood Killer? How does the Goatman fit into this scenario?"

"You didn't read any of the newspaper clippings or watch any of the news feeds I gave you, did you?" Cat asked. Her voice was more than a little agitated. "Jesus, Adam, I bet you didn't even watch any of the *YouTube* videos, did you?"

"Look, darling, I operate the camera," Adam retorted matter-of-factly. "I don't do research or extra studying I don't have to."

"Don't call me darling," Cat snapped.

"Sorry, babe," Adam chuckled. Cat stopped walking and shot the camera a dangerous look. Adam immediately responded with, "I'm sorry, okay? But seriously, how are the two connected?"

"Diana Roa, the sole survivor of *the Pelican Bay Massacre* spent the next two months living with her sister, her twin sister, Christmas Roa," Cat explained.

"If you had done any reading at all, you would know that Christmas Roa was murdered in her home by the Goatman. It is the first reported killing involving the Azlewood Killer on record."

"Holy shit!" Adam exclaimed.

"That's right, holy shit," Cat nodded then continued. "Now, the media claims the attack is coincidence, but I know they are somehow related. That's just too big of a coincidence for me. There must be a connection and if we can find it out here then we have an ending for the documentary, an ending with a real kicker." The next few steps were spent in silence and then Cat asked, "Do you want to know how he did it?"

"I'm not sure," Adam's voice was shaky. "Okay, yes. Tell me."

"Christmas was standing in her own living room," Cat explained. "Jesus, can you imagine? Your own living room should be the safest place in the world. She was facing the wall, straightening a picture frame on the wall, a picture of her and her sister. She had her back to the front door when the killer crept in, walked right up behind her unnoticed, and strangled her to death with his massive, dirty hands. She couldn't scream as he squeezed the life out of her. All she could do is stare into the eyes of her killer until the light in hers went out."

"Jesus," Adam breathed. "How do you, and the police for that matter, know these details?"

They paused for a moment at the post with the arrow shaped directional signs and Cat explained.

"Because there was an eyewitness," she said. "Standing off to the side, shrouded in darkness, and unseen by the killer, Diana stood frozen with fear and watched as her sister was murdered. Her experience with the *Pelican Bay Massacre* was still so fresh in her mind that her body just froze. She watched as the Goatman strangled the life out of her own sister and then let her limp form fall to the floor in a lifeless heap. And then, without a word, he just turned and left."

Adam asked from behind the camera, "That's a horrible story, but how does that story connect the Goatman murders to this place?"

"It's all right there in the details," Cat said holding her hands up. "Look, for a second, let's just set aside that the two victims involved are sisters, but it's in the way he went about murdering Christmas."

"What do you mean?" He asked.

"All of the Azlewood murders on record have a brutality, an almost animalistic quality to them," she explained. "They are wholesale slaughters with absolutely no fucks given for human life. They are just random acts of violence, but this one wasn't. It was not

247

random at all. Christmas was murdered in her home, and she wasn't stabbed or skinned or pummeled to death. No, she was murdered with her killer's hands wrapped around her throat. No, this attack was personal." Cat paused for a moment to rub her chin and look at the derelict campgrounds. "If we can somehow figure out why and how and prove those two incidents are connected then we will have just the capper this documentary needs."

"Oh my God!" Josh's voice came from somewhere far away, off camera.

The camera whipped around to show Josh stand way up the hill at the entrance to the Town Center building. He was wildly gesturing for them to come hither. Without a word Cat darted away and the camera followed. For the next minute, the picture was violently shaky and a bit disorienting until they reached their destination. Once they were at Josh's side, the camera stopped shaking, but it was not quite steady as the cameraman's deep breaths caused the picture to oscillate a little.

"What is it?" Cat demanded. "What did you find?"

Josh pointed to the door that led into the Town Center. "In there," he breathed and swallowed hard.

The camera followed Cat as she carefully made her way up the steps and to the front door of the building.

As she peered into the room beyond the portal she gasped and brought her hand up to her mouth.

"Oh my God," she breathed as she slowly entered the darkness beyond the doorframe.

The camera looked over at Josh who just shook his head and said, "I don't know what to say. You'll have to see for yourself."

The camera then turned back toward the doorway, navigated the steps leading up to it, and followed Cat into the building.

Inside, the building was shrouded in almost complete darkness. Both Cat and Josh had powerful flashlights and the camera had its own lighting for just such a situation. The picture was almost as clear as if they were still outside in natural light. They were in a small foyer. The receptionist's desk was covered in dust and vines and other plant life had already invaded the space from the open windows and cracks in the wooden floor. On the walls were rows of framed pictures. They were also covered in dust and dirt. So much so that it was next to impossible to make out who were in the pictures. Presumably, they were past staff members. This was confirmed when the camera came to rest on the last picture which had an embossed tag that read *Sonny Peterson – Camp Director*.

What was of interest in this room was the animal hide strung up taunt by several pieces of rope. It was positioned directly in front of the window where the setting sun was showing through.

"What is that?" Cat asked.

"It's deer skin," Adam answered from behind the camera. "Somebody is tanning the hide." When Josh and Cat both looked at the camera sideways, Adam explained, "My dad was a big-time hunter when I was a kid. Sometimes he'd take me. This is how the hide of an animal is dried out and then used to make things like clothing. My dad would do this and make rugs and stuff."

"Well, this is fresh because it's still dripping," Cat pointed her flashlight to a small puddle of deer blood gathering from a slow drip off the stretched skin.

"What is that?" Josh gestured to the floor with his flashlight.

The camera panned downward. Coming into frame, scrawled across the floor was some sort of drawing. It was a large circle, the circumference of which engulfed nearly the entire lobby. Within the circle there was a continuous line that branched in three different directions creating almost arrowhead shapes. At the center of the large circle was a rendering of what appeared to be a star-like shape. Its six appendages were all curved giving it a look as if it were spinning. And finally, at the center of the spinning star was a single dot.

"What is that symbol?" Adam asked. He moved the camera back and forth over the symbol to show the scope of it. All three of them were standing within the circle.

Josh knelt and ran his finger over the star and the dot at the center of the circle. He rubbed his fingers together.

"Sticky," he said. He brought his fingers up to his nose and took a sniff. "Ah, Jesus!" He exclaimed.

"What...what does it smell like?" Adam asked.

"Like your grandma's dirty diapers," Josh snapped as he vigorously wiped his fingers against his jeans.

"I don't like this," Cat stated flatly.

"What's that?" Josh asked, still wiping his fingers on his pants leg.

"That symbol," she pointed her flashlight down to the markings on the floor. "There's something, I don't know, ominous about it. It almost looks like a giant eye. I feel like, I don't know, I feel like maybe something is watching us."

"It's just graffiti, Cat," Adam assured her. "Probably just some local high school kids jacking around."

"I don't think so, man," Josh interjected. "Wait until you see what's in the next room."

Josh led them into the next chamber. It was a large hall that ran nearly the length of the building. The dying illumination of the setting sun provided dim light through the four large windows that lined the west wall. In this room were three more skins from animals stretched taunt and displayed in front of the windows. The floor, walls, and ceiling of this room were covered in many symbols like the one they had encountered in the lobby. Some of them were just smaller variations of the first one, but there were many others of varying sizes and with different configurations. Animal bones and skulls were littered here and there and some even stacked in neat piles in two corners of the hall. The camera panned from side to side giving a good look at the spectacle these filmmakers had stumbled onto.

In the center of the room was a circle of blackened stones and in the middle of those stones were the ashy remains of whatever was burned there. Hanging from the ceiling and nailed to the walls in several places were small ornaments and figurines constructed out of straw and sticks. Cat reached up and snapped one free of the string it was attached to. She looked at the figure up and down, seemingly mesmerized by it.

"It kind of looks like a man with no arms or legs," she said in a low voice.

"Ah, Jesus Christ!"

The camera whipped over to see Josh standing at the furthest window seal. The camera followed as Cat came to stand beside Josh. Cat brought her hand up to her mouth and gasped. The camera followed their shocked gazes to the window seal. Sitting on the seal were three large glass jars. The jars were full of what looked like dirty water. However, it was what was floating in the water that caused the cameraman to wretch and the camera to shake violently for a moment. When the picture finally came back into view, it focused on what was floating in the water of those jars. The first jar was full of severed ears, the second was full of what appeared to be tongues, and the third jar was full of what appeared to be eyeballs.

"No fucking way this is real," Josh shook his head in disbelief.

"Those can't be human parts, can they?" Cat buried her face into Josh's chest clearly not wanting to face the truth of the macabre scene presented before her.

Adam simply said, "No."

The camera veered back toward the animal skins that were stretched out in front of the windows. The picture focused on the closest skin. Adam could be heard gasping for air as the camera focused on what appeared to be two nipples on the skinned torso from a human being.

"We have to get the fuck out of here!" Josh declared and quickly led Cat out of the large room.

The camera followed but stopped for a moment as the camera man's foot scrapped the floor and caught a notch that caused him and the picture to jolt. When the picture came back into focus it showed that a portion of the large circle that adorned the lobby floor had been scuffed away. The camera looked forward out the front entrance and then quickly back in toward the great hall.

"Fuck," Adam's voice could be heard from behind the camera and then the picture cut out.

The camera cuts to Cat standing with her hands on her knees.

She is breathing hard and there is a look of dread on her normally jubilant face. Josh is standing close at her side not looking much better as his head darts from side to side. It is obviously sometime later as the sun has set. Darkness has engulfed the forest and all the nocturnal denizens of nature can be heard in the background. The night vison of the camera showing the filmmakers in as much detail as if they were standing in the noon day sun.

"This can't be happening," Cat said in-between deep breaths.

"This doesn't make any since whatsoever," Josh added as he continued to look over his shoulder.

The camera is oscillating slightly as the heavy breathing of Adam can be heard. "What the hell is going on here?" Adam asked, his normally flippant tone replaced by a more serious one.

"We've been walking for hours," Cat explained catching her breath. "This makes no sense."

"We went right back the way we came," Josh added as he dropped his backpack onto the ground. "How the hell did we get so turned around?"

The camera panned to the left and the derelict campground of Pelican Bay came into view. All the buildings were cast in shadow and the campsite took on an even more ominous look in the dark of night. It was a picture of isolation and despair. The camera swung back around to find Cat vigorously tapping away on her phone.

"Fuck!" She screamed in frustration. "No signal!"

"This makes no sense," Josh repeated. "How in the hell did we circle back around and end up back here?"

Adam's voice sounded from behind the camera. It was very evident to everybody he was trying to project an air of confidence. He said, "Let's just remain calm. None of us are very familiar with these woods. In the dark, it's possible for us to have gotten turned around."

"But that's impossible," Josh shot back. "We never strayed away from the path. We never left the path. We should be at the sheriff's station right now reporting what we saw."

"I understand, Josh," Adam's voice was showing signs of losing calm. "But there is no other explanation. Somehow we got turned around."

"No…no…this isn't right, man," Josh began repeating himself and walking in a small circle. "This just isn't right, man. No…no…something is wrong here."

"Well, we're not going to get far in the dark," Adam said.

"So, what are you saying?" Cat asked looking a little more than just concerned.

"I say we set up camp and try to hike out in the morning by the light of day," Adam answered. "Who knows, maybe we'll run into some hikers or maybe that cool ass Texas Ranger from earlier. I don't know, but we can't just keep walking around in circles in the dark. It's too dangerous."

"Dangerous?" Josh scoffed. "Do you remember what we found in that campsite earlier? That wasn't some leftover evidence from something that happened years ago. Nah, man, that shit was recent. Fuck this shit, man. This just isn't right."

"What are you saying, Adam?" Cat asked again as the desperation in her eyes grew.

"I say we hold up in one of the buildings over there, barricade the doors and windows, and wait until daylight and get the hell out of here."

As Adam laid out his plan the camera veered over to the campgrounds. Then the camera swept back around to show Josh and Cat's exasperated faces.

"Have you lost your fucking mind?" Cat hissed. "There is no fucking way I'm staying here for the night."

"Ditto," Josh growled. "Whoever is keeping a collection of human parts will come back and I for one have no intentions of ending up as somebody's lampshade. We're getting the fuck out of here right now."

The picture cuts out.

The camera cuts to Cat and Josh hugging each other.

Cat is crying hysterically, and Josh is trying in vain to calm her down. The camera moves away from the couple and pans to the left. Coming into view is the dark, barren structures that make up the condemned Pelican Bay Summer Camp. Adam begins to speak off camera in low tired voice. His voice is horse and raspy. His breathing is heavy.

"We have been walking for what seems like hours upon hours. It's hard to tell what time it is. None of our phones even have power anymore. As you can see, we have somehow ended up right back at this damn campsite. It truly is baffling how we could have possibly gotten turned around so badly. We're going to set up the tent here on the outskirts of the campsite. None of us want to sleep there for the night. And none of us wants to be alone so we will all be squeezing into one tent. I hope in the morning we get our bearings and find a way out of these godforsaken woods. Look at this." For a moment, the camera veers to the night sky to show a large full moon hanging overhead. Somewhere off in the distance, a wolf howls. Then the camera comes back to settle on the dark foreboding looking campgrounds and Adam begins to speak again. "It's a funny thing, but I could almost swear, the moon has not moved from that spot all night. I have a weird feeling out here. Something isn't right. I have never been what somebody would call a religious man, but, God, if you are up there," the camera veers back toward the night sky, "if you are up there and listening, please, help us."

Somewhere off in the distance, a wolf howls again.

The picture cuts out.

The camera cuts to an extreme close-up of Cat and Josh huddled together in a small tent.

"What the hell are you doing?" Josh snapped.

"I want to get this on film," Adam snapped back.

"Will you two be quiet?!" Cat cut them both off. "Listen. There it is again."

They all fell silent. Josh and Cat were cocking their heads and listening. Then, there was a sound, a very vague noise from a great distance off.

"What the hell is that?" Cat asked.

"It sounds like…," Josh closed his eyes tightly and concentrated, and then he said, "It sounds like an animal. I don't know, a goat maybe?"

"It sounds like a baby crying," Adam said from off camera.

They all jumped as that animal bleating suddenly rang out very close to their tent.

"Oh shit!" Josh nervously uttered. "It's getting closer."

"Here," Cat pulled her handgun out, cocked it, and offered it to Josh. "Go out there see what the fuck that is."

Josh vigorously shook his head. "No fucking way," he said holding his hands up. "No fucking way am I going out there."

"Come on, you limp dick," Cat scolded him. "Get your ass out there and be a fucking man."

"Why can't Adam go?" Josh pointed toward the camera.

Cat offered the gun.

"Nope," Adam's voice came from off camera. "Not going to happen."

"*Shhh*," Josh whispered and made an exaggerated motion with his finger. "Listen."

The wind outside the tent picked up. The fabric of the tent began to quiver. Suddenly, the entire tent began to shake violently. That bleating sound was seemingly right outside the tent flap. Josh, Cat, and even Adam screamed. Then, just as suddenly as it began, the shaking stopped, and the tent returned to a slight quiver in the evening breeze.

"Oh God, oh fuck, oh god, oh fuck," Josh was whimpering.

Cat was weeping as she clutched her handgun tightly to her chest. The camera was a bit shaky. It was obvious that Adam's nerves were getting the better of his normally steady hands. Then all at once it fell silent in the tent. In that terrifying moment, that awful sound, that mix between the crying of an animal and infant rang out once more, but again it was a great distance away.

Cat looked directly into the camera and with tears streaming down her face she said, "I don't want to die."

The picture cuts out.

The camera cuts to Cat who is in a state of hysteria. Adam can be heard trying to console her from off screen.

"It's okay, honey," he said reaching over to touch her shoulder. "It okay."

"It's not okay!" Cat screamed. She was weeping, cradling her gun, and rocking back and forth on her knees. "He's gone, don't you get it? We're next. We never should have come here. We never should have come here…" She repeated over and over.

"Look, you stay here, and I'll go find him," Adam said. "He probably just went to take a piss."

"No!" Cat screamed. "Don't go! Then you'll be gone too, and I'll be all alone. Please…please, don't go Adam. Please."

Cat leaned in real close to the camera as Adam took her in his free arm.

"It's okay, honey," he said as he reached into his pocket and pulled something out. "Here." He handed her his little green plastic lighter. "This is my lucky charm. It's the first lighter I ever bought; I just keep refilling it. Here, you take it. It will bring you luck."

Cat took the small lighter and stared at it. She seemed to calm down, if just for a moment. Both jumped at a sound. It was far away.

"What is that?" Adam asked. "It's not the same as before."

"*Shhh*," Cat waved her hand and cocked her head. "Oh my God! That's Josh. That's Josh!"

Before Adam could respond, Cat dashed out of the tent on all fours. The camera quickly followed. The picture shook violently as the cameraman gathered himself and got to his feet. Cat was standing a few yards away. Her head was cocked. She was listening. Then, on the wind a voice came. It was very far away and weak.

"Help me!"

It was barely audible.

"It is Josh," Adam said from behind the camera. The view swept around showing the black forest. The wind whipped through the trees and brush making it hard to discern where the cries were coming from.

"Help me! Please!"

The cry was so soft, so far away. The camera swept to the left and landed on the Pelican Bay campgrounds.

All the buildings were covered in darkness. However, up the hill, past the dormitories, past the showers and cafeteria, at the top of the hill, a weak light was coming from the windows of the Town Center.

"Oh my God," Adam breathed. "It's coming from there."

"Josh!" Cat screamed. "Josh, I'm coming!"

Brandishing her gun, Cat sprinted off toward the campsite. The camera followed close behind. The picture shook violently as they raced past the wooden pole with the many arrow-shaped signs and up the hill toward the Town Center. As they drew closer, Josh's cries grew louder.

"God help me! Please, God!"

Adam's breathing was manic as he raced up the pathway behind Cat. Her breathing was a mixture of wheezing breath and whimpering.

"HELP ME! NO! PLEASE GOD NO!"

They reached the steps to the entrance. Cat darted up the steps with the agility of her namesake. Adam the cameraman must have tripped because the camera tumbled forward. The camera darted down and showed that Adam was in fact on his knees. As he quickly gathered himself, Cat could be heard screaming from within the building.

"Cat!" Adam called out. "Cat hold on, I'm coming!"

The camera raced into the dark foyer where the large symbol was edged into the floor.

"Cat!" Adam cried out again. "Where are you?"

The camera raced into the main hall and came to a sudden halt. Cat was to the left. Her face was contorted into agony and pure fear. Strung up in the middle of the room and pulled tight by two large wooden beams was what appeared to be the skin of Josh's face, neck, and torso removed from his body and still dripping wet with blood.

There was a loud thud and the camera crashed to the hard-wooden floor. In the far corner of the room, the sickening remains of Josh's mutilated body could be seen leaning against the wall. Cat could be seen to the left, but the camera was lying on its side causing the picture to fall askew and out of focus.

"Adam!" Cat screamed.

A sheer look of horror came over her face. She held her gun up in front of her and fired off two rounds. The deafening blast echoed throughout the chamber. Something reached out from off camera, something powerful, and snatched Cat right out of the frame. For a moment, there was the scuffling sound of resistance. Cat could be heard screaming and fighting violently.

Then there was no sound at all.

A few moments later, from somewhere outside the building, a vague bleating sound could be heard ringing out in the night.

The camera picture paused.

*****

Sheriff Wyatt was holding a remote control. As he walked over and turned the monitor off, he said, "There is nothing else. The camera runs for another three hours before finally losing power and shutting down." The large lawman placed the remote on top of the monitor and then shuffled over to his desk and sat down. "Two days later, after the events you just saw, Caitlin Bachman was discovered standing on the roadside outside of town, covered in blood, and completely catatonic. Her camera man, Adam, is still missing, presumed dead. The other boy's remains, Josh, were never found, neither was any of the other skins or jars. The whole building had been cleared out by time we got there to investigate." Sheriff Wyatt rubbed the rough five o'clock shadow of his beefy chin.

"Well, bless her little heart," Ranger Maverick said. The renowned Texas Ranger could not stand violence against women of any sort of nature let alone an incident as violent and traumatic as this one.

265

"She was found standing on the side of the road by ole Pete Groves on his way into to town," Sheriff Wyatt said, his hands visibly shaking. "She was covered in blood, her clothes torn and ragged, and she was completely catatonic. Officers were immediately called out but every time someone tried to approach her, she would break out in wild fits of hysteria."

"Sheriff, was she raped?" Special Agent Edison asked.

"She was sent over to Arcadia General with a guard at her door," the sheriff responded. "Tests have come back and not all the blood on her clothes belonged to her. She was suffering from severe dehydration, a sprained ankle, one broken wrist, and numerous lacerations and multiple contusions." Sheriff Wyatt continued, "She'll fully recover from her physical injuries the doctor said, but he's concerned for her mental wellbeing. What happened to those kids out there has left a permanent scar on her psyche. For a while, she was under twenty-four-hour surveillance for suicide watch."

"Sheriff," Special Agent Edison leaned forward and asked again, "was she raped?"

The old lawman swallowed hard and rubbed his eyes with his meaty hand. His voice broke as he answered, "Yes…yes, multiple times." His big brown eyes started to well up. "My god, she was out there for two days…" His voice trailed off.

"It's alright, Marcus," Ranger Maverick said standing and putting on his hat, "we have heard and seen enough here. Thank you for your time."

Agent Edison also stood and said, "Thank you for your cooperation, Sheriff."

Ranger Maverick tipped his hat and exited the Sheriff's office with Agent Edison close behind him. As the door closed, the Sheriff immediately started feverishly searching every drawer in his desk looking for that emergency pack of smokes he knew he would need one day.

As they exited the Sheriff Station, Agent Edison turned to his partner and said, "I'm going to want to see these campgrounds."

"I assumed you would," Ranger Maverick nodded as he retrieved his phone from his shirt pocket and pressed the speed dial. "Katheryn," he paused as a voice came cascading back from the other side. "Yes, honey, I realize I have paperwork piling up. Now, listen, I need the ATVs pulled out of the garage, gassed up, and loaded up onto the trailer. Special Agent Edison and I are going to go for a ride."

Chapter 6: Mr. Nobody

A small flock of Northern bobwhite quail that were pecking along the trail suddenly took flight, startled by the roar of the ATVs. They landed in nearby trees, looking down at the curious machines and the humans that road them. Their signature black, white, and brown feathers ruffled and settled as the ATVs motored down the woodland trail, that annoying shriek of the humans' motors now fading into the distance.

Texas Ranger Emmitt Maverick and Special Agent Christoph Edison brought their 4-wheelers to a stop where the trail opened. They had reached their destination, the condemned site that was once known as Pelican Bay Summer Camp. Ranger Maverick dismounted his ATV and stomped his cowboy boots hard on the ground. Then he stretched his long limbs to the sky. He removed his cowboy hat for a moment to wipe the sweat from his wrinkled brow with a handkerchief he pulled from his back pocket.

"Damn things always rattle my bones," the older lawman said as he placed his hat back onto his head. His long gray hair hung out the hat and framed his grizzled face like a lion's mane. "I tell you this, though; I'd rather rattle around on one of those 4-heelers for an hour and half than have to walk out here."

Special Agent Edison bounced off his ATV with the spring of a much younger man. Ranger Maverick scoffed. Agent Edison was dressed in a black T-shirt, black jeans, and black tennis shoes. His side arm was holstered on the backside of his black belt. His mop of jet-black hair fluttered in the wind. His chestnut brown eyes searched the surrounding landscape with eagle-like precision. Directly to his left was the post with numerous arrow-shaped signs, the same signpost from the video.

"You said that the road leading to the campsite had been closed," Agent Edison said as he walked over to the sign. "You said ATVs would be the best way to reach the campsite."

"Yeah, not long after the incident that closed this place down, the campsite fell into disarray and was condemned," Ranger Maverick explained. "The dirt road that once led here is all but grown over now, see."

He pointed to the far side of the campsite where a dirt path, not much bigger than the one he and the ranger had just come down led into the woods, but about ten feet in, the grass and brush had grown over all but concealing the road. There was a large wooden sign erected at the entrance that read ROAD CLOSED. The sign was covered in spray paint of assorted colors. There was a picture of a hangman's noose, the words *Dead Man's Camp* scrawled in red, and other various graffiti. Agent Edison noticed that several of the buildings on the campgrounds as well as the signposts also bore similar markings.

"Sometimes local kids make their way here and tag the place," Ranger Maverick explained. "It's some kind of rite of passage thing. They dare each other to come here and those that do, to prove that they were here, usually spray paint some sort of name or symbol. It's the reason why that trail we took in is still so maintained…all the foot traffic."

The grass in the area was much higher than it was in the student's film. Moss and ivy covered the derelict buildings. The pathways that led from building to building and down to the shoreline of the lake were all but gone.

"What is it you are hoping to find out here?" Ranger Maverick asked.

"I'm not searching for any particular clue or revelation," Agent Edison replied. "I just wanted to get a feel for the scene."

"Fair enough," the old lawman said as he retrieved his cantina and took a hardy swig.

He watched intently as Special Agent Edison moved through the thigh-high grass. The young man was studying the grounds intently. What crime scene tape remained flapped in the wind, hanging and tattered from door jams and window seals.

"Why?" Agent Edison asked.

"Why…what?" Ranger Maverick assumed he was speaking to him.

"Oh, sorry," Agent Edison looked over his shoulder. "I was just thinking out loud."

"Do share, Special Agent Edison," the older lawman said as he walked over to stand next to the younger man.

"Going over the case files I came across many similar circumstances," Agent Edison said as he scanned the campgrounds. "What I didn't see in the reports, nor have I come up with a reason of my own, is why…why are these murders happening? What are the killer's motives?"

"Oh, right," the old ranger nodded with understanding. "We have been trying to figure that out ourselves. Once we connected the Roa and Lawry murders we called in the U.S. Marshalls. They conducted a manhunt, but no joy. The sheer enormity of these woodlands is staggering. I'm still getting reports of Goatman sightings coming from Tyler to Austin to Beaumont to everywhere in-between. Most of the time the reports turn up empty, college kids pulling pranks or olds thinking they saw something they didn't. What we have narrowed it down to is that these attacks seem to be concentrated in and around the Eagle Mountain

Lake area. Also, every time there is an attack, it correlates with the fact that there's a full moon."

"Every time?" Agent Edison asked.

"Every single time," Ranger Maverick confirmed. "You saw the police sketches, right?"

"Yes," the young man shook his head. "Monstrous."

"Well, yeah," the old ranger continued. "Using eye-witness reports and going on what those girls over at the Lawry Household had to say, our artists have been able to cobble together a composite pic of what this son of a bitch may look like."

"Has the animal skull he uses for the mask been identified yet?"

"No," Ranger Maverick scratched his grizzled chin. "We've called in animal experts from all over the state and nobody yet has a clue. Maybe some kind of mutated horse, or cow, who knows?"

"Well, what we do know is our killer has something to hide," Agent Edison paused and then said, "or, he is hiding from something."

"How so?"

"Why the mask?"

Ranger Maverick shook his head and said in all honesty, "Because it's scary."

"Maybe," Agent Edison replied. "But I'm sure once we know the reason, we'll be much closer to finding him."

"Maybe he's protecting something?" The older lawman added.

Agent Edison looked over at his counterpart and smiled. "Why, Ranger Maverick, you sound like you may have a theory."

"I might at that," Ranger Maverick replied.

"Anything you'd like to share with the classroom?"

"I just don't think you're ready to hear it," the older man scoffed.

"Now you have to tell me," Agent Edison insisted.

"Alright." Ranger Maverick clasped his hands and said, "*Draugr*."

"What?"

"*Draugr*."

"Please, explain," Agent Edison asked.

"*Draugr* are the dead who have risen from the grave to plague the living," Ranger Maverick explained. "They

273

reek of death, possess inhuman strength, and they are known for slaying their victims in an extremely cruel manner."

Agent Edison just stood there blinking his eyes. "I feel like you are fucking with me," Agent Edison said after a moment of contemplation.

"Perhaps," Ranger Maverick's face showed no signs on whether he was serious, or not.

"So, you are trying to tell me that our killer is some kind of zombie from a child's storybook?" Agent Edison's eyes squinted. His brow furrowed.

"No, I'm just fucking with you," the older man smiled. "Besides there haven't been any *Draugr* sightings in these parts for over a century."

He padded Agent Edison on the shoulder and strode past him. The younger man shook his head and chuckled.

"The really scary thing is I can't tell if you are serious or kidding," he whispered to himself as he followed the older man up the vanishing trail that led to the buildings.

"You go on and have a look around," Ranger Maverick gestured to the buildings. "I'm going over yonder to drain the lizard."

For a moment, Agent Edison watched the tall, lean Texas Ranger stride away. Then, he just shook his head and thought *what a strange old man*. First, he entered the boys' dormitory and searched the entire rundown building. Nothing out of the ordinary jumped out at him. There were empty beer cans and wine bottles strewn all over, an old mattress tossed in a corner, and some cigarette butts here and there. He found what looked to be a shattered bong. Resin stained the wood panels surrounding the shattered glass. He proceeded to the girls' dormitory and then to the councilors' cabin, both buildings were in just as much disarray as the first. But still, nothing to help him with the case.

He entered the cafeteria. A faint smell of musk and rot filled his senses. What tables and chairs remained in the main hall were cracked, broken, or turned on their sides. Everything was covered in a blanket of dust and dirt. Cobwebs were as thick as bed sheets. Just another shabby, rundown building. Agent Edison exhaled, and his shoulders slumped. Then a shuffling sound caught his attention. It was coming from the kitchen. He all but convinced himself that it was probably just a raccoon or some rodent scavenging. Carefully, and slowly he made his way to the swinging door that led to the kitchen. He leaned in close and listened. He heard more of the same, only louder. Agent Edison swung the door open and standing directly in front of him was a very tall man, a man that stood nearly an entire foot taller than Agent Edison. This tall man was just standing there, his hands clasped behind his back. He was just standing there, smiling.

275

"Hello there," the tall man smiled.

It was an off-putting smile, a smile that stretched inhumanly far from chick-to-chick. Not only was the sheer height of the man and his otherworldly smile off-putting, but his eyes, they were set deep in his alabaster face and cast almost in shadow. They were amber in color and hypnotic. Agent Edison felt lightheaded. His vision began to blur. The tall man's attire almost seemed to shift before his eyes from a long flowing crimson gown to a mundane outfit comprised of a worn button up shirt, suspenders, and black pants. His long jet-black hair hung down to the floor and seemed to billow around the tall man as if with a life of its own.

"Who are you?" Agent Edison heard someone ask. There was a moment of clarity and he realized that it was his voice asking the question.

"Me?" The tall man gestured to himself with a finger that was far too long to belong to a human being. "I'm Nobody."

Agent Edison rubbed his eyes and stumbled back into the main dining hall. As he fell back, he watched as the tall man moved forward toward him. His movements were precise and elegant, nothing was without purpose. He almost seemed to be gliding on air rather than walking.

"What are you doing here?" Agent Edison heard his own voice again, but the question seemed to come from a million miles away.

"I warned them," the tall man said. Though he was standing over him, Agent Edison felt as if the tall man were whispering right into his ear. He could feel the tall man's breath on his neck. A strong aroma of cherry filled the air. The tall man continued to speak, each word making the hair on young agent's neck stand up. "I warned them, but they would not listen. Heed my words, Special Agent Christoph Edison. When the moon is full, the coven shall crumble."

Agent Edison's ears began to ring, the way they do after a loud gunshot or when a nearby explosion goes off. He stumbled and struggled to recapture his footing. He blinked his eyes several times to try and clear them. As he did, he saw the tall man cascade toward the exit.

"No!" Agent Edison could barely hear his own voice above the ringing in his ear. He removed his revolver from its holster and brought his firearm to bear. "Freeze!" He heard himself say from far away.

The tall man turned to face Agent Edison. His vision still blurry, Agent Edison could not be sure but the tall man's attire continued to shift. One moment he was wearing the flowing crimson robes from earlier, the next he was clothed in a nice black suit and tie.

"We shall meet again, Special Agent Christoph Edison," the tall man's voice was like sweet music. "When you have a better understanding of the path before you, but mark this. Your mentor knows more."

"Don't move!" Agent Edison shouted, at least that is what his mind told his mouth to do, but the words came out as audible as a whisper.

"Remember, Special Agent Christoph Edison," the Tall Man said, "With the full moon comes the fall."

That inhuman smile spread across the Tall Man's face and then he dropped back through the doorway. Through Agent Edison's blurred vision, the Tall Man seemingly dissipated into the sunlight. His ears still ringing, and his balance not fully recovered, Agent Edison stumbled to the doorway.

"I said freeze!" He called as he stumbled down the wooden stairs leading out of the cafeteria, his sidearm held out in front him with shaky hands.

"Whoa, easy partner," said the dark, blurry blob standing directly in front of Agent Edison.

The young man blinked his eyes feverishly. He took his pinky and wriggled it around in his ear. The disorientation lasted a few more moments before Ranger Maverick started to come into view. The older man had his hands held up with a very perplexed look etched across his grizzled face.

"Take it easy there, partner," Ranger Maverick coaxed. "We're all friends here."

Agent Edison holstered his firearm and slumped down on the steps. He suddenly felt very tired, but his vision and hearing were coming back to normal. He used the front of his T-Shirt to wipe the sweat from his face. He looked up at his partner with an exasperated and confused expression on his young face.

"You want to tell me what the hell that was all about?" Ranger Maverick asked.

"Where did he go?" Agent Edison asked looking past the ranger and searching the grounds.

"Where did who go?"

"The Tall Man," Agent Edison replied as he tapped his ears. The ringing was faint and fading quickly.

"The Tall Man?" The ranger's question sounded more like recognition than it did an inquiry.

"Do you know him?"

Ranger Maverick stroked his long handlebar mustache for a moment. He turned his hawk-like gaze to the left and right and scanned the campgrounds.

"What did this *Tall Man* say to you?" He asked.

"I don't remember exactly," Agent Edison said and slammed his fist on the step next to him in frustration. "I became so disoriented. It was like I was drugged. Do you know him?"

"He's Nobody."

"That's what he said," Agent Edison said, rubbing his blistered knuckle. "Who is Mr. Nobody?"

"He's a troublemaker," Ranger Maverick said sternly. "Is there nothing else you can remember about your encounter?"

Agent Edison closed his eyes and concentrated really hard.

"Yes," He answered. "He said something about the full moon and a coven."

"Always riddles with that one," the old ranger muttered under his breath. He reached into his shirt pocket and retrieved a pack of cigarettes. Pulling one out he offered it to Agent Edison who waved it away. "Soot yourself," Ranger Maverick said placing the cigarette to his chapped lips, striking a match, and lighting it. "Don't let it rattle you too much, kid. We should be getting back if we want to hit town before dark. We don't have the right equipment to be out here in these woods after dark" As the ranger turned and started to stride toward the ATVs, Agent Edison could not help but wonder if he was just referring to camping gear or something more. After a few steps Ranger Maverick stopped, took a long drag off his cigarette, and then half turned back toward Agent Edison. He said, "You know, tonight is the full moon."

Then, he turned and strode away.

Agent Edison stood up. The ringing in his ears was now a faint memory and his eyesight had finally cleared. He brushed off his pants and shirt. Before he started after the old Texas Ranger he turned and looked back through the doorway to the cafeteria. *With the full moon comes the fall*, this Mr. Nobody had said. Agent Edison could almost hear the Tall Man's voice in his head as clearly now as when he said it. He then turned to see Ranger Maverick mounting his ATV. That's when he recalled something else Mr. Nobody had said.

Your mentor knows more.

Chapter 7: Tesla's Story

18 months before the trap…

The dance and crackling of the fire were hypnotic to her. The warmth it provided was a nice bonus, but for some reason she could not explain, Tesla always found the visual presence of flame alluring. This fascination with flame goes back to her childhood when her father would take her camping. She would help him gather wood for the fire while her mother prepared herself a glass of wine. She never partook in the gathering. No, that was something Tesla only shared with her father.

He father was a great outdoorsman. He knew exactly which wood to pick and which to leave alone. He showed Tesla the best way to erect a campfire and the safest way to extinguish it.

"Never leave the campsite with embers still smoldering," he would say.

He would build the best campfires. Tesla would sit for hours without ever saying a word or moving from her spot.

"Honey, your hot dog is burning," her mother would say.

Tesla would not even notice that the frank had long since turned black and shriveled. It was the fire. The flames. There was just something about the way they danced and rolled over and through the logs, the snapping sound each flame would make when it licked the cool night air, like a tiny whip. The fire captured her imagination like nothing else on Earth. A numb, tingling feeling would rise in her throat like when she would go in for a doctor's visit. Sitting there staring into the fire, it was as if the rest of the world went mute and fuzzy and her senses all became hyper focused only on the dancing flame.

Tesla blinked her big brown eyes, jolting back to actuality. She could not even begin to surmise how long she had been sitting there lost in the *Dance* this time. For a moment, a fleeting moment, she almost felt sad. When she was lost in the *Dance*, all is right in the world, or rather, she is not thinking about all the trials and tribulations life can throw her way. For a moment, she stared back into the flames of the brick fireplace, but then shook her head and smiled. She had to turn away for fear of getting pulled into the *Dance* once more. Fear? No, fear was not the right word. She felt anything but fear when consorting with the flames. No, it wasn't fear that kept her from reengaging the flames. It was an obligation.

She could hear her husband's voice coming from the shower down the hall. Ross Lawry, the famous science fiction novelist. Winner of such awards as the *Mary Shelley Award, Nimbus Award* for *Best Science Fiction Short Story*, and multiple *Bifrost Awards*, his name is spoken with as much reverence as Martin Harlan and

Ellison George. He is singing at this moment because he just finished his latest novel, *Saucer City*, an existential and theoretical exploration of the universe and mankind's place in it, of course set against the backdrop of interstellar civil war. Tesla, despite her dour mood, smiled.

"You always did have a way with words, Professor Lawry," she said to herself.

Outside, the chilly rain pelted hard against the large casement windows. The windows were fogged over. Like he always does, right when he was about to finish a book, Ross had brought them to their house in the woods. He says he likes the quiet and serene setting. It helps him to concentrate when he is on what he calls the *Homestretch*. Tesla loved their woodland abode. It was always such a nice break every time they came down from the hustle and bustle of Dallas.

Tesla pulled her knitted blanket tight around her slender shoulders. The rain against the window poked at her conscience, and the crackling from the fireplace called for her to escape. The sudden silence coming from the shower down the hall told her the time was nigh. Ross Lawry, renowned author, on a day of celebration, was about to receive very shocking news.

He was still humming when he came into the living room, a towel wrapped around his waist and drying his hair with another. He was a very attractive man. The fact that he was fifteen years older than her never bothered Tesla. His curly black hair was showing signs of greying as did his well-groomed beard and mustache. He put on his glasses. This too did not deter away from his attractiveness. In fact, it only added to his distinguished look. Their age difference may have been a hurdle in the beginning, especially since she was a student in his mythology and folklore class, but that was five years ago, and they had been married now for two years. Besides, the fact that they were an interracial couple always raised more eyebrows than the difference in their ages.

Tesla felt something nudge the back of her neck. She smiled as Ross gently ran the rose over her shoulder and down her arm. The sensation was tingly. He leaned over the back of the love seat and kissed her on the neck. The whiskers from his beard tickled and enticed her all at once.

"Good evening, my queen," he whispered into her ear. His hot breath caused her to involuntarily gasp. "I hope I did not keep you waiting long?"

His long, strong fingers rubbed her neck and shoulders with the skill of a classical pianist. For a long, wonderful moment she was lost in his touch. Then, the weight of her news came roaring back to the forefront of thought. She tensed up and leaned forward out of his reach. Undeterred, he stalked around the love seat and sat down next to her. The look in his eyes told her all she needed to know about what he had in mind.

"Honey, we need to talk first," Tesla insisted.

Ross slowly shook his head and flashed that wicked grin that she had come to love so much. He leaned in real close, his body heat engulfing her. His lips barely touched her ear as he spoke.

"Now is not a time for words, darling," he said as he gently pulled her to him. "I have traversed oceans of stars to behold your beauty, and now, in the presence of such angelic splendor I am overcome with a desire and passion no mere mortal man has ever experienced before. I need only a glimmer of truth, a compliance of passion from my goddess to fulfill my quest."

"You always did have a way with words, Professor Lawry," Tesla smiled and fell into his arms.

He gently unwrapped her knitted blanket from her shoulders and laid it out on the floor. He guided her down to the soft blanket and kissed her neck, her breasts, and her stomach. As sensations of passion rippled through her body, Tesla allowed herself to give into the moment. They made love with the warm fire crackling next to them, the cold rain pelting against the window glass, and a woman's guilt momentarily restrained.

Afterwards, they lay on the floor, their chests heaving, their bodies glistening in the light of the fire. Their heavy breathing joined the sounds of the flame and the rain to orchestrate a kind of romantic symphony. Tesla lay there staring at the ceiling, a river of emotions flowing through her mind. She was all at once relaxed, happy, sad, and scared. She truly loved this man lying next to her and she truly regretted what she was about to tell him.

Ross propped up on his elbow, leaned over and kissed Tesla on the lips, smiled and looked into her eyes. "I love you," he said as earnest as any man has ever said those words to a woman in the history of mankind.

Tesla replied, "I'm pregnant."

For nearly an hour they just sat in silence. After Tesla had dropped her bomb, Ross, without a word, stood up and walked out of the room. He returned a few minutes later fully clothed. Tesla had retreated to her spot on the love seat in front of the fireplace. For a while, Ross paced around the room, but ultimately, he settled in at the dining table, his hands clasped in front of him. He just sat there and just staring straight ahead.

In her mind, Tesla had made the decision to not speak first. She needed to gage his reaction. She had long ago already made her mind up about the baby. She was keeping it. Knowing the precarious spot, she has left him in, knowing how much she loved him, all Tesla could do now is wait for his response. She sat and waited. On the outside, she tried to protrude a look of calm, of patience, but on the inside, she was a jumble of emotions. She felt a tremendous amount of relief to finally have unburdened this secret she was keeping.

She also felt a tremendous amount of guilt for what this revelation would do to the man she loved, and what it meant for their future moving forward.

She turned her gaze back to the flames in the fireplace and begged for the release the *Dance* could offer. Then, he began to speak.

"Would you like to know what's really funny?" Ross asked rhetorically. "There was a split second there, after you said what you did, where I was genuinely happy. The thought occurred to me, oh my god, I'm going to be a father, I'm going to have a baby, and it is with the woman that I love, but that was a fleeting notion, a fool's folly. That's when the reality of your news really set in, because as we both know, I am unable to have children." He took a moment to remove his glasses and rub his eyes. Then, he said, "Jesus, it's why Joan left me. She wanted children and I…and I could not provide that for her."

The sound of his first wife's name caused Tesla to wince. "I have always felt like you would still be with her if you could," Tesla said as she continued to stare at the fire. "Sometimes I feel like our affair was just a way to allow you to let her go. You sleeping with one of your students would allow her to divorce you guilt free and seek out someone who could provide for her what you could not."

There was absolutely no malice in Tesla's voice as she spoke. It was a matter-of-fact tone. She was just stating things they both already knew.

"We both know the baby isn't mine," he said. "I lost the ability to reproduce to Testicular Cancer when I was twenty-two. You knew that before we ever started up." Ross stood and crossed the room to stand before her, and he asked, "So, who is he? Who is the father?"

Tesla sat in silence for a long uncomfortable minute, pondering over the best way to respond, and then she decided, "It doesn't matter."

"It doesn't matter?" Ross snapped back. "You reveal to me that you are having an affair, an affair that results in a pregnancy, and you can sit there with a straight face and tell me it doesn't matter?"

"You don't know him," Tesla said.

"Oh well, that makes all the difference in the world," Ross was extremely animated as he spoke. He was flailing his arms and contorting his features. Then he began speaking in a mocking voice. "Hello. How you doing? No, no, I don't need to know your name, good sir. Please, enjoy my wife, will you?"

"Did I ever get to meet the whore you fucked while on a signing in Philadelphia?" Tesla snapped back. As she was saying the words, she instantly regretted it, but she maintained her rigid exterior.

Ross' hands fell to his sides in defeat. "Is that what this is about?" He asked. "Was this supposed to be revenge? Yes, that happened, over a year ago, and you forgave me for it. We had gotten past it. I know I fucked up, and I've regretted it every single day since it happened. But we worked on it. You forgave me."

Her heart began to break as the look on his face shifted suddenly from anger to utter despair. Tears were welling in his big dark eyes. He quickly removed his glasses and wiped his eyes on the sleeve of his sweater. When he put his glasses back on that look of anger and betrayal had returned. He stormed back into the dining area and began to pace. His steps took him into the kitchen then up the stair to the rooms above. She could hear his steps stomping up and down the hallway as he was going from room to room. Then, there was silence. For a moment Tesla could almost swear she could hear the slight sounds of sobbing. Then, she was startled and jumped up as his suitcase, fully packed by the sounds of it, was tumbling down the stairs. Once it reached the bottom of the stairs the suitcase continued end over end until it slammed hard against the island in the kitchen, chipping the wood siding.

Moments later, Ross came stomping down the stairs. He was completely flustered. He looked around wildly until finally finding his keys. He opened the coat closet and retrieved his trench. He wrestled with the coat, struggling to get his left arm through the sleeve. Finally, he won his battle with the trench. He stood motionless. Then, he turned to face her, the flaps of his coat fluttering into place at his sides.

"I don't think I should be around you right now," his voice was shaky. She could tell his anger was the only thing keeping the tears at bay. He tossed the keys onto the counter then he continued. "You can stay here, of course, as long as you'd like. You always did like this place more than I. I'm heading back to Dallas tonight. Don't worry, I'm leaving the car. I just need to get the hell out of here."

"It's raining," was all Tesla could muster through the lump which was growing in her throat.

"Yeah," Ross said absently looking over his shoulder out the window on the backdoor. "I think a nice long walk in the rain will do me some good. I need to cool off and I have some thinking to do. I'll call for a cab once I reach the main road and my cell can pick up a signal."

He turned and retrieved his suitcase and then turned toward the back door.

"Wait," Tesla called out.

Her words stopped him in his tracks. He looked back over his shoulder. The bottom part of his chiseled face was covered by the collar of his coat. All she could see were his eyes, those eyes that once upon a time had reflected such love and passion for her. Now, those eyes were clouded with such anger and pain.

"Give me one good reason to stay," he stated flatly.

Knowing exactly how he felt in this moment, the only word she could utter was, "Please."

He closed his big dark eyes for a moment, then turned and stormed out the back door.

Tesla, in the living room wrapped in her knitted blanket, watched through the small window on the back door as he simply stood there. His head was hung low. The rain poured down mercilessly, pelting him. With the warmth of the fireplace at her back, she watched in silence. Her lip was quivering as her heart shattered. A tear rolled down her cheek as she watched him hold his suitcase high above his head and then slam it to the ground. He let out a primal scream. The rain continued, oblivious to his cry. He just stood there. For what seemed like an eternity in her eyes, Ross just stood on the back porch, his back to the door, and let the rain wash over him. Then, she saw the rise and fall of his shoulders as he took a deep breath.

She exhaled as the doorknob turned. The backdoor opened slowly. Ross stood in the frame, the rain roaring and pouring down in sheets. Lightning flashed, silhouetting his figure in the doorframe, giving him an ominous look. He stepped into the kitchen, his wet shoes making a squeaking sound with each step he took. Shutting the door behind him, the sound of the storm outside became muffled.

His clothes soaked, rainwater pouring down his face, and his glasses completely fogged over, he asked, "What have you decided to do about the baby?"

Tesla rushed to the hall closet and retrieved a towel. She brought it over to him. He accepted it. Removing his glasses, he wiped his face with the towel.

"Come on, honey," she said as she helped him out of his drenched trench coat.

He absently pulled a small flash drive from his pocket and handed it to her. It obviously held the contents of his latest manuscript. She led him over to the bathroom and as he took off his soaked attire and dried himself off, she ran upstairs and retrieved some dry clothes for him from the guest room. A few minutes later he was sitting on the love seat in front of the fireplace with her knitted blanket wrapped around his shoulders. Tesla went into the kitchen and started a pot of coffee.

When she returned, she sat on the love seat beside him. She could feel his body stiffen.

"You never answered the question," he said, staring straight ahead. "What have you decided to do about the baby?"

Tesla took a deep breath, swallowed, and replied, "I'm going to keep the baby."

"Does your lover know yet?" he asked without a hint of ire.

"No," she answered. "Not yet. I have not told him."

Ross sat there in silence. Tesla went back to the kitchen and poured him a cup of coffee, three sugars and one cream. She brought it back and handed it to him.

"Careful," she warned. "It's hot."

As the mug in his hand smoldered, a swirling wisp of steam rose upward and dissipated into the air. Ross sat in silence and just stared into the flames of the fireplace. The flames were beginning to subside as the fire was beginning its slow journey to embers.

"The *Dance*," he said as he blew at the rim of his cup.

"What was that?" She asked.

"The *Dance*," he repeated. "That's what you called it, right? Those long silent moments when you are staring into the flames, once, you referred to it as getting lost in the *Dance*." She nodded. "What is it you think about in those moments? What do you see in your mind's eye?"

"Nothing," she replied. "It's not that I see anything or make some sort of internal discovery. No, that is not what the *Dance* is for me. It's not some sort of meditation or self-discovery exercise."

"Then what is it?" Ross asked as he sipped the hot coffee.

"I don't know really," she said. "In those moments when I'm engaged with the flames, the entire world around me just seems to fade away. When I'm really locked in, all my cares and worries just seem to disappear."

Ross smiled. "That must be nice," he said taking another sip of coffee. Then, his face contorted and for a slight moment it looked like he might break down and cry. Then, he straightened in his seat and his face returned to normal. "I'm hurt, honey," he said. "I'm utterly devastated in a manner I know all too well that you know." He slowly reached over and took her hand in his.

His touch was warm, soothing, and she welcomed it.

"I never intended for this to happen," Tesla said. "I was angry, and lonely, and…"

He held up his hand and interjected, "The reasons are not important right now. We obviously have a lot to work on, but I know two things. I love you with all my heart, and even though I am gravely wounded at this moment, I truly don't want to spend the rest of my life with anyone else on this earth other than you, and I hope you feel the same way." Her eyes were welling as she nodded. Ross continued. "Second, this baby needs a family. I am your husband. I love you, and I promise you, this baby is a part of you and that means I will love this baby, too."

She smiled, but then a look of concern crossed her face and she asked, "And, the father?"

Ross rubbed his curly beard for a moment then asked, "Are you in love with this man?" Tesla shook her head. "Then, his involvement will be entirely up to him. This will be a hard road ahead. We'll have to work out all the details, but I know I love you. I'm extremely hurt and angry and confused right now, but I know for sure that I don't want to lose you."

Tesla did not even try to fight back the tears. They began to flow freely. She leaned in and he took her in his arms, wrapping the blanket around them both. For a while, they sat there on the love seat holding each other in silence and watched as the flames in the fireplace began to slowly die. A wave of chill washed over her body and Tesla involuntarily shivered.

"The fire is getting low," Ross said. "Here, let me step out to the bin and grab some more logs for the fire." He stood up and wrapped the entire blanket around her. "I'll be right back, honey."

He leaned down and kissed her on the cheek. Then, he turned to retrieve his shoes from the kitchen. They were still soaked from earlier. There was a squishy sound as he squeezed his bare feet into them. As he reached for the doorknob on the back door her voice came from the living room.

"Ross," Tesla called, "honey, please take the umbrella this time."

Ross smiled. He opened the coat closet and retrieved the large black umbrella they kept there. He unfurled it and opened the backdoor.

First, there was the stench, that putrid, horrible smell of rank death. Ross' nostrils flared and his eyes immediately began to water. The stench wafted over him and caused him to gag and fight the urge to vomit. The stench was followed by the thunderous sound of rain as the storm seemed to have increased in intensity. A flash of lightning glinted off a metal blade poised for a strike. Ross on instinct alone brought the umbrella up in front of him to parry the killing blow. However, the blow struck with such force that Ross was sent stumbling backward and he tumbled end over end over the kitchen island, disappearing behind it with a loud thud.

Tesla screamed.

The killer entered their home, his hulking frame barely able to traverse the frame of the backdoor. He looked like a monster of myth and legend as he wriggled his way through and into the kitchen. For a moment he just stood there, dripping wet. A damp musk added to the dizzying stench that already filled the air. This thing that stood like a man slowly turned his head from side to side, taking in the abode. He wore the skull of an animal over his face which was adorned with a large mane of animal hair. His enormous barrel-shaped chest heaved, and his breath was like a foghorn with each exhale. In one of his monstrous hands, hands that were gnarled and filthy with chipped, blackened fingernails, he held a large hunting knife. That sinister bone face slowly scanned the room and then his gaze came to rest on Tesla in the living room. Though she could not see his face, she could see his eyes, deep in the shadows of that macabre mask, were the blackest, most soulless eyes she had ever seen in her life.

Tesla, confronted with this monstrosity, gasped, unable to scream. Sheer fear had stolen her voice.

The killer turned in her direction then marched right toward her. Two long strides later he was already just on the other side of the love seat from her. In one swift movement, this monster that walked like a man knelt and with one mighty gesture flipped the love seat to the side. Tesla fell back a step as there was nothing between her and certain death. Her hand brushed the handle of a metal poker. But she whimpered as she knew that would be useless against such a foe. The killer raised his knife high over his head. Tesla held her hand up in front of her.

"No!" Ross cried out as he flung himself across the living room and plunged the pointy end of the umbrella deep into the killer's shoulder.

The monster growled in pain as he stumbled forward to one knee and dropped the knife. However, he recovered almost instantly. The killer swung his monstrous hand in a wide arc connecting with a backhand that sent Ross airborne across the room. He crashed hard into the refrigerator. Stunned, he slid to the tile floor in a daze. The killer quickly retrieved his knife and stomped toward Ross, who was absolutely in no condition to defend himself.

With one hand, the killer hoisted Ross up off the floor by his neck and leaned him against the refrigerator. Ross' head bobbled as the writer struggled to clear his senses. For all the good it would do him, the killer was not going to allot him the time. The beast once again held the knife up, but just as he was bringing it down for the killing blow, the killer was struck hard in the side of the head. The blow caused him to release Ross who slumped back hard against the refrigerator.

The killer shook his head. The blow placed a small crack in the side of his skull mask. He looked back over his shoulder to see Tesla standing behind him holding a metal poker. The killer made a *snort* sound akin to that a bull would make. Out of the hallow nostrils of that horrible skull mask erupted a very small spout of blood. Not fully recovered but alert enough, Ross seized the moment and kicked the killer in the crotch with all his might. The monstrous beast in front of him stiffened for a moment and inhaled. That seemed to be the extent of the smaller man's attack. Ross, however, knew instantly that he had just broken three toes.

The killer plunged the knife forward. Instinctively, Ross was able to duck out of the way. The knife plunged hilt-deep into the freezer door. Frustrated the killer broke the knife off at the handle, tossed the useless handle aside, seized the refrigerator with his enormous hands, and slammed the appliance to the floor. While the killer was momentarily distracted, Ross scrambled to his feet and ran to Tesla's side. He grabbed her by the hand, and they darted for the front door. Ross was limping severely. Just as they reached the front door, Tesla looked back over her shoulder to see the killer was nowhere to be seen. Her gasp caught Ross's attention. He stumbled to a halt and pulled her to him. She was shaking.

"Where is he?" she asked with quivering lips.

They both scanned the living room, dining room, and kitchen. He was nowhere to be seen. The only clues that he was ever there were the cast aside love seat, the demolished refrigerator, and the severe aching in Ross' right foot. The backdoor was still wide open. The rain outside was relentless.

"I don't know," Ross answered. Then he looked over his shoulder and said, "He must have circled around front to head us off." He pulled the curtain on the large window beside the door and looked outside. "I can't make anything out through this rain."

Then a flash of lightning followed by an explosion of thunder took the electricity. The only light in the house came from the dying embers in the fireplace.

"What are we going to do?" Tesla was becoming frantic. The fear along with the cold was threatening to send her over the edge.

"We have to stay calm," Ross insisted. "Our wits are the only thing that may keep us alive." Ross looked once more out the window and shook his head. "Here's what we're going to do," Ross said as he turned to his wife and clasped her by the shoulders. "Look at me…Tesla, look at me. We're going to get out of this. I promise you. All we have to do is make it upstairs. I have my father's revolver stowed away in the bedroom safe. Look at me, honey!" His hands were now on her face. "We can do this, okay?" She nodded weakly. He said, "Okay, let's do this. Tesla, I love y…"

There was a loud crash as the killer came bursting through the window behind them with a monstrous roar. His hulking weight landed on top of them both. Tesla felt a stinging pain in her abdomen as she crashed to the floor. She struggled back to her feet. Ross and the killer were tumbling across the floor striking each other with blows. Tesla went to take a step but stumbled as the strength in her legs began to give. A pain from her abdomen shot up and spread out over her entire body. She looked down in horror to see the blade of the hunting knife buried half the length of the blade into her stomach which was hemorrhaging at an alarming rate. In a state of total shock, Tesla wrenched the knife from her stomach, an act that made her scream in excruciating pain.

Her world began to spin. Ross and the killer were coming in and out of focus as she slowly made her way over to them. The killer was on top of Ross and had him pinned to the floor. Tesla was barely conscious when she plunged the knife toward the killer's neck. However, her aim was compromised by her fleeting consciousness and the knife gashed across the killer's shoulder instead. The monster let out a growl of pain.

The killer swatted Tesla with a backhand that sent her flying backwards and crashing hard into the brick of the fireplace. She crashed to the floor with a sickening thud. Just as her senses began to dissipate, she saw that Ross had gathered up the knife, but the killer had him by the wrist, and then her world went black.

Tesla awoke with a screaming gasp. The paramedic at her side immediately tried to keep her calm.

"Lay back down, honey," the paramedic tried to speak in docile tones, but Tesla's struggling was making it difficult. "Please, Mrs. Lawry. Please, I need you to remain calm." Tesla was proving to be more than she could handle. "Sonny…Sonny! Get in here!" The paramedic called.

Another paramedic leapt into the back of the ambulance and helped the first to restrain Tesla as gently as possible. While the second paramedic held her down, the first one administered a shot into Tesla's I.V.

"This will help you calm down a bit," the first paramedic said.

Tesla felt herself relaxing, but then a thought occurred.

"No, please," Tesla pleaded. "Please don't give me any drugs. I'm pregnant. I'm pregnant!"

The two paramedics shot each other a dower look that did not go unnoticed by Tesla.

"You've been through quite an experience, Mrs. Lawry," the first paramedic said as she brushed the hair from Tesla's glossy eyes. "We really need you to remain calm."

Tesla looked around the back of the ambulance wanting to focus on something. Then a slight pain from her abdomen drew her attention. She gasped to see the second paramedic working feverishly to stop the bleeding from her midsection. Tesla's head fell back. She was weak. Tears began to flow as she looked over at the first paramedic who looked down at her with eyes full of sympathy.

"I lost the baby, didn't I?" Tesla asked. Her voice was extremely weak.

The paramedic's welling eyes confirmed her fears. Tesla began to cry. Then, she gasped.

"What about Ross?" She sat up again, an act that caused great pain in her stomach, and more blood seeped forth from her wound. The second paramedic was already replacing the first bandages which had soaked through. "Where is he? Where is Ross? Ross! Oh God, where is Ross?"

"We have to get moving or she won't make it," the second paramedic said as he desperately tried to keep Tesla's bleeding under control.

"Let's go!" The first paramedic cried out and banged her fist on the side of the ambulance. The back of the ambulance slammed shut and the engine fired up. As they began to move, the first paramedic administered another shot to Tesla's I.V. "Please, Mrs. Lawry, I need you to try and not move and above all else stay calm."

Tesla's world began to spin away once more, but just before it faded to black, she asked once more, "What about Ross?"

Outside, as the ambulance with Tesla sped away, the grounds of the house were alive with activity. The rain had settled down into a light cool drizzle. Lights from half a dozen police cars illuminated the front yard with an eerie red and white glow. All the commotion was veering toward and encircling one primary location on the grounds of 308 Saranell Ct. Off to the side a rookie was vomiting. Every few seconds a flash from a crime scene photographer's camera would illuminate the area in a white glow. The forensics team was darting this way and that trying to keep the other on looking officers from contaminating the crime scene.

One officer leaned to another and said, "The neighbor, a Ryan Carpenter, lives a few miles east of here drove over to check on the Lawry's when the electricity was knocked out by the storm. Said he wanted to check in on them knowing they were in from out of town."

"Oh, I know Ryan," the other officer said. "Good man."

"Yeah, the first officer retorted. "He found Mrs. Lawry inside the house. He tried to stop her bleeding as best he could and immediately hauled on back to his place and called us in on his CB radio." He nodded to the middle of the gathered police officers. "What on God's green earth could have done this?

In the middle of the circle, strung up between two trees with ropes tied to his wrists and ankles pulled taunt, was the world-famous author Ross Lawry. His nude, bloody body oscillated in the cool night breeze. The skin of his torso, from his waist to his neck, front and back, had been excoriated and removed.

Off to the side, a ten-year veteran of law enforcement was vomiting beside a rookie.

*****

"Tes…Tes…Tesla?"

Tesla was completely lost in the dance. She sat on the couch, wrapped in her favorite knitted blanket, and staring deeply into the fireplace. The fire's hypnotic dance was reflected in her big brown eyes. The warm glow illuminated her round, sad face. She was completely detached except for a vague chirping coming to her from some great distance. The chirp was relentless and persistent. Then, a sudden realization struck her, and Tesla realized that the chirping was someone calling her name. Her consciousness gradually made its way back to what is perceived as reality. She blinked her eyes which were watering.

"Tesla?" She heard Diana's voice. It had that signature Diana sternness mixed with a slight dash of concern. "Welcome back to the present, honey. Tes, it's time."

"Time?" Tesla asked as she rubbed her eyes. "Sorry. I was just lost in…," she hesitated, "…lost in thought."

"It's time to discuss what we are going to do," Diana said. "Everybody is waiting at the table."

"Yes, of course," Tesla smiled.

She stood and suddenly felt a chill. She pulled the blanket tighter around her shoulders. She followed Diana over to the dining room table where Anne, Cat, and Autumn were already seated and waiting. As Tesla took her place next to Autumn she reached over and stroked the young girl's hair.

"How are you doing, sweetheart?" she asked as she shuffled her chair up to the table.

Autumn smiled weakly. "I'm just really tired."

"I know, honey," Tesla replied in that doting manner of hers. "The last couple of days have been quite stressful to say the least. Don't worry though; it will all come to an end very soon."

"It could come to an end right now," Anne interjected. The look on the younger woman's face told Tesla that Anne was not kidding around. Anne continued, as her usually cheerful face twisted in annoyance. "Come on, Diana, let's take that hand cannon you carry at your side and go downstairs and do what we should have done yesterday."

"And what exactly is that, Anne?" Tesla asked sternly.

Anne shot her a look that would suggest that the two women were not close friends at all but bitter enemies. However, nothing could be further from the truth. The five women siting at that table had become something akin to family over the course of the last year. They were as close as friends could possibly be without being blood related. They all shared a bond nobody else in the world could ever understand. They all had suffered at the hands of the monster chained up in the cellar.

"Anne, take it down a notch," Diana said tapping her finger on the table. "We're all in this together. We all agreed to this."

Cat reached over and placed her hand on Anne's trembling arm. The hair on Anne's arm stood up at her touch. "We all feel the same pain, Anne," Cat said. "We've all suffered. Don't forget, it was Tes and Diana who brought us together. We are all much stronger now than we were before."

As Cat spoke, the sleeve on her shirt receded slightly. Anne could see the beginning of what were rows of small pink scars lining the inside of the woman's arm. Anne's expression softened. She placed her hand on Cat's and gently squeezed it.

"Right, right, of course," Anne smiled. "I'm sorry, Tes."

"Of course, honey," Tesla smiled and reached across the table to place her hand on top of Anne's.

"Okay, we all know what we are going to discuss here," Diana said. "I'm not going to beat around the bush here, we have to decide if we are going to hand that bastard over to the authorities or are we…." For a moment, Diana's normally stern face softened, and she swallowed hard.

"You can't even say it, can you?" Cat asked.

"Of course not," Tesla said matter-of-factly.

"Well, I can say it," Anne slammed her hand on the table. "Kill the fucker! We go downstairs, place both barrels of that shotgun you have hanging on your wall over there against his head, and we blow that son of a bitch out of existence."

"Anne, I cannot believe you mean that?" Tesla was almost pleading.

"I cannot believe you can sit there and not be thinking the same thing," Anne snapped back.

"It's because I still have a soul," Tesla replied in earnest. "Anne, honey, if you cross that line then you'll be no better that that killer down there."

"That's not true," Anne shot back. "That thing is nothing but a rabid animal and needs to be put down."

"It would be doing the world a favor," Cat interjected quietly.

A look of concern etched onto Tesla's round face. "Oh, Cat?" She said as she leaned back in her chair. Her shoulders slumped as the weight of the world suddenly became almost too much to bear.

"See, Cat agrees with me," Anne said. She leaned back in her chair with her arms crossed, a look of triumph marking her features.

"Yes, I believe the world would be a better place without the Goatman in it," Cat proceeded, "but that doesn't mean I want to be the one to pull the trigger. We have laws in a society that separate us from animals like him."

Anne's triumphant look was quickly replaced by one of betrayal. "Anyone of us would have ended that fucker on the night of the attacks if we had half a chance to save those we lost," Anne said defiantly, pointing in succession at each woman sitting at the table. "Hell, Autumn came the closest. She blew the fucker out of a second story window with a shotgun. Autumn, don't you wish you had ended him right then and there?"

Tesla instinctively threw a protective arm around the young girl's shoulders. Autumn had been quiet up to now. She leaned forward in her chair. She was the youngest member of the *Survivors Club* by far.

"I owe a great debt to each one of you," Autumn said softly. "Y'all have become like sisters to me, especially Tesla." Autumn looked over to see Tesla's warm and reassuring smile. "You all have truly helped me through something I thought may have destroyed me. If Tesla and Diana had not come over and brought me into the fold, I would probably still be in a padded cell over at the Gaia Institute, drooling on myself because of over medication, and concentrating really hard to stay inside the lines in my adult coloring book." Autumn paused for a moment and smiled as if remembering something, then her smile vanished as quickly as it came. "Anne, you're right," she said, her face as stern as Diana's. "I would have killed him that night if could have. Hell, I tried. But I was in survival mode, and I had my little brother to protect. It was all just pure instinct. To be honest, I can't even begin to know how I survived the experience, but what you are thinking of doing is wrong. It's premeditated."

"Well said, honey," Tesla said as she rubbed Autumn's arms.

"We are not judge, jury, or executioner," Cat added.

Anne crossed her arms again. She was shaking her head. Her barefoot was tapping so hard under the table that everyone could hear it. Finally, she leaned forward and pointed at Diana.

"What do you think?" Anne asked. "You have been quiet this whole time. What's your solution? I mean why bother with all that working out and gun training and Tai chi bullshit then?"

Diana had her elbows on the table, her hands clasped together in front of her, her fingers interlocked. She was carefully studying each woman, weighing on all the words that had been said. She quietly contemplated each of the women sitting at that table and what they had come to represent in their little club.

Tesla had taken on a motherly role, doting on the rest of them. Perhaps it was because as the oldest member of the *Survivors Club,* Tesla was the most mature, or perhaps it had to do with some sort of guilt over the unborn child she lost during the attack. Anne had come to represent the group's collective anger. Nobody wants to be victimized. As contemptuous as Anne could be sometimes, Diana understood where that fire came from. Cat, poor Cat, she perhaps suffered the worst of them all. She bears the scars physically that reside on all their souls. Her self-cutting is a reminder to them of all the damage done to their psyches. And finally, Autumn. Autumn represents the innocence lost, but her defiance in the face of repressive terror also shows a strength and resolve unheard of in a girl her age. Autumn gives them all hope. She represents the light at the end of this nightmarish tunnel. Through her strength, the rest of them will come out the other side stronger and better despite their shared harrowing experiences.

And now it is time for Diana to do what it is that she does best – lead.

Diana slowly placed her palms face down on the table and said, "I love every one of you. Without you, I would be lost. Together, we are far stronger than any individual. Together, the five of us pulled off a miracle. We did what the law could not accomplish. We tracked down and captured the Killer of Azlewood, the infamous Goatman." Diana's face grew even more stern than usual. "It's time to put this to a vote." She turned her left palm facing up and said, "On one hand we turn the killer over to the authorities and let the law of the land handle him." She turned her right palm face up. "On the other hand, we take the law into our own hands and pass decisive judgement. All those in favor of the law raise your hand."

Going around the table, one-by-one Diana, Tesla, Autumn, and Cat all raised their hands. Anne just sat in her chair dejected, arms crossed, and shaking her head. She stood up and leaned forward, her hands on the table.

"We are all going to regret this decision," she said.

Anne turned around and marched away. She retrieved her sandals, grabbed her keys, and stormed out the backdoor. They heard her car engine fire up and the tires throw up gravel as Anne sped away into the night. Off in the distance, the ladies could hear thunder.

Chapter 8: Anne's Story

By the time Anne had reached her destination the rain had really started to come down. Through the fog of her windshield, she could make out the lit-up sign - *The Vikings Hub*. The Hub, as the locals called it, was located on the side of the highway coming into town on the north side. Though far from a centralized location, it was in fact a very popular establishment among the folks of Glen Haven. Its five-thousand square feet interior provided plenty of space for a main bar, a side bar, a dance floor, and a stage for a band. It had three billiards tables, a line of dart boards, and seven large screen TVs with satellite so the local chapter of the Minnesota Vikings Fan Club never has to miss a game of the team they support.

Anne made a mad dash across the parking lot; she had to park quite a way out because the joint was jumping tonight. Standing in the doorway ringing out her long brown hair, she caught the attention of many of the menfolk. It took her a moment to realize that her already tight white half shirt was soaked and wet and leaving nothing to the imagination when it came to her female attributes. Any kind of embarrassment, if there was any, was fleeting. Anne smiled. She enjoyed the attention of men. She always had.

"Here you go, honey," Marge, the owner of the Hub said, offering Anne a towel. "It must really be coming down out there?"

Anne accepted the towel and padded herself dry, much to the chagrin of a few leering patrons.

"Come on, darling," marge guided Anne toward the bar, "have a seat. Let ole Marge get you something to warm your bones."

"Tequila," Anne called to the large woman as she took her seat at the end of the bar.

Marge nodded knowingly and poured her young friend a shot. For years, Marge had been a sympathetic shoulder to cry on, an ear to bend, and a motherly figure doling out advice for any of her patrons in need. Anne liked her, a lot. She was there for her after she survived her encounter with the Azlewood Killer. On nights when Anne had run from her thoughts and fallen too far down to the bottom of the bottle, Marge was always there to pick her up and give a warm, safe place to sleep it off, usually in the guest room in her small cottage she lived in behind the Hub.

Marge was the widow of Big Earl Thompson. Big Earl's grandfather and grandmother were Scandinavian immigrants that came to America in the 1920s. They made their way west and settled in the small town of Two Harbors along the shores of Lake Superior. Big Earl's grandfather worked on the docks, loading ships.

His father also worked the docks. This was to be Big Earl's lot as well, but it seemed fate had other plans for him. In 1995, while on a trip to Dallas to see the new home of his beloved Minnesota North Stars, Big Earl met and fell in love with a young, big eyed Texas beauty whose passion for Hockey rivaled his own.

Big Earl did not think twice. He bid the Great Lakes goodbye and moved to Texas where he married that beauty whose free spirit had captured his heart and soul. Fifteen years ago, the bank agreed, and Big Earl opened the Vikings Hub in his bride's hometown of Glen Haven. It quickly became the town's number one drinking hole. The townsfolk loved Big Earl. He was a friendly, gentle giant of a man who just had a way of befriending everyone.

Two years ago, Big Earl went missing in the woods that surround this quiet hamlet. Those woods have always just had a way of swallowing some folks up. Marge has been running her missing husband's business ever since.

After what happened to Anne and her sister, Marge had become very protective of the young woman.

"You want to slow down, honey, and tell ole Marge what's wrong?" She asked after Anne downed her third straight shot and was gesturing for another. "Honey, your arms and legs are all scratched up. What is going on?"

"Sorry, mom," Anne answered as she caressed the shot glass Marge had just refilled. "You wouldn't even begin to believe me."

Marge chuckled. "Honey, I live in Glen Haven. I've seen things…we've all seen things we can't explain. Try me."

Anne stared at the shot in front of her. Her eyes came up to meet the motherly gaze of the woman that had become like a mother to her, yet she still could not bring herself to tell the truth. She was probably not ready yet to admit that the events of the last two evenings were entirely real. The weight of Marge's sincere concern was beginning to weaken Anne's resolve. It was time for misdirection.

"I see you have the candle lit," Anne nodded to the large wax candle fluttering in the window seal over the backdoor exit.

"Marge followed her young counterpart's gaze and inhaled deeply. "Yes," she replied longingly. "You know I light that candle every night and I have every single night now for two years. I want Big Earl, wherever he is, to always know that someone is waiting for him." Marge's gaze came back to meet Anne's and her voice became a little sterner. "But you already know that," she said. "So, when you are ready to talk, you know where I am." Marge used the white rag she always carried to wipe down the bar and then walked away to service other customers.

Anne felt a little ashamed. She needed a distraction from her thoughts. She downed the shot and then laid her head down in her arms. She reached out with her senses, letting the cacophony of the Hub drown out her own thoughts. One conversation caught her attention. She swiveled around on her stool to see three young men playing pool, drinking beer, and cutting up. They looked like college types. Which should come as no surprise since many of the students from the university one town over, which is in a dry county, make their way over to the Vikings Hub to cut loose on the weekends.

"I just don't get it," a very agitated guy with an unkempt beard was saying as he was lining up his next shot. "We live in Texas. How in the hell is there a Minnesota Vikings Fan Club smack dab in the middle of the Lone Star State? Shit!" He cursed as his errant shot sinks the eight ball. "Motherfucker!" For an instant, it appeared as if he were going to break the pool stick with a downward swing, but his friend placed a hand on his shoulder which seemed to have a calming effect. The shorter, bearded man gestured violently at the nearest widescreen television and said, "I'm just saying, would it kill them to play the Cowboys game here in Texas. Hell, I'd even take a Houston Texans game over this Vikings bullshit."

The irate man's tall, heavy-set friend chuckled, as he deposited a few quarters and started to re-rack the balls. "Why the hell are you so worked up about this, Rick?" The taller man asked as he steadied the balls in the triangular wood frame. "So, this is a Vikings joint...we are in Glen Haven after all. You know this town has a heavy Scandinavian ancestry."

Rick cocked his head for a moment and then shot back, "What the hell does that mean? Is that supposed to be some big brain learning thing you're doing off at college...you mocking me, son?"

The taller man, obviously accustomed to his friends fits of outrage, only chuckled. "No, no," he said motioning for the third member of their party to come over and break. "I'm just saying - we are visitors here, man. Relax. Bret, it's your break."

Rick, still seething a bit, tossed his pool stick into the corner and walked away to the restroom.

The third man, Bret, was average height with a lean build. Not overly handsome, but not bad on the eyes either. Anne dialed in.

"Is he wound tight, or what?" Bret asked as he leaned over the table to line up the break. There was a thunderous crack as the cue ball smashed into the rest of the pool balls, scattering them in all different directions and even sinking a few.

"You're stripes," the taller man declared, absently chalking his stick. "Rick's okay, man," he assured his younger friend. "He's just still sour because Beaumont lost to Glen Haven in the State Championship his senior year."

"Oh, well then I'm so glad you brought him along then," Bret teased as he sunk another ball.

"Well, we would have won that damn game if the refs had gotten the call right," Rick announced his return with a clarification of his side of the story. "It was a catch!"

"Yeah, yeah," the taller man dismissed.

"You shut the fuck up, sasquatch," Rick mockingly threatened his friend. "Don't make me climb your big ass and bring you back down to earth."

The three men laughed.

"Hey, Dan, I have a question," Bret said to the tall man.

"Yeah, what's that?" Dan responded.

"Well, actually maybe both of you can answer it," Bret added as he sunk yet another ball.

"Jesus, slow down there, champ," Dan chuckled, astonished at the run his younger friend was on. "What's your question?" he asked, continuing to chalk a stick he was quickly realizing he may not get to use this turn.

"Do y'all believe in parallel worlds?" Bret asked with all sincerity.

"Parallel worlds...what the fuck?" Rick exhaled and walked over to their table to refill his glass with beer, all the while shaking his head.

Without batting an eye, Dan retorted, "My physics professor talked about parallel worlds in class, but do I believe they exist?" His brow furrowed in contemplation. "Maybe," he said cautiously.

"Well, I believe in parallel worlds," Bret said with confidence, as Rick refilled Dan's glass for him. "And, I believe we all have access to them, every single one of us."

"Do tell," Dan said sipping his refreshed glass of beer.

"Yeah, Einstein," Rick said sarcastically between healthy gulps, "do tell."

"I have a theory that our dreams are the key," Bret said. "When we are sleeping, our dreams are windows into alternate realities, a multiverse of infinite possibilities. Haven't you ever had a dream where you were the President of the United States, or you were the MVP of the Super Bowl, or you were running for your life from a bear...I believe all those things are events that have happened or are happening to an alternate version of yourself that resides in an alternate reality adjacent from our own."

"What the fuck are you talking about?" Rick asked, shaking his head once again in disbelief.

"What about Freud's belief…that dreams are the mind's unconscious attempt for wish fulfillment?" Dan asked. "Or Jung's belief that dreams are a way for the mind to resolve emotional problems or fears?"

"I don't think either of those theories conflict with my own," Bret answered. "In a multiverse of endless possibilities, endless worlds with countless shifts in actions, reactions, and outcomes, there are bound to be worlds where someone has lived a life or many lives where the best possible outcome is the order of the day, thus wishes do come true, and as for the second…watching through the mind's eye an alternate version of yourself as he deals with the conflicts and challenges presented to him in these alternate realities, if you pay attention, may give you a better understanding on what you are dealing with in our reality and how to proceed."

"Are these words actually coming out of your mouth right now?" Rick asked before downing his beer and refilling his glass for another pass.

"So, you believe in parallel worlds is what you're saying?" Dan asked.

Rick choked on his beer. "Don't encourage him, you fuck," he said through a series of coughs.

"Oh, yeah," Bret answered as he lined up another shot and sank another ball. "In fact, just last night, I witnessed a version of me somewhere out there in the multiverse, a super version of me, who has slept with every single woman I've ever met in my life. Not just my ex-girlfriends from school and the few one-night stands, but he slept with them and all the ones that got away. He even bagged the girls I have just fantasized about, even the girls whom I might have if I had any more balls than just saying hello to them." Dan was laughing hysterically. Even Rick was getting amused by the joke. "I was sitting there watching this super George Clooney version of myself and wondering out loud what it must be like to be so cool, and that's when he looked over at me."

"Oh shit, he saw you?" Rick asked, now completely engaged in the story.

"Yes," Bret answered as he lined up the eight ball. "I asked him - what was it like being so fucking cool?"

"What did he say?" Rick asked.

"He said – exhausting," Bret said and sank the eight ball.

The three guys broke out into a fit of laughter. Rick, wiping tears from his eyes, took the empty pitcher over to the bar for a refill. Dan leaned over and nudged Bret on the arm.

"Hey, Quantum Leap," he said, "I think you have an admirer." He motioned Bret's attention toward the bar.

Sitting facing them, leaning back with her elbows on the bar, her long, toned legs crossed, her damp tight white shirt still leaving little to the imagination, Anne smiled a devilish grin.

"Holy shit," Bret breathed. "I know that girl."

"What are you waiting for?" Dan nudged him again. "Go over there and talk to her."

"Don't be ridiculous," was Bret's response. "That girl is way out of my league."

Rick had returned and was refilling everyone's glasses. "I can't believe you," he scoffed. "What are you, a puss-in-boots? If some fine ass broad was giving serious fuck-me eyes like that, I sure as hell wouldn't be wasting my time with you two yahoos."

"Come on, McFly," Dan urged Bret again. "Since when does an opportunity like this come up for you?" He chuckled for a moment and then answered his own question, "Except in an alternate dimension of rainbows and unicorns."

Bret was practically frozen with a severe case of shyness, but then the most unexpected thing happened. The very attractive young lady at the bar motioned him to come join her. Handing Dan his stick, Bret swallowed hard and walked over, not even noticing his pals were high fiving behind him.

"Hey, McFly," Rick called after him, "don't cross the streams."

"Wrong franchise, ass," Dan scolded his bearded friend.

"But…," Rick began to explain."

"Just rack them," Dan motioned him to the pool table as he began to chalk his stick.

Even though the walk over was only a dozen steps, to Bret, it felt like an eternity. "Hello," he sheepishly said.

"Hello there yourself," the attractive young woman replied.

"May I join you?" he asked, gesturing to the stool next to her.

"Please do," she nodded. She swung around on her stool and motioned to Marge with two slender fingers. Marge obliged by pouring them two shots. "Thanks, mom," the girl said as she slid the second shot over to Bret.

"The owner of the Vikings Hub is your mother?" Bret asked.

"She likes to think she is," the girl answered. "I'm Anne by the way."

Bret nodded absently. "Yes, I know you," he said. Anne's brow furrowed. "We went to high school together, but I don't blame you if you don't remember me. You were a cheerleader and prom queen and dating the jocks and going to all the big parties and dances, and I…well, I was also there."

Anne laughed. "Were you always this funny…?" She nodded her head waiting for him to fill in the blank.

It took him a second to realize, but then he stammered, "Oh yeah, I'm Bret…Bret." He repeated himself.

Anne giggled again. "Will you join me in a drink, Bret?" He followed her gaze to the shot of Tequila in front of him.

"Sure, sure," he replied reaching for the shot glass. "What are we celebrating?"

"Your lucky day," Anne said as she toasted him.

"What do you mean?" He asked.

Anne smiled the kind of smile that gets the blood of men pumping. Bret blushed. "We're going to down about three more shots and then we are going back to my place and see if we can't give that alternate version of you a run for his money," she answered.

They drank their shots and followed them with three more. Slamming the shot glass top down on the bar, Anne called out to Marge, "Bar Keeper, put them on my tab." Marge just smiled weakly and shook her head. "Come on Chet," Anne said as she grabbed his hand and led him to the door.

"Um, it's Bret," he corrected her as she easily pulled him along.

"Whatever," she replied as they exited the bar, "let's go."

"Yahoo!" Rick shouted from behind. "Get you some McFly! But don't feed her after midnight!"

"Dammit, Rick!" Dan exclaimed.

"What?" His bearded friend asked sheepishly.

"Wrong fucking franchise!" Dan answered, shaking his head. Rick shrugged his shoulders apologetically. "Just rack the damn balls, you Goon," Dan teased as he chalked his stick.

With *The Viking Hub* in the rearview mirror and the sounds of Gwen Stefani coming out of the radio, Anne drove a few miles north on Route 666 then made a left onto Nine Mile Road. This was a rural barely two-lane road that led deep into woods. About five miles in, the smooth pavement gave way to gravel which eventually gave way to an old dirt road which ultimately comes to

327

a dead end amongst a cul-de-sac of trees. Local teens are known to hold bonfire parties at the end of Nine Mile Road, but not tonight. The weather had seen to that.

Anne came to a stop at the dead end and put her car in park. The rain began to pick up again. The heavy drops landed on the roof and hood of the car with a sound akin to a Snare drum. The occupants inside the vehicle did not notice the sudden surge in the rainfall. They were quite preoccupied.

The windows of the car had fogged over. The cramped quarters of the car's front seats made for awkward yet effective positioning. Anne pulled Bret in close and pressed her lips against his. She reached out for his hand and brought it up to cup her left breast. Her clothes still wet from the rain, clinging to her toned body like a second lover. As he kissed her on the neck, Bret gently lifted her soaked shirt up releasing her ample breasts from their confinement. He inhaled deeply at the sight of them. They were quite exquisite. Bret gently reached up to cup them in his hands. Anne moaned audibly as his thumbs skillfully pressed against and rubbed over her nipples.

"I can't believe this is happening," Bret breathed into her ear. "My god, I've had a crush on you since grade school."

Anne covered Bret's mouth with her own, her tongue darting into his mouth and caressing his tongue. For several moments, they petted and caressed each other. The rain outside adding its own rhythm and seemingly picking up pace to the sound of their heavy breathing.

"I can't believe this is happening," Bret repeated between kisses.

Anne leaned back, a perplexing frown on her face. "I hope you realize that you are less and less attractive the more you speak," she scolded as she pulled her top back down, covering her breasts.

Bret had the look of a child that had just been caught with his hand in the cookie jar. "I'm sorry," he apologized. "It's just that I can't…"

"…believe this is happening," Anne finished his sentence for him. "Well, nothing is happening, yet." Anne pulled a pack of cigarettes from the console and lit one.

For several moments, there was silence between them. The only sounds were the radio and the driving rain outside. Anne sat leaning against the door, one hand on her forehead, the other bringing the cigarette up to her lips. Her brow was furrowed in contemplation. Bret sat staring at the front windshield, unable to see beyond due to the fogginess. His hands rested in his lap with his fingers entwined and his thumbs dancing nervously in circles around each other.

"I knew Angela," Bret finally said in a low voice. "We were in the same homeroom class together. We were friends."

Anne exhaled, filling the cabin with smoke. She cracked the window and tried to direct the smoke out of the vehicle, cursing as the driving rain splashed her in the eyes.

"Yeah, I remember seeing you around sometimes," Anne responded as she wound the window shut. She reached into the glove compartment and pulled out a napkin to wipe her face. "You came over to the house a few times, didn't you?"

"Yes," he responded. "Sometimes when your folks weren't home, Angela would invite us over to jump on the trampoline and swim in the pool."

"Oh yeah," she smiled absently.

"I remember one time," Bret continued, "we were all in the pool splashing around and acting out and then you came out of the house and started sun-bathing." Bret could not control the smile that spread across his face. "You were absolutely gorgeous."

Anne's cheeks blushed. She looked over and studied him for a moment. The memory of that hot Texas summer day came back to her. "Oh right," she smiled. "I remember that day. I thought you boys wouldn't mind the view."

"No, we didn't," Bret chuckled. "You had already graduated high school two years before us. I had always had a crush on you from afar, but I never dared to act on it. You were the cool chick, the prom queen. I was just another guy."

"Ah, you're probably right," Anne teased, reaching across to pinch his cheek, "but look at you now, all grown up."

It was his turn to blush.

"Yeah, I remember Angela got so mad because you were drawing all the attention from the guys that day," he recalled. "She never let me forget that one. We dated for a while but after that day it was never the same again. We broke up a week later. We remained friends though, even went to the same college and hung out on campus." He began to wring his hands, searching for the courage to ask the next question. "Anne," his voice was low, "what happened?"

She was silent. This was by far and away not the first time someone had asked this question, and more than likely would not be the last time. It was just that considering the events of the last two days, Bret's question struck her in an odd way. Though it was a question many before had asked, in this moment, in this situation, it caught her off guard.

"What do you mean?" she asked, knowing full well what he was asking. She could not even begin to say why she volleyed his question with one of her own. Just stalling perhaps, for she knew the dark path this line of questioning would take her, and she was not quite sure if she was willing to go there, again.

"A little over a year ago," he said, "Angela and I had just finished our sophomore year at A&M. She came back home for summer break. I stayed on campus that summer taking some summer classes. She came back here, and I never saw her again." Bret straightened up in his seat and faced her. "Of course, I saw the news reports and read accounts on the web, but you were there. What happened?"

Anne sat in silence just staring, not at anything, just staring. She swallowed hard then replied, "Why do you need to know this?"

Bret reached over and stroked Anne's shoulder. In spite of herself, she found the gesture comforting. "I know she was your sister and whatever happened must have been terrible," he said, "but Angela was my friend and one day she's here and the next day she's not. I'm just trying to make sense of it all. The reports say it was an attack perpetrated by some sort of insane person, a murderer that was never caught…a lunatic that is still out there somewhere."

Anne's body stiffened. She lit another cigarette to calm her nerves. After a couple of deep puffs, she said, "Are you sure you want to hear this. God, I'm not even sure I want to talk about it."

"Please," he replied.

Anne paused and took several more drags off her cigarette. She cracked the window and deposited the smoking stem outside getting pelted by rain drops in the process. Bret had already retrieved another napkin from the glove compartment and was handing it to her by the time she had wound the window back up. Anne padded her face and neck.

"Alright," she said. "I'll tell you."

She swallowed deeply, took a deep breath, and began her tale.

*****

"It was just like you said, Angela was home for the summer. The first week she was back, we barely spoke a word to each other. We've always been competitive, going all the way back to childhood. All those things you said about me...popular, prom queen...that may have been true at school, but at home I was anything but the best. You see, all my life, my parents rode me hard about school, boys, my clothes, my hair. Nothing I ever did was good enough for them. Angela on the other hand was their little *Ms. Perfect*. She was smart, good in school, hell; she was even good in sports.

Do you have any idea what it's like to live in somebody's shadow?"

She paused for a moment. Bret began to answer but was quickly cut off.

"I'll tell you what it's like," Anne said, "it sucks. It weighs heavy on your soul, and it sucks your will to live right out of you. You start to question everything about yourself, every single decision you make. I resented her for a long time. She made me feel...," Anne drifted off for a moment. She rubbed her forehead as thoughts of her childhood came flooding back in waves. Bret reached over to place a comforting hand on her shoulder. She exhaled slowly, a long-drawn-out breath. She smiled weakly and then continued. "She made me feel small, and the worst part about it is she did not do it on purpose. There was not a mean bone in that kid's body. She excelled in life, and she was leaving me behind. I hated her for that.

We were riding our bikes on the trails in Azlewood. For the very first time in a long time, we were laughing and enjoying each other's company as if we were kids again. We were heading to the lake for a swim. As we zipped along, the trees of the woods flying by in a blur, Angela squirted me with her water bottle, then like a child, she laughed and sped up. I caught up to her; she could never outrun me, and I dumped the contents of my water bottle over her head. We went back and forth like this for a good way. So, caught up in the competition to drench each other, we came flying around a bend and nearly slammed headlong into a group of college kids walking up the path.

Angela and I both skidded to a stop just short of the group; our eyes were wide with terror, the terror of the travesty we just barely avoided. Then, we looked at each other. We were both drenched and despite the almost calamity, we began to laugh hysterically. The two guys at the front of the group stepped forward. The first guy was tall with shoulder length blonde hair, very muscular, very attractive. The second guy was even taller, muscular, but not as big or ripped as the first guy.

'Are y'all alright?' the first guy asked, holding his hands up in a helpful manner.

'Yeah, you girls were really flying,' the second guy said pointing back up the trail from where we came from.

'We're okay,' Angela said still giggling. 'We're really sorry about this.'

'Yeah,' I said, 'we were just goofing around. I'm glad we saw y'all before we crashed right into you.'

'Yes, we're glad to,' said a tall dark-haired girl. She reached over and grabbed ahold of the guy's arm to her right. She glared at me as she pulled him closer to her. He was extremely built and even though he could probably toss her in the air, he allowed her to manipulate and control his posture.

'Think nothing of it, darling,' the first guy smiled and winked.

I felt my uterus skip, goddamn he was so sexy.

He said his name was Kevin. The second guy introduced himself as Mikey B. He said it was his handle or something and that one day he planned to be a sports talk personality, whatever that means. He was always quoting something called the *Ticket*. We gave them our names and Kevin proceeded to introduce us to the rest of their party.

The tall girl with her talons in the guy next to her was Avery. She smiled politely, but her cold eyes told a different story. Her man's name was Robin. Cute kid well built, even more muscular than Kevin. He was a loud, boisterous sort. Robin would always end his jokes with a machinegun-like infectious laugh. Robin was cool. Sorry, I could not say the same for Avery.

Let's see," Anne paused and began tapping her fingers on her leg. She bit her lower lip and furrowed her brow desperately trying to recall the others' names. "Is it sad that I don't recall their real names?"

Bret did not respond.

"Is it sad that I was there for their last moments of life and all I can remember is the silly nicknames they called each other?" Anne sighed. "The next girl in the group was Barbie, but they called her Barbarella. She was an amazon of a woman, tall, very in shape, with a flat stomach and legs as toned and muscular as I've ever seen. She literally looked like she stepped right off the cover of a Vogue magazine. Her incredible body was made even more statuesque, even more hourglass like by the immaculate breasts implants that crowned her chest like two perfect globes. She wore these huge lens sunglasses. Barbarella was a fitting nickname.

Next there was Lando. He was as tall as Mickey but nowhere near as muscular or cut as the other guys in the party. He wore a loose T-shirt he had bought two sizes too big. A mop of curly hair adorned his large head. He was cute but extremely shy. He was extremely polite and as I recall, he took quite a liking to Angela right away. He sat on a 4-wheeler that was hitched to a smaller trailer loaded down with camping supplies. Angela and I breathed a sigh of relief we didn't crash into him. We could have been seriously hurt.

The two last members of the party were a couple of little party girls that could be mistaken for sisters if you didn't know any better. They were Buttercup and Blossom. They took their nicknames from a cartoon they loved as kids. Buttercup and Blossom grew up together and were BFFs, and they were quite literally the life of the party. Their water bottles were full of wine. Their pudgy little cheeks had a rosy glow. They both wore their long dark hair in a tight ponytail. Arm-and-arm they would giggle and poke at each other and speak nonsensical words. They were so close that on occasion they'd be so in sync that they could finish each other's sentences. It was impossible not to fall in love with their fun-loving spirit and outgoing personalities.

Like Angela, they were all on summer break from college. They were a close nit group of friends, and they were ready to blow off some steam before returning to school for their senior year. They went to Baylor I believe they said. They were on their way to Padre Island, but first they wanted to stop over in infamous Glen Haven and campout on the shores of the notorious Eagle Mountain Lake." Anne paused and slowly shook her head. "They had no idea…we should have known better…."

She paused again. Putting her face in her hands, her body was shivering. Not from being cold, but from the horrible visions passing in front of her mind's eye.

"They invited Angela and me to join them," Anne continued. "At first Angela declined, but Kevin was insistent, and charming, and I wanted to, so we agreed. 'Besides,' I asked her, 'why else did we wear our suits under our clothes then?' We walked our bikes along with them; Lando was bringing up the rear very slowly with his payload. The trail eventually led to a secluded beach on the shore of the lake. There we all helped to unload the trailer and set up camp.

Kevin and Mikey set about erecting the tents. Angela helped Avery and Robin arrange the ice chests, towels and camping chairs, and the keg, which Robin hoisted as easily as a child hoisting his favorite toy, was placed in a large tub of ice. Lando set about digging a hole for the campfire and then scoured the nearby brush for wood. I helped Barbarella set up a net for volleyball. Blossom and Buttercup immediately headed for the water and splashed around with all the joy and delight of children."

Anne started to smile at the thought of those two little balls of joy, but her smile quickly faded, and she continued.

"I got to talking with Barbie as we set up the net. She was currently going through a rough break up with her boyfriend who was back in Waco.

'That douchebag trashed my apartment and stole money out of my bank account,' she told me. 'Yes, I cheated on him, twice, but damn…he didn't have to wreck the place.' I gathered from our conversation that when her relationships ended, they always ended badly. 'Train wrecks,' is what she called her break ups. She had done some modeling in Dallas, Houston, and Austin. She told me she had a fling with Mikey, but nothing ever came of it. She was very protective of Buttercup and had absolutely no use for Kevin. 'He's just another college douchebag with a tan and muscles…thinks he's god's gift to women,' she said.

Even as she told me this, I found myself just staring at Kevin. The wind coming off the lake whipped through his shoulder-length blonde hair. His muscles were tan and dark, glistening with sweat as he hammered in a tent peg. Douchebag? Not at first look. Bronze god was more like it.

These kids were great. They were a friendly, outgoing bunch of college kids just looking to blow off some steam in-between semesters. Mikey cranked music out of the old school portable radio he brought. Robin and Lando grilled hamburgers and hot dogs. I noticed Angela had become quite involved in conversation with Lando. The way she laughed at his jokes, the way she found an excuse to constantly touch his arm. I can't explain why but seeing her and him get on like that brought that tinge of jealousy within me back to the surface. God, I feel so guilty about it now. I am such a fucker."

Anne bit her lip and smacked her thigh in frustration. Bret remained silent. Once she was ready, Anne continued.

"We all spent the day swimming, drinking, smoking pot, playing volleyball. Everyone was super cool, even Avery. Though she spent most of the time clinging to Robin and staring daggers into anyone that walked by too close, especially me or Barbie. Even Avery aside, it was one of the best times I ever had in my life.

Later in the afternoon I came across the *Terror Twins*, as Mikey and Lando called them. Blossom was completely sprawled across her beach towel passed out. Her sun hat rolled away down the beach in the wind. Her sunglasses were askew across her reddening-by-the-minute nose. Her left hand was tucked awkwardly under her back while her right hand lay flat in the sand with an empty margarita glass lying just out of reach.

Oh, and poor Buttercup. She was in bad shape. Partied out. She was sitting in the sand, right next to Blossom, her elbows covered in sand resting on her knees, her head hung low. I asked her if she was okay. It took several attempts to get her attention, but even when she looked up at me, the look in her eyes, which I could barely see because her eyelids were almost closed, she was gone…, toast…she'd been abducted.

Right at that moment, Kevin strutted by and handed her a small paper cup. He smiled and said, 'If you're going to spew, spew in this.' He laughed as he backed away.

Buttercup smiled and flipped him the bird. 'Get your *Wayne's World*-loving ass out of here," she slurred as she weakly tossed the cup after him. Barbie came to stand next to me. She was concerned for her friend.

Buttercup reached down and dug a small hole into the sand. She leaned forward and puked into the hole.

Then, bless her little heart, she did the most bizarre thing. She covered up the vomit like a cat or a dog, hiding it. She padded the ground and stared at the small hump of sand now hiding her unfortunate expulsion. 'There,' she said proudly. She looked up at us and smiled. 'Now, where's my margarita, bitches?' The look on her little round face was priceless. Then she lay back on the sand and passed out. Barbie and I were in tears we laughed so hard.

The boys gathered up the *Terror Twins* and placed them in their little triangle tent where they slept the rest of the afternoon away. As the sun began to set, Lando and Robin gathered wood and started a fire. We gathered around the campfire, sitting on blankets and folding chairs. Kevin came over and sat next to me. To my right Robin and Avery snuggled together. On Kevin's left, Barbie and Mikey sat chatting. Across the way, I could see Angela and Lando engaged in conversation. They were really hitting it off.

'You really are quite an attractive woman, Anne,' said Kevin, leaning in as he spoke. I could feel his breath on my cheek. He had a really aggressive nature. 'You know,' he smiled, 'you and Angela can stay here tonight.'

'Oh?' I feigned surprise. There was no denying my attraction for the kid, but I still loved to play the game. I reached over and gently stroked his well-tanned, well-muscled arm and asked, 'And, whose tent would we be sleeping in. You see, we did not bring a tent of our own. We had no idea we'd be sleeping out here tonight.'

Kevin smiled a smile that could charm the devil. 'Well, I was thinking maybe you could sleep in my tent. It's just that I really like you and I would not want you to have to try and make your way home in these dark, scary woods. Oh, and don't worry. I'll keep my hands to myself…promise.' He held his hands up innocently and gave me a wink that made my skin boil.

'That's a very nice offer,' I said then nodded toward Angela, 'but what about my sister. Where will she sleep?'

His brow furrowed for just a moment as if trying to recall a thought that had escaped his mind. He looked over at Lando and Angela locked in conversation. Then he smiled and turned back to me. 'Oh, I'm sure she'll be just fine. We have plenty of room, really.'

I smiled. He leaned in real close, and I thought he was going whisper in my ear but instead he nuzzled my ear with his nose. His five o'clock shadow tickled my chick. I almost swooned as he gently kissed me on the neck. His hot breath sent goosebumps up my arm.

'Oh, I suppose spending a night out by the lake wouldn't be the worst thing in the world,' I said as he leaned back and smiled.

Kevin laid his strong arm across my shoulder and pulled me closer to him. I prepared myself for a kiss, but instead, he said, 'Good. Now remember, this is just one friend doing a favor for another friend…solely plutonic. I'm not just a piece of meat mind you, so please, do try and keep your hands to yourself.'

'Kevin, are you using that lame ole plutonic line again?' Mikey teased. 'Get some new material, chief.'

Kevin removed his arm from around my shoulders and clasped his hands in front him. He was blushing. Everyone was laughing. Mikey and Barbie, who had apparently been watching our exchange the whole time were laughing even harder than the others.

Kevin held his hands up and said, 'Hey, I was just trying to be a nice guy. You want to let these two beautiful young women go home alone in the dark?'

'Yeah, that's you all over, Kevin,' Robin chimed in, 'Mr. Chivalry.'

'Don't worry, honey,' Barbie said to me, 'we have plenty of space. We'll find a spot for you and your sister to sleep…without the pawing hands of this horn-dog trying to get at you.'

'Hey,' Kevin scoffed. 'That's not cool.' He turned back to me with the biggest innocent look and said, 'I am a gentleman. Ask anyone. Hey, Lando, who is the biggest gentleman you know?'

Lando looked over and contemplated for just a moment and answered, 'Sir Patrick Stewart.'

'Nah, come on, man!' Kevin exclaimed. 'Who is the biggest gentleman you know?' He really emphasized those last few words.

Without hesitation, Lando responded, 'Mikey B.'

'That's right, my man,' Mikey laughed as he and Lando exchanged a high-five. Mikey then turned back to Kevin and pointed his finger. 'Busted, chump!'

'Ah, whatever,' Kevin threw his hands up in defeat. 'Juke on you guys.'

Kevin stood up and stormed off toward the beach.

'Kevin! Kevin!' Mikey called after him. 'It was just a joke. Kevin! Big Dog?' Mikey shook his head and stood to go after him, but Barbie caught his hand.

'Just let him go cool off,' she assured him. 'You know how sensitive he gets.'

Mikey stood there for a moment looking in the direction Kevin walked off. He sat back down beside Barbie and nodded his head. 'Yeah, he'll be okay.'

Suddenly, Robin and Avery broke out into an argument, an extremely heated argument.

'…whatever!' Robin had just emphasized some point I didn't hear.

These two people who were all snuggly and lovey-dovey just a second ago were now screaming as if they hated each other.

'Oh, was that supposed to make me mad like it does you because if so, it didn't work,' Avery shot back with pure venom. 'Maybe you should try asking me if I'm off my meds and see how that one works out for you.' She curled her lip and then a sudden calm came over her. In a tone so calm it was unsettling, she asked, 'So, I guess we need to figure out a time to talk.'

'Let me guess…break-up, take a break, take a step back…am I close?' Robin rattled off the list as if for the hundredth time.

'Nah, let's just keep going on like everything's great until one of us gets to the point that we just don't even like each other anymore,' Avery's words were sharp as knives, but if they affected Robin, I couldn't tell.

His voice dropped and through clenched teeth he said, 'Then go ahead and get it over with already.'

'No,' Avery held her hand up and shook her fist. 'I'm quite serious.' Her whole body was shaking.

'Just get it the hell over with!' Robin's composure was waning by the second. I saw his body begin to shake as well. This was not just some typical lovers spat, they were angry.

'What the hell?!' Avery crossed her arms. 'I said that is not what I am doing.'

'And, I'm saying get it over with already,' Robin shot back. 'I don't feel like arguing with you anymore.'

'Oh, okay, so YOU want to break it off then?' She turned abruptly putting her back to him.

'Of course not,' Robin's stance immediately softened. He reached over and placed his hands on her shoulders, 'but I'm sure that's where you're going with this. I don't have the energy for the fight, so just get it over with already.'

'I'm confused,' she said with her back still to him. She reached up with her right hand and placed it on his for a moment. Then she gently shrugged herself free and turned her back to him again. She was not crying, but her big brown eyes were welling up. 'I said that's not what I'm going to do, but you keep saying do it, and get it over with, so if that's what you want then you just do it.'

'Look, come talk to me whenever,' he shook his head and turned to walk away, 'but don't come overlooking for a fight because I won't.'

'I wasn't looking for a fight to begin with,' she reached out and touched his arm, a gesture that stopped him in his tracks. 'You are the one who is saying let's just get it over with so then just do it yourself.'

For a long excruciating moment, Robin just stood there, his back to her, and us. Everybody around the campfire was silent. Angela was, of course, writhing in her seat. Arguments between couples always made her nervous. Barbie and Lando just shook their heads. They gave each other a knowing look and just threw their hands in the air as if to say *what can you do?* Mikey on the other hand was enjoying the show. He had a big ear-to-ear grin on his face. He kept nudging Lando and pointing as if to say *this is going to be good.*

'So, are you going to do it or what?' Avery's voice was harsh. She crossed her arms and tapped her foot in the sand expecting an answer now.

Robin put his hands on his hips and exhaled hard. He turned to face her and replied, 'Look, I don't want to break up. I don't want to fight. I love you. And you can talk to me whenever you like. Was that clear enough?'

'Then why the fuck can't we just get along because I don't want to be in a relationship that is a constant battle,' Avery said, her voice escalating with each word.

'There is a lot of drama going on all around us,' Robin said. 'If we can just remember we love each other and get through these troubled times together and intact then we will be stronger than anything.' It was like watching an episode of *90210*. The tension was so palpable. Robin continued, 'I know where I want to be and that's standing at your side. I guess you just have to decide if it's what you want.'

'What I want is to be happy and enjoy life and not be constantly having arguments and constantly having to ask what's wrong, because you always act like things are irritating and that you are just going through the motions. I want to laugh and be able to smile.' Her last few words stung him the most. I could see it on his face.

'Honey, I want that for you, but life isn't always smiles. There are downs, too. There are things that when it comes to our relationship that aren't normal. That puts extra strain. Either we decide it's worth it to work together and move forward or it won't work.' He reached for her, but she did not budge.

'It's not about it being worth it as opposed to I can't handle it,' she said, her arms still firmly crossed.

'Lean on me instead of pushing me away and let me lend you strength,' he reached for her again.

'No, I tried opening up to you,' she shook her head and turned away from him, 'and look where that got us.'

349

Her head fell and her body began to quiver as she began to cry.

Robin, with mighty arms that looked like they could easily crush her, reached over and ever so gently embraced her in a loving hug. Her stance softened and she turned and fell into her arms. She allowed him to lead her away from the campfire and they disappeared into the tent several yards away.

'Well, that was exciting,' Mikey laughed. 'Damn, I knew I forgot something.'

'What's that?' Lando asked with a smile saying that he already knew the answer.

'The popcorn!' Mikey exclaimed. He and Lando broke out into laughter.

Barbie just shook her head and apologized to Angela and me. She said, 'I'm sorry about those two. I wish I could say this never happened before but...'

'This shit happens all the time,' Mikey finished her thought.

'Yeah, unfortunately,' Lando added. 'I just don't understand those two. They're toxic for each other. Avery by herself is a wonderful girl. Robin by himself is the best. But, put them together and sooner or later *BOOM*. Toxic.'

'Should we check on them?' Angela asked genuinely concerned.

'No,' Barbie answered. 'They'll be fine. This is what they do. The best thing we can do when they get like that is just to stay out of the way.'

'Yeah, that's a lesson Barbarella here learned the hard way,' Mikey teased.

'Nice,' Barbie smiled. In a quick move, she reached over and placed Mikey in a headlock. 'Maybe I just keep you like this for the rest of the night.'

With the side of his face firmly pressed against her left breast, Mikey responded with a smile, 'Yes, please.'

Barbie released him. 'Jerk,' she said, playfully shoving him away.

'Yeah, we've all been there,' Lando said as he threw another log onto the fire. 'It's just something they are going to have to figure out for themselves.'

Just then, a loud moan resonated throughout the camp. It was the unmistakable moaning of a woman in the throes of lovemaking. It was Avery's voice, and Avery was loud. Angela and I looked at each other. She was blushing. Barbie, Mikey, and Lando just shook their heads knowingly and laughed. The moaning went on for a few minutes then died out as suddenly as it began.

Lando tossed another log onto the fire and, shaking his head, said, 'The only thing more obnoxious than one of their arguments is their aggressive make up sex.'

'Yeah, but at least it's always quick aggressive make up sex,' Mikey added. We all began to laugh."

Anne paused and allowed herself a moment to smile reflecting on the moment.

"They were really a great bunch of kids," she said, her smile quickly fading. She looked over at Bret who was staring at her intently. "They didn't deserve what happened to them." She swallowed hard. "Angela didn't deserve that…." Her words trailed off.

Bret reached over and placed a comforting hand on her trembling shoulder. "Anne," the earnest tone of his voice caught her attention, "what happened?"

"We continued sitting around the fire talking," she continued. "Blossom came stumbling into the scene. She almost fell face first into the fire pit and would have if Mikey hadn't reached out and caught her. She plopped down next to Mikey and laid her head on his shoulder.

'What'd I miss?' She slurred, still obviously drunk.

'Well, you missed face-planting right into the fire there by a hair, you freaking idiot,' Lando teased her the way a big brother teases his little sister.

'Shut up,' was her response.

Mikey wrapped his arm around her shoulder and squeezed her. 'You went hard today, my girl,' he teased. 'The Terror Twins went hard!'

Mikey and Lando laughed. Barbie even smiled.

'I swear sometimes you girls worry me,' Barbie said. 'At least we're out here in the middle of nowhere where y'all can't hurt anyone but yourselves.'

'Whatever,' Blossom dismissed the teasing. Rubbing her nose, she asked, 'Did I hear Robin and Avery fighting?' We all nodded. 'What was it about this time?'

'Who knows,' Mikey replied. 'With those two it could have been Robin saying yellow when he should have said six, or something.'

'Typical,' Blossom said. Then she sat up and pointed at Angela. 'You are cute. What's your name?'

'Angela.'

'Blossom, you idiot,' Lando chimed in. 'You met her on the trail earlier. Jeez, you know you are killing brain cells when you drink that much? You know that, right?'

Blossom scoffed.

Mikey hugged up on her and said, 'Not my Blossom. Isn't that right, my girl?'

'Whatever,' she blew off the teasing again. It was clear that she was quite used to it.

'How did all of y'all meet?' I asked.

'We all met in school,' Lando said. 'Freshman year, we were all assigned to the same dorm. Mikey and I were roommates. Our room opened into a communal area with a TV and couch, and a couple of chairs. It connected to another room where Kevin and Robin were roomed together. Right across the hall the girls were set up in a similar fashion. Barbie and Buttercup were roommates, and Avery and Blossom were in the same room.'

'Yeah, we all just started hanging out and have been ever since,' Mikey added.

'Y'all seem pretty close,' Angela said. 'You really have a tight knit group.'

Barbie chuckled. 'It wasn't always like that.'

'Oh?'

'Yeah, as if you couldn't already tell, Avery can be a tough pill to swallow sometimes,' Barbie said, rubbing her chin.

'Holy shit that's an understatement,' Mikey interjected. 'In this corner, we have Avery the Man Killer, and, in this corner, we have Barbarella! Grab your popcorn, ladies and gentlemen, and let the hair-pulling and name calling begin!'

'Ding-ding, fight…!' Lando added with glee.

Ignoring their taunts and noticing the puzzled look on my face, Barbie explained, 'Avery and I kind of got into a fight once.'

'Once?' Mikey asked with fake exasperation.

'Okay, twice,' Barbie corrected herself. 'She can be a real bitch sometimes, but we're all good now.'

'Why did y'all get into a fight?' Angela asked.

'To be honest,' Barbie said, 'it was really over nothing. I think it had more to do with us all living together. You know, we are just kids and for the first time we're thrust into this situation where we are living with strangers and having to deal with all that comes with that. I think it was just some things that had built up over months and the reason why we ended up going at it was just an excuse, really.'

'So, why did it happen?' Angela persisted.

'Let's just say, we all know Robin and Avery's relationship is toxic, and sometimes it has a way of poisoning those around it and drawing them into their dysfunctional little soap opera,' Barbie said.

'You see how we responded to their fight earlier, right?' Mikey asked.

Angela and I both nodded.

'Yeah, the best thing to do is just stay out of it,' Blossom said. 'Don't get in the middle of it.'

'I learned that lesson the hard way,' Barbie said rubbing her chin.

'Don't sell yourself short, doll face,' Mikey said as he reached over and rubbed her chin playfully. 'You represented well.'

'I did get some good shots in, didn't I?' Barbie asked.

'Yeah, you did,' Mikey laughed and hugged her.

'But we're okay now,' Barbie reassured us. 'In fact, I'd say we're all closer than ever.'

'We're like family really,' Mikey added.

'You don't live with each other as long as we have and go through the things we have together and not form a strong bond,' Lando said.

'You mean like the bond you and Mikey form every night right before bedtime,' Blossom chimed in with a hic-up.

'Right,' Barbie added, 'so have y'all decided who's going to be the big spoon and who is going to be the little spoon tonight?'

'Lando is the big spoon,' Mikey answered without hesitation, 'always.'

'You know it,' Lando said hi-fiving Mikey.

Many minutes passed by before someone spoke again.

'So, Angela, Anne, as locals, what do y'all know about these woods?' Lando asked.

'Yeah, is it true they are haunted?' Mikey asked.

Angela and I gave each other a knowing look.

'Come on, don't hold out on us,' Mikey said. 'Are these woods haunted?'

'Is it true what they say about…about what happened here?' Barbie asked. 'Is there really a serial killer that roams these woods?'

'The Goatman…' Lando added. 'They call him the Goatman, the Goatman Killer of Azlewood.'

'Now that's just creepy,' Blossom said as she snuggled closer to Mikey. 'What the hell is a Goatman?'

'I hear that he's a demented hillbilly that lost his mind,' Mikey said. 'I don't know, he got cabin fever or something and went all cannibalistic and shit.'

'Cannibalistic?' Blossom asked.

'Yeah, he started killing people for food,' Mikey replied.

'That's disgusting!' Blossom face scrunched in disgust.

'That's not what I heard,' Barbie said.

'What did you hear?' Mikey asked, truly interested.

Barbie swallowed hard and replied, 'I heard he was once a family man. His family, wife, son, and baby girl were all killed in an accident somewhere in these woods and the incident drove him insane. Now, he prowls these woods looking for anyone that crosses his path so he can murder them and ease the pain he feels. The problem is every time he murders someone it doesn't ease his pain, it, I don't know, kind of feeds it and makes him even crazier. So, he'll never be sated and his lust for revenge will go on forever.'

'Accident,' Lando asked shaking his head, 'what kind of accident?'

'What?'

'You said his family was in an accident,' Lando explained. 'What kind of accident were they in?'

'I don't know,' Barbie answered honestly. 'A car accident, the children drowned, I don't know?'

'That makes no sense whatsoever,' Lando scoffed. 'Your family dying in an accident, though tragic, is by no way a reason for a man to go insane and go on a nearly two-year killing spree.'

'How do you know?' Barbie shot back. 'How do you know how you'd react to a tragedy like that?'

'I know I would simply lose it if my family were to die,' Blossom added. 'I'd simply lose it. No doubts.'

'Who knows why he went nuts,' Barbie continued to argue her point. 'Maybe he blames the locals for the accident. Maybe he blames the government. I don't know. I'm not crazy.'

'You sound crazy,' Mikey interjected followed by laughter.

'Dick,' Barbie smiled and playfully punched Mikey on the arm.

'Quick!' Mikey exclaimed as he cowardly leaned away from her jokingly. 'Quick, somebody help, she's crazy!'

'Do y'all want to know what I heard about the killer that stalks these woods?' Lando asked.

'What'd you hear, my man?' Mikey asked as he hugged it out with Barbie.

'I actually looked into it before we headed down here,' Lando said leaning forward. 'Do you know why they call him the Goatman?' Everyone just shook their head. 'They call him the Goatman because he's a satyr.'

'…a what?' Mikey's eyebrows came together when he asked, 'He's a what?'

'A satyr,' Lando answered with confidence.

Mikey and Barbie looked at each other skeptically. Then Mikey asked, 'What the fuck is a *salt-tear*?'

'He's a satyr,' Lando said again, 'from Greek Mythology. They are half man, half goat.'

'Which half…?' Blossom asked.

'From the waist up, he's a man,' Lando explained as he ran his hands from his stomach up to his neck, 'and from the waist down,' he lowered his hands down to his thighs, 'he has the legs of a goat.'

'Gross,' Blossom's nose crinkled.

'Greek Mythology,' Mikey shook his head, 'what the hell are you talking about?'

'I'm telling you,' Lando did not back down one bit. 'The Goatman is a satyr. I'll do you one better. I'm going to solve this mystery right here and now. Do y'all want a hot sports opinion?'

'…a what?' Angela asked.

'Just let him go, darling,' Mikey reassured, 'he's on a roll.'

'The Goatman Killer of Azlewood is a Cryptozoic!' Lando declared.

'Okay!' Barbie threw her hands in the air. 'Now, you're just making words up.'

'No, I'm not,' Lando replied. 'Let me ask you this. Have you ever heard of Bigfoot or the Jersey Devil, how about the Loch Ness Monster?' We all nodded. 'History is full of unexplained phenomenon. These creatures are just evolutionary freaks. They're mutants.'

'Like the X-Men?' Mikey asked.

'Yes!' Lando exclaimed.

'So, you're saying the Goatman has superpowers?' Blossom asked with all sincerity.

361

'Yes, no, I mean, I don't know,' Lando shook his head. 'What I mean is we're not talking about a man at all. What we are talking about is a creature not on the evolutionary charts that is wandering around these woods and is probably just as scared of us as we are of it.'

'But that doesn't match any of the reports on the news,' I said.

'News…?' The word was like bile in Lando's mouth. 'Do you believe everything you hear on the news?' He did not wait for a response. 'Don't you know the news is owned by Big Business and the government? Do you think they want the normal people of the world to know that there are actually living, breathing monsters roaming our backwoods, mountains, and swamps?'

'I'll tell you what I can't believe,' Mikey answered. 'I can't believe these words are coming out of my best friend's mouth right now. Bigfoot, satyr, holy shit! Next thing you are going tell me is that the Chupacabra is the Goatman's arch nemesis.'

'The goatsucker…?' Lando shook his head. 'No, he lives much further south than this, closer to the boarder.'

'Oh my god,' Mikey turned to Barbie, 'help! My man here has been abducted and replaced by an alien or a robot, or something!'

We all started laughing. Everyone was laughing hysterically, everyone except Lando. He sat back down next to Angela, utterly defeated.

'Satyr, I'm telling you, I'm telling you,' He repeated. 'Mark my words, the Goatman is a satyr.'

He was so cute.

'So, now you've heard our theories. What can you or Angela tell us about what y'all know about the Goatman?' Barbie asked.

I shook my head, 'Sorry, I don't know any more than what y'all do. I only know what the news tells me.' I shot a playful smile in Lando's direction. He playfully shrugged. 'However,' I continued, 'Angela does have an interesting story that may shed a little light on these woods being haunted theory.'

Angela's eyes went wide.

'Really,' Mikey asked the question that was on all their minds, 'will you tell us?'

'Yes, please,' Barbie added as she placed her hands in front of her ample breasts in a prayer fashion.

'It's really not a big deal,' Angela said shyly. 'It's just something that happened to me when I was a girl. Y'all wouldn't even believe it to hear it.'

'Oh, now you can't have a build up like that and not tell us the story,' Mikey said.

'Yes, please, please, please…,' Barbie pleaded. 'Please, tell us your story.'

'Yeah,' Lando nudged her gently, 'it can't be any worse than mine.' He chuckled, and she smiled.

Angela shot me a look as if to say *I'm going to kill you for this.*

'Ok, I'm going to tell you this how I remember it, so it's not my fault if y'all don't believe me,' Angela said, straightening up in her chair. 'Wow, this goes back a few years. I think I was like seven or eight years old. Our grandfather…'

'Poppy George,' I interjected.

'Yes,' Angela nodded, a smile spreading across her face. I could tell she was having a fond memory of our poppy. 'Yes,' she continued, 'Poppy George brought Anne and me along with him to go fishing at Eagle Mountain. Poppy knew these woods well, and he knew the best spots for fishing. On that day, he took us deep, deep into the woods. I remember him telling us stories about the woods and the town of Glen Haven. Do you remember what he said?' She asked me.

'Some of it,' I answered. 'I remember him saying things like never taking from the land what can never be replaced. Things like that. Oh, I also remember him talking about the history of Glen Haven and its relation to these woods. I remember him saying that the woods themselves were not inherently evil and that if you respect the spirits of the woods, the spirits will leave you be, or something like that. I don't remember exactly. It was a long time ago.'

'Poppy George was part Native American,' Angela continued, 'a descendant of the Caddo tribe which used to be indigenous to these parts many years ago. He knew a lot of things about the land, and he knew a lot about how to navigate it. Well, on this day, he took us with him to go fishing. He shook us awake before the sun had even come up. We drove into the woods until the paved road became a dirt road and then we drove until there was no road at all. We walked the rest of the way. It seemed like hours before we arrived at his special fishing spot. We walked along a trail he said had been there for a long, long time.

When we arrived at his special fishing spot, Poppy provided us with poles and taught us how to bait the hooks and how to cast them into the water. Before every cast, he would recite a prayer. I don't know what it was he was saying. I could not understand the language. I just assumed it was some sort of Native American trick. A few hours in, Poppy and Anne between them had already caught five fish. I, on the other hand, had caught none. As you can imagine, I got bored. I remember setting my pole down and wandering the shoreline picking flowers. To this day, I can't tell you why I did it, but for some reason I wandered off back up the trail.

I was fascinated by the woodland surroundings, the trees towering overhead, the dense brush framing the pathway, the ambient sound of life all around. However, as I walked along the path, I suddenly had this overwhelming sense that I was not alone. The woods seemed to grow darker, colder. I started to become afraid.

I continued along the path. On the side of the path was a pile of stones. I didn't recall seeing this wall of stones when we were walking to my Poppy's fishing spot. They were stacked very neatly. They were large, smooth stones. They were stacked and made a little wall about three feet high and, I don't know, five or six feet long, I guess. I became fascinated by the little stone wall. I reached out and touched it. Its surface was ice cold. I ran my fingers along the smooth face of each stone until I came to the center. Right in the middle of the wall there was a stone missing, but the hole was not empty. There was something inside.

I don't know what possessed me, but I reached in and touched something, something warm, something alive. Startled, I jumped backward. What happened next was so terrifying; y'all are not going to believe me.'

'What happened?' Barbie asked.

'I really don't know how to explain it,' Angela replied. She rubbed her forehead. 'The thing in the wall, whatever it was, started to, I don't know exactly how to say this, but it started to breathe. I sat there, terrified, yet transfixed. Right in the center of this wall there seemed to be a mouth, and it was breathing.'

'Holy shit!' Mikey exclaimed. 'What was it?'

'I don't know,' Angela answered honestly. 'For years, I've gone over this incident over and over in my mind, and to this day I cannot tell you exactly what it is I saw that day.'

'What happened then?' Blossom asked.

'I stood there staring at this mouth,' Angela continued. 'I have no idea how long I stood there, but I just stood there, staring. Looking back on it now, I think I was hypnotized by this thing. I just stood there looking at this mouth and it just breathed. I began to have this out-of-body experience. I was hovering just above and looking down at myself staring at this wall. A wave of fear poured over me and I began to scream. Suddenly, I started, as if awaking from a dream and I was back, standing on the path and staring at the wall. The mouth was gone.

Beyond scared now, I ran back up the path, back the way I came. I ran and ran as fast as I could. I had run so far so fast that I was sure by now I should have been back to my Poppy's fishing spot. I was scared, more frightened than I've ever been in my life. I looked back and the trail ran on until disappearing on the horizon. I looked forward to being greeted by the same sight. I thought I might be losing my mind.

I cried and continued running. I ran and ran, and I ran until finally I collapsed on the ground in a heap, utterly exhausted. I curled up into a small ball, shaking and crying and I must have passed out from exhaustion."

'Oh my god,' Blossom exclaimed, 'what happened next?'

'I don't really know,' Angela replied. 'When I woke up, I was in a hospital bed with my parents and a doctor standing over me. The doctor said I had suffered severe shock and severe dehydration along with a few minor cuts and bruises from my fall. He said I should easily recover given time and rest.

My parents stood there with tears in their eyes. They kissed me, hugged me, and told me how grateful they were that I was alright. Then they scolded me for wandering off and getting lost in the woods. They told me I had somebody to apologize to, and they left the room along with the doctor. Sitting in a chair by the window was my Poppy George.

He smiled warmly at me, stood up, and came to stand next to my bed. *Had yourself quite a scare didn't you*, he said. I nodded. *Do you know what it is you saw?* I shook my head. He stared back down at me for a moment, rubbing his chin. I feel like he was searching for the right words to say, the right words that would not frighten me as much. When he began to speak again, his posture changed. It was as if a heavy weight now resided on his hunched shoulders.

Honey, there are things in this world that are unexplainable, things both terrible and great, he said. *There are certain places in this world where the realm of mortals and the realm of spirits intersect and in places such as this mortal man must tread very lightly and with great care. Do you understand what I am saying?* I nodded. *Honey, you were very fortunate today. Here, I want you to have something.* He reached inside the collar of his shirt and pulled a necklace up from around his neck. *This is a totem. Do you know what a totem is?* I shook my head. *A totem*, he explained, *is a talisman, a charm that bestows upon its wearer protection. I want you to have this totem and may it bring you the same protection it has me for oh so many years.* And he handed me this.'

Angela pulled her necklace out from under her T-shirt. It's a leather strap necklace with a small angry looking bird carved out of wood dangling from it.

'What is that?' Lando asked pointed to the small carving.

'It's my totem,' Angela replied. 'It's what the Caddo called a Thunderbird. My Poppy gave it to me that day and he said it's supposed to protect me or give me strength or something.'

'It's pretty,' Blossom said, reaching over to touch it.

'So, does it work?' Barbie asked.

'I guess so,' Angela replied. 'Nothing bad has ever happened to me since then.'

'That's an understatement,' I scoffed. 'Sister, you live one semi-charmed kind of life.'

'What do you mean by that?' Angela asked, taken aback by my comment.

'Oh, don't get me started,' I retorted. 'Straight A's, honor role, class president, full ride to any college of your choice, shall I go on?'

'Hey, I worked hard for all of that,' she shot back.

I can't explain why I was acting the way I was. Maybe it was because of all the attention Angela was getting from telling her story. But that didn't make sense because it was I that suggested she tell it in the first place. Whatever the reason for my sudden jealousy, I didn't hold back.

'Worked hard?' I snapped and made a gesture with my hands as if giving a hand job. 'Is that what we're calling it now?'

'You bitch,' Angela retorted.

'I love a good catfight this time of year!' Mikey broke the tension with his signature mirth.

'May I take a look at your totem?' Barbie asked.

'Yeah, yeah, me too?' Blossom added.

'Sure,' Angela replied without hesitation. She removed her necklace and passed it over to Blossom. Angela shot me another glare then stood up and straightened her shorts and shirt. 'I'm going to go for a walk,' she said.

'Would you like some company?' Lando asked.

'No,' Angela snapped a little harsher than she probably intended. Her anger for me unintentionally was extending toward Lando. 'No,' she repeated, this time her tone was much softer. 'I just need to cool off for a bit and simmer down.'

Angela shot me one last glare then stormed off toward the beach. Lando watched her as she walked away. He caught me staring at him and quickly turned his gaze away. While Barbie and Blossom cooed over Angela's necklace, Mikey lit up a joint and began passing it around.

'So, what brings y'all to Glen Haven and Azlewood?' I asked after a bout of coughing. 'I mean it's not exactly what you would call a summer destination.'

Lando took a deep drag off the joint before passing it back to Mikey. He held it in for an excruciatingly long time before exhaling without even the slightest hint of a cough.

'Curiosity, I would say,' he answered with a billow of smoke. 'See, Mikey and I have always been fascinated with hauntings and alien abductions and possessions, things like that. Back in the dorm, we watch all those ghost-hunting and sightings of the unexplained shows that come on late at night. Well, on one of those shows…,' he paused for a moment, trying to recall. 'Mike, do you recall what show we saw that on?' Mikey's eyes were glazed over, and he had the widest smile spreading across his face. Lando asked again, 'Mike! Hey, hophead! Mikey, what show was that we saw Glen Haven on?'

'I don't know,' Mikey replied through a fit of giggles. 'Oh wait! I do remember.' He straightened up and suddenly got serious. 'It was *The Top 5 Most Terrifying Places to Visit in America*.' Mikey took another drag then passed the joint on to Barbie who was still examining Angela's totem. 'Yeah, one was somewhere up north, some haunted summer camp or something,' Mikey explained. 'Another was in Illinois somewhere, I can't quite remember the name of the town, but it was some small town where a bunch of babysitters were murdered. Real downer shit, man.'

'Yes, another one was on some street where this guy was abducting and murdering the neighborhood kids and all the parents got together and took him out,' Lando added.

'And the other one was an island community that was being terrorized by sharks,' Mikey said. 'Fucking sharks…,' he trailed off.

'So, yeah,' Lando continued, 'so, anyway, the last place on the list was Glen Haven, or more specifically these woods…Azlewood. It talked about the Goatman killings and how this area has had a long history of macabre and supernatural unexplained occurrences.'

'Yeah, is it true that nearly the entire community was wiped out back in the late 1800s by a mass murdering?' Mikey asked. 'Or that there have been no less than seventy-five unexplained disappearances in the last century alone?'

I just shook my head. 'Like I told y'all earlier,' I said. 'I don't know any more than what the news reports say. Y'all probably know more about this stuff than I do.'

'But Angela's story…?' Lando asked leaning forward. 'If it's true, and I have no reason to believe she's not telling the truth, if it's true, then surely these woods must be haunted, or at least some kind of nexus point for the supernatural.'

I just shook my head. 'Yeah, I just don't know anything about it,' I said. I was beginning to worry about Angela. I looked over my shoulder but could not see through the darkness where she went.

'Will you two stop pestering her with your voodoo bullshit,' Barbie scolded as she tossed the last nub of joint into the fire.

'Hey!' Mikey exclaimed with his hands spread out wide in protest. 'That was still good!'

Barbie shot him a look I assumed he'd seen many times before because his protest was short lived. He just pulled another joint from his pocket and smiled.

'Here's what happened,' Barbie said reaching over to touch me on the shoulder. 'We are all on our way to Padre and the whole ride down, these two fucks won't shut up about the *haunted woods of Glen Haven* and how we have to stop and check them out. Believe me, if you hear these two wailing and complaining like a couple of five-year olds with skinned knees for a few hundred miles, you'd give in too. So, we all agreed that we'd stop over for a night and visit the haunted woods.' She made quote signs with her fingers and rolled her eyes.

'I smell pot,' said a pixie-like voice from behind.

We all turned to see Buttercup wrapped in her beach towel and sluggishly shuffling over to join the circle.

'There she is!' Mikey exclaimed. He jumped up and hugged her, an embrace that lifted her up off the ground.

'Get off!' She protested, as she giggled.

She sat down on Mikey's right side. He put his arms around Buttercup and Blossom and pulled them close and with a big smile he declared, 'My girls!'

Barbie reached over and pulled a twig out of Buttercup's hair. 'Really?' She scoffed, tossing the twig aside. 'Did you pass out in a bush? You look like hell, darling.'

'Bitch,' Buttercup said playfully as she shot her friend the bird.

'Let's do this, girls,' Mikey said lighting the second joint.

As they began passing the joint around, I waved off my turn. I stood up and brushed myself off and headed off toward the beach. 'I'm going to go check on Angela,' I told them.

As I walked along the path that led to the beach, the night got darker as the light of the campfire disappeared in the distance behind me. When I got to the beach, the lake was calm. The night sky was clear with a billion stars all around. The moon was full, just like it is tonight. With no wind to speak of, the waters barely rippled. I did not immediately see anybody. For a moment, I was concerned. As I walked along the shore for a little way my concern was instantly replaced by confusion, hurt feelings, and ultimately anger.

Up ahead, not far from a wooden lifeguard stand, standing knee deep in the calm waters of the lake, silhouetted by the moon's light, I could see two bodies embraced. They were kissing and groping each other passionately. I swallowed hard when I realized they were Angela and Kevin. Stunned, I just stood there staring. They were oblivious to my presence, and I think that upset me even more. So, caught up in my own drama, I didn't hear the footsteps coming up behind me.

'This is not surprising, really,' I started at the sound of Lando's deep voice. He came up to stand beside me and was watching with the same contempt I had. 'Sorry, I didn't mean to startle you. I just wanted to bring you this.' He handed me Angela's totem necklace. 'I figured I better bring it over before one of the girls decided to claim it as theirs.'

I took the necklace from him. Our eyes went back to Angela and Kevin.

'I'm sorry if this hurts you,' he explained gesturing toward them. 'This is so typical Kevin. He loves to play the victim but, in the end, he has no code when it comes to girls. You see, women are just pawns to him, pawns in his little game of getting laid as much as possible without any regard for the feelings of others, least of all those around him.'

'You have no idea,' I said as I turned and walked away. Lando walked along beside me as we made our way down the beach. 'She does this to me all the time,' I said aloud. 'My whole life, she has always one upped me every single step of the way. I mean, do you have any idea what it's like to live in someone's shadow?' Lando nodded. 'My whole life, Angela is the pretty one, Angela is the smart one, and Angela is going to be anything she wants to be. Jesus, sometimes they treat me like I don't even exist.'

'Don't I know it,' Lando replied. 'Try being friends with a guy that will try to fuck your mother if you leave them alone together too long. Every girlfriend I've had in the last three-and-a-half years, hell, every girl I just talked too has been hit on and/or bedded by my so-called best friend. It's almost like another part of his game. You know, I get it, you're a good-looking guy and women dig you, but you don't have to be a complete douchebag about it. You don't have to have all the women in the world.'

We walked along the beach for a long while, leaving the campsite and the source of our ire way back behind us. As we walked along, I absently tied Angela's necklace around my neck. Lando and I walked a little further before sitting down on the soft sand. For a while we continued complaining about our perceived nemeses. Then, at some point, and I cannot tell you who made the first move because I don't remember, but at some point, we started to make out.

I think we just took comfort in each other's arms. We both needed to feel something in that moment other than anger, disappointment, and jealousy. We needed to feel wanted. One thing led to another, and we began to make love. He was so sweet. He rolled up his shirt and placed it under my head. Lando was a big guy, much portlier than the guys I usually hook up with, but in that moment, I didn't care. I just needed him, and he needed me.

The moment was fleeting. He lay on top of me breathing heavily. I wiped his sweaty, curly hair out of my face and that's when I saw him. Standing directly over us was a giant man. He was holding something prone right above us. I barely could make out that awful mask he wore, a mask carved out of the skull of some long dead animal.

'Oh, God…!' I screamed.

'What is it?' Lando asked leaning up on his hands.

That son of a bitch brought that object he was holding down with all his might and impaled Lando through the back. The impact of the blow slammed Lando's skull into mine. I was instantly knocked unconscious.

I have no idea how long I was out. When I came to, my head was pounding, but as my senses came back to me, I suddenly realized the true horror of my situation. Lando was still lying on top of me, and he was dead. I tried in vain to move him off me, but he was too heavy. His limp body barely budged when I tried with all my might to push him away. I could see the object used to murder him still impaled in his back. It was a metal pole, like a fence post. Oh god, the wound was spilling blood out everywhere, all over me.

Panic started to set in when suddenly I heard them. I heard the screams coming from the campsite. I have no idea what was happening and the images my mind came up with were chilling me to my very core. I was helpless. All I could do was lie there and listen to the terrified and dying screams of those innocent college kids. Then, I thought about Angela, and I knew I had to move.

Adrenaline must have kicked in because suddenly I had the strength to move Lando's large, limp body just enough so that I could squirm out from under him. I winced in pain as I suddenly realized that the pole that killed Lando had gone all the way through his body and the sharp end had in fact cut into me. It pierced my side. I could feel it scrapping up against my rib. I began to cry. The pain, the realization of the wound was overwhelming, but I heard more screams coming from the campsite. I had to do something.

God, it hurt so much, but I gave it everything I had. I was able to position my right foot onto Lando's side and I pushed for all I was worth. As Lando's body rolled away, the sharp end of the pole gashed and tore away a nice chuck of meat. I screamed through clenched teeth.

I laid there for a moment to catch my breath. Realizing precious too many moments had passed; I drug myself to my feet. Even in the dark, I could see my naked body covered in blood. As fast as I could move, I gathered my blood-soaked clothes. I pulled on my shorts and T-shirt. I grabbed Lando's shirt and tied it tight around my midsection to help stop the bleeding from my wound. I look down at Lando's motionless naked body. Seeing him lying there with that metal pole rammed through him; I was overcome with a bout of nausea. I threw up, an act which only served to remind me of my own wound. The retching caused muscle spasms which then sent waves of pain all throughout my body.

As I wiped the vomit from my lips something else suddenly occurred to me. I suddenly noticed that I did not hear any screaming anymore. I cannot tell you to this day what was worse, hearing the screams, or not hearing them. With my hand placed firmly against my side, I stumbled back up the beach, back toward the campsite. I dreaded what I would find.

As I limped slowly into the campsite, the gash in my side sending waves of pain throughout my body with each excruciating step, I mentally and emotionally tried to prepare myself for the worst. I was nowhere near prepared for what I found.

As I stumbled past the first tent, lying on the ground in a heap of blood and gore was Robin. His body had been impossibly bent backward and broken in half in the middle. His head rested by the heels of his feet. His face expression locked in a twisted mix of horror and pain. What could have possibly done this to him? Robin was in great shape and very strong. What kind of monster could have overpowered him in such a fashion?

Suddenly my senses were overwhelmed by the putrid smell of burning flesh. I gingerly made my way over to the campfire. Lying on her back, lifeless, was Barbie. Her throat had been cut and gouts of blood were still pouring forth from the wicked wound. The flames of the fire crackled and another waft of burning flesh engulfed me. As hard as I tried, I could not hold it in any longer. I threw up.

As I sat there on my hands and knees, each wretch caused my wound to spasm. My senses were being overwhelmed and I nearly passed out from the pain. Wiping my lips, I glanced over at the fire. Somebody's body had been thrown into it. Their remains were a blacked, charred mass. I could tell by the feet which lay just outside the licking kiss of the flames that the victim was male. Mikey, I assumed.

At this point, I was completely numb, physically, and emotionally. I struggled back to my feet. A few yards beyond the campfire I found what was left of Blossom and Avery. They were lying in a heap, Blossom on top of Avery. They had been hacked to pieces. Something was very odd by the way they lay there. Avery hands were wrapped around Blossom's arms in a death grip. It was almost as if Avery was using the smaller woman as a shield or something. It apparently didn't help. Their bodies were mutilated with dozens of deep gashes and cuts. Poor Blossom's head was nearly cut clean from her neck. It was only clinging on by a thin strip of flesh. I felt another wave of nausea wash over me. I didn't even fight the urge.

When I was done, I saw something lying on the ground right at the perimeter of the campfire's light. I limped over to discover Buttercup's remains. A large beach towel was wrapped around her small frame. Her skull was severally fractured. I could see bone fragments and brain matter matted in her dark hair. The tree trunk next to her body showed signs of chipping and trauma. My god, it appeared as if someone had wrapped her in the towel and then smashed her against the trunk of that tree over and over. I fell to my knees, and I began to weep.

Suddenly, panic washed over me. Where was Angela?

'Angela!' In my mind I shouted her name, but my voice was horse. My body was not responding like it should. 'Angela!' I cried out again, but my voice was barely audible above the crackling and snapping of the campfire. My god, where was she. Had she gotten away, or…or...?

Once again, I struggled back to my feet. Making my way back the way I came, back through the carnage, the slaughter, I limped back toward the pathway that led to the beach. I was trying to run, but my physical wounds and emotional trauma were keeping me from moving any faster than a brisk limp. Nearly falling twice, I managed to make my way back to the beach. I headed in the direction where I had seen Angela and Kevin earlier. I could see the lifeguard stand silhouetted in the distance, a black shadowy beacon calling out to me in the darkness.

As I drew nearer to the stand, I suddenly found it hard to breathe as another wave of shock and fear came over me. I screamed. I screamed as loud as I could, but I no longer had a voice. I fell down face first into the sand and cried. I no longer felt the pain from the gash in my side. My body began to wretch uncontrollably. My mind was wiped of all rational thought. The only thing I could even see, hear, or feel in that moment was all encompassing grief. Utter madness threatened to consume me.

Kevin's hands were nailed to the wooden legs of the lifeguard stand. He hung there, crucified. His stomach

383

had been sliced open crossways just below his ribcage and all his insides had spilled out into a gory mess onto the sand. As my eyes searched the lifeguard stand, my gaze came to rest upon the image that finally broke me. Sitting there in the seat, placed with great care, was the severed head of my baby sister. Blood dripped down between the cracks of the wood and splashed upon her estranged body. Lying on the sand, just beyond Kevin's guts, was a woman's headless body. It was Angela's headless body. The waves of the lake washed in and carried away with it the pools of blood that were draining from her lifeless body.

The world lost all meaning to me. I lay there in a heap of hysteria, whimpering and shivering like a child in the dark.

I really have no recollection of how long I laid there, but it was that sound that brought me back to my senses, that awful sound. It was like an animal call, but it wasn't an animal. Don't ask me how I knew, I just did. It was like the baaing of sheep and the whimpering of an infant rolled into one haunting sound. It was impossible to tell just where that sound was coming from, but it was off in the distance, and it was coming from the darkness of the woods.

It seemed to be coming from quite a distance away. Then suddenly, it was coming from the campsite. A few moments later, that awful sound was coming from the direction where I had left Lando's body. My head started to swim. I fought through the dizziness and got back on my feet. I wasn't even consciously in control of myself. I really don't know how to explain it other than I was afraid, and I was fleeing from that sound.

I ran through the woods, not having any idea where I was headed or even which direction I was going. As I moved as quickly as I could through the darkness, Angela's totem bounced off my chest and hit me in the mouth, cutting my lower lip. I started to remove the necklace with plans of tossing it aside, but I stopped myself. I don't know why. As I continued into the darkness, I tucked the totem into my shirt.

That horrible sound was still echoing in the night, but it was much further away now. The further from the campsite I fled, the further away the sound was. I stumbled blindly for what seemed like hours. Far past exhaustion, I can't even begin to tell you what kept me going. It must have been adrenaline.

I suddenly realized that I couldn't hear that awful sound anymore. This did not comfort me. Azlewood was cast in a thick shadow that was almost blinding. If it weren't for the starlight and full moon up above seeping in through cracks in the branches, then it would have been. I suddenly had a very scary feeling. I was alone in this darkness, but I wasn't alone. Somewhere out there, out in that black was another…the man, the thing that murdered those poor kids, that monster that murdered my sister.

For a moment, I slumped against a large tree and began to cry. I reached up to place my hand on my chest and my fingers fell upon Angela's totem. I felt its hard texture, through my shirt, my fingers running over the grooves of the carving. A sense of calm came over me, but it was fleeting. Noises of things moving in the brush, in the trees above, in the darkness brought me back to the reality of my situation. I darted off into the black once again.

I have no idea how, but I found my way to the main road. There I collapsed on the side of the road until a passing car stopped. The man driving the car was a gas station attendant on his way home after his late-night shift. After seeing my wound, he called for an ambulance and the police. Thinking I was safe, if even for a moment, I let the darkness take me. I passed out, finally overcome by my experience.

When I awoke, I was lying down in the back of an Ambulance. Flashing red lights poured in through the windows of the ambulance. I could see police cars and officers outside the back just as a paramedic closed the back door to the ambulance. The loud sound of activity from outside was instantly muffled. It took me a moment to realize where I was. A paramedic was sitting next to me. I winced in pain as she stuck me with a needle which was attached to a long tube that led to an I.V. The pain and aches of my wound and numerous cuts and bruises shot through me. I started to whimper and squirm.

'Just relax, honey,' the paramedic said, as she rubbed my arm. Her voice was calming. 'You've been through a lot.'

I lay back, but suddenly, the night's events came flooding back into my mind. 'Angela!' I screamed. I sat up quickly, nearly tearing the needle right out of my arm. 'Angela!' I pleaded. 'Where is she? Where's my sister?'

Gently but firmly, she clasped me by the shoulders and coaxed me back into a lying position. 'Please, honey, try to remain calm,' she said. Her voice was quiet and calm. 'You have suffered a deep cut in your abdomen. I have the bleeding under control, but if you keep squirming, we'll have to start back at square one. You are severely dehydrated as well. Try to relax as much as possible and let the fluids rehydrate you.'

For a moment, I struggled against her. 'You don't understand,' I protested. 'Angela is still there!'

She pulled out a syringe and gave me a shot in the arm. 'This should help calm you down,' she said. 'Try to get some rest, sweetie.'

'But…but she's still there,' I repeated as I suddenly became very groggy.

As the injection started to take effect, the events of the night suddenly came rushing back to my mind. I saw them. I saw them all…murdered. As the darkness came to me, the last image I saw before drifting off to sleep was the severed head of my baby sister."

*****

Anne looked out the driver-side window, her breath fogging the glass. For a long moment, they were both quiet. The only sound was the thudding of rain drops on the car's roof, hood, and windows. Bret swallowed hard and contemplated whether he should even say what he was thinking.

"Jesus," he whispered. His eyes darted left and right as he desperately searched for words.

When he was ready to speak again, he turned to face Anne and was met by a kiss, a deep, hard kiss. Anne pressed her lips against his so hard that it was painful.

"Please," she said leaning in closer and closer. "Please, don't talk. No more talking. Not right now." She climbed over to the passenger seat and positioned herself on his lap facing him. "Just help me feel something else right now. Make love to me?"

Bret wanted to protest, but he could not. Anne represented something he had always desired and, in that moment, as seemingly inappropriate as it was, he could not possibly deny his want, or Anne's. Her nimble, lithe fingers reached down and unfastened his belt. In one apt movement, she had unbuttoned his jeans and released his member. For the next few minutes, their passions took over and the memories of her horrible tale floated away.

Afterwards, for a few long moments they just sat there holding each other. Anne resting her head on Bret's chest. She was listening to his heartbeat. It was racing. The sound of it gave her comfort. For a moment, she smiled. However, her moment of comfort was fleeting, as the memories of her tale came flooding back. Anne eased herself off Bret and rolled back over into the driver's seat. She started the car's engine, then turned the defrost on. All the windows of the small car were now completely fogged over.

Bret pulled his jeans back on and exhaled a deep breath. He looked over at Anne who smiled back at him. He smiled. Then, she pointed at something on the floorboard. Bret followed her gaze to what she was pointing at. It was her shorts and panties. He quickly reached down to retrieve them and handed them back to her.

"Sorry," he said as his face blushed.

"Sorry?" Anne laughed, taking her garments from him, and showing great dexterity, pulled them back on with little effort. "Honey," she said leaning over to kiss him on his rosy cheek, "we're way past being shy now."

Bret smiled. He wanted to tell her something but stopped himself short. Anne caught it and asked, "What? What is it you want to say?"

In that moment, he felt a connection between them, a bond that allowed him to open up. He decided not to hold back. She had been so open and honest with him that in that moment he decided he could not be any less to her.

"I was in love with you, Anne," he said as he stared out at the rain-soaked woods. Anne's head snapped around. He swallowed once more and continued. "I was so in love with you. Of course, you didn't know it. There was no way for you to know it. Angela knew though. The whole time we were dating, she knew. In the end, it's what broke us up. We never even had a fight or a coarse word between us. She just knew I could never love her the way I was in love with you."

"But…but…" Anne repeated to herself several times before she could articulate her thoughts. "But we barely know each other."

"I know," Bret said. "It's definitely something I can't explain. Do you remember the very first time we ever saw each other?"

Anne's brow crinkled. Then she smiled and answered, "Yes, it was at Jack Smith's house…the bonfire party senior year. Y'all were freshmen. Angela brought you over and introduced us."

Bret smiled weakly. "No, that was the night Sam Crawford nearly took my head off because I accidentally scuffed his new snake-skinned boots."

"Oh, right," Anne chuckled. She quickly straightened up. "Sorry about that."

"No, no," he shook his head. "You saved me a beat down by talking him into throwing me into the creek that ran outback of Jack's house instead."

"That's right," she smiled. Then her brow furrowed once again. "For the life of me I can't remember what happened after that."

Bret sighed. "You rewarded that Neanderthal by sleeping with him in the back of Kyle Crawford's pickup truck within earshot of the rest of the party."

"Oh, that's right," she said as the memories came flooding back. She started to laugh but her outburst was short-lived as she noticed Bret's sullen expression.

"The very first time I ever saw you, it was two years earlier," he continued. As he spoke, he wrung his hands in his lap. "I was skating around my block to go to the skate park and then I saw you. You rode by me on a ten-speed, your long hair flipping behind you in the wind. You were wearing the shortest shorts I had ever seen and a half-shirt tank top that hugged your body and rippled in the breeze. The way the sun shined down on your tanned skin; it gave you a kind of glow.

You looked like a goddess." He smiled. "My teenage pants were going crazy." He straightened up in his seat and continued. "You said hello to me as you zoomed by me and my board. I was in such a la-la daze that I swerved out into the middle of the street, not looking where I was going, and was suddenly struck hard from behind. Angela was riding up after you on her bike and my dumbass and board swerved right out in front of her. She couldn't stop in time, and we tumbled to the ground in a heap.

Most girls her age would have been a blubbering mess after a collision like that, but not Angela. She was so strong, even back then. Even with two skinned knees she did not shed a single tear. She was more concerned about how I was doing, and apologetic. You zipped back and as you rode in circles around us, asked if we were okay. Physically stunned by the incident and mentally stunned by your beauty, I could only muster a nod. Angela assured you she was fine, and you got a good laugh at our expense before you zipped off on your way. That was the day Angela and I became friends, and that was the day I fell in love with a goddess named Anne."

Anne smiled, and then frowned. "I remember that day, but I had no idea that was you. Sorry."

Bret shook his head. "Why would you even bat an eyelash my way? You were a goddess in high school. I was just some skinny little kid with pimples struggling with seventh grade Texas History. Angela helped me with that, too. She helped me pass Mrs. Nutt's Texas History class and I rewarded her by incessantly pelting her with questions about her gorgeous older sister."

Anne started to laugh and Bret, despite himself, started to laugh as well.

"Do you still have her totem?" Bret asked.

"Yes," Anne replied as she pulled the small carving out from under her shirt and let it hang.

"May I?" Bret gestured toward the small wooden figurine.

Anne hesitated, but only for a moment. "Of course," she answered. She pulled the necklace up over her head and handed it to Bret.

For a few moments, Bret studied the little figurine. It was a majestic bird carved out of solid wood. The figurine itself was only about two inches long and maybe an inch wide, but for something so small it was quite detailed. Bret could see that whoever made this trinket took great care in doing so. He could make out every single feather every single minute detail.

"It's beautiful," Bret declared.

"Yes, it is," Anne said absently as she lit another cigarette. She cracked the window and blew a wisp of smoke out into the rain. "Our grandfather gave it to

Angela. He said it was a charm or something. He said it would protect her." She scoffed. "I only keep it around because it meant so much to Angela."

"Right," Bret replied still running his fingers over the wooden figurine. "She had also told me that story. The one about the day she got lost in the woods. She loved this necklace. She was such a sweet girl, an innocent...,"

Bret did not finish his sentence. He closed his eyes and clasped the totem in his fist and squeezed as hard as he could. He squeezed until the pain in his palm forced him to stop. He opened his eyes and his hand. The wooden figurine had left pink and red marks on his palm. The point at where the bird's beak had been had even drawn blood.

"You're bleeding," Anne observed. "Here..." She reached over and pulled a napkin from the glove compartment.

Bret sat the necklace down on the seat between his legs and let Anne take his hand into her hands. She applied a little pressure and wiped the small amount of blood away from his hand.

"They never caught the son of a bitch," Bret spoke through clinched teeth.

"What?" Anne was startled not just by Bret's sudden change in demeanor but by the question itself.

"The police, they never caught that son of a bitch, the son of bitch that murdered Angela," Bret clarified. "They act like we are stupid, but we know the truth. We all know the truth. Anybody who has lived in this shit-hole town knows the truth."

Anne leaned back in her seat. She was not frightened or angry or even startled now. She sat there and listened and observed.

"Angela wasn't even the first," Bret continued, "and she wasn't even the last. There was that writer, what was his name?"

"Ross," Anne answered.

"That's right, Ross, Ross Lawry," Bret said. He was becoming quite agitated. "Ross Lawry, a famous writer, was murdered and they never caught the person who did it. There was also some poor teenager last year. That poor girl's father was massacred right in front of her, and they never caught the son of bitch responsible for that one either. I know there have been others too. Someone should do something about this. Somebody must stop the killing. They're all connected. Someone has to find this son of a bitch and stop him!"

"What would you do if you could get your hands on him?" Anne asked. Her voice was so calm, so relaxed. She surprised even herself with how calm she sounded.

"What was that?" He asked. Her demeanor was so infectious Bret could feel its soothing calmness.

"What would you do if you could get your hands on the son of a bitch that murdered Angela?" She asked.

Bret sat staring at her. Then he smiled and shook his head. He even managed to chuckle a little.

"Wow, girl," he said as his smile grew bigger. "I almost took your question as more than a hypothetical."

"Amuse me," Anne smiled back, a wickedly delightful grin that gave him goosebumps. "What would you do?"

Bret brought his hand to his mouth and thought about her question for a moment.

"I tell you what I'd do," he said once he had it all figured out. "I'd chain that son of a bitch down onto a table and make him feel all the pain and misery he has ever visited upon others. This wouldn't be no quick stab and done *Dexter*-style either. No, I'd take my time with this fucker."

Anne's big eyes got even wider. "Tell me," she said, her breath getting rapid, "tell me what you would do once you had him tied down?"

Bret began to explain in detail what it was he would do.

"The first thing I would do is use a nail gun to nail his feet and hands into place. That way every time he squirms, he'll feel even more pain. Then, I'd use some needle-nose pliers and slowly pull each one of his toenails out, one-by-one. Then, I'd do the same thing to his fingernails. Then, I'd take a pair of gardening sheers and snip off his pecker and shove into his mouth, make him eat it."

"What else," Anne could not hide her excitement.

"Well, by that time, he'd probably be a whimpering mess," Bret said. "So, I'd go medieval on his ass. Yeah, I'd place a block between his ankles and hobble the motherfucker *Misery*-style. And when he's lying there covered in blood and piss and his own shit, begging me to stop, I'd take a sledgehammer and bash the fuck's knee caps to powder. I'd spend time breaking that son of a bitch down to the point where he'd be nothing more than a pile of whimpering jelly. He'd beg me to put him out of his misery, but like I said, there isn't going to be a fast way out, not for this creep."

"How would you end him?" Anne asked.

Without hesitation, Bret answered, "I'd douse his quivering mess in gasoline and light the fucker on fire."

"You're Goddam right you will!" Anne exclaimed.

She put the car in reverse and backed up and turned the car around.

"Buckle up, honey," she leaned over and kissed him on the cheek.

"Where are we going?" he asked.

"Just relax, baby," Anne replied as she planted her bare foot on the gas. "I'm about to make both our wishes come true."

The tires of the little car kicked up rocks. Once they grabbed, the little car sped off into the darkness.

Chapter 9: The Final Chapter

The pleasant aroma of hot chocolate filled their senses. Tesla and Diana, sat on the couch in the living room in front of the fireplace, both smiled as they each took a steaming mug from the tray Cat was carrying.

"Girl, you are a blessing," Tesla smiled as she held the rim of the mug just under her nose. "You are going to make some man very happy one day."

"Oh, I almost forgot," Cat said as she plucked a marshmallow up off the tray with a silver prong and dropped it into Tesla's mug. "There you go, Tes, the finishing touch to any great cup of coco." She plucked another marshmallow and dropped it into Diana's cup.

These were not the tiny little treats one might sprinkle on top of a cupcake. No, these were jumbo marshmallows the size of a big toe. For a moment after being placed in the steaming coco, the jumbo marshmallow floated. Then, as it absorbed the liquid, it expanded to nearly twice its already jumbo size. All three women giggled with delight as the marshmallows finally gave way to their destinies and melted, seamlessly mixing their sweetness with the hot chocolates.

"Y'all enjoy," Cat said as she headed back toward the kitchen.

"Cat, won't you join us?" Tesla asked.

"Maybe in a minute," Cat replied. "Let me take care of the dishes first."

As Cat headed back to the kitchen, Diana and Tesla both took their first sips of the hot chocolate. The satisfied look on each of their faces told the other just how good it tasted. Then, a look of concern suddenly came over Tesla. She half turned on the couch and looked over at the kitchen. Cat was running the water in the sink and Autumn was retrieving the liquid soap from underneath.

"What is it?" Diana asked, noticing her friend's concern.

Tesla leaned in close and whispered, "There are knives in the sink tonight."

"It's okay," Diana assured her. "I can see from here. Don't worry. I'll keep an eye out. Besides, Autumn is with her."

Tesla leaned back onto the couch. She took another sip of the hot chocolate. The sensation of taste brought a smile to her smooth, round face. She looked over at the fire and for a fleeting moment she thought she might pursue the *Dance*. However, she had other concerns pressing on her mind.

"Where do you think Anne ran off to?" she asked, blowing at the rim of her steaming mug.

"Oh, you know that girl," Diana replied. "She's just out to blow off some steam."

"Mothers of Glen Haven, lock up your sons and husbands," Tesla's reply drew laughter from both women.

"That girl is most definitely a free spirit," Diana chuckled. Then her face grew stern once more. "Tes, do you think we are doing the right thing…turning that monster over to the authorities, I mean?"

"Absolutely," Tesla answered without hesitation. "What is it Nietzsche said? Ross used to quote this all the time. Oh yes, I remember, he said, 'Whoever fights monsters should see to it that in the process he does not become a monster…if you gaze into the abyss, the abyss will gaze back into you.' Or something along those lines. I never really understood that quote until today."

"You are so strong, Tes," Diana said. "How is it you were able to come back to this place after what happened?" Diana waved her hand in a wide arc gesturing to their home.

Tesla thought for a moment and then said, "Because this is my home, and now it is your home too, and Autumn's, Cat's, and Anne's, as well. To be honest, I probably could not have done it without the *Survivors Club*. Y'all gave me the strength to reclaim my home. Thank you."

"You don't have to thank me, honey," Diana replied with a crooked smile. "This endeavor may have been my idea, but none of this happens without your funding."

"Ross was a highly successful novelist," Tesla nodded absently at the fireplace. "I'm sure he's happy knowing that his money is going to a worthy cause. Not only did it bring the five of us together, but it was also instrumental in providing the necessary equipment and training to capture his killer. Despite what Anne might think, we are doing the right thing here."

"I wonder if Christmas would say the same." Diana's words were uncharacteristically soft.

"What?"

"Or Autumn's father, or Anne's sister, or Cat's friends," as Diana spoke, Tesla could almost see the wheels turning in her mind. "What about all those innocent kids he murdered. Should nobody avenge them? When do the scales balance?"

"Diana, honey," Tesla reached over and stroked her friend's arm. "We can't lose hope. We stopped the monster. Tomorrow we'll turn him over to the people that can deal with him properly."

"You're right, of course," Diana reached up and squeezed Tesla's hand. "You and Autumn are the bravest women I know. I wish I could have been as brave as you two." Tesla's brow furrowed. Diana explained, "Y'all fought back. In the most desperate moment of your life, a loved one was in danger and both of you fought back as hard as you could to try and save them. When my moment came, I was frozen with fear."

"Oh, honey," Tesla said in that motherly way only she could. She set her cup on the side table and put her arm around Diana's shoulders. "Don't do this to yourself. You'll just drive yourself crazy. Nobody ever knows how they will react in a life-or-death situation."

"That's just it," Diana's eyes were beginning to well up. "I did nothing. I just stood there and watched as that maniac murdered my twin sister."

"Honey, if you had reacted you would probably not be here today," Tesla tried to comfort her.

"Maybe I shouldn't be," Diana retorted, wiping her eyes.

"Don't say that," Tesla replied. "Don't ever say that."

"I swore I would never be a victim again," Diana said as she leaned back and placed her head on Tesla shoulder. "After the incident at Pelican Bay and then witnessing the murder of my sister, I swore I would never be a victim again. Even before I sought you out, for six months, I trained in firearms. I was at the gun range four nights a week. The other three nights a week I trained in Taekwondo and boxing. I read all the survivalist books I could get my hands on. I would hang around the V.A. listening to the stories of old soldiers and learning from their experiences of survival. Christ, I don't know what I was doing."

"Training to become Batwoman?" Tesla said with a wry smile.

Diana laughed despite her dour mood. "Yeah, maybe," she said. "I really didn't have a vision, at least until I saw your story on the news. From the description on the broadcast, I knew that the killer who attacked you had to be the same as the one who attacked my sister. And then shortly after the story about Anne's attack hit the news. I had no idea what it all meant but I knew one thing and that was I had to reach out to you, all of you. I had to connect."

"Thank God you did," Tesla said. "Because of you we all found each other and are now stronger for it. Because of our shared experience we, better than any doctor or family member, can relate and know what it was like to have gone through what we did."

"Yes," Diana sat up and looked Tesla directly in her big brown eyes. "Now, thanks to all that training and studying I did and thanks to your funding we were able to finally put an end to that monster's reign of terror."

In that moment, the two women connected on another level. Before either of them even knew it, their lips touched. It was not the passionate kiss of lovers, nor was it a simple peck of familial affection. It was an understanding between two people who both experienced something only they could possibly ever comprehend.

"We are doing the right thing," Diana said confidently.

Cat cleared her throat to draw the women's attention. Diana and Tesla both straightened up. They each retrieved their cooling cups of hot chocolate. Cat and Autumn were both now standing in front of them. Cat was smiling awkwardly while Autumn was looking a bit ragged.

"Are you feeling alright?" Tesla asked.

"I'm just tired," Autumn said as she leaned forward and kissed Tesla on the cheek. "I'm going to turn in for the night."

"Would you like me to walk you up?" Tesla asked.

"I'll be fine," Autumn smiled and started for the stairs. "Goodnight, everybody."

"Goodnight," Cat called after her.

"Goodnight, honey," Diana said.

As Autumn disappeared up the stairs, Cat sat down in a chair facing Tesla and Diana. A big smile crossed her alabaster face.

"So, ladies, what shall we talk about?" She asked.

*****

Fifteen minutes later, Anne and Bret arrived at the house.

"Where are we?" Bret asked. "Whose house is this?"

"You probably wouldn't believe me if I told you," Anne replied as she put the car in park and unfastened her seatbelt. "Come on, but quietly."

Bret just sat in his seat as Anne got out and walked around to his side of the car. She opened his door and unfastened his seatbelt.

"Come on," she whispered.

"Come on?" He asked. "Come on where?"

She pulled him out of the car and led him around to the side of the house. Unnoticed by both, lying there on the passenger seat was Angela's totem.

"Whose house is this?" Bret asked again.

"Keep your voice down dammit," she shot back at him.

Anne got on her tiptoes and peered in through a window into the kitchen of the house. Since there was nobody there, Anne assumed the other women were in the living room.

"Okay, the coast is clear," Anne grabbed Bret by the hand.

"What do you mean the coast…Anne, what the hell is going on here?"

She took him by the chin, not roughly, but firmly. "Listen to me," she whispered. "I'm going to show you something that is going to blow your mind, but in order for that to happen I need you to shut the fuck up, follow my lead, and be quiet about it." She kissed him firmly on the lips. "Okay?"

All Bret could do in that moment was nod. Anne slowly opened the back door and led him into the house. They stayed low and curved around the island counter of the kitchen. Bret could hear voices coming from another room, female voices. Up ahead there was another door. Anne gestured for him to stay put. She quietly walked over and opened the door. Bret could see that it opened into a stairwell which led down.

Anne looked over into the living room. The kitchen view of the kitchen was mostly covered by an outcropping wall which separated the two areas. However, the door to the cellar was in full view of the living room. Anne could see Tesla and Diana sitting on the couch, their backs to her. On the far side of the living room, sitting in a chair was Cat. Cat was too busy flicking her lighter to notice anything.

Anne motioned for Bret to come on. She placed her finger on her lips to signal him to be quiet about it. Bret, as quietly as he could be, scooted over to Anne and through the door. Anne quickly and quietly shut the door behind them.

For a moment, Cat thought she had caught something out of the corner of her eye. She looked into the kitchen and saw nothing out of place. She looked over at Tesla and Diana to see if they might have seen or heard something. They were still wrapped up in telling each other their origin stories. Cat just rolled her eyes and went back to flicking her lighter.

Halfway down the stairwell, Bret stopped and grabbed Anne by the arms.

"Enough, Anne," he said in a harsh whisper. "What the fuck is going on? Who were those women? Where in the fuck are we? Whose house is this?"

"This is Ross Lawry's house," Anne answered.

"What?" Bret retorted, releasing his grip on her.

"Ross Lawry," she repeated. "This is Ross Lawry's house, that writer who was murdered."

Bret just stood there blinking his eyes. He suddenly felt a wave of nausea start to build up in his stomach.

"One of those women upstairs is Tesla Lawry," Anne began to explain. "She also survived the Goatman's attack. All of us, we are all survivors, and we all lost someone because of it, because of that…that monster."

"Survivors…? Goatman…?" Bret's head was swimming. "Anne, what the hell are you talking about?"

"Don't worry, sweetie," Anne smiled and kissed him. "Come on. I have something to show you."

Anne pulled a key from her pocket and unlocked the padlock on the door at the bottom of the stairs. She led Bret into a cellar. When she shut the door behind them, they were left in complete and utter darkness. All Bret could hear was breathing, but it wasn't his breathing. Anne's? No, the breathing he heard was deep, like a large animal. The pitch black coupled with that disembodied breathing sent shivers up and down his spine. Bret suddenly felt very scared, and very alone.

There was the sound of a switch being thrown and suddenly the cellar was illuminated by a large bulb hanging directly overhead.

"Sorry about that," Anne smiled. "Sometimes it takes me a second to find that damn switch."

Bret rubbed the spots out of eyes. It took a moment for his vision to adjust. The first thing he saw was a giant wooden work bench. Hanging on the wall was every conceivable tool, screwdrivers, saws, hammers, pliers, and more. Leaning next to the bench were brooms of assorted sizes and shapes, an old tired looking mop, and an empty bucket. All along the walls of the cellar were metal shelves filled with boxes. Along the back wall hung assorted gardening tools such as rakes, shovels, and a weed-eater. In fact, this was quite a typical storage area, nothing out of the ordinary except for one small thing – the giant, dirty man wearing an animal skull-mask who was chained to a metal chair right in the center of the room.

"Holy shit!" Bret exclaimed.

"Keep your voice down," Anne scolded.

"What the…what the fuck…?" Bret began to feel very dizzy.

"This is him," Anne gestured toward the Killer. "This is the son of a bitch that murdered my sister."

Bret felt his mouth go dry. He was staring at the Killer and the Killer was staring right back into his eyes, into his soul. The dark hypnotic stare of his black shark-like eyes stared right back at him, and Bret suddenly felt very weak.

A melting pot of emotions washed over Bret as his head tried to wrap around the current events of his life. All at once he was cycling through the fear, confusion, panic, and lust as they hammered his senses wave after wave. His world was spinning. The touch of agile fingers unbuttoning and unzipping his jeans brought his focus back to reality. He looked down to see the woman of his dreams smiling back up at him. His blood began to pump, and he felt his control waning as she pulled his jeans and underwear to his ankles and seized his maturing manhood.

"No," he pleaded weakly. "This isn't right." He looked over at the macabre monstrosity chained to that chair. Bret's knees buckled as that monstrosity stared back at him with cold black eyes from behind an animal skull mask. "No, we can't…do this…" he protested weakly, but his resistance faded quickly when she took his manhood into her mouth.

Bret's world was spinning. The alcohol he consumed that evening was coursing through his veins as his blood began to pump furiously. Anne reached up and guided him by the waist. Having lost all since of control, Bret welcomed her assistance as she guided him back down onto the mattress she had unrolled. The fear and absurdity of the moment was lost in the carnal sensations now enveloping his being. At this point, Bret had no fight left in him. He gave into the very thing he had always wanted since he was teenager.

Anne removed his boots and jeans. She stood up and her cutoff shorts and panties fell to her ankles. She deftly stepped out of them. She pulled her soaking wet half shirt off and dropped it to the cold basement floor. For a moment, she just stared down at him, all her amazing womanly attributes on full display.

"Oh, my god," Bret breathed.

He was completely overwhelmed with lust. She was beautiful. His eyes closed and he braced himself for her touch. Anne looked over at the Killer who simply stared on in silence. She extended her middle finger and winked. Then, she knelt and crawled across Bret's waiting body with the agility of a jungle cat. Straddled on top, she reached back, once again seizing control of his manhood. They both groaned in pleasure as their bodies interlocked. Their worlds drifted away in that moment. The only thing that mattered in that moment was them, together.

The sounds of their lovemaking echoed throughout the basement. Slapping sounds of passion that could only be drowned out by their moans and groans of pleasure. So, caught up in their throws of passion, neither of them even noticed the presence of another entering the basement. Neither of them noticed the restraints that kept the Killer imprisoned loosen and slump to the floor. All they knew at that moment was each other. Their passion built and built until climax was reached in an instant of intense muscle spasm.

Their young naked bodies glistened with sweat. Their chests heaving as they both tried to catch their breath. Bret opened his eyes and stared up at Anne who was smiling down at him.

"Now, that was hot," she said between heavy breaths.

He smiled back at her. God, she was beautiful.

Then, his smile turned to terror as two monstrous hands suddenly wrapped impossibly large, dirty fingers around her head. In one violent jerk, Anne's head had been completely twisted one-hundred and eighty degrees in the opposite direction. If her life had not already expired, she would be staring into the cold black eyes of her murderer. Anne's lifeless, limp body flopped forward. Her head, now facing the wrong way on her body, slammed into Bret's face, breaking his nose.

"Oh, god!" He called out. Only moments before he was using this exclamation to illustrate his pleasure. Now, it had taken on a whole new meaning. "Oh, god, oh, god…!"

Blood ran down his face as he desperately tried to pry himself free of his dead lover's embrace. He rolled out from under her only to be seized by the neck by the very thing that had murdered her. Bret fought back with all his might, but in the hands of this monster he was like a child fighting against an adult. His world spun as he was violently hoisted off the ground and slammed hard onto the nearby workbench. He continued to struggle in vain to free himself from his attacker's viselike grip. As he kicked his legs and torqued his body, thrashing about, splinters from the wooden bench began to stab into his exposed flesh.

With one hand, the Killer held Bret in place. With his free hand, he reached for one of the many tools hanging on the wrack above the bench. Taking hold of a nail gun, the Killer secured Bret's hands to the wood bench with two very painful volleys. As Bret cried in pain and terror, the Killer tossed the nail gun aside and grabbed a rubber mallet from the wall. With a thunderous smack, he clobbered Bret in the skull. The blow sent Bret reeling.

It seems the Killer was not too happy about being held prisoner and now he planned to take out some of that frustration on Bret. So, they would not be disturbed, the Killer reached into Bret's mouth and in one violent motion tore his tongue out. Now, the Killer could begin his macabre work. Bret was barely conscious when the Killer reached for the handsaw.

*****

The rain outside started to really come down. Raindrops pounded against the window like a million tiny out-of-sync drums. Autumn walked toward the window. She pulled the wool shawl tight around her shoulders. The temperature in the house was dropping rapidly. Her breath left small fog condensation on the cool glass. For a long moment, she stared. Then, all at once it happened.

The light coming in from the hallway behind her was obscured. There was movement in a blurred reflection on the glass. The sound of familiar deep breaths filled her ears. Her mouth went dry, and her body began to tremble with fear. For an instant, she closed her eyes as hard and as tight as she could, praying under her breath, praying that this was only a dream. She opened her innocent eyes wide and knew instantly that she was not alone in the room.

Autumn slowly turned around and there looming large in the doorframe of the room was the Killer. His barrel chest was heaving. His black shark-like eyes stared down at her from behind that macabre animal skull mask. For a moment that lasted for an eternity, they stood staring at each other. The light from the hallway set his massive frame in silhouette and gave his already intimidating size an even more terrifying presence. Autumn shook her head and then she screamed!

The Killer lunged for her. In a desperate attempt to avoid his monstrous grasp, Autumn threw herself backwards. Her violent momentum carried her back right through the window, shattering glass, and frame alike. She tumbled out into open space, end over end, until her descent from the second story window came to a sudden and abrupt halt upon the cold, wet ground below. Her right leg was twisted and bent in an unnatural way. Blood escaped her lips as she struggled to retrieve the air that had been violently knocked from her lungs when she landed. Two broken ribs scraped against the wall of her left lung threatening to seal her fate. The rain poured down upon her broken frame with an unyielding, uncaring indifference. Up above, on the second floor of the house, standing in the very shattered window frame she had just fallen from was the Killer, staring down at her.

Autumn could not help but be reminded of the very first time she came face-to-face with the Goatman of Eagle Mountain Lake.

"Autumn!" She could hear Tesla's voice call out to her from inside the house. "Honey, are you alright?"

Though she could not see her from her vantage point, she could envision her friend calling up the stairs. She knew Tesla's concern for her wellbeing would soon bring her to the room. That room where the Killer waited. With all the effort she could muster, and every single movement was excruciating pain, Autumn attempted to call out a warning.

"T-Tesla!" Blood spat from her lips and her body wrenched with pain with each syllable. "Tesla, please...d-don't go upstairs! Oh, God," she began to weep as much from fear as from the pain. "G-god, Tesla, please...!"

She called out with all the might she could muster but the pain of her wrecked body only allowed a marginal sound, and the unrelenting roar of the rain and thunder drowned out any hope of her being heard by those inside the house. Autumn could hear Tesla's voice once again.

"Autumn!" She called up the stairs. "Autumn, I'm coming!"

"Tesla, wait!" She could hear Diana's stern voice calling out now. "Let me grab my gun!"

Tears began to run down Autumn's face, mixing with and disappearing amongst the unrelenting rain drops. Autumn looked back up to the second story window from wince she had fallen. For just a moment, the Killer stared back down at her. Her blood ran ice cold as the Killer slowly melted back into the shadows of the dark room and only a moment later, she could hear Tesla's voice as she entered the room.

"Autumn!" Tesla called out as she ran into the dark room. She was brandishing a knife she had grabbed from the kitchen before ascending the stairs. Her eyes went wide, and her heart stopped when she saw the shattered glass and broken frame of the bedroom window. "Oh, my god, Autumn!"

Tesla raced over to the window. Torrent rain and wind greeted her, soaking her sweater. A flash of lightning and a thunderclap took her breath away as she peered down to the muddy ground below. She brought her trembling hand to her mouth as she stared below at her young friend's broken body lying helpless in a bloody and muddy heap. Autumn weakly and with great effort brought her hand up out of the mud and pointed, trying to warn her friend of the imminent danger she was in. Autumn's trembling gesture came too late.

"Oh my god!" Diana's voice could be heard from downstairs. "He's free!"

Before Tesla could even turn around and dart to Autumn's side, she heard the creak of the bedroom door as it closed behind her. Her blood ran cold as she suddenly could hear that familiar and awful heavy breathing. She gripped the handle of the kitchen knife tight and with all her strength she whirled around intending to strike with the blade. The Killer was faster and far stronger than she could imagine. He caught her hand in his and held the knife at bay. He reached out with blinding speed and wrapped his monstrous free hand around her neck. With strength not of this earth, he hoisted her up off the ground. Her bare feet kicked in vain trying to find the floor. Slowly, the Killer bent her hand, the hand with the kitchen knife, bending it back bringing the tip of the stainless-steel blade to rest against her stomach.

"No," Tesla pleaded through clenched teeth and jerked her body and legs in one last vain effort to break free from the Killer's vise-like grip.

There was a flash of lightning and for a moment the blade of the knife reflected the heavenly light and illuminated the dark room. There was a sickening sound as the blade plunged to the hilt into her stomach. Tesla eyes rolled back, and her tongue extended from her mouth as the Killer, with her hand in his, slowly sliced her from her navel to her sternum. Her limbs went limp. The Killer then sliced a wicked cut horizontally across her ribcage. All her fears, hopes, and dreams faded away, and Tesla's world went black as her insides spilled out onto the floor.

Below, Autumn just stared helplessly up at the black window frame. Then suddenly, an object flew out of the window from the darkness and landed with a wet thud only a foot from where Autumn lay. With great effort, she turned to stare into the lifeless eyes of Tesla's severed head. A flash of lightning was quickly followed by an explosion of thunder that drowned out her screams.

*****

After that last crash of thunder, the electricity in the house went out. Now fully armed with her .44 holstered on her side and brandishing a pump-action shotgun, Diana was racing up from the basement. She was sweating and breathing hard.

"Oh, god," she breathed as she took a moment to lean on the kitchen counter and gather herself.

"What is it?" Cat asked from the living room.

Diana looked over with an expression of utter despair on her face. She just shook her head and could barely utter the words, "Anne…Anne…she's, she's…"

Cat knew, even without an explanation, she knew. Then a loud thud came from the second floor. Diana wiped her nose on her sleeve, gripped the shotgun hard, until her knuckles turned white. That familiar stern look of determination came over her face and without another word she raced up the stairs.

"Wait," Cat called after her, but she was already gone.

Cat walked over and grabbed the revolver that was sitting on the mantle above the fireplace. She checked to see if it was loaded. Then she pulled her pocketknife and released the small blade from its casing. As lightning flashed, a look of dread soured her normally pretty features.

To nobody else at all, she said aloud, "We're all going to die."

Upstairs, Diana came to the top of the stairs and gasped as the Killer's heavy frame darted across the hall about ten feet in front of her from one room and into the adjacent one. She raised the shotgun and fired a blast that only hit the door frame to the room he had darted into. There was a bright flash, a loud explosion of gunfire, and wood splintered into the air.

"You son of a bitch!" Diana called out. "I'll kill you, you son of a bitch!"

The barrel of the shotgun smoking, Diana gripped her weapon and carefully, slowly, made her way down the hallway. The room the monster disappeared into was Tesla's. Diana stopped just short of the portal and listened. She held her breath but all she could hear was the relentless pounding of rain on the roof and walls of the house. She clicked on the flashlight which was attached to the barrel of the shotgun. A strong beam of light illuminated the upstairs hallway. From Tesla's room came only silence and darkness.

"Tesla!" Diana called out.

No answer.

Diana placed her back against the wall of the hallway opposite the open portal leading into the lair of the beast. Sliding slowly down the wall with the shotgun to bear, she tilted her head to try and gage the situation on the other side of that dark frame. Her mouth dry and her hands trembling, Diana took a deep breath to steady herself. *Remember your training*, she thought. Her hands steadied, she stepped forward cautiously toward the portal.

Shining the beam into the room, nothing seemed out of the ordinary. Tesla's night gown was laid across the foot of her bed which was still made. Her room was always the cleanest, the tidiest, everything put away in its proper place. There was no sound save for the torrential storm outside. Then a small creaking called out and the flashlight's beam streaked over to rest upon the closet door which was slightly ajar.

Diana cocked the shotgun and aimed it right at the closet door. She took one more step further into the dark room to fully put her target in front of her. She held her breath, but just as she was about to pull the trigger, she heard the breathing. The Killer's distinct muffled, heavy breathing revealed his location. He was behind the door. Diana cried out in defiance and whirled to fire. The door slammed into her with such force that the blow sent her flying through the air, across the hallway, and through the open door into Autumn's bedroom.

Diana landed hard on her backside with a loud splash. She barely had time to gather herself when the Killer stepped out into the hallway. He loomed like a shadowy giant in the doorway to Autumn's room. Without even the slightest hesitation, Diana brought the shotgun to bear and fired. With inhuman speed, the Killer lunged to the left avoiding the blast. Instead of slaying her foe, Diana's shot blasted a basketball-size hole through the door to Tesla's bedroom nearly blowing the door off its hinges.

"Shit!" Diana exclaimed as she quickly stood up.

She quickly realized her backside and hands were wet. When she took her first step forward there was a sickening, squishy sound as her bare foot stepped on something soft and wet. Something oozed and squeezed between her toes. She shined the flashlight down on the floor to see she had landed in a grisly pile of blood, fluids, and human organs. The beam panned over and shined down on a headless, disemboweled body.

"Tesla," Diana breathed. "No…no…no…" Her protest was barely audible. Then a rage swept over her, and her cry of fury could be heard over the thunder. "No!"

Her feet sliding, Diana came crashing headlong into the hallway and thudded hard against the far wall. She saw the back of the Killer's head, that massive animal's mane, as he disappeared down the stairs. Off balance, she fired the shotgun, missing her intended target but splintering the top step. She unsnapped the flashlight from the shotgun and threw the cumbersome weapon to the floor in frustration. A bout of nausea hit her when she felt the squishy remnants from Autumn's room oozing between her toes. She unsheathed her .44 and set off down the stairs.

Flying down the stairs in pursuit so fast that when she hit the kitchen floor, her slick feet nearly flew out from under her. Catching herself on the kitchen island, Diana searched downstairs frantically for her adversary. Her eyes landed on Cat who was in the living room. Cat was frantically pointing toward the basement door which was still open.

Without a word, Diana gathered herself and lunged toward the portal. Crashing through, she slammed against the wall at the top of the stairwell. The stairs descended into darkness. Diana shined the flashlight down the stairwell.

"There's nowhere left for you to run, you son of a bitch," she called down. "You hear me? I'm going to kill you!"

Cocking the hammer on the .44, Diana, slowly, carefully, started to descend the stairs.

*****

With the power off, and the flames in the fireplace dying out, the living room was covered in darkness. With no hum of central heat or kitchen appliances droning, the stark silence was alarming. The only sound was the driving rain outside which seemed to be gathering steam with each drop. A flash of lightning illuminated the room with a white light, a fleeting light. Cat was left alone once again blinking her large green eyes to adjust to the sudden shift back to darkness. She retrieved her small plastic lighter from her sweater pocket and clicked the flint.

There was nothing, barely a spark. What a terrible time to run out of fluid, she thought. There was loud billowing thunder that seemed to roll across the heavens. A distant memory brought a fleeting smile to her face. When she was a child, her father used to tell her that thunder was the angels bowling. "You hear that?" He would ask. "Sounds like Gabriel just bowled a strike." As she grew older, Cat realized that it was his way of assuring her that she was safe. Cat's happy memory vanished quickly because her instincts told her she was anything but safe at this moment.

Gripping the handle of her pocketknife calmed her, centered her, but that feeling too was fleeting. Deftly using her thumb, like she had done some million-million times before, she flicked the blade in and out the housing of the black handle. The clicking sound as the blade locked into place was comforting to her in the dark. For a long moment, she stared at the blade which flickered in the dark every time distant lightning flashed. She could feel her breath quickening and her pulse begin to race. She needed to calm down, she needed to...to...she was not quite sure what she needed to do.

Absently she brought the steel three-inch blade to her forearm. Before she even realized she had done it, she made several small, shallow cuts just above her wrist. It was not pain she felt at this moment, nor shame, not even arrest, no, what she felt in that very moment was calm. The slight sting of her self-inflicted wounds focused her, brought her into the moment, and that is when she heard the sound.

She had heard that sound before. It preceded the most terrible events of her life. It was an awful sound, and no amount of self-cutting would ever be enough to distract her from its hideous meaning. It was that awful mixture of a lamb screaming and a baby crying. The hairs on her arm stood up. Her mouth went dry. She spun around in the darkness, checking all her corners. As far as she could tell, she was alone in the room. The sound was not coming from inside the house. It was coming from outside.

Cat stared at the large window, rain pounding relentlessly against the glass. The awful sound was coming from out there. Once again, lightning flashed, illuminating the room, but the light was fleeting. The sound, unfortunately, was not. Again, and again it resonated over the rain, chilling her to the bone. Placing her lighter back in her pocket, Cat retrieved the revolver she had taken from the mantle from her pocket. With her knife in one hand and the revolver in the other, Cat slowly began to walk toward the living room window.

Each slow step was an effort. As she made her way across the room and drew closer to the large window, her resolve was tested by thunder, by lightning, and by that sound. God, how could a human being make such a noise? And how could that sound possibly be coming from the front yard? She reached the portal. The glass was foggy. Using the sleeve of her sweater, Cat quickly wiped the glass then scanned the front of the house searching for the source of that tormenting sound.

She would not have to search long for standing straight ahead, next to Diana's truck, was the Killer. He stood there in the mud, rain pouring down on him in sheets. He just stood there, hands at his sides, his massive barrel chest heaving with each breath. In one hand, he held a hunting knife. His breath could be seen exiting the front of that awful animal skull mask. He just stood there, staring back at her.

The front hood of the truck flipped up. From her vantage, Cat could see that the engine had been dismantled. Anne's small car parked next to it was also in the same state. If there was to be an escape, it would not be found with the vehicles. Cat gripped her knife tight. Absently, she was gently slicing the blade across her upper thigh. She brought the revolver to her chest making sure the Killer could see the weapon. If it gave him pause, she could not tell.

That awful sound began to resonate from the Killer once again. Each time the noise came, a billow of breath escaped the mask. As unnerving as the sight of the Killer was, Cat was surprisingly calm. Her shallow cuts kept her focused. She had a gun, and she had that son of a bitch right in her sights. What would prevent her from just opening the front door, walking right up to that bastard, and putting a bullet in his head?

But could she do that? Could she take a life?

For a few moments, the two adversaries stood and stared at each other. A single tear streamed down Cat's face as that awful sound began to unnerve her. Unintentionally, she cut too deep with her knife and the sharp pain caused her to wince. Suddenly, her vison was clear and her perspective strong. In that moment, she knew what she had to do to put this nightmare to rest. No longer was there any doubt. With her thumb, she cocked the revolver and clicked off the safety. But just as she took one step toward the door, something quite peculiar happened. No, peculiar was not a strong enough description of what Cat witnessed in that moment. Something astonishingly horrible happened.

Cat's large green eyes grew even wider, and all the air left her lungs in one single gasp. Utter confusion and terror gripped her as she stared out the window, and as the Killer stood there in the rain making that awful sound, his sound was answered by another. Stepping out from behind the truck and walking up to stand right next to the Killer was another. Another man of equal size with the very same attire, boots, pants, suspenders, and a macabre mask fashioned from the skull of an animal. The second man's husky voice joined the Killer's as their animalistic call grew in crescendo.

Her mind began to reel. Her brain was having the most challenging time of processing what she was seeing. There are two of them? Have there always been two of them? Was what she is seeing even real, or had she finally gone mad? She felt sick. She wanted to vomit, but before she could follow through, her world became even more confusing, and terrifying. That awful sound, that animalistic cry of the Goatman, was now coming from inside the house.

"Oh, God!" She exclaimed.

What was happening? None of this made sense. She could still see the twins on the front lawn, yet that awful sound was now resonating from behind, and inside the house. Cat whirled around and a flash of lightning revealed the Killer standing at the top of the stairs. He stared back down at her with those black eyes. The animal sound coming from him was guttural. She could hear his heavy breathing which was given an echo by the skull-mask he wore.

Cat's legs went numb, and she leaned back against the cold glass of the window. Her mind was racing. She looked back over her shoulder to see the twins still standing next to the truck, in the rain, still calling out with that terrible noise. Only now they had been joined by two more, two more Killers! There were four of them?!

Then another call came from inside the house, and then another, followed by yet another. Cat spun back around, and her world had no meaning anymore. Standing in the kitchen holding a large kitchen knife was the Killer. Standing by the back door, holding an axe, was the Killer. Standing at the top of the stairs, holding a machete, was the Killer. Their cries merged to create a deafening cacophony that engulfed Cat's very being and left her utterly shattered.

Through her hysteria, Cat realized the subtle differences between her tormentors. Her hand shaking, she brought the barrel of the revolver up to her temple. In those last few moments of her life, Cat had deciphered the secret of the Goatman of Eagle Mountain Lake. As the Killers slowly advanced, Cat pulled the trigger and took that secret to her grave.

*****

Standing at the bottom of the stairwell at the entrance to the basement, Diana heard a gunshot echo throughout the house. She turned around swiftly and looked back up the stairs which now ascended into darkness.

She shined the flashlight up the stairs and called out, "Cat! Cat, are you okay?! Cat, answer me!"

Diana started to go up the stairs to investigate, but then she heard the breathing, and it was not coming from upstairs. It was coming from the darkness behind her. That unsettling breathing, muffled by an even more unsettling bone mask was resonating from the basement. Diana took a deep breath, held her .44 close, and ventured forward into the darkness.

She whimpered as the first thing her beam caught in its light was the twisted remains of Anne. Beyond that, on the large wooden workbench, were the mutilated remains of some poor young man whom Anne had brought into this situation, a situation that boy could not have possibly comprehended. The heavy breathing drew the attention of the light. Diana stepped into the basement slowly but stopped in her tracks when the light came to rest on the Killer. He was standing motionless beside the chair he was once chained to, motionless except for the rise and fall of his massive chest.

He pointed his large finger with a chipped blackened fingernail that was more like a claw than a fingernail. He pointed toward the wall next to Diana. She carefully looked over to see the switch on the wall. The switch that would have electrocuted the Killer if the women had been so inclined. To her dismay, the wires connecting the switch to the chair had been severed.

Diana quickly brought her attention back to the Killer. She aimed her .44 for a kill shot, right between the eyes. Those cold dark, soulless eyes. The Killer just stood there, unflinching.

"I have you now, you son of a bitch," she spits through clenched teeth as she took very careful aim.

There was a sickening thud as the blade was driven with great force through Diana's back. The curved tip of the hunting knife protruded from her right breast. A gout of blood erupted from the wicked wound. Diana felt her legs go numb. Her world was spinning, and her big brown eyes rolled into the back of her head as the ground rushed up to greet her.

She hit the floor. Lying in a heap of blood and her own bodily fluids, Diana gasped for air. As she lay there, unable to move, and breathing her last breaths, her vision came into focus on the Killer. He had not moved from the spot where he stood. Then, she heard a voice. A voice she realized she recognized. It was the unmistakable voice of an elderly woman. It was the voice of Salvia Vasa.

"There, there," the woman said. "Did that bad girl hurt you?"

Diana knew the question was directed at the Killer, who stood unmoving, staring down at her with those cold, dark eyes.

A small figure came into view, an elderly woman with stringy gray hair, her spine wickedly bent by age. She shuffled across the floor to stand beside the Killer. Diana, still gasping for air, watched as this old woman reached up with old, withered hands, hands gnarled into wicked claws by arthritis. With those gnarled hands, she lovingly stroked the Killer's blood-splattered, bone mask. His dark eyes never showed expression, never changed.

"Don't worry, my boy," the old woman reassured the Killer of Azlewood. "She won't hurt you anymore. None of them will ever hurt you ever again."

The old woman turned her gaze toward Diana. She tilted her head as if examining Diana. Her face was withered but unnaturally warm. In fact, she bared the resemblance of a typical woman of advanced age. She could have been somebody's grandmother, anybody's grandmother. There was nothing out of the ordinary about her at all except her eyes, those cold, dark eyes, like staring into a void, those same cold, dark eyes that she had passed down to her son.

Diana breathed her last breath through blood encrusted lips, and her world went black.

Epilogue

The ride out to the house was spent in uncomfortable silence. In his brief time in town, Special Agent Christophe Edison had never seen Ranger Maverick this solemn, this intense. The older lawman stared out the front windshield of the Bronco with a hawk-like gaze. There was a frown on his grizzled face that made his handlebar mustache seem even longer than usual. Agent Edison did not push for answers.

The only sound in the cab of the Bronco came from the radio. In the crosstalk chatter Agent Edison kept hearing two phrases over and over – an address: 308 Saranell Ct., and a code: 187. Agent Edison got a queasy feeling in his stomach. Outside the Bronco, the trees of the woods were almost a blur as the ranger guided the vehicle down the dirt and gravel road probably faster than humanly safe. The flashing red lights mounted on top of the Bronco mixed with the blur of the trees and was almost hypnotic. The young agent shook his head several times catching himself drifting while staring at the fuzzy red lit landscape.

The chatter from the radio grabbed his attention again. *308 Saranell Ct. 187.* The code, 187, he, of course, recognized as the police code for murder. Unfortunately, in his line of work, and even in the short two years since he graduated from the Academy, Agent Edison has been privy to all too many 187s.

That was its own animal. What made the young man's stomach turn was the other statement coming through the radio – *308 Saranell Ct.* It was an address.

"We were just here this morning," Agent Edison said aloud. "What in God's name is going on in this town, Emmitt?"

The veteran Texas Ranger remained stoic in his posture, stern in his appearance, and unfaltering in his piercing gaze. The young F.B.I. agent's question would have to go unanswered. For now.

In the distance, Agent Edison could see the two-story house coming into view. There was already a half-dozen police cruisers parked in a semi-circle on the front lawn. The lights to all the cars flashing, their headlights and spotlights illuminating the grounds. Both deputies and state troopers were hustling back and forth across the lawn and in and out of the house. Up above, a police helicopter circled the grounds shining a spotlight down, adding to the light below. The rain from earlier in the evening had died down to a light sprinkle. Lawmen were outfitted in bright yellow ponchos with hoods for their hats to protect them from the wet and cold.

The Bronco came skidding to a halt and Ranger Maverick exited the vehicle without a word. A young deputy rushed over and offered the tall grim ranger a yellow poncho. A quick glare told the young lawman that he was not interested in the attire. The young deputy came around the Bronco and offered Special Agent Edison a poncho as well.

Agent Edison held up his hand and said, "Thank you, No." He preferred the freedom of movement his trench coat gave him. A bit dejected, the young deputy darted off back the way he came.

Agent Edison came over to stand next to the stern Texas Ranger. Their breath was quite visible in the cool evening air. Ranger Maverick studied the grounds with the intensity and focus of a bird of prey. Next to them was a small red car. Its hood was raised, the belts had been cut. The windows were a bit foggy but something in the passenger seat caught Agent Edison's eye. He reached over and was delighted to learn the door was unlocked. He opened the passenger side door and reached down to retrieve the item. It was a small wooden carving of a bird. It was attached to a leather string.

"Huh, a necklace," Agent Edison said out loud.

The old ranger looked down at the trinket and his face grew even dourer. "That's not a necklace," he said, his voice low and throaty. Seeing the younger man's perplexed expression, Ranger Maverick explained, "That's an extremely powerful talisman."

"A talisman?" Agent Edison asked, studying the little wooden figure. The young agent had, of course, heard the word before, but he had never heard it used out in the world so casually.

"Yes, it's a charm of protection," the ranger replied turning his gaze back toward the house.

Without another word of explanation, the Texas Ranger marched toward the crime scene. Agent Edison took a moment to study the little wooden figurine again, and then he placed it in his pocket and walked on after the older man.

As they walked by the two other civilian vehicles in the driveway, they noticed that their hoods were also raised, and like the little red car from where Edison had pulled the charm, their belts had also been cut. They walked over to where a police photographer was snapping photos around the area of a plastic bag. He was aiming his camera up at a second story window. The wooden frame was broken, and the glass shattered. Their gaze tracked from the window down to the bag. Inside the bag was an object about the size of a basketball. As they drew closer their eyes went wide with shock. Inside the plastic forensic bag was the severed head of Tesla Lawry.

Agent Edison grimaced. Ranger Maverick knelt, his hand absently stroking his mustache, as he examined the wet ground.

"There's an indention in the ground here where someone jumped or was thrown from the window," the ranger observed. "Where's Tesla's body?" He asked the nearest deputy.

The lawman cleared his throat and said, "The rest of this victim's remains are up there…on the second floor."

Ranger Maverick's eye darted to the front door of the house. He immediately made a B-Line to the entranceway. Halfway there, Sheriff Wyatt intercepted him. The sheriff's girth was quite apparent, even under the cover of the extra-large poncho. Breathing quite heavy, his breath came in wave after wave of billows on the crisp night air.

"Ranger Maverick, my god, it's a slaughterhouse in there," the sheriff breathed. He was visibly shaken. His big brown eyes welled up as he continued. "My god, what kind of monster could do this? Those poor girls?"

"Were there any survivors?" Ranger Maverick asked in a calm but stern voice. The sheriff's face contorted into agony. His breath quickened as his words would not come out. The ranger reached over and placed two large steadying hands on the sheriff's shoulders. This seemed to have a calming effect on the veteran lawman. "Marcus, were there any survivors?" Ranger Maverick asked again, his voice even more stern than it was before.

However, before the sheriff could muster a response, a voice rang out from across the yard.

"We've got a survivor!"

Ranger Maverick and Agent Edison left the quivering old sheriff where he stood and rushed over to where the call came from, several other lawmen on their heels. A small group of lawmen were gathered around a large wooden box. It was a four-foot-by-three-foot-by-three-foot chest-shaped storage box used for housing chopped wood. Ranger Maverick forced his way to the front. Inside the wooden box, illuminated by the flashlight of the lawman who found her, was the shivering, whimpering figure of a teenage girl.

Ranger Maverick's heart broke to see her like this. He reached in to retrieve her. The instant his hand touched her arm, she let a banshee scream. She hid her face behind matted hair and her hands that were cut up and bleeding.

"It's okay, baby," Ranger Maverick coaxed. "It's okay. Autumn, you're safe now, darling. I promise you, honey, you're safe."

There was something about his voice that reached through her hysteria and clicked a switch of recognition. The veteran Texas Ranger very carefully peeled her injured and limp frame from the wooden box. Having no strength left to resist even if she wanted to, the battered teen allowed him to bring her out into the open.

"My god, how did she cram herself into that box?" A young deputy, the same deputy who had offered the ponchos earlier, asked.

Agent Edison reached over and took one of the deputy's extra ponchos and ordered him, "Go get a blanket for her."

"Yes, sir," the deputy replied without question and darted away.

Agent Edison handed the poncho to Ranger Maverick who slowly wrapped it around the frightened teen. When the young deputy returned with the blanket, Maverick wrapped her in that as well. He could still feel her shaking under the blanket as the paramedics came rushing over. A few minutes later, she was safely secured in the back of the ambulance. As one paramedic administered an I.V., the other was briefing Ranger Maverick and Agent Edison on the situation.

"She has a broken left ankle, several cracked ribs, a separated shoulder, her index and ring fingers on her right hand are broken, she has multiple contusions, and maybe a punctured lung," the paramedic paused and looked over at the teen and smiled. "We won't know for sure the full extent of the injuries until we can get some x-rays, but I'll say this, that is one tough little cookie."

"She's a survivor," Ranger Maverick added. He reached into his pocket and pulled out the keys to the

Bronco. He tossed them to Agent Edison and said, "I'm going to ride in the ambulance with Autumn to the hospital and make sure she's taken care of." He stepped up into the back of the ambulance.

"Emmitt?" Agent Edison had to ask. "How do you know her?"

"Autumn is my granddaughter," Ranger Maverick replied with a grimace as he looked over at the battered teen.

Absently, the young Special Agent reached into the pocket of his trench coat. His finger wrapped around something hard. He pulled the talisman from his pocket, the very trinket he had recovered from the little red car upon first arriving at the house. He remembered what the Texas Ranger had said about the item and smiled.

"Emmitt!" Agent Edison called out before the paramedic closed the door. "Here." He handed the ranger the wooden talisman.

The older lawman looked down at it for a moment then asked, "Why Special Agent Edison, don't tell me you are starting to believe in spirits, are you?"

Agent Edison paused for a moment and then replied, "Let's just say I'm starting to keep an open mind."

"Fair enough," the ranger replied with a wry smile as the paramedic closed the rear door.

As the ambulance drove away, Agent Edison could see the old Texas Ranger fastening the charm around Autumn's neck.

Agent Edison watched as the ambulance drove off down the gravel, dirt road that led away from the house, but then, something caught his eye. Standing amongst the dark tree line staring right at him and smiling was an unmistakable presence. It was the Tall Man. None of the officers seem to take any notice of this strange visitor. In the cold and rain, his form took on an even more ethereal look. His form seemed to fade in and out of focus. He seemed unaffected by the weather. It was almost as if he existed between rain drops. Agent Edison felt a little uneasy as this man held a long finger, a finger much too long to belong to a human being, up to his impossibly wide mouth as if to say *shhhh*.

Agent Edison was startled as two state trooper cruisers flashed in front of him as they sped down the road, following the ambulance. When he looked up, nobody was there. The Tall Man was gone.

Agent Edison pulled his trench coat tight around his lean frame. The cool night air was biting. Correction, the morning air, as he noticed dawn's light cracking the eastern horizon. He turned back toward the crime scene and realized that the demise of this *Survivors*

Club was not an ending…it was only the beginning. There was a lot of work to be done here. He would notify the Home Office as soon as he got back to the Ranger's office.

As he marched back over toward the house, Special Agent Christoph Edison remembered Ranger Maverick's words when they first met. He shook his head.

"Welcome to Glen Haven indeed."

July 2017

Page 185 Goatman Art by Michael Breakfield

ISBN: 9780692921685

Read the whole story!

Available on mycomnicshop.com, Amazon, or wherever books are sold online.

Autumn Dawn: A Glen Haven Tale: Book 2 By Michael Breakfield

Over a year has passed since the Survivors Club's fateful showdown with the monstrous Killer of Azlewood. One woman is left to pick up the pieces. Racked with guilt and paralyzing fear, can she even begin to process those harrowing events. Or have her experiences left her broken and too far gone to recover from injuries, both physical and psychological?

A Texas Ranger and Special Agent of the F.B.I. begin to piece together the puzzle that plagues this mysterious rural community, as another massacre leaves this small-town reeling and on the verge of collapse.

Meanwhile, a new monster stalks the dark woods surrounding the town. And a new killer leaves a grisly trail of bodies in his wake as he slowly makes his way toward a terrifying final reckoning.

Return to Glen Haven and catch up with the brave survivor girl, Autumn, and those stalwart lawmen, Texas Ranger Emmitt Maverick and Special Agent Christoph Edison. Revisit all the eccentric and peculiar residents of that small east Texas hamlet we know and love and, along the way, meet some new faces.

Another full moon has already begun to rise…

Eden: A Glen Haven Tale: Book 3 By Michael Breakfield

Glen Haven.
A town barely hanging on. As the Goatman killings continue, this warm community is on the verge of collapse. Amidst the tragedy, Autumn has resurrected the Lawry House and turned this location of a massacre into a safehouse for other survivors like her. Texas Ranger Emmitt Maverick struggles to tap the power of the *Eye of Odin*, an ancient artifact with the gift of sight, but that gift comes at a terrible price. Special Agent Christoph Edison finds his reason challenged as the supernatural endangers his hold on what he thought possible.
As community and sanity threaten to crumble, the final showdown is about to take place.

The origins of evil.
From the ashes rises a new Survivors Club.
What price would you pay to stop the killing?

Autumn, Christoph, and Emmitt are joined by new allies, face dangerous new challenges, and risk everything to end the evil that haunts the small east Texas town of Glen Haven forever!
But first, they must unlock the secrets of EDEN.